Chiefless of Acora

Chieftess of Acora

TRIBES OF CHALENT
BOOK 1

Judy Lynn

Infinitely Wandering Books LLC

First Printing, 2022

ISBN 979-8-9860598-0-8

Cover Art by: SelfPubBookCovers.com/ Viergacht

Proofreading by: Laurie Castaneda

Infinitely Wandering Books Logo art by: Veronica Lynn Ah-Mann

To
Ina-Robin Schuyler Williams
You know what you did.
<3

Contents

CHAPTER 1

23rd of 10th Lunar, 521 AC
Western Kelvia

Maleen urged her massive graebig beast faster, charging through the trees toward the meeting place where her uncle, Noture, would be waiting. It had been nearly a year since she'd last seen him, but he'd promised to wait for her there at this time every month. Before this, she'd only sent him a message. But not this time.

It was time to go home.

Her pursuers' mounts thundered somewhere behind her. The graebig she rode was fast, but it was growing tired. *Just make it to the clearing*, she begged silently.

Maleen ignored the chafing of her thighs as she rode the broad animal bareback. She ignored the beast's long gray hair whipping into her face. Her own auburn hair escaped her braid and snagged on the low tree branches. She fought the compulsion to look back, knowing they couldn't be far behind. She concentrated on gripping what was left of a wagon harness as she directed the beast to safety—she hoped.

She came into view of the clearing at a full gallop. Noture waited on the far edge. He mounted his beast, face beaming. With him was another saddled graebig, waiting in anticipation of Maleen's homecoming.

"It's about time." He grinned as Maleen slid from the winded beast she'd taken from the garrison. Despite graebigs being massive, strong beasts, they were also fast. But before she procured this animal, it had already pulled a wagon for an unknown distance. Even with a head start, it might not have been able to outrun pursuers for the six miles home, and without a proper saddle, it would be difficult for any rider to hold on over the rough terrain.

Noture's smile faded, seeming to sense her urgency.

"I'm not alone," Maleen warned. She mounted the fresh beast in time to see her pursuers gallop into view on the clearing's edge. Noture urged his graebig into motion as an arrow sailed through the air, hitting Maleen's beast in the leg.

The animal let out a low grunt and stumbled. Maleen called out to her uncle as it went down, and she rolled clear of the two-and-a-half-ton animal. She reached up to grab Noture's outstretched hand and pulled herself up behind his saddle. Despite the animal's height, six feet at the shoulder, a full two inches taller than Maleen, she executed the maneuver quickly. However, the few seconds it took, allowed Fanton's men to circle them and cut off their escape. Fanton, sub-chief of Western Kelvia, stopped his graebig directly in their path, his beast breathing heavily.

Maleen grabbed Noture's bow, never one to have her reaction time slowed by fear. As she nocked an arrow, Fanton did the same. Searing pain told her he was faster. The bow fell from her hands, Fanton's arrow lodged in her right shoulder. She made only a whisper of a sound, nearly falling from the graebig. Maleen gritted her teeth, cursing her luck that Fanton, the garrison's best marksman, had joined the chase.

Fanton and two other warriors dismounted. The other two halted their graebigs close to her mount while Fanton stepped forward and yanked Maleen from it, shoving her to the ground. Maleen bit her lip to keep from screaming when the arrow bit into her shoulder.

"Is that necessary?" Noture yelled, sliding off his mount. The two Kelvians grabbed his arms before he could reach Fanton. Noture didn't fight them. "Whatever she's done, you've caught her."

"What concern is it of yours?" Fanton asked, nostrils flaring. The man stood six foot two. His brown hair was sprinkled with gray. The usually light complexion of his face was bright red from both exertion and rage. He yanked her to her feet.

Maleen lashed out at Fanton with her left hand. Even being

ambidextrous, the pain in her injured arm prevented any power behind the swing. Fanton deflected it and held her arms behind her at a painful angle until she desisted.

Considering the penalty, attempted desertions from Kelvian garrisons were rare. As far as the leadership would admit, no one from the western one had ever succeeded. Fanton wouldn't allow her to be the first, a thought which made Maleen's stomach clench into an icy knot.

Fanton's son, Lenet, looked at Noture with a scowl. "I know you. You're one of Acora's warriors," he accused, never dismounting, his hand staying close to his bow. "A high-ranking one, if memory serves."

"And I believe you're the whelp I put in his place at the Equin competition a few years ago?" Noture glared at the younger man.

Lenet's scowl deepened. "What connection do you have to our deserter?" He looked at Maleen. "Or is my father correct about an infiltrator?"

"I saw a woman running from several pursuers and thought I'd give her a hand," Noture answered calmly, not resisting the hands that held him.

Maleen cringed inwardly. His excuse sounded flimsy, but she wouldn't have been able to come up with anything better. The plan had been to mount the fresh beast and make it across the border without anyone realizing who she was. There was no backup plan and no plausible story.

"I didn't know she was yours, and I didn't know her pursuers were the sub-chief and his son." Noture all but spit at the titles linked to both men, but he gave no indication he was concerned about what happened to Maleen.

"Why are you on Kelvian land?" Lenet challenged.

"After a stray graebig." Noture indicated the fallen one that came to its feet with no outward sign of distress.

"I don't believe you." Lenet's hand inched closer to his bow.

"Makes no difference to me what you believe." A stubborn note entered Noture's voice, demonstrating his refusal to be intimidated by this Kelvian, barely old enough to have been named Heir to his province.

Lenet's bright red hair and freckled face made him look much younger than his twenty-one years despite his fully mature stature. Broad shoulders and well-built arms hinted at the raw power the young man possessed and often wielded with arrogance and superiority.

Fanton's grip loosened, likely paying more attention to Lenet and Noture than to his captive. Maleen pulled free from him, but before she could run more than a few feet, another man urged his graebig in front of her.

She slowed only enough to change directions, but it gave Fanton the opportunity to grab her again. He shoved her back to the ground. When she tried to get up, he kicked her in the stomach, sending her backward.

He glared down at her. "Are you from the Acora tribe?"

Maleen refused to answer, struggling to get up again.

Fanton grabbed her injured shoulder. "I want to know what tribe you're from!"

"I'm Kelvian," Maleen said through clenched teeth, cradling her arm. She wouldn't give Fanton the satisfaction of crying out, though the throbbing in her shoulder matched the pounding of her heart. She couldn't raise a hand to him, much less draw a bow. She already felt light-headed from the blood loss.

"Why did you run?"

When she remained silent, Fanton squeezed her injured shoulder.

Knowing he wouldn't stop until he got an answer, Maleen let out a cry and pretended to faint, slumping to the ground. Had these men genuinely known her, they would have realized it was an act. They would have known she was trained to endure more pain than Fanton was delivering. She'd made sure none of them had gotten to know her that well.

Someone jammed bandages under her shirt and around the open wound, doing a poor job applying a field dressing. Rough hands lifted her to the back of a graebig and a strong arm went around her. Maleen didn't have to open her eyes to know who it was.

Lenet held her in front of him, his grip unyielding—she would not be going anywhere until he said so. Maleen shifted, giving away the fact that she was conscious. Lenet reached up, his hand grazing where it ought not, before applying pressure to the wound to slow the bleeding. Maleen resisted the urge to recoil.

"You will accompany us back to the garrison," Fanton ordered, glaring at Noture. "You can do it sitting on your beast or lying across it." He nodded to the warrior, still mounted, with his bow ready.

"Well, since you asked so politely..." Noture said.

Maleen stole a look at him. Having had experience with these Kelvians before, there was no reason to think Fanton was bluffing. Noture showed no fear of them, but resisting would mean putting her in the middle of an unbalanced fight, something she knew he'd never willingly do.

Maleen could usually hold her own, even against most men, but not after this injury. Noture ran his hand through his hair, looking from Fanton to Lenet. He mounted his graebig and followed the sub-chief and his son.

After fifteen minutes, the trees thinned, and Maleen caught a glimpse of the main road. She considered jumping from Lenet's fast-moving mount. The leap would have to be well-timed, or she would have more than a hole in her shoulder to contend with. She would have to land, roll, and run into the woods before anyone had time to react with a bow. The Kelvians didn't yet know the connection between her and Noture. His escape would be easier if he didn't have to worry about her, which she knew was the only reason he cooperated.

Her muscles tensed in preparation.

Lenet hissed in her ear, "Don't think *you* are going anywhere." He tightened his arm around her, his hand clasping her injured arm, ignoring her small gasp of pain. She'd only been this close to him once, and it hadn't been voluntary. If it hadn't been for someone else coming into the otherwise empty barracks, Lenet would have gotten even closer and taken what he wanted.

Even if she managed to break his hold, she wouldn't be able to regain her footing fast enough after the six-foot drop to avoid Fanton's arrow. Of course, she'd only have to worry about the arrow if she didn't roll on the wrong shoulder and black out from the pain. The risk was too great, and she resigned herself to returning to the garrison with the man she abhorred and feared.

Once within the garrison's wooden walls, Maleen saw the incredulous stares and shaking heads of the young people she'd trained alongside for the past year. Their looks meant nothing to Maleen. Neither did their opinions of her.

No one had expected her defection because none of them knew the truth about her. Amid the confused trainees, a merchant woman, Kanda, stood in front of the garrison commander. She berated Commander Rundel about the loss of her beast. His apologetic tone assured Maleen the garrison leadership wouldn't accuse Kanda of conspiring with a deserter.

The garrison prison was small—one room, divided in half, with wooden bars for the cell. Behind the bars, there was only a cot. Outside was a table with two chairs, out of arm's reach from the cell.

Maleen and Noture were shoved into the cell. Lenet took the lead, not giving Fanton the opportunity to start the interrogation.

"Who sent you here?" Lenet demanded, standing within the confines of the cell, his vest covered in Maleen's blood.

Other Kelvian guards stood by, at full attention, white knuckles showing how tight they gripped their staffs. Maleen would have no opportunity to slap the son of a troll, even if she had the courage for it.

"No one." Despite her growing sense of dread, she answered without a trace of fear in her voice. "You recruited me yourself from the village over a year ago." She scowled, feigning anger at the way her supposed tribesmen were treating her. Acting angry wasn't difficult. She was furious with herself for getting arrested, and for taking Noture down with her, but her defiant attitude only irritated Lenet more.

He grabbed her arms, holding her in front of him, making her look at him as he yelled, his face inches from hers. "Who planted you there?"

"No one!" she yelled back, gritting her teeth, biting back a wince of pain. She would not give him the satisfaction of showing pain or fear, though what she really wanted to do was cry out and run away. "I was there because I knew you'd be there to recruit trainees from the games at the village's Equin Festival. I knew I was good enough to be a Kelvian warrior. I only needed an invitation to the garrison. You've seen how hard I've worked, trying to live up to your standards." She tried to pull away from him—knowing what he was capable of even without a weapon in his hand—but he held on tightly.

"If you truly want to be a Kelvian warrior, why did you leave four days before your test?"

When she didn't answer, Lenet shoved her against the wall. Her head erupted in pain, and Maleen struggled against his strong grip. With the use of only one arm, she couldn't maneuver out of his hold. She lashed out with one foot, but Lenet swept her other one out from under her. When she landed hard on the dirt floor, Noture moved slightly, his fists clenched. It had to be taking everything he had not to pummel Lenet, with or without the other guards nearby, but they couldn't afford for him to give himself away.

Lenet stared down at her. "Were you afraid again?"

"No." She paused, deciding to change tactics. "Not of the test." Maybe appealing to the man's ego was her better option.

"Of what then?"

"Of you." Showing less anger, she let her shoulders slump, eyes on the floor, and added quietly, "You made no secret of how badly you wanted me." A lock of auburn hair fell across her face. She showed only a hint of the fear he caused her but hid her revulsion and loathing.

"Why should that scare you into desertion?" The vein in his neck pulsed.

"I heard about Natra." She met his eye, watching him bristle. "And how badly you treated her, until your father sent her away."

"I see someone has a big mouth," he growled. "But Natra was small and weak. It was easy for things to get out of hand. You're neither." His voice lost a little of its edge. "Why would you be afraid of me when even the best of our instructors can't scare you?"

If they didn't believe her, Maleen was dead and, likely, Uncle Noture with her. Even if they never discovered the relation, he would be guilty by association. Fanton would never believe Noture had been unlucky enough to be in the clearing at the precise moment Maleen attempted to desert.

"I've always known I could best any of the instructors if I wanted to," Maleen mumbled, never taking her eyes off her feet. "But I've seen you in the ring, with and without a staff. I wouldn't have a chance." She looked at the floor, allowing her voice to falter. The reasons she gave Lenet barely scratched the surface of why she would never consent to be with him. "If I had agreed to be with you, I'd always be in fear of your temper, your greed, and your lust. I knew you wouldn't take no for an answer much longer." She looked up at him, hoping he bought the emotion she put behind her words.

"So, I looked for an opportunity to leave." Maleen wrapped one arm around herself and allowed a slight tremble in her voice and body. She remained seated on the floor, allowing Lenet to exert dominance. "When I saw that the merchant used a quick release loop on her harness and the gates were still open, I ran." She put a hand over her face and sobbed.

***

Noture was impressed by his niece's theatrics. They'd apparently served her well over the past year. If only the Kelvian knew she would never be afraid of him. Or, more precisely, she would never let it show unless it was intentional.

Cold rage gripped his stomach at the idea that this depraved man had pursued his niece, but he could say nothing without incriminating both of them. So, for the moment, he sat aside and pretended indifference, struggling to keep his expression neutral.

As Maleen sat on the floor sobbing, the door opened, and two people entered the small prison. A young man, wearing a physician's jacket, saw the arrow still protruding from Maleen's shoulder and hurried into the cell to investigate. He knelt next to her, oblivious to the fact that Lenet was also covered in blood.

Noture recognized the other person as Kayla, daughter of Sub-chief Fanton. Her reaction was distinctly different from the physician's. When Kayla saw whom she was to interrogate, she laughed.

"I heard there was a runaway, but I didn't know who it was," she said to her brother. She peered down at Maleen. "After all this time, I finally get to speak with you." Kayla smoothed the green scarf she wore draped over her shoulders. The adornment marked her as a Grand Voyant, working for the garrison leadership.

"We can't determine whether this woman is a deserter or an infiltrator," Fanton said, clearly less convinced by Maleen's act than his son. "Find out for us."

"The object of my little brother's lust?" Kayla said.

Noture saw the annoyed look Lenet shot her, but Kayla either didn't see or didn't care.

"Now that I'm in the same room with her, she's as easy to read as if I've known her my whole life. She's just never let me get close enough to talk to her." Kayla knelt down. Though wooden bars separated them, the two women were at eye level. Brushing her bright red hair from her face, Kayla asked, "Have you been truthful to my father and brother?"

Noture's heart sank. Maleen was found out. She couldn't answer the question truthfully without incriminating them both. He glimpsed the terror that flickered across her face for a split second.

"Yes." Maleen gave a simple answer, but in that one word her death sentence had been pronounced, and maybe his.

"Liar." Kayla stood up, arms crossed. She took a step back with a smug grin. She turned to Fanton and Lenet. "She's terrified of you both. More than she'd ever let on." Standing straight with an air of confidence, she looked down at Maleen. "I suppose now we all know why you've avoided me since you got here. And I thought it was because you didn't want me to know how much you hated my brother."

"Liar, maybe," the physician said, "but a wounded one. Get out of the way." He helped Maleen onto the bed to better examine the wound.

Is that sympathy? From a Kelvian? Noture tried not to let his surprise show.

"It's just an arrow wound," Fanton said, with a sneer.

The physician spun around. "And a poor job of dressing it. Do you have any idea how quickly infection can set in?"

"Just bandage her up so she doesn't bleed to death before her *public* execution, Phillip." Fanton turned to Noture with hate in his eyes and a growl in his voice. "Explain yourself. Why did the Acorans send a spy into my garrison? If this whore isn't Kelvian, that's the only explanation."

Kayla turned to look at Noture, frowning.

He had to choose his words carefully. While still young—early, maybe mid-twenties—the woman could easily have enough experience to be proficient at using her gift. He'd deceived voyants before, but too much was at stake to take any chances. It could mean the difference between execution and survival. Covering the fear he felt for Maleen with anger at Fanton and Lenet, Noture answered, "I already told you why I was out there. Before returning to my own garrison, I saw a woman coming toward me at a full gallop, with five men in pursuit. I tried to help her."

This time he didn't claim not to know the woman, or who the pursuers were. He chose his words to be sure they were true, even though his intent was not. Kayla looked at him. Noture didn't meet her gaze. There was something in the eyes which made detecting deceit easier for voyants.

Fanton and Lenet both looked at Kayla.

"I don't know," she said after a long moment. "He's an unreadable. But he won't look me in the eye, and that says volumes." Turning back to Maleen and stepping into the cell, Kayla asked, "Maleen, could you be so kind as to tell me who this man is?"

"Lenet said he was a high-ranking warrior for the Acorans," she answered, looking at the ceiling, avoiding Kayla's eyes. Her technique was right, but she didn't have Noture's innate ability to control the emotions voyants read. Most people didn't. Her acting skills could fool anyone else, but not a voyant.

"You dodged my question," Kayla pressed.

At that moment, Phillip poured a cleaning concoction on Maleen's wound.

Maleen groaned. "Ow! What did I ever do to you, Physician?"

"You bled all over me," Phillip scolded. "Hold still."

Was he trying to get her out of the questioning? If so, it would only be temporary. Noture stood watching, leaning on the wall, still pretending he didn't care.

"She's not going to live long enough to die from infection—get the arrow out and stop the bleeding," Fanton growled.

While Phillip worked, Kayla stood over Maleen.

"How do you know the Acoran warrior?"

"He tried to aid me," Maleen answered with no emotion in her voice, still refusing to meet Kayla's gaze.

"And?"

Maleen said nothing.

Kayla turned to her father. "We're not getting an answer, but what do you think? Same auburn hair, same blue eyes. Her father, maybe?"

"He's not old enough," Fanton said, looking from Maleen to Noture. "But certainly related. I should have noticed earlier." The resemblance didn't stop at the color of their hair and eyes. When Maleen clenched her jaw in her refusal to answer Kayla, Noture knew her look mirrored his own as he evasively answered Fanton's questions.

"Big brother? Cousin? Uncle?"

Noture kept his barrier up but, unfortunately, Maleen had none.

"Uncle," Kayla deduced. "Definitely uncle." She smiled unpleasantly.

"Good to know." Fanton narrowed his eyes at Noture. "Thank you, my dear." He offered his arm to his daughter, and the pair left the prison. "Commander Rundel!" he called to someone outside as the door closed behind him.

Having removed the arrow, stanched the blood flow, and wrapped the wound in a bandage, Phillip looked at Maleen for a moment. There was more to his expression than sympathy for an injured person. His shoulders sagged as he carefully packed away his medical tools for cleaning. He stood and followed Kayla and Fanton.

Lenet's expression had changed. Any sympathy he may have had for Maleen was gone. The look he gave her was pure hatred.

Apparently, Maleen was done being docile. She sat up, giving no indication of how much the movement must have hurt her arm or how dizzy she must have been from blood loss. She stood on legs that shook and faced Lenet. He drew back a left-handed fist. She instinctively tried to raise her right hand to block his blow, but her arm wouldn't cooperate. Before she could compensate, and before Noture could step in, Maleen was out cold.

***

"A pretty face!" Fanton yelled at his son across the desk in his office. "You realize all the careful plans that have been waylaid in the past year, every failed excursion into Acora, were because you were distracted. By a pretty face."

"Wanting a woman isn't the same thing as being distracted by her," Lenet growled.

"You couldn't be content with what you already have. What's wrong with Jewel that you couldn't be satisfied? Too big? Not endowed enough? Hair too short? Too light?"

Lenet punched the wall. "Enough!" His father was right. He'd been fooled by a pretty—no—a beautiful face, but it would be a warm day in the arctic before he'd admit it to his father. "Her looks had nothing to do with it. She's an incredible warrior. Maybe even better than Jewel. She's been at the top of her training regiment. There was no reason to think—"

"No reason except we knew there was an informant." Fanton stood and paced the length of the room. "Besides, she failed her test."

"She said it was nerves."

"And you believed her without question." Fanton leaned close to his son's ear. "Because you were more concerned with her other assets."

Lenet clenched his fists. His father had no idea how much restraint it took to resist hitting him. Or maybe he did know, but also knew he was the only person in this garrison who could get away with belittling him.

"You knew that Acoran warrior." The accusation in Fanton's voice was unmistakable.

"I've met him in the ring."

"How did you not realize she was related?"

"You didn't even figure it out when she was standing right next to him until Kayla pointed it out."

The door opened, and Commander Rundel stepped in with another warrior whose name Lenet didn't care to remember. Maleen's uncle was between them. The man wasn't exceptionally tall, barely six feet. His build, however, was every bit as strong as a Kelvian warrior's. While the man tried to appear casual, the rigid way he carried himself said otherwise.

"Who are you?" Fanton demanded.

"Your daughter already determined I'm Maleen's uncle. And I believe it's only been two years since I claimed the championship at the Equin festival. I'm sure your son remembers me for that."

Lenet's scowl deepened.

"What are you doing in my garrison?"

"You insisted I come." The man smirked. Lenet punched him in the stomach. He recovered and took a step toward Lenet. Rundel and the other guard grabbed his arms.

"What are you doing in Kelvia?" Lenet stood inches from the restrained man.

"At the moment? Being questioned by a son of—"

Lenet punched him in the jaw.

"Enough, Lenet," Fanton growled.

"I haven't even gotten started." Lenet drew his fist back again.

Fanton caught his arm mid-swing. "I said that's enough. The day will come when you do things your way. Until then, we *start* with diplomacy." He turned back to the Acoran. "What was that woman doing in my garrison? Did your chief send her?"

The man remained quiet. Lenet stepped up again, but Fanton put his hand in the center of his chest and pushed him back. Lenet seethed. How dare his father reprimand him like a child in front of two warriors and this prisoner?

"Let me get answers." Lenet clenched his fists.

"You'll get your chance." He turned to the man. "Unless he wants to come clean without bleeding."

Still the man said nothing. He lifted his chin and stared at Lenet.

Lenet saw it for what it was. An invitation. He was daring Lenet to take another swing. It was stupid. There were four Kelvians in the room. Not that Lenet would need their help to take out one Acoran. He'd improved immensely since the last time they'd faced off in a tournament. This man had only gotten older. He was at least thirty-five, maybe closer to forty.

"Call Kayla," Fanton ordered the guard.

"That's useless." Lenet sat down. "She said he was an unreadable."

"You'd rather beat him senseless? That only serves to make him tell us what we want to hear." He looked at the Acoran. "Sit down."

"I'm comfortable standing, thank you."

Ignoring the man's protest, Rundel shoved him across the room to a chair.

It was only a moment later when the guard returned with Kayla.

Leave it to her to have been listening by the window.

It was to their father's detriment that he only used Kayla for her voyant abilities when she was capable of so much more. She was more intelligent than any other woman Lenet knew, and more cunning than most men.

"I need to know his thoughts," Fanton said to his daughter.

Kayla sighed. "Father, you know it doesn't work like that."

"All right, I need to know his emotions then."

"I can't. He's blocking me out. I can't tell if he's afraid of you, or confident. Ask all the questions you want, but I can't tell you if he's lying. Maybe with time—"

"We don't have time!" Lenet yelled. "If the Acorans are planning an attack, we need to know."

Kayla took a step back as if he had hit her. She fidgeted with the end of her scarf. Lenet regretted his burst of temper. He hadn't meant to yell. His sister was one of only two people he could count on to follow him to the ends of the world.

"I'm sorry," Lenet said softly. She was also the only one who would ever hear an apology from him. "Do your best. It'll have to do."

"When the other prisoner is conscious, you'll need to be in the room when we interrogate her," Fanton said.

"Her I can read." Kayla's smug smile returned.

The Acoran shifted uncomfortably.

Lenet smiled a little. "What's wrong? Don't think she's as stubborn as you are?"

"She's *more* stubborn than I am. Family trait. The women are always more stubborn."

"But she can't get anything past me," Kayla scoffed.

"No? Then how is it she's been here for ten months?"

"Avoidance and deception are two different things," she said through clenched teeth.

"Why is that girl here?" Fanton demanded.

"Girl? She's of age. Ask her if you think you can get her to tell you." The Acoran crossed his arms and sat back in his chair.

"Did Rabe send you?"

He remained quiet.

"He's a practiced unreadable," Kayla said. "If he was natural, he'd be able to state a lie as if it were nothing."

"Did your chief send you?" Fanton asked again.

"Send him a message and ask him," the man said, evading the question.

"You realize without a claim to your chief's orders, you will be tried and executed for espionage."

"If I say 'Yes, Chief Rabe sent me,' you go to war and we're the first casualties. If I say 'No, we acted on our own,' you execute us. Better not to give an answer."

"Not giving an answer can be dangerous." Fanton looked at Lenet. "We'll question the girl first. Then he's yours."

Rundel and the other guard grabbed the man's arms and dragged him out of the room.

"You should have let me get answers." Lenet made no effort to keep his voice down.

"We're not ready for a war," Fanton said. "Not when we've had a spy in the garrison for a year. At least one. We need to know if there are others."

"Father's right, Lenet." Kayla put a hand on Lenet's arm. "You question her. I'll know if she's telling the truth. Even if she doesn't answer a single question, I'll know."

"I'll be the one interrogating her," Fanton said. "You've been taken in by that woman too much."

"You imply—"

"I'm not implying anything. I'm coming out and saying it. I don't think you can be impartial. I'll ask the questions. You'll sit there and be quiet, or you won't be there at all." Fanton walked out.

Lenet gripped the back of a chair until his knuckles turned white. "One day soon..."

"One day soon, you'll be the sub-chief, and we can do things your way." Kayla squeezed his shoulder in support.

CHAPTER 2

Kelvia, Western Garrison

Regaining consciousness on the cold dirt floor, Maleen began to stir.

"Pay attention to the game, or forfeit," Piel's irritated voice echoed in Maleen's head, snapping her attention back to the Calbo game in front of her.

No, the game wasn't in front of her. Maleen struggled to draw her mind away from the memories of earlier in the day. Moments before this nightmare had begun.

She moved a game piece.
"You're distracted, girlie." Piel laughed, countering her move and taking a step closer to victory.

Lying in the cell, Maleen tried to clear her head. Tried to open her eyes. Tried to wake up and bring her mind back to the present.

She moved another game piece, countering Piel. All afternoon there'd been an unusual quietness in the air. People were going about their business. Watchmen on the towers were relieved by those with fresh eyes and alert minds. She and Piel sat at a table in the shade of the dining hall, the Calbo game between them. Other trainees watched or wandered the courtyard, exhausted after a taxing drill session. Those whose performance was unsatisfactory in the session still ran laps while instructors yelled insults.

No, she wasn't outside. She was in a cell.

Piel kicked her foot under the table to draw her attention back. "Where's your head?" he asked.

Pounding! Maleen couldn't think straight.

She moved another game piece as she watched the stable master and his subordinates take the graebigs from the front gate back to the stables, replacing them with fresh ones.
Their readiness had been to her detriment.
"Are you playing or not?" Piel kicked her foot again.
Maleen tried to ignore her apprehension and concentrate on the game. To everyone else, it was just another day.

"Think they're getting any information from her collaborator?" That voice was much clearer than Piel's. Much closer.
"No. If he's Acoran, he won't give up anything, easily."
"Lenet's not likely to go about it easily."
"Good point. But they need evidence. They can't use Kayla's testimony to connect him to her."
"Not legally, but since when have you known Lenet or Fanton to care about a little detail like that?"
Maleen still couldn't shake the darkness surrounding her as memories of her failure plagued her and she drifted in and out of consciousness.

The supply wagon rolled into the garrison. She ignored the tightening in her chest. Kanda was here. Once more she considered her options. It was broad daylight, but if she waited for nightfall, the gate would be closed. It and the back gate were too well guarded to hope to sneak out after dark. She had to do it in plain sight of everyone. She wouldn't get a second chance.

"I suppose we should go help unload?" she suggested to the other young warrior trainees. Paying no attention to the jeers from Piel and the spectators accusing her of quitting the game for fear of losing, she stood up.

Commander Rundel emerged from a building. "You know what to do," the rough, middle-aged man yelled at the trainees. "You haven't earned your colors yet." He gave a forceful nudge to the trainee standing closest to him.

They all knew better than to grumble about the task of unloading the wagon. Their battle test was coming in four days' time and those who passed would receive the green-trimmed vestments of Kelvian warriors. After the test, there would be a new group of trainees to do the grunt work, such as unloading supply wagons.

Kanda approached casually, giving no indication to anyone else she even knew who Maleen was. Maleen leaned over to remove a rock from her boot, standing up just as Kanda was passing by, bumping into her.

The force of the collision was minor, but Kanda leaned in close. "Are you all right, young lady?" In a discreet movement, Kanda held out her hand.

Instead of slipping the usual note into Kanda's open palm, Maleen said quietly, "I need out."

Those were the only words Kanda needed to hear. She handed Maleen a brush and asked her to take care of the graebigs that pulled the wagon, giving her an excuse to use a stepstool to raise herself closer to the beast's six-foot-high back. Maleen stepped up into position. Kanda took a box from the back of the wagon and, while handing it to a young trainee, dropped it. Fruit scattered in every direction while the merchant demeaned the young man for his clumsiness in a voice that carried across the courtyard.

Maleen pulled the quick release knot on the beast's harness and urged the graebig into motion, pulling herself up onto it. She'd nearly run down other trainees, but Maleen bolted out the gate before the watchmen had time to close it.

She startled and sat up. The pain exploding in her head reminded her of Lenet's reaction to her espionage. Other details of her failure were unclear, but that much she remembered.

The setting sun gave a little light through the small window. She'd been out cold for hours.

Having been so close to finally going home, only to have been thwarted by men who would now want her dead, was a devastating blow. Maleen's head felt like a barkpecker bird was knocking, and her shoulder throbbed as she tried to think clearly.

"Where is the man who tried to help me?" she asked the guards, pulling herself up from the floor onto the cot.

"The chief is questioning him," one replied.

Maleen closed her eyes and sucked in a deep breath. Fanton knew Noture was Acoran. Thanks to Kayla, he knew they were related. She took little solace in the fact that he'd been in better condition to withstand an interrogation.

A guard lit a lamp, turning it up bright. "Tell the chief she's awake," one guard instructed the other. "How's the arm?" he asked Maleen with arms crossed and half a smirk on his face.

Maleen laid down and draped her good arm over her eyes, not giving him the satisfaction of responding.

Moments later, the prison door opened. Noture was shoved into the cell. He turned to glare at the men who locked the cell before they walked outside. When there were no Kelvians left inside the small building, Noture plopped down on the cot. His lip was swollen, but he didn't look like the interrogation had been too serious.

Maleen sat up and whispered, "I'm sorry."

"For what?" Noture inspected her injury as best he could without removing the bandage.

"I still can't control emotions."

"There aren't many people who can deceive voyants." He gently pulled her close to him, mindful of her shoulder. "Don't worry about me. Fanton will use diplomacy for as long as he can. When he's tired of not getting answers, that's when we worry."

Maleen couldn't help but wonder if she should have jumped from Lenet's graebig. Taking the risk seemed better than sitting helplessly in a cell. Then again, Fanton was the one person who could probably outshoot her. A moving target was nothing to him. He'd have taken her down long before she reached the cover of the tree line.

"Whatever happens," Noture took a steadying breath, "remember, you did everything for the right reasons."

His words did nothing to alleviate her fear of a painful interrogation, followed by an extraordinarily painful and public execution by slow strangulation. Most likely for both of them. The Kelvians would not take kindly to an infiltrator.

Kelvians, particularly those in the Western Province, were known for being brutal. Their tribal leadership was always at risk from those who would seek to unseat them. The threats were usually internal, a faction within the tribe who was unhappy with the current leadership. Now they found an outsider who appeared to be trying the same thing. Fanton would most certainly make an example of Maleen *and* Noture.

"Now that they know I'm Acoran...will they make a charge against Chief Rabe?" She leaned against Noture's shoulder, speaking without emotion, refusing to give any indication of how she felt, even to one who knew her as well as her uncle did—but she'd be foolish not to have any fear. An involuntary shudder gripped her.

"The Chiefs' Council at Equin is still three months away. I don't think Fanton will wait that long." He shook his head sadly, running his hand through his short hair. "Not to mention he's only a sub-chief, so he'd have to go to his brother and explain how his own actions led Acorans to do this. It's better for Rabe if they don't know *how* connected you are to the leadership. But...since you're not a member of the chief's family yet, the trial will be quick. They can't technically use the voyant's testimony to convict you of anything. But the trial will be a mockery anyway."

"One judge, instead of a ten-man jury?" Maleen said. "When *isn't* a Kelvian trial a mockery?"

"You may have more of a chance if you admit to being sent by Chief Rabe as one of his Elites," Noture added. "*If* Fanton follows the *Code of Conduct*, he'll have to contact Rabe. Considering it's you, the chief may come himself, but even if he sends Commander Nell, it'll still give him time to get a message to Chief Tyndall, asking him to step in. Fanton *shouldn't* be handling this on his own anyway."

"I can't do that."

"I know." Noture sighed. "Doesn't mean I can't want you to."

Maleen couldn't make such a confession without making trouble for the Acoran chief with the entire Kelvian tribe, not just the Western Province. She wouldn't let her fear of death be the cause of so much turmoil. And there was absolutely no way she could reveal how close she was to the chief's family.

Maleen longed to be home, in her own garrison, surrounded by her tribe and people she loved. She'd been gone since the day after she came of age, almost a year ago. When she'd seen the supply wagon that afternoon, she had been elated, having already planned to leave as soon as her contact arrived. Now there was a very real possibility she would never see another Acoran again.

"How is everyone at home?"

"They're well. They're looking forward to seeing you again," Noture said with a mischievous grin. "One young man in particular, who still hasn't forgiven his father for sending you on such a dangerous and prolonged mission alone. What was that young man's name?" His teasing did nothing to diminish the tension they both felt, but it did make Maleen give a half-hearted attempt to smile.

"Leave it to Cutter." She sighed. "The only one who can give the chief an unrestrained piece of his mind and still be standing afterward."

"He's a strong and steady young warrior." Noture had never made a secret of his approval of her intended. "It's too bad he doesn't aspire to be Chief."

"He's a great warrior and an even better man, but his diplomatic skills aren't any better than yours, and we won't even talk about his skills with strategy." She chuckled. "We've known for a long time he doesn't belong in the chief's seat." Her smile disappeared at the thought that she might never see her love again. "Did Chief Rabe name Asher as his heir?"

This was the first chance in months she'd had to receive any news from home. Her betrothed's cousin was next in line for the chief's seat if Cutter allowed it to pass by him. Asher had been old enough to be named Chief Heir only a month after Maleen left for Kelvia. When his birthday had passed, she'd regretted not being there to celebrate his coming of age, but she'd been given a job to do. At the time, she had still been looking for a way to get into the Kelvian garrison.

Currently, it seemed all the information she had gathered over the past year would be wasted.

"Rabe hasn't made the announcement yet," Noture said. "Everyone expected it at Asher's twentieth birthday, especially Asher's wife, but I suppose Rabe feels he has plenty of time to choose his successor, even if we all know who's next in line."

She sat quietly for a moment, contemplating the wisdom of the Chief Heir being married so young to a woman like Denetra.

"I joined the warriors' council this year," Noture continued. The idle conversation was easier than dwelling on what awaited them when Fanton came back. He wasn't likely to be as civil as he'd been at the first interrogation. "I go from teaching children to be warriors in the daytime to being treated like a child by older warriors in the evening."

Maleen smiled again. Fifteen was the youngest any student could become a warrior, though few ever graduated so early. Twenty years of being a warrior made Noture eligible for the council at only thirty-five. Despite his experience and his proven strength, being the youngest member meant it would be some time before the older warriors accepted Noture's voice.

"Why didn't you bring Cutter to the rendezvous point?" It was sentiment that brought her back to thoughts of her betrothed, but at this point, she didn't care. It was likely she would never see him again. Talking about him was as close as she could get.

"It's bad enough to send a close relative who's recognizable to the Kelvians but imagine the diplomatic nightmare of our present situation if the Acoran chief's son was with us."

"Understood." She chewed her lip. Maleen often forgot herself when it came to thoughts about Cutter. She should have realized how ridiculous her question was before she asked it. Cutter may have declined the chief's seat, but that would matter little in diplomatic circles if he were found in the rival tribe's territory uninvited.

"I thought I taught you strategy a little better than that," Noture said.

"I'm out of practice. I haven't been able to get any good opponents to play Calbo with."

"When was the last time I won a game against you?" He chuckled. Noture had taught her the strategy game at an early age. Good opponents were rare for someone with her skill and intelligence.

"I guess you taught me too well." She laughed a little. "Do you know how difficult it is to let inferior opponents win Calbo without looking like a complete dunce?"

"You let them win?"

"I had to, at least part of the time. I had to get them to talk to me. Most of these warriors and trainees grew up here. I was an outsider. There are more Lady Warriors in this garrison than we have in the entire territory, but there's something about them that makes the men treat them like men...until they want the comfort of a woman."

Maleen had a feeling it had to do with the fact that they had to act like men or be treated as inferior. Not all tribes respected their women the way the Acorans did.

Acora was far from egalitarian, but her own family was a prime example of Acoran family life. Her parents were farmers. Her stepmother was also a midwife but spent most of her energy on the domestic workings of the household. Maleen's father provided for and protected the family, encouraging his three daughters to pursue less dangerous professions, but he did it out of a protective heart, not out of the need for dominance that seemed to be prevalent in tribes like Kelvia—and he never considered stopping his eldest daughter from training to be a warrior as he had once been.

Noture stood up, eyeing the window. He didn't really think she could fit through that, did he? It was too small for even her thin frame. He lowered his voice. "So, enough sentiment. You're the resident expert on the Kelvians. How do we get out of here? Unless you intend to sit by, feeling sorry for yourself, waiting for an execution."

"Phillip," she said, a surge of strength going through her at the realization that there might be one Kelvian in this place who would be willing to help her.

"The physician?"

"He's the only one I would trust at this point. He's always known I had some sort of façade going. He even asked me about it once or twice, but never mentioned it to anyone." She eased herself to the edge of the bed, trying not to move her arm. "He's particularly vocal about his feelings on the way Fanton crosses the border without just cause. He's no warrior, but he's no coward either."

"We'll only get one chance at this. If we fail, we don't reach a trial. Mockery or otherwise. Are you sure he'll help?"

"You noticed his crest." She sighed.

"How could I miss it?"

Phillip's family crest, sewn on the shoulder of his physician's jacket, was a blend of Fanton's and another which would only be recognizable to those who knew the family.

"He's the adopted son of Fanton's sister," Maleen explained. "The other half of his crest is his adopted father's family."

"I also noticed the look he gave you before walking out of here."

"A look I never encouraged." Her chest constricted a bit at the memory of the hurt in his expression as he had walked out of the prison. "I'll ask for help. *If* he says yes, then I trust him to do it. Betrayal isn't his style."

"We can't wait until morning. Fanton will be back by then. How do we get your friend in here?"

"Very painfully." Maleen prodded at her wound. Fresh blood stained the bandage and a larger swath of her torn shirt. She let out a loud, exaggerated cry of pain and fell to the floor.

"Guard!" Noture yelled, loud enough to be heard through the brick walls and wooden door. When a young warrior answered the summons, Noture shouted, "She's bleeding again."

The guard picked up the clean bandages Phillip had left on the table. "Put pressure on it," he ordered, handing them through the wooden bars.

"It's too deep. We need the physician." Noture appeared to be putting pressure on the wound, though, in reality, he was allowing the blood flow to continue, soaking the fresh bandage in a short time.

Maleen let the mask of composure she wore slip and allowed the Kelvian guard to see the pain in her eyes and the sweat glistening on her face. She needed it to look convincing.

When the guard hurried out to find Phillip, Noture did put pressure on the wound.

"If a prisoner dies before a trial, it'll make Fanton look bad," Maleen said through clenched teeth. "That fellow knows it, and knows if Fanton looks bad, it'll come back on him." She tried to chuckle but groaned as the prison door opened again and the guard stepped back in with Phillip.

He opened the cell door for Phillip then stood back at a distance.

"I need more bandages." Phillip showed him the bloody cloths. "She's losing too much blood. Get more from the infirmary."

The guard paled at the sight of the blood, but still had the presence of mind to bolt the cell door closed before leaving to retrieve fresh bandages.

"I'll never understand it." Phillip chuckled. "You're all trained to shed blood, but some can't handle the sight of it."

When the guard was gone, Maleen grabbed the edge of Phillip's jacket, leaving a bloody handprint on the green trim. "We need your help."

"I know," he said quietly. He pulled clean bandages from his bag and tried to stop the flow of blood from Maleen's shoulder. "Help is coming."

"Who?" Maleen couldn't imagine anyone else in this garrison who would be willing to help her now that they knew she'd spent the past year lying to them.

Phillip hesitated before answering, "Jewel."

"Jewel? Are you *insane*? The woman wanted me dead the moment I got here."

"Who's Jewel?" Noture asked.

"The one woman in this garrison who could give Maleen a good fight," Phillip said. He pressed a crot leaf to her shoulder. "It'll slow the bleeding, but I'll have to clean the wound again," he warned. "Before Maleen came, there wasn't a woman here who could beat Jewel. And few men."

"She fought long and hard for her status," Maleen pointed out. "And she's got very few other qualities to be proud of."

"And the attention Lenet gives you doesn't help matters any," Phillip added.

Maleen groaned, more from Phillip's reminder than from the heat of the treatment he applied to her shoulder. She had watched the jealousy eat away at Jewel every time she saw Lenet talking to Maleen. To think Jewel would betray Lenet was inconceivable. Even more unlikely was that Jewel would be willing to help *her*.

"Regardless of how she feels about you, she wants out, same as us."

Phillip's use of the word "us" did not go unnoticed. Phillip was unhappy here, but Maleen had not expected he would want to leave his home.

"Jewel has been coming to see me lately. She's pregnant and doesn't want to raise a child in a garrison, at least not in this one. Neither does Sampton. They need somewhere to go where they won't be tried for desertion. They wanted a diplomatic way out before she started showing but haven't found one."

"Sampton and Jewel?" Maleen narrowed her eyes. The pair seemed unlikely. "I don't trust that combination." She didn't know Sampton other than by name, but there was no reason to expect him to turn on his sub-chief or have a relationship with Jewel. And there was no way Maleen would ever trust Jewel, no matter what man she was running around with.

"I don't know that we have much of a choice," Noture said as the door to the prison opened and the guard stumbled into the small room, propelled from behind.

Sampton smashed the handle of his knife into the back of the guard's head. "Sorry about that. I know you're only doing your job." Unbarring the cell door, he asked the prisoners, "Ready to get out of here?"

"If Maleen doesn't bleed to death first." Phillip helped her up from the floor.

"I'm fine." As soon as Maleen tried to stand, however, she realized she wasn't fine. She'd lost too much blood to be steady on her feet. Seeing her waver, Phillip and Noture each took an arm and helped her follow Sampton out of the prison. On the way out, Noture grabbed his bow and quiver, which had been placed on the table when he'd been escorted into the cell.

Night had fallen, and few people wandered the garrison. Most of the torches were extinguished.

"Jewel is on duty at the back gate," Sampton explained as they made their way through the shadows.

"Who else?" Maleen asked. Those guards had been the reason she hadn't tried to leave at night, under the cloak of darkness.

"Does it matter?" Sampton laughed, glancing over his shoulder.

It would be slower going on the back trail, but the rear gate was small. Not even wide enough for a graebig, it was less guarded and there was no watchtower. The trek through the woods would take much longer but would be safer than the main road.

Jewel was waiting at the gate, an unconscious watchman at her feet. "Let's go." Her voice was harsh, but quiet as she tossed a pack to Sampton. "So much for our marksman," she said, looking at Maleen, who leaned heavily on Phillip.

After a year of putting up with Jewel's insults, Maleen had finally stepped up to her two days before, but Phillip had stopped the fight before it started. At the time, he'd refused to tell her why. Jewel's cold blue eyes told Maleen she'd not forgotten and would take the first opportunity to rectify it. Apparently, Maleen would have nine months to recover well enough to take her on.

Jewel grabbed a torch from the sconce on the wall nearest the gate.

Noture snatched it from her. "Are you trying to give away our position the second anyone discovers we're gone?" He jabbed the tip into the dirt, smothering the flame, and shoved it back at Jewel.

"Do you have any idea how hard it is to get to the alchemy chemicals to treat those torches?" she hissed, examining the ruined tip.

"Better than being seen," Noture muttered.

Jewel wore a cloak with a hood that would hide her light skin and blonde head. Sampton's much darker complexion allowed him to nearly disappear in the shadows, but he handed the other three dark-colored cloaks.

As they stepped out of the gate, Maleen turned to Phillip. "Don't come unless you're sure. No one else knows you're involved. It's not too late to go back." She saw the look in Phillip's eyes that she'd tried to ignore for the past several months. "I'm engaged. Don't leave your home because of me." She removed her arm from his shoulder and leaned on her uncle for support. Phillip hesitated for only a moment, then followed them.

Due to the animosity between the tribes, there were only two roads that crossed the border. Kelvia had built guard towers at both. The small back trails which ran through both territories, connecting village to village, never crossed the border. So, it was through the woods that they made their escape.

***

Ten minutes outside of the garrison, the trail ended at a creek. On the other side of the creek was a wide clearing. It would be at least fifty yards before they'd be able to find cover. That was fifty yards of vulnerability with a full moon in a cloudless sky.

"Here they come." Sampton looked back the way they'd come. A group of people moved covertly, but not completely silent, somewhere behind them.

"Hurry," Noture hissed, waiting as the group stepped tentatively across the stones of the creek. Once across the creek, there was no trail. The water marked the boundary between Acora and Kelvia. Noture doubted the boundary line would be a hindrance to the pursuers. The last one to cross, he glanced over his shoulder. Shadowed figures approached. No one carried a torch. Even through the trees, the moonlight was sufficient.

Smart, Noture thought. The flickering flame of a torch would only serve to hinder their night vision. He crouched behind a boulder. Nearby, Maleen crouched near the physician. The other two Kelvians darted behind a large bush.

The group of pursuers stopped at the creek. Noture could make out five searchers. Against himself and only two other capable warriors, their chances were not good, even if he could trust Jewel and Sampton.

"Surrender and return. We won't hesitate to cross the border to seize fugitives." Noture thought he recognized Fanton's voice, but without being able to see, he couldn't confirm. Instead, he knocked an arrow to his bow. It was risky, but the only way out.

The arrow sailed through the air and hit the speaker. The man cried out, and his companions drew near to inspect his injury.

"Run," Noture whispered to his companions. He'd shot over the border. If they hadn't already planned to pursue, Noture had just given them a reason.

"We'll pick up the trail in the morning. Get my father back to the garrison," a firm, commanding voice said.

"The physician is with them. We need them first." This speaker sounded older, his voice just as commanding.

"No," the first voice replied. "Back to the garrison. Now."

To Noture's relief, the entire group gathered and returned up the path. He waited a moment before turning and leading the way to the thicket.

"That was Fanton," Maleen panted, still recovering from the mad dash to cover.

"You shot Fanton?" Jewel demanded. "We're not in a deep enough pile of graebig dung as it is? You had to heap more on the pile?"

A sense of dread filled his gut. There was no escaping the consequences. Now he had to warn his tribe that an attack may be imminent. "We have to get to the garrison."

Maleen stood, wavered for a second, then fell to her knees.

"Maleen?" Noture called.

"I'm fine." Her voice cracked.

"No, she isn't," Phillip said, helping her to her feet. "She's lost too much blood. The crot leaf only works for so long. If infection sets in, the damage to her shoulder could be permanent."

"My shoulder feels like I got stabbed, then stung by a swarm of fire beetles," Maleen admitted.

"Not surprising. The heat is from the crot," Phillip said. "It clots the blood but can cause infection if not cleaned out properly. When we get somewhere I can get supplies, I'll have to clean it again and check the tendon and muscle tissue. Otherwise, you may never draw a bow or swing a staff again."

Such news could be devastating to a person of her skill, but a good physician wouldn't hide the truth. Maleen only nodded.

Good girl, Noture thought. *Wait and see before you react to that piece of information.*

Her face said that right now it took every ounce of strength she had to stay on her feet without vomiting or passing out. Or both.

Noture took her good arm and swung it over his shoulder. "If it's all the same to you, we'll have our garrison physician examine it when we get home." These Kelvians had quite likely saved their lives, but for a seasoned warrior, trust didn't come easily. Particularly for one from Fanton's family.

"Where's home?" Jewel asked, shifting her weight and fidgeting with the straps to her pack.

"Northern Garrison, Acora," Noture said. It was too late for secrets, whether these three were trustworthy or not.

"That's only two hours by the main road on foot," Sampton observed.

"It'll be a lot longer through the woods, but we can't risk the road." Noture's tone left no room for argument. Their escape had come far too easily. One more reason not to trust their rescuers.

"And a lot longer than that if you don't want Maleen to bleed to death before we get there," Phillip warned. "We'll have to take it slow."

"Well, we're not getting any closer standing around talking about it." Jewel started walking.

Throughout the trek, the three men endured angry protests from

Jewel at their slow progress and frequent moans from Maleen as she tried to push through the pain and dizziness. Noture fought back the urge to slap Jewel multiple times through the night. The woman made so much noise stomping through the woods, that it gave a warning to anyone of their location. When she voiced what felt like her fiftieth complaint about their pace, he clenched his fist. He did not like her and trusted her even less.

***

After three bandage changes, the group saw the northern wall of the Acoran garrison. It was the first time Maleen had seen her home in over a year. Her heart longed for the people inside. Sitting in that Kelvian prison, she'd been sure she would never see any of them again. The sun had barely risen. Though its light did little to warm the frigid air, it did fill Maleen with a different kind of warmth to see it shining on the walls of her home.

"We should go around to the front gate, before we're mistaken for trespassers," Maleen warned. Neither she nor Noture wore the Acoran purple which would identify them from a distance. She knew the danger if the watchman on the tower saw the Kelvians' green-trimmed vests before recognizing that she and Noture were with them, but she didn't care to insult their rescuers by asking them to remove their colors.

As they approached the front gate, a watchman issued a challenge, "You in the shadows, come into the clearing where I can see you."

Noture complied.

"Commander!" Maleen's former classmate climbed down from the tower and opened the gate. "Chief Rabe sent a search party after you at first light, but no one would say where you had gone. What happened?"

"This happened." Noture waved to the rest of the party. Maleen came out of the shadows, leaning on Phillip, with Sampton and Jewel close behind.

"Maleen?" The watchman hesitated. "It *is* you." He held his arms out to her. He would have had no idea where she'd been for the past year. "Rumors have run rampant, but anyone who knows you knows better than to believe them," he prompted, his voice earnest, apparently hoping for an explanation.

"Hello, Tobal," she said as she hugged him with her good arm. At his tight embrace, she gave a small gasp of pain.

"What happened?" He looked at her face, then her blood-soaked shirt, fresh blood amassing over what had dried on the long walk.

"Long story, my friend. Thanks to Phillip here, I haven't bled to death yet, but I'm afraid my uncle won't relax until I see Batal." She wavered a bit.

"The physician went out with the search party this morning. Unless they see your tracks heading this way, they won't be back until nightfall."

"We tried not to leave any tracks," Maleen said. "Any we did leave won't be noticeable unless they knew where to look." She glanced at Phillip.

"Maleen can't wait that long," Phillip pleaded with Noture. "The longer we wait, the higher the risk of infection and the less likely I'll be able to repair any damage."

Noture looked at Maleen.

She nodded to him and turned to Phillip. "In Acora, I can make my own decisions, with or without a male relative nearby."

Phillip's cheeks turned slightly red, and he nodded. "We need to get started quickly."

Noture transferred her arm from his shoulder to Phillip's. As he did, he leaned forward to whisper, "The physician's assistant doesn't leave your side, understand?"

Maleen's nod was barely perceivable. She trusted Phillip, but she'd give her uncle the simple concession to set his mind at ease.

As Maleen leaned on Phillip and gave him directions to the infirmary, a crowd formed. At first, everyone wondered why Noture brought three Kelvians into the garrison, then whispers started as they recognized Maleen among them. Noture issued orders regarding precautions for the other two visitors. Jewel's grating voice rose in complaint at being treated as disreputable visitors, instead of the pair who'd saved their lives. Noture's response was lost to her as Maleen and Phillip entered the infirmary, but she had a feeling it was less-than-diplomatic.

***

"Drink this," ordered Mattie, the physician's assistant and daughter. She handed Maleen a mug of thessel tea Phillip had prepared.

Maleen refused the sedative. "Not until I see—" Her sentence was cut short by someone bursting through the door with a complete disregard for whom he might be disturbing. "Cutter!" Maleen's joy at seeing him knocked out all the emotional defenses she tried so hard to maintain. The tears over the whole ordeal flowed as he embraced her. Embarrassed, she wiped them away.

Cutter brushed her hair back and leaned down to kiss her. For a moment, Maleen had no other concerns. The surgery she urgently needed, the two untrustworthy Kelvians outside, the rigorous debriefing that was to come, even the backlash they could expect from Kelvia all faded away as she kissed Cutter for the first time in over a year.

The moment was cut much too short when Phillip cleared his throat.

"We need to get started on that shoulder." Phillip gently laid a hand on Cutter's arm.

Maleen saw the invisible mask Phillip put up, hiding his feelings.

"If you find Noture, he'll explain everything." Phillip nodded toward the door.

"I'm not going anywhere," Cutter said, eyeing the green trim on Phillip's physician's jacket. Cutter took the mug of thessel from Mattie and handed it to Maleen. "You take this, and I'll see you when you wake up." Maleen complied and lay down.

Cutter bent to kiss her one more time. His face was the last image she saw as the sedative took effect. Smiling, Maleen closed her eyes, feeling safe for the first time in an incredibly long time.

CHAPTER 3

When Maleen began to stir, Cutter stopped his pacing and sat on the edge of her bed before Phillip could move closer.

He wants his face to be the first thing she sees. Phillip tried to smile, pushing back the hint of jealousy.

Mattie, the young woman who'd assisted him with the surgery, closed the book she'd been reading. "I'll go tell her uncle and the chief she's awake." She slipped quietly from the room.

Maleen opened her eyes. She looked up at Cutter, unfocused.

"It seems you have a fine physician here." Cutter brushed Maleen's matted hair away from her face. "A wound like that, taking so long to be treated...but he beat the infection."

As she tried to sit up, Maleen grimaced and lay back down. "How bad was it?"

"The arrowhead missed the bone," Phillip reported, coming to check her bandage. "I got the wound clean on the inside, where infection is likely to start."

Chief Rabe and Noture entered the room. Instead of the physician's assistant, an elderly woman followed them in.

"How long until my favorite Elite is on her feet?" the chief asked.

"For show? Another hour or so and she'll be fully awake," Phillip said. "I would have expected it sooner, but she's slow to come out of the sedative. I don't usually like to use thessel when there's so much blood loss, but I had to probe around for any splinters left behind. I had no choice. Nobody wants to be awake for that."

"I have a vulnerability to thessel," Maleen said. Her eyes drooped a little and she stifled a yawn. "One time when I broke my arm, Batal gave me just enough for pain when he set the bone. I slept for two hours. Scared him to death."

"That would have been nice to know before I made it so strong," Phillip said. "You should have a much weaker dose, even for a surgery." He supposed the physician's assistant couldn't keep track of who had an issue with what. He certainly wasn't going to insult her. She had been a great help. He wondered if there was a record somewhere he should have consulted. Few physicians kept as careful records as he did. "In that case, a couple of hours more sleep, and she can be on her feet. She'll be weak from the blood loss for a week or so and shouldn't exert herself. We'll have to immobilize the arm for a week, maybe two. After that, I'd like to evaluate her movement range, and have her do basic exercises to build back strength and flexibility before *slowly* resuming any sort of normal workout routine." He stared at her when he emphasized the word, but he didn't expect Maleen would listen to his recommendation.

He paused, tugging at his jacket before continuing. "We have to be diligent about keeping it clean and not risking tearing it open again. If even a little infection sets in, you could lose the use of your arm."

"You'll do us the favor of keeping that piece of information in this room," Cutter instructed, sitting on the bed, stroking Maleen's arm. "And I'll still feel better when Batal gets back to examine you."

"That's not necessary." Maleen reached up and brushed Cutter's blond hair away from his brown eyes and laid her hand on his cheek. "Phillip has my complete confidence."

"It is necessary," Chief Rabe said, looking at her firmly. "We don't know anything about the people you brought with you."

Phillip sighed as the chief indicated his own family crest and nodded slightly in Phillip's direction. Cutter gave a small nod. Did the two men think he wouldn't notice the gesture? He was Kelvian. Half his crest matched the Kelvian chief. That fact alone would make earning their trust difficult, if not impossible.

"I *do* know them," Maleen insisted. "You can't trust the other two, but I've watched Phillip's skills as a physician and grown to know his character over the past year. In the last several months, since his father died, I've seen him act as the sole garrison physician, with twice the number of warriors to look after as Batal. I count both his skill and his honor as an asset to this garrison for as long as he chooses to stay." She set her jaw in confidence.

Phillip wondered at the tone she used to speak up to the chief, essentially inviting Phillip to stay with them. He appreciated she didn't put him in the same class with Jewel and Sampton. But had she overstepped bounds? Fanton wouldn't have taken that tone from anyone but Lenet. Not even the woman everyone had thought Lenet would end up marrying.

"Don't hold his family of origin against him. He's nothing like Fanton or Lenet," she finished.

"It's all right, Maleen." Phillip patted her hand but drew back as Cutter's posture stiffened. Phillip only knew the Acoran chief's son by reputation. His broad shoulders and six-foot-three frame could intimidate, but Phillip was more concerned about the reputation Cutter had made for himself as one of the best hand-to-hand fighters at the last few Equin Festivals. "They obviously care about you and the safety of the garrison. They'd be remiss not to take precautions."

The flash of red in Cutter's face told Phillip just how much the other man cared about her. Phillip took a step away from his friend's bedside. He was tall and as strong as any warrior, but he was a pacifist, almost to a fault. A woman's attention wasn't something he was willing to risk a confrontation for. From what he'd observed, Maleen returned this man's affections.

"We have guards escorting both Jewel and Sampton," Cutter said. He looked at Phillip. "And another is assigned to you as soon as you step out of this room."

Phillip understood. They were right to take safety measures.

"Our escape was too easy," Maleen said, pausing long enough to stifle another yawn. "A single arrow sent the entire troop of pursuers back to the garrison. That's not like the Kelvians."

"It was Lenet who called the retreat," Phillip said. "That doesn't sit right. I'd have expected Lenet to send one or two people with Fanton back to the garrison and continued his pursuit more fervently than before his father was shot."

"What can you tell us about the other two who helped us?" Noture asked.

"If you call a voyant into the room, I won't be insulted," Phillip said, before realizing that if they intended to use a voyant, they wouldn't care whether he was insulted or not.

"Winloen," Rabe said to the old woman who'd set about cleaning the room, "Come here, please. No need for a ruse."

Winloen didn't wear a purple scarf, which would identify her as a Grand Voyant. Apparently, Chief Rabe had brought her in under false pretenses. If a person didn't know he was being read, he was less likely to have a guard up against a voyant. It was a common tactic among many tribes, though he was mildly surprised that the Acorans would use deception. Maleen had said nothing when Winloen entered the room.

Phillip glanced at Maleen. *Smart lady.* For these men to trust Phillip, he had to prove his character. Not warning him about a voyant was one way for Maleen to help him earn their trust. Phillip didn't know how strong Winloen was, but he would answer honestly and completely because it was the kind of man he was. If there were tribal secrets he wasn't willing to share, he would say so. He would not lie about it.

The infirmary was a casual place to hold an interrogation, but there were no other patients in the small room, and the physician's assistant hadn't returned.

"Jewel and Sampton were both in the garrison before I was adopted and apprenticed by the previous physician," Phillip began. "Jewel and I were only children. Sampton was a young adolescent. I knew Jewel's father. He was *not* a nice man. Jewel has an obvious attachment to Lenet. She always has, even as an adolescent, but more so since Lenet stood up to her father a couple of years ago, expelling him from the garrison. Not that he treats her any better than her father did."

"I know that attachment is part of the reason she hates me so much," Maleen interjected. At Cutter's questioning look, she took his hand.

"Lenet was attracted to me. Don't worry. I was careful, but it was no secret. Supposedly it was an honor of some sort." She grimaced.

Phillip tried not to laugh aloud at the look on her face. The other Lady Warriors and trainees in the garrison had been split between disbelief that she would turn Lenet down, and warnings about crossing Jewel.

"Jewel's dislike for Maleen, because of that attraction, was just as obvious," Phillip added. "That's why I was so surprised when Jewel came to me and offered to help her. I wasn't sure I could trust her, and I'm still not." He looked the chief in the eye. "But I didn't see any other way to get the two of them out. I don't fight and, because of our friendship, I'd be a suspect when she was discovered. Even if he didn't have me arrested, Fanton would have had someone watching me by morning. We couldn't wait."

"Maybe this woman wanted the competition out of the garrison?" Cutter suggested.

"That's not how Kelvians operate." Maleen tried again to sit up with Cutter's help. "If they want a competitor gone, it's *not* by seeing them out of the garrison, unless it's on a funeral bed."

"Jewel came to me a week ago about her pregnancy, before your infiltration was known," Phillip said. "That's why I stepped between the two of you the other day. At the time she didn't tell me who the father was. I assumed it was Lenet, but now she's claiming it's Sampton."

"So, she *is* pregnant?" Noture asked.

Phillip shrugged. "She wouldn't let me examine her. She said she'd seen the midwife. My father always preferred it that way when our ladies were pregnant, and I had no issue with continuing the policy."

"What reason would she have to lie about it? At least to you?" Maleen asked, her eyes drooping.

"That's a legitimate question," Phillip said. "To a woman like Jewel, pregnancy would be an inconvenience and motherhood even more so. Kelvia has extremely strict rules regarding pregnant Lady Warriors. Not only are they not allowed to fight, they can't even hold a staff until the child is weaned. I think that law was passed to ensure mothers are no longer fit enough to regain the position of a warrior by the time their first child is a year old. It doesn't make sense for Jewel to fake it." Phillip shrugged.

Sampton's claim to fatherhood was hard enough to believe. The fact that Jewel hadn't shared the information with anyone else made it more unbelievable. Keeping such a secret was a risky endeavor for someone who was prone to provoking fights. "When she said she wanted out of the garrison, I suggested she go to Fanton. He wouldn't want his son to marry one of our own ladies. It would serve no diplomatic purpose. I figured he'd send her away, even if Lenet didn't. But if Lenet's not the father, it would explain why she refused. Given the differences in their appearances, there is no way Sampton's child could be mistaken for Lenet's."

"What about the man? What can you tell us about him?" Rabe asked.

"Sampton keeps to himself, mostly. I barely know him," Phillip said. "Until last night, he never gave any indication of disloyalty. His desertion surprised me more than Jewel's."

"Fatherhood can change a man's priorities," Noture said.

"*If* he is the father." Maleen squeezed her eyes shut for a second. It was surprising she was able to keep her mind clear enough to follow the conversation. "I never saw them together."

"I'm not convinced he is, but if I were him," Phillip said, staring at nothing in particular, "I wouldn't want to get on Lenet's bad side by being seen with Jewel. You saw what he did to Jidad when he caught him just flirting with you. And he's been attached to her much longer."

"So, if we assume the worst, and they aren't here to avoid having a child grow up in the most corrupt garrison on Chalent, why are they here and why did they help us?" Noture looked at Phillip, who could only shrug and hope they were not as suspicious of him, though it was likely.

"To get a spy in here?" Cutter asked hesitantly.

"Doesn't make much sense." Noture shook his head. "It won't be long before we'll know for certain if they lied to get in here. They won't have much time to gather the information they're looking for. For that, they help a known spy escape?"

"Doesn't sound like something Lenet would agree to," Maleen said. "And the father does nothing without consulting the son."

Phillip nodded. "He is his mother's son," he muttered.

"Meaning?" Cutter asked.

"If you believe the rumors, the only reason she married Fanton was because he was a brother to Tyndall. She convinced Fanton to ask his brother to divide the territory into provinces and give Fanton the most strategically placed one as a sub-tribe. That was more than twenty years ago. Even after she died, Lenet still takes the lead in much of the havoc they rain on the surrounding tribes. There's a reason Lenet has the reputation he does, even at his age."

"So, *if* they weren't sent as spies and *if* Jewel isn't pregnant, then why did they risk everything to help us?" Noture asked.

"Sabotage?" Cutter asked, his voice barely above a whisper. "Maybe they didn't risk anything because Fanton sent them."

For a moment, no one moved or spoke.

At last, Phillip broke the silence. "Well, unless you have more questions, I'd better get out of here. I'm sure you'll want to analyze everything I said." He nodded acknowledgment to Winloen.

"Phillip." Maleen smiled sadly.

"It's all right, my friend. Thank you for your trust, but it'll take time to build with your people." From the looks Cutter continued to give him, Phillip realized he shouldn't stay in the Acoran garrison long enough to earn that trust.

"I have one more question for you, young man," Chief Rabe said. "We have reason to believe the Kelvians are getting information about us from somewhere. Do you know where?"

"No, sir," Phillip said honestly. "What I know about Acorans is only what I overhear careless warriors say. They never seem to know where their information comes from." He stood, nodding to Rabe and Cutter. When he exited the hut, he wasn't surprised to see a guard by the door. "I'm going to the dining hall. I suppose you'll be joining me, so you may as well show me the way." The guard chuckled at Phillip's candor and gladly obliged.

***

"Every word he said is true," Winloen said, as the door closed behind him. "He was open, quite easy to read. He was appalled, but not surprised, by the suggestion of sabotage."

"If he was working with the other two, he probably wouldn't have shared his concerns about them with us," Rabe said.

"So now will you trust him?" Maleen asked both Cutter and Rabe.

"We'll see." The chief patted her hand.

"Good enough." She closed her eyes and, in an effort not to fall asleep, she quickly opened them again, sighing deeply.

"We'll discuss it more when you're a little more lucid." Noture kissed her forehead. He and Rabe left the room, with Winloen following close behind.

"The search party who went looking for Noture will be back soon. I know there's at least two people who will be disappointed if you don't stay awake long enough to greet them." Cutter's voice sounded far away. Maleen's eyelids refused to stay open, and she couldn't answer him.

***

When she woke in the dimly lit hut, Maleen could see that her betrothed slept on a cot on the other side of the room. She smiled at the sight of him. He hadn't left her side. It didn't surprise her. Cutter was as compassionate as he was strong and as loyal as he was brave.

By the time Cutter was seventeen, Chief Rabe had given up trying to shape him into the next leader of the tribe. His encounter with Phillip was only a minor example of his lack of diplomacy. But Cutter wasn't bothered by it, he was only bothered by disappointing his father.

Only a day after his proposal, they'd had to postpone their marriage plans when Maleen had been ordered to infiltrate the Kelvian garrison. He had been furious with his father and the council, yet he supported her choice to go where she was ordered, knowing that, as an Elite, she'd vowed to put duty before anything, just as he had.

It had taken time to convince people she was as capable as her status suggested, but she'd passed the same tests as any male Elite. Few people expected her to pass, even among those who supported her right to test. Once she wore the Elite patch, her skills were at the disposal of the garrison commander, Nell, who took pride in his Elite force.

Only a handful of people outside of the council knew where she'd been sent. Maleen hoped Cutter hadn't had to endure too much gossip with her unexplained disappearance from the garrison. Only those who didn't know her would dare to make any assumptions. Still, when she left the garrison unexpectedly for a prolonged period, there was bound to be talk. The "official business" excuse would only have gone so far.

As the sun rose, the garrison began to stir. A piece of her felt strange to be waking up in her own garrison again. For months she'd woken up among Kelvians, always dreading the possibility she would be discovered. Though she knew she was safe here, she couldn't shake the fear that haunted her.

Outside, Maleen could hear shouts from training unit commanders, disciplining students who were slow to get into line. Noture's strong voice issued orders for extra laps before the morning workout even started. He worked with the newest of the students, many of them not yet in their adolescent years.

Maleen often watched their training and wondered if she and her brother had been as unruly. The one time she asked Noture about it, he'd laughed at her. Tian had been a model student for much of their training, just as he had become a model warrior. She, on the other hand, had frequently been in trouble for starting fights, both verbal and physical, not only in Noture's unit but in all three levels of training.

The shouts woke Cutter, and his eyes flickered open to meet Maleen's across the room.

"Now there is a sight to wake up to." He smiled at her. "I could get used to waking up to that beautiful face."

"Well, maybe we should make a habit of it." Maleen sat up, pulling the blanket around her. The movement made her head spin. Despite Phillip's warning about weakness from blood loss, it was still a disturbing sensation.

"Well, then." Cutter stood up and came over to kiss her. "I guess I'll have to marry you." He brushed her cheek with his hand.

"Now that, I can get used to." Maleen smiled up at him as his lips brushed hers. She was finally home. Finally back where she belonged. In Acora. In her own garrison. In Cutter's arms.

The door to the hut opened. A cheerful voice called out, "Anyone awake in here?"

"Tian!" Maleen greeted her elder brother joyfully. She'd missed him as much as she'd missed Cutter.

"Ready to go to the dining hall?" Tian grinned. He was only a couple of inches taller, and their resemblance had often been referred to as uncanny. This morning, his shortly cropped auburn hair was unkempt and his blue eyes looked a little bleary. Perhaps he had stayed awake all night worrying about her. He *was* the worrier of the family. He'd always claimed that being the eldest meant it was his job to worry.

"You mean have breakfast with my two favorite men in the entire world for the first time in a year? Absolutely. Give me a chance to get to the barracks for clean clothes."

"Done." He handed her the bundle of clothes she hadn't noticed. He pulled the privacy curtain around the bed.

Maleen gritted her teeth and began the long arduous process of dressing with only one hand.

"No peeking," Tian said. "At least not yet."

Maleen could imagine the impish grin.

"With her big brother in the room? I wouldn't dream of it." Cutter's deep laugh was like music.

Despite the laughter, Maleen knew Tian's protectiveness wouldn't be tempered by the fact that Cutter was the chief's son or the fact that the two men were best friends. But even before Cutter had seen Maleen as anything other than his friend's little sister, he had *never* treated her as anything less than a lady, a fact Tian was well aware of. To compare Cutter to the class of men in the Kelvian garrison would have been like comparing a lalot bird with a graebig beast. Still, Maleen was grateful for the friendship between these two.

Several requests for help with a button and the sling later, the three of them were on the way to the dining hall. Maleen studied her brother. In the year apart, he had grown to look even more like Noture. They had the same hair, face, and mannerisms that were prominent in the men of the family. Noture was much younger than Maleen and Tian's father, making him closer in age to them than to the head of the family.

As the aroma of sizzling food filled her nose, Maleen realized she was famished. She'd eaten nothing the day before, having spent most of the day sleeping. Tian and Cutter chatted idly about happenings in the garrison over the past year. They were at the age when most of their peers were finding wives. Some of the pairs they told her about surprised her, but most didn't.

"Oblam's ten now." Tian reminded her about one of their little brothers. "Mother doesn't want him to come to the garrison yet."

"I'm sure Uncle Noture will convince Father." Maleen laughed. It had been Noture's persistence that had convinced their father that Maleen and Tian were ready to begin garrison training at ten and eleven years of age. "And Mother will relent when father agrees."

"And Mother's pregnant again." Tian grinned.

"What?" Maleen's eyes went wide. "At forty?"

Tian nodded, shoving mush into his mouth.

Watching her finish her hearty meal, Tian looked at Cutter, a sly smile on his face. "So, when are you getting married, so I can stop playing chaperone?"

"How about today?" Cutter smiled at Maleen.

"Today?" Maleen's spoon clattered to her bowl, her eyes wide, not sure whether to laugh or cry.

"We said we'd do it the day you got back, but yesterday was a bit of a chore, so how about today?"

Maleen made a deliberate effort not to stare. Cutter had proposed before she'd been assigned the mission. When they said goodbye the following morning, he'd promised her they would get married the day she got back, but she'd been gone for a year. She was still getting used to being home. She attempted to keep her sentiment in check, but as the realization of what Cutter was suggesting sank in, she failed.

"Yes, let's do it today! Think your father will be available?" She stood, her thoughts going to her belongings, which she assumed were still in the barracks. She only owned one dress. It would need to be aired out. Maybe she could borrow something from Mattie or Denetra? No, Mattie was heftier, and both ladies were much shorter. The one in her trunk would have to do. Her hands shook with excitement.

Cutter stood up and pounded his mug on the table to get every-one's attention. "May I have your attention?" he shouted. "You are all formally invited to the wedding of Cutter, son of Chief Rabe and Lady DeLean; and Maleen, daughter of Sonley and Lesney. The ceremony will commence in the courtyard this afternoon."

"Right this way, Madam." Mattie, Lady DeLean, and a few other women appeared out of nowhere, apparently already expecting the an-nouncement, and led Maleen to an adjacent hut.

A tub of warm water waited for her. Mattie helped her wash her hair and gently combed out the extensive knots from the ordeal of the past day and a half. When they were done, Mattie pulled out a dress. Never had Maleen worn a gown like the one Mattie showed her.

"Your stepmother sent it months ago, after she got your letter about your engagement," Mattie said. The leather was soft, giving the skirt a fullness, which provided movement and allowed a warrior to also be a lady. The bodice was trimmed in Acoran purple. On it was embroidered her family crest and the symbol for an Elite. The thoughtfulness of it touched her deeply. Maleen knew how her mother felt about having two grown children in the garrison, yet she supported them both in all their endeavors.

As Lady DeLean laced the bodice, Mattie wove flowers into the small braids that circled Maleen's head while the rest of her auburn hair was allowed to flow free, a rare but beautiful sight. Maleen winced, not for the first time, as Mattie secured the sling holding her arm close to her body.

"Don't be surprised when people start putting the title of 'Lady' before your name," Lady DeLean advised her as they worked. "I can think of few women who deserve it more."

"Thank you, ma'am." Maleen smiled. "It's all right if I still call you that, right?"

"For now." The chief's wife smiled at her.

"Now those of us who grew up with you have to start calling *you* ma'am?" Mattie teased, bringing a laugh from all the ladies in the room.

"Please don't." Maleen both groaned and laughed at the idea. She was marrying the chief's son, but since he wasn't going to be Chief, she wasn't going to be the next Lady of Acora. She would still have the same status as any other warrior, certainly nothing to make others call her ma'am. Not unless she managed a promotion to commander. Even then, it would only be the warriors who were expected to honor it.

Lady DeLean took Maleen's hand in hers. "We have missed you. It's good to have you home. I know you will bring honor to our family." She blinked rapidly and cleared her throat. "What do you think?" She turned Maleen around so the bride could see herself in the reflection glass.

In the reflection was a completely transformed woman. A lady who would become the daughter-in-law to the chief. It wasn't a position she had ever coveted, but it was also one she would not take lightly. Until Rabe announced his heir, Cutter was still next in line. She vowed she would make them both proud.

After applying light cosmetics and putting finishing touches on her hair, the ladies walked outside. Tian was waiting for Maleen and escorted her to the courtyard. She gasped at the changes. Flowers and colorful streamers of fabric hung from tree branches and the overhang of the buildings that surrounded the courtyard, all beautifully arranged.

"This is why you brought me a change of clothes this morning." Maleen smiled at Tian. If she'd gone to the barracks, she would have had to cross the courtyard to get to the dining hall, and the surprise would have been spoiled. "I can't believe he did this all in one night. I thought he never left the infirmary."

"Mother sent the dress months ago," Tian said. "The rest was easy enough. You were asleep when I got back with the search party last night, and Cutter told us his plan for this. We had a lot of volunteers who are glad to have you home safe, and who wanted to do something special for you both. And...some with the need to demonstrate an apology for their assumptions of *why* you disappeared."

"Were the rumors that bad?" she asked.

"No one who knows you gave any credence to them, but I broke Avron's nose when he implicated Asher in your need to disappear."

"Asher? Anyone seriously thought that?" Maleen laughed, despite the insult.

Tian laughed with her now, but she'd bet everything she had that he hadn't been laughing at the time. It wasn't often he acted out of anger. Her best friend, Asher, however, probably *would* have laughed it off.

"Denetra must have had a meltdown." Maleen looked around the gathering crowd to find Asher and his wife.

"She may not like you, but she trusts him." Tian chuckled. "She even defended you among the kitchen staff."

Lady DeLean took her seat in the front row, and Cutter and his father stood in front of the entire garrison of warriors and support staff.

"Ready? Last chance to avoid being in-laws with Denetra," he teased, offering his arm.

It looked as though anyone who wasn't on watch was here. Not one thing was out of place. Maleen could not have dreamt of a better wedding —and she'd done a lot of dreaming in the past year.

Maleen's new father-in-law presided over the ceremony. He spoke beautiful words of family, honor, and esteem. His smile, reflected in his eyes, showed his delight as he welcomed her into the family. Cutter presented Maleen with an intricately carved marriage armlet. Burned into the smooth wood was Rabe's family crest, alongside her father's. The two crests blended together, symbolizing the blending of the two families, but the chief's crest was the more prominent.

"Anyone who sees this will know instantly you are now a part of the chief's family. Today and forever," Cutter said quietly.

"Today and forever," Maleen repeated the simple traditional words that would change their lives.

Cutter smiled as he tied the leather cords of the armlet around her upper arm and kissed her to the cheers of the entire gathering.

In that moment, the crowd disappeared. Chief Rabe disappeared. Tian, standing in her father's place, disappeared. For a long moment, there was only Cutter and Maleen. And now, they were one. Two hearts, never to be separated, no matter where their duties took them.

The kitchen staff had a feast ready, with dessert for a flourish. Maleen had missed the joy of community that was so alive in her home garrison. This kind of closeness was a foreign concept in Kelvia. There was a camaraderie between warriors and between the trainees, but the support staff was only there because it was their job. There was little interaction between the three groups.

After dessert was served, Chief Rabe stood up to make a toast. "To my son. May he always deserve the beautiful young woman sitting beside him. And to my new daughter, who, with the council's approval—" He grinned at Maleen "—will be my new Chief Heir."

Maleen sat dumbfounded. Her jaw dropped, and she stared wide-eyed at Rabe. Had she heard correctly? Had her new father-in-law just broken tradition and made her his Chief Heir? Meaning, if the nomination was approved, when he retired, she would be the first woman ever to lead the Acoran tribe? To lead *any* tribe. The silence from the crowd pressured Maleen to say something. Anything. But no words came.

"Maleen, say something," Cutter urged. "My father just named you Heir." His lips turned up. He'd known this was coming. How could he not have told her?

Maleen moved her lips, but no sound came out. Murmurs moved through the courtyard. No one would speak out on their wedding day, but there were many who would not sit by and allow such a break with tradition to go unchallenged.

At last, Maleen found her voice. "Thank you, um...Father. May I always bring honor to your family. And may it be many years before they call me Chieftess." She raised her glass, and others followed suit. Maleen looked to where Cutter's cousin, Asher, sat with his wife. Both wore stunned expressions. Apparently, Asher had not known this announcement was coming, effectively removing his claim to the chief's seat.

Denetra's expression changed. Her face flushed red, and she narrowed her eyes at Maleen. Asher quickly masked any emotion from his face, but Maleen recognized the clenched fists and blank stare as barely controlled rage he'd never before directed at her.

CHAPTER 4

Maleen woke up early in her private quarters. It was still a strange sensation. She was home. She no longer had to worry about being discovered. She no longer had to be afraid of Lenet.

She pulled the blanket to her chin. The greatest change was Cutter, sleeping next to her. *That* had been worth waiting for. She smiled.

What she had not noticed the previous night was the furnishings of the bedroom. The headboard had fine carvings that matched the frame of the reflection glass. She traced her finger around a delicately carved vine that wound around the bedpost.

"Like it?" Cutter leaned over and kissed her bare shoulder.

"I love it. It's beautiful." She rolled over to look at him. "You did this?"

"It took me months to make the headboard and the frame." Cutter's smile broadened. "Everything else was done by some of the very talented ladies of *your* garrison."

"*My* garrison?" She laughed, putting her good arm around him, looking up into his eyes. "You knew your father was going to do that."

"Only since you got home." He leaned in for a kiss that said she should not speak at the moment.

***

Some time later, Maleen finally set her feet on the thick rug next to the bed. She pulled the blanket around her, leaving Cutter to either dress or endure the cold. In the front room, she knelt next to the fireplace and stirred the hot coals from the night before then added a log.

Cutter came into the room behind her. "*You* are supposed to be taking it easy."

Maleen smiled as she stood. "And you are going to become as big a worrier as my brother if you're not care—" A wave of dizziness hit her.

Cutter supported her and urged her toward the nearest chair. "Let me do this?"

Warmth seeped into her being that had nothing to do with the fire. Had she really been gone so long that Cutter's thoughtfulness would surprise her? It had been a long time since she'd felt so cared for.

Once they were both clothed, Cutter tried to be gentle as he brushed out her hair, but his fingers felt more than a little clumsy as he wound a fresh braid. When he finished, she didn't check her reflection. It was probably good that she didn't care what it looked like. She could ask Mattie to fix it before she had to face the council mid-morning.

In the crowded dining hall a few minutes later, Chief Rabe and Lady DeLean joined the newlyweds for breakfast. Cutter greeted his parents with a smile. Maleen took his hand as she greeted them.

"I want to thank you, Father," Maleen said. "Yesterday I was so shocked at your announcement I was speechless. I'm afraid my expression of gratitude was wholly inadequate."

"You weren't the only one surprised, my dear." Rabe laughed. "The warriors' council knew months ago that I intended to do it, but I don't think they expected me to make it public before they'd confirmed it."

"Months ago?" Cutter was incredulous. "And you only told me the night before?"

"I made my choice the day you told me you intended to propose. I took it to the council then, even though she wasn't old enough, yet. I knew it would take a while to convince them. Let's face it. You have no aspirations to be Chief. I promised your mother a long time ago I wouldn't force you to be something you're not." He reached for De-Lean's hand. "I want the chief's seat to remain in my line, but I'm not waiting for a grandchild to come of age before I retire."

"Everyone expected it would be Asher," Cutter said. "Especially Denetra and Uncle Brice."

"My brother has more ambition for his son than his son does for himself. It was more fun to shock Brice and the rest of the council than to wait for their confirmation. Though, in hindsight, I suppose I should have warned Asher. It's true that traditional succession would mean that after you, he would be next in line, but since when do we do anything traditionally in this family?" He chuckled.

Cutter and Maleen laughed with him, knowing Rabe had been the younger son, chosen before his elder brother, and had always found bucking tradition amusing. Now, Chief Rabe had made his son's new wife his heir. He had too much respect for the position to have done it strictly for amusement, but it seemed to entertain him, nonetheless. And it appeared to delight Cutter.

"Asher would have made a fine chief, but his humor only goes so far to defuse tense situations. He's too passive. He'd rather talk when everything has already been said. Maleen will make a better chief, so I named her. She can beat any man here with a bow, and most men with a staff. She may not be the strongest, but she's quick and agile, everything that makes a good warrior. She's also intelligent, an excellent strategist, and an expert in diplomacy. Why do you think you were sent on the mission to the Kelvian garrison?" Rabe continued, looking at Maleen. "Think about it."

There were no official "tests" chief heirs had to pass, but there were a number of requirements heirs must meet to ensure they would be strong enough to lead.

"There's the small issue of her not being a man. The council argued long into the night about that. Most women can't compete with a man for strength. So, I argued that leadership is not about swinging the largest stick or shooting a bow, but about intelligence, and making difficult decisions. The position in Kelvia gave you the opportunity to demonstrate those skills."

"So, the mission to Kelvia was a year-long test?" Cutter clenched his fist. Across the table, Lady DeLean shook her head slightly. Maleen took Cutter's hand. They could discuss it later, in private. Yelling at his father in public was not wise.

"No. We need the information she gleaned," Rabe said. "The council had already discussed sending a spy, even before the attack on the garrison last year, but we hadn't decided who the best person was. It couldn't be you or Asher. You'd both be recognized. Sending her rather than one of the other Elites proved to the council that her strength of character, strength of will, and strength of mind far outweigh the necessity for strength of body."

***

An hour later, back in proper attire for an Acoran Elite warrior, Maleen headed to the council hall. She buried her anxiety under a façade of confidence. Cutter would see through it. So would Uncle Noture. Hopefully, no one else in the room would.

Even if Chief Rabe could convince the Acoran warriors' council she was the best choice, he'd have to convince the leaders of the other nine tribes at the annual Chiefs' Council during the next Equin Festival. Maleen took a deep breath. One obstacle at a time.

Over her shirt, she wore her warrior vest with purple trim for the first time in over a year. On one shoulder of her vest, one of the ladies had sewn a patch of the chief's family crest in place of her father's. She was now a member of his family. If Kelvia wanted to make an issue of her crimes against them, they would have to deal with the Chiefs' Council. Fanton was not likely to do that.

On her other shoulder, hidden beneath the sling, was the patch identifying her as an Elite.

The Acoran warriors' council sat in three rows of chairs, forming a semicircle around Maleen. They would start with a debriefing of her mission. Chief Rabe sat in the center of the first row, the eldest warriors around him. Noture, the youngest and one of the newest members of the council, was relegated to the back row with others nearer his age and experience. Not being members of the council, Cutter and Asher stood in the back of the room. Asher was here. There was a third person who would certainly see through her well-composed mask.

The family resemblance between the cousins was clear. Asher had the same blond hair and brown eyes. Anyone who didn't know the family could easily mistake them for brothers. While Asher did have a thinner build that he'd gotten from his mother's side, he was still a strong man, his rippled arms telling the story of his status among the Elite warriors. Despite his youth, there were few people in the garrison who outmatched him. Cutter was one of them. Noture was another.

Before the debriefing started, the cousins stood talking amicably to each other. Asher gave no indication that he was angry about Chief Rabe's announcement the previous day. The fact that he was here, however, told Maleen that either his father or his wife had insisted he not stand by and do nothing. Probably both of them.

Maleen eyed him from across the hall. She hoped her year-long absence and her new position wouldn't change their friendship. She wished her friend would tell her his thoughts on the matter. She also wished she'd had the opportunity to tell him she hadn't deliberately sought to take the position from him.

Maleen spent the next two hours in the council hall discussing everything she knew about the Western Province of the Kelvian tribe; their tactics, their plans for an upcoming attack, the personalities of their leadership, their numbers, and even recruiting and training methods for young warriors which differed greatly from Acora. Most important was information she had gathered on their readiness. At any point, they had only to decide it was time, and Acora could be overrun.

"They had an attack planned for tomorrow. An attack on *this* garrison. It was to include trainees and seasoned warriors. The sub-chief's son was going to lead it himself. I could not let the attack happen without bringing you a warning. And I would have been forced to be a part of it."

"If you were only a trainee, how do you know their plans of attack?" an older warrior asked.

"In the past, I was able to get the information from warriors who were happy to impress a young woman with their daring plans."

"They told an untested student when and where they planned to attack?"

"I'd let them buy me a drink, and spill more than I drank, but I'd act a little tipsy, flirt a little, let them get drunk off their stool trying to impress, and they would tell me most anything. Well, some of them would. It didn't take long to figure out who developed loose lips with a little liquor."

Chief Rabe interrupted Maleen's narrative. "Let that be a lesson to any of you who think my ban on alcohol use in the garrison is too harsh."

Using her femininity to acquire information would be repugnant to some of the older warriors. Maleen wasn't proud of the methods she'd used, but it had worked, and she wouldn't apologize for it, though she realized her flushed face would give away her embarrassment at her behavior.

"Did you ever, at any time, compromise yourself for information?" an old warrior asked, severity in his tone.

Maleen's eyes darted over the heads of those seated to Cutter. He pushed away from the wall he leaned on. Asher put a hand on his arm and said something Maleen couldn't hear. Rabe and Noture both moved closer to the edge of their chairs.

"No, sir." Maleen kept her voice even, but her narrowed eyes said volumes. She had flirted, made men think she was offering more than she was willing to give, but she had *never* spent the night with a single one of them. A part of her was insulted that he'd ask such a question, but she supposed it was logical. Such an intimate act made for an easy way to get emotionally involved with those she was supposed to be gathering information about.

"What made you decide it was time to come home?" a warrior sitting next to Noture asked. "Surely you could have sent a message through Kanda about the planned attack. Now that you are here, they will certainly change the timing of their plans."

"If my departure had gone as planned, they wouldn't have known I'm Acoran, but either way, my usefulness in their garrison was at an end. As I said, the attack will include testing for the trainees." Maleen took a deep breath. She'd never had an issue with speaking in front of people but speaking in front of the warriors' council and having them judge her actions was another matter entirely.

"Those who fail their battle testing will no longer be candidates for Kelvian warriors," she continued. "They'll be sent to the kitchen or stables. To Kelvians, it is a demotion of the greatest dishonor. They don't see their support staff as key members of the community, but rather as second-class citizens. I'd already failed once. The only reason I was still in training was because the sub-chief's son had an interest in me."

"*You* failed a warrior's test?" A surprised hum spread throughout the room.

"What kind of test do they require that you were not able to pass?" a warrior from the middle row asked.

"Their tests are always on the field of battle. If I had not failed it, Commander Krish would be dead." She nodded to a warrior in the front row. "As would my uncle."

"Explain," Commander Krish insisted.

"Being a marksman, I was assigned the task of picking off the two lead riders of a caravan we were to raid. Those riders were you and Noture."

"I remember," Noture spoke up. "She sent word about a road which was being watched for caravans, so they could raid them. We took a caravan of empty wagons, to lure them out of hiding. At the start of the battle, an arrow barely missed me." Noture recounted the incident. "Asher was driving the wagon behind my mount and later reported that when he'd aimed up the embankment where the arrows had come from, he was fairly certain he had caught a glimpse of Maleen, standing with Fanton."

Maleen nodded, grateful Asher had been one of the few people who knew where she had been. "And the second arrow almost hit you," she told Krish. "I shot those two arrows. You know me. I do not miss. I convinced my trainer it was nerves. I needed another chance to prove myself. Lenet usually has no tolerance for fear or failure, but he made sure I got the chance. His father, on the other hand, is paranoid. Fanton already suspected there was a leak of information. The fact the wagons held nothing but Acoran warriors ready for battle confirmed it.

"After watching me miss an easy target, he became suspicious of me," she continued. "Tomorrow was to be another test. If I'd stayed, then my refusal to kill my own tribesmen would have sent me to the kitchen at best, but more likely I'd have been imprisoned or executed for treason or espionage. Either way, I was no longer of use to you there."

"You have performed your duty admirably," Brice, the chief's brother, spoke up. "However, we will need to debate a bit more about this Chief Heir business. If you and your husband will take your leave." He indicated the door.

Brice was well respected. Nearly as well as Chief Rabe. Had it been anyone else, someone would have brought up the fact that no one asked Brice's son to leave.

Maleen took Cutter's arm, and together they walked out of the hall as Noture insisted that no further debate was needed and protested the injustice of debating in her absence.

"He'll defend me to his dying breath." Maleen smiled. The smile did nothing to hide her nervousness from Cutter.

"Forty-five warriors. Two for you, two against, and forty-one more to convince." Cutter took her hand. Maleen was grateful he said nothing about the slight tremble. "My father can be very persuasive, but so can Uncle Brice. This could take a while."

***

True to Cutter's prediction, the council was still debating that evening at suppertime.

After the meal, Phillip, still followed by a guard, found the newlyweds. "I need to change your bandage and check the stitches," he told Maleen.

"I kept my word." Cutter chuckled, placing an arm around Maleen. "We were careful."

"I never doubted you." Phillip's small smile looked forced as they entered the infirmary. "If you're a good enough man for Maleen, I'll never doubt a word you say."

Maleen looked at Phillip, dread grasping her heart. Did he understand what he sounded like? Whether Phillip realized it or not, Cutter must have heard the same tone of affection Maleen did.

"I think we need to clear the air, Physician," Cutter said brusquely, closing the door harder than was necessary.

"By all means." Phillip turned to meet Cutter's stern look with one of his own.

Maleen had never seen Phillip stand toe-to-toe with anyone as dangerous as Cutter. They were well matched in size, but not in skill. Maleen moved forward to take a step between them but changed her mind. For Cutter to even begin to respect Phillip they had to do this on their terms, without her interference.

"Maleen and I have been friends for a year," Phillip said, without apology. "I'm her physician. Your garrison physician said himself he couldn't have done what I did. As far as any personal feelings I may have had regarding her, I didn't know she was engaged to be married. I didn't pursue her in Kelvia because not only did she make it clear that the attraction was one-sided, but I respected her reputation too much. Kelvian Lady Warriors do *not* associate with non-warriors. Now we're here, and she's married to you, so I'd like your permission to continue to be her friend in addition to being her physician."

Maleen held her breath. Phillip didn't break eye contact. Cutter could have pounded him into the ground if he were so inclined, but if Phillip backed down, he'd never earn her husband's respect.

Cutter's stance relaxed, and his face softened. "That was the most I've heard you say since you got here. Well said, Physician...Phillip." He held out his hand and Phillip shook it, firmly.

Maleen let out a relieved breath as their truce was sealed, however tentatively.

"I won't choose my wife's friends for her," Cutter promised.

Behind Cutter, at the desk in the corner, Maleen caught a glimpse of Mattie, the physician's assistant, trying to hide a smile. When Maleen saw it, she almost smiled herself, but it would not help the situation to laugh at her husband and friend.

Moving on from the tension in the room, Mattie grabbed clean bandages and handed them to Phillip.

As Phillip unwound the old bandages, there was a knock on the door of the hut. He pulled the privacy curtain around the examination area. Cutter showed just how tentative their truce was when he moved to stand on the same side of the curtain.

"Enter," Phillip called.

"We're looking for a young lady who wants to be Chief." Noture's voice sounded like he was keeping it deliberately lighthearted.

"She also claims to be my sister or something, but she spent the last year forcing me to make excuses to Mother about why she hasn't written." Tian pretended annoyance, but Maleen recognized his voice for what it was—nervous.

"I sent her a message yesterday, Big Brother." Maleen laughed. "I even used an expediated courier."

"This same young lady seems to think my cousin was worth marrying for some reason."

"Asher?" Maleen was surprised to hear her friend's voice. "I thought you'd still be in the council meeting, listening to your father list all the reasons why you'd make a better chief than me."

"After the third listing, I thought I'd better leave while my ego still fit through the door." His tone gave no indication he was angry with her. "In your defense, the only qualifications on his list you can't compete with is that I'm male and Rabe's blood."

"Think it'll be enough to sway the council?" She chewed her lip.

"The part about being a blood relation *shouldn't* matter," Noture said. "Rabe pointed out that historically, chiefs without sons have named sons-in-law as heirs. This is no different. The seat will revert to Rabe's bloodline when your own child succeeds you someday. And about the gender issue, the chief argued that if we're willing to let Lady Warriors fight, and perhaps die by our side in battle, then we ought to be willing to let them lead us in and out of battle."

"Leave it to my father to be poetic about it." Cutter chuckled. "But he's trying to convince the same men who would keep women out of battle altogether if they had the choice."

"My father among them," Asher said, an apology in his tone.

"And Commander Nell," Maleen added. "Both of their opinions will carry a lot of weight." Her nervousness had to be showing through her façade. The men in this room all knew her too well to fool them, whether they could see her face or not.

"When I left twenty minutes ago, they'd just declared a recess. The split seems to be fairly even. It could go either way." Noture sighed. "Now with all the facts and opinions in the open, everyone has to wrestle with his conscience before voting. They should have gathered to take the vote about five minutes ago. Which, I might add, they've excused me from."

"I was counting on your 'no' vote," Asher complained loudly.

Maleen heard the sound of a fist on flesh.

"Ow!" Asher and Noture both laughed.

"With a situation like this, a close family member has to be excused," Noture explained. "Suppose I voted her in, then because she was Chief something was to happen to her? I'd forever be blaming myself for helping her win the position."

"No one asked Uncle Brice to abstain?" Cutter asked.

"At this point, it's only a yes or no for Maleen. Everyone knows who's next if they vote no, but technically Asher has no stake in it, so Brice—well, let's just say no one has the courage to ask him to abstain. I, on the other hand, have little influence with or without a vote."

"But if you voted her down, you'd be protecting her and...giving me a chance, then..." Asher paused dramatically. Another punch and laughter followed.

"I've been gone a year, but some things never change," Maleen said.

Another knock came on the door of the hut. "They're ready for you," a youthful voice said. "They want both Asher and Maleen."

"Almost done," Phillip said.

"Shall we walk in together?" Asher called through the curtain. "Regardless of the outcome, we will still be fighting side by side." Asher paused, and Maleen could only guess he was smiling that crooked, guilty grin. "Besides, it'll rankle my father to no end."

"It's an excellent gesture." Cutter stood to leave, kissing Maleen. "I'll tell them you'll only be a minute. Coming, Noture?" Cutter stepped around the curtain and out of the room.

"No. Regardless of the outcome, I don't think Brice and I should be in the same room when it's announced." Noture sighed with regret. "It could be hazardous to the peace."

"He's that bad?" Maleen asked. "You two used to be such good friends."

"Have you never met my father?" Asher asked with a sarcastic chuckle. "This is supposed to be a vote about whether or not to confirm you as Heir. My father has tried to turn it into a vote of me versus you."

"You two don't act much like rivals." Phillip finished wrapping a clean bandage.

"You'll eventually get used to Acoran politics." Maleen winced as he helped her put her arm through her shirt and vest. "In Kelvia, when a chief makes an announcement, like appointing an heir, there is no discussion. Here, the chief has to submit to a vote by his warriors. It keeps a chief from wielding too much power over those he administrates. So, even though the chief announced his choice of heir, he still has to get approval from the veteran warriors."

"I've just never seen two rivals be so civilized."

Asher snorted at Phillip's observation.

"You'll find a lot of politics are different here than in Kelvia," Noture said. "But it's not always so peaceful. When Cutter and Asher's grandfather named his second son as his chief heir, there was quite a bit of boorish behavior. At one point it even looked like Brice was ready to resign from the garrison altogether."

"According to Aunt DeLean, it was my father's less-than-gracious behavior that convinced the council Grandfather's choice had been correct. But he's been grooming me for this ever since Cutter announced he didn't want to be Chief."

As they explained, Maleen wondered how much Phillip needed to know about Acoran politics. He couldn't go home, but she didn't think he would be comfortable staying here, either. For the moment, she was grateful Asher wasn't treating him as an outsider and Noture seemed to have relaxed. A little.

"Asher and I have been both friends and competitors since we were ten years old," Maleen told Phillip. "In warrior's training until we were fifteen, then we competed for who would become an Elite first."

"And for who would get married younger," Tian chuckled.

"Father decided that one for us." Maleen sighed. Her father had made it perfectly clear she would not get married until she hit the age of maturity. Asher's father, on the other hand, had agreed to him and Denetra getting married at only eighteen.

"So, who became an Elite first?" Phillip asked.

"That would be me," Asher said proudly from the other side of the curtain, earning a laugh from both Tian and Noture and an eye roll from Maleen.

"Only because at the ceremony, the names were listed alphabetically." Tian laughed as Phillip fitted Maleen's sling. "By Asher's account, my little sister was an Elite before me, just because her name comes before mine."

"But alas, how can I compete with a beautiful woman who bewitches the chief's son?" There was no malice in Asher's comment, only humor.

"With a staff." Maleen laughed. In a mock whisper to Phillip, she said, "He's one of the few men who can beat me, but don't let word of *that* get around."

"Well, I'm done here," Phillip said. "You two go find out your fate." He pulled back the curtain.

"Shall we?" Asher stood to her right, making a show of offering her his arm then of dancing around to the other side, so she could take it with her good arm.

"Always a gentleman." Maleen's lighthearted laugh was fake. Phillip, Noture, and Tian all knew her well enough to see it for what it was.

So did Asher. "Nervous?"

"I feel like I'm going to be sick," she admitted. "Before yesterday, I never even dreamed of being in this position. Now I find myself wanting it more than anything."

"You will make Acora proud."

Was Asher going to concede? She couldn't imagine the chief's nephew being willing to step down. Then again, Asher always strove for what was right.

The fact that the council had asked to see both Maleen and Asher was *not* a good sign for Maleen. Currently, Asher had no tangible claim because Chief Rabe had named her. If they wanted him in the hall when they gave her their answer, it could be because they wished to impart the position to him, making Rabe's appeal less effective.

"If they refuse to confirm you, you do know I'll accept the position?" Asher asked, his tone turning serious. Noture and Tian walked behind them.

"I know." She nodded. "If they refuse to confirm me, I won't hold you responsible. Your father on the other hand..." she teased, then turned serious. "I didn't know Chief Rabe was going to make that announcement. I would've warned you if I had."

"I know. Tian pointed out how rare it is to see you speechless. Your reaction at the announcement yesterday tells me you had no idea. I'm sorry I didn't welcome you home properly yesterday, but I didn't get the chance before the wedding, and I was too incensed after." He sighed thoughtfully. "I was up all night, being angry. Just when I thought I'd come to terms with it this morning, Denetra woke up and her hostility got me angry all over again. Then my father came by for breakfast and the pair of them..."

He paused. "I'm not mad anymore. I stood in the council room, hearing everything Uncle Rabe said about you, and hearing everything my father said about me... Their lists of qualifications—the ones that matter —are identical...but you're Rabe's choice. If the council honors it, so will I. Can we make an agreement right now, before we know the selection, that whatever happens, *nothing* changes our friendship?"

Maleen nodded. This was Asher. The one person she'd always confided in. One of the few who never doubted her abilities. One of the three who never hesitated to swing if she stepped in the ring. After all that, why could she not be more secure in the belief that their friendship would endure, whichever of them was selected?

In the moonlight, they could see Cutter approaching the council hall, fifty yards away. At the other end of the building, they could also see a figure moving in the shadows. Maleen squinted in the dark, wondering who might be trying to get a look into the council hall. The feminine figure ran, putting as much distance between herself and the hall as possible. A moment before the concussive blast hit them, the council hall was engulfed in an explosion.

CHAPTER 5

The council hall was an inferno. Cutter hadn't yet entered the building, but he'd been close enough to be knocked off his feet by the blast and showered with burning debris.

Maleen sprinted toward him. Amidst the ensuing chaos of screams and cries from men, women, and children alike, she felt like she was moving in a daze. She was only vaguely aware of Tian charging in the direction they'd seen the dark figure heading seconds before the explosion. No matter how fast Maleen moved her legs, she couldn't get to Cutter's side quick enough. Her chest constricted and she fell to her knees by his unconscious body. Cutter was severely burned but breathing. Her entire world lay on the ground in front of her. She'd just come back to him. She could not lose him.

Phillip, Noture, and Asher were right beside her the next moment. "I'll take care of him," Phillip assured her. "You need to act like a chief now and a wife later." He squeezed her good shoulder, calling men nearby to help move Cutter to the infirmary.

Thankful for his wisdom, Maleen took a deep breath. There was nothing she could do for Cutter at the moment, and she trusted Phillip to do everything he could. Setting aside her fear for her husband, she stood up and took a step back. Before she could turn, an arrow whizzed past her and struck the ground where she'd been kneeling a second before.

Instinctively, she reached for her bow and winced as her shoulder screamed a painful reminder of why she did not carry it. Her arm may not have worked, but her eyesight was intact.

"There." She pointed to a rooftop where a dark silhouette reached for another arrow. Noture and Asher reacted quickly. Noture shot straight and true, while Asher grabbed Maleen around the middle and yanked her out of the path of the next arrow, released a moment before Noture's reached its mark. The figure fell, tumbling down the sloped roof.

Pushing aside Asher's arm and the jolt of the assassination attempt, Maleen issued orders. In their shock and confusion, no one questioned her right to do so. Even Asher followed her orders without question.

Behind her, a woman's wail sounded over the roar of the fire. Maleen turned to see Lady DeLean kneeling on the ground. In her hysteria, she was oblivious to the frantic activity around her.

Maleen knelt beside her. "Lady DeLean?" She laid a hand on the woman's shoulder. "Mother?"

Lady DeLean looked up at her. Her tears tore through Maleen's heart. *Hold it together*, she scolded herself. But DeLean was not a warrior. She couldn't be expected to have the same emotional control. "Go to the infirmary." She took hold of the woman's arm and lifted her to her feet. "Be with Cutter. He needs one of us. But I need to..." She cleared her throat. She needed to think clearly.

"You need to be Chief." DeLean laid a hand on her cheek and turned toward the infirmary.

Maleen turned her attention back to the blaze. Twice someone tried to enter the council hall. Twice they were repelled by the intensity of the flames. Long before the flames abated, the roof collapsed. Maleen felt sick. There was no hope. No one inside could survive that.

There were many outside the hall injured in the explosion. Men, women, and children helped one another get to the infirmary, where Phillip prioritized injuries and barked commands while he attended to everyone he could reach. Batal, the garrison physician, had been in the council hall, and few of the injured were willing to trust Phillip, so anyone with any knowledge of the healing arts was recruited to help him and Mattie.

"Double the guards on the towers," Maleen ordered one man, the sub-commander of a unit that had just lost its commander. "And I want a continuous patrol around the garrison all night."

The warrior looked from Maleen to Asher. "Sir?"

"Do as you're told!" Asher barked.

Maleen gave him a grateful look as the man hurried off. Having his support meant everything to her at the moment.

"That's going to happen a lot," Asher warned.

"Your response was perfect," Noture said. "That will be what makes or breaks her leadership."

"Find Jewel," Maleen ordered Noture. She didn't have time to worry about bigotry or rivalry. "I have a strong suspicion the one you shot is Sampton." It had been a masculine form that had fallen from the roof.

Noture hurried off in the direction Tian had gone.

"And Phillip?" Asher asked the question Maleen should have seen coming. Phillip would have had nothing to do with the massacre that had just taken place, but if she were to be Chief, she couldn't let her personal feelings make decisions for her.

"Check in with the guard assigned to him, make sure he hasn't left his side all day. Phillip will need his testimony. Either way, put a full guard detail around the infirmary." Those guards would be as much for Phillip's protection as for showing that she was taking precautions.

"Yes, Chieftess." Asher hurried off, leaving Maleen wondering if, by using the title, he conceded his claim to the chief's seat. There'd been no hint of joke or mockery in his voice, and even as silly as Asher had a habit of being, this wasn't the time.

The council was dead without their vote being announced. Many of the remaining warriors had supported her through her training and as a young warrior. She'd earned their respect a long time ago. It'd been much easier to earn than the respect of the older warriors. They hadn't seen her in over a year, but by now everyone knew why. Would they follow her as their chief?

What about the warriors in the Southern Garrison, where few of them knew her? Was she even ready for this? She was only twenty-one years old. Chiefs were supposed to mentor their heirs for years before handing over leadership. Rabe had been over thirty when his father retired.

If a chief died before the heir was ready, his successor should at least have had the council of warriors to guide him. Acoran tradition required the council members to be twenty-year veterans. Now Noture would be the oldest member of the council at only thirty-five. Every other council member would have been in that meeting. With a vote for the chief heir hanging in the balance, not one of them would have missed it, whichever side of the debate they were on. That was the opportunity a saboteur would look for. Noture had only been spared because he'd been dismissed from the vote.

For a moment, Maleen stood, staring at the burning rubble.

Alchemy. Few people across Chalent would have known which chemicals to mix in what quantities to get that kind of explosive reaction. Alchemy was closely guarded by those who knew its secrets. Why had it not occurred to her that she'd heard rumors of Jewel being a third-generation alchemist? Then there'd been the torch Jewel had when they left the Kelvian garrison... Her reaction at Noture's destruction of it... She'd even mentioned it had been treated with alchemist chemicals. Yet no one had checked her or Sampton's packs when they'd entered the Acoran garrison.

Her negligence made Maleen ill. She had never trusted Jewel and didn't know Sampton. Why hadn't she taken more precautions before taking the sedative for the surgery?

Maleen shook herself out of her contemplation. She needed to focus on the present. As she saw people kneeling where Sampton had fallen, she hurried over to see if he would be capable of telling them anything.

***

A moment before the explosion, Tian had considered confronting the woman who appeared to be eavesdropping on the council. A moment after, he was pursuing her through the garrison. He dodged both people and objects flung into his path by his quarry. Tian caught up as she reached the shadows between the barracks and a row of private quarters. He reached out and was only able to grab a handful of clothing.

The woman spun around, fist flying. It was one of the Kelvians who'd helped Noture and Maleen. Ducking her blow, Tian did not hesitate to swing back. He sparred with his sister often enough to know hesitation was dangerous. Woman or not.

Jewel was stronger than Maleen, but she wasn't as fast. Tian's fist landed solidly on her jaw. Jewel stumbled before landing a foot in the center of Tian's chest, sending him back into a wall. As he recovered, Jewel turned and ran. He pursued, his chest aching from the kick.

How does she have that kind of endurance? Tian thought, giving chase again. He rounded the corner around the back of the barracks where he'd seen her slip into the shadows. Seeing no one, Tian stopped to listen, slowing his breathing to hear. He crept along the space between the garrison wall and the barracks wall. His lungs burned. Squeezing between a pile of crates and the wall, Tian swore as he realized his mistake. Jewel was hiding behind the same crates and slid the top one as he came through the narrow space, pinning him to the wall while Jewel continued on.

The crate wasn't heavy, but by the time Tian maneuvered around it, Jewel was halfway up a rope, secured to the top of the garrison wall.

Tian scurried after her. If she got over the wall, he would never catch her on the other side. Inches from the top, Tian grabbed her ankle, his head low enough to avoid a kick from her other foot as she clung to the rope.

Fast and strong, Tian thought when Jewel didn't lose her grip. Tian gripped her foot tighter and let go of the rope. His full weight made Jewel let go, nearly landing on top of him. Tian recovered faster than Jewel and stood over her, his arm drawn back.

"You really want to get back up?" he dared her as she lay on her back, winded, with a bruised jaw, but otherwise uninjured.

***

Cutter awoke to the sight of Mattie and Phillip hunched over a small boy on a mat beside his bed. "Why am I in the infirmary?" he asked weakly. His ears rang and his head hurt too much to see straight, but he could tell where he was. His ribs felt like he'd sparred with a Gantin lizard. When he tried to sit up, the pain in his abdomen made him want to swear.

"Lie still," Mattie ordered. "We'll be there in a moment." The child cried out as Mattie held him down and Phillip set the bone in the boy's leg.

"What happened?" Cutter could barely get the words out through his pain. His mother was by his bedside, tears streaming down her face. As he asked the question, relief replaced some of her anguish.

"You're awake!" She grabbed his hand and quickly loosened her grip as he bit his lip against the pain.

"What happened, Mother?" Cutter asked again.

Lady DeLean sobbed again, and he got no answer from her.

After directing Mattie to splint the boy's leg and to give him thessel, Phillip stood and came to the bedside. "It seems my tribesmen were, in fact, sent here to sabotage your garrison."

He explained to Cutter about the explosion and the assassination attempt. "They must have mistimed their attack. I guess they expected both candidates to be in the council hall, but when they weren't... The first arrow only missed Maleen because she moved at the last second. Asher saw the second one coming and got her out of the way. He's lucky it didn't hit him. Thanks to Noture's quick response, there wasn't a third."

"Have they been caught?"

"The guards who were supposed to be staying with Jewel and Sampton were found dead. Either Noture's arrow or the fall from the roof killed Sampton. By the time they brought him in here, there was nothing I could do for him. Tian caught Jewel trying to climb the wall to get out. And Maleen took the proper precautions here. She knows me, knows I would never have had anything to do with this bloodbath, but as acting Chief, she placed a guard detail around this building. I'm not going anywhere, even if I wanted to."

"Acting Chief? So, my father..." His voice caught, and he tried to sit up.

"No one inside the council hall survived the explosion." Phillip paused.

Cutter took a deep breath, painful as it was. His father was gone. The reality hit hard, more painful than the bruises and the burns.

Phillip continued softly, his eyes full of pity. "Jewel has training as an alchemist. She knew exactly how to set it up to make sure there were no survivors inside. And unless you want your bride to be a widow, you will lie still." He put a hand on Cutter's shoulder to make his point. "If you'd been a few feet closer, I would have had one fewer patients, and we'd be burying one more warrior."

"She's an alchemist? And you didn't see fit to tell us that before?" Cutter hurt too much to put any force into his angry words.

"I never even thought about it. She's so dangerous in person, I didn't even imagine she had other ways to hurt people." Phillip said. His shoulders drooped. Clearing the emotion from his throat, he added, "I honestly don't know why that fact didn't occur to me sooner."

Maybe he's not the enemy. Cutter tried to sit up again. He certainly *looked* sincere. "Why do I feel like I fell off a cliff?" he asked as Phillip put pressure on his shoulder, insisting he lay still.

"The blast caused internal bleeding. I had to do repair work in your abdomen. Remember all those stitches I used in Maleen's arm? You have a whole lot more in your gut. Not to mention broken ribs, a concussion, severe burns, and a wife who needs to concentrate on her duty, not worry about you."

As Phillip moved on to another patient, Mattie came over with a mug, handing it to Cutter.

"Thessel?" he asked.

Mattie nodded. "Just enough for pain, and to help you rest."

"I need to see Maleen first." He tried to get up again.

"You need to lie still." His mother sounded stern, getting her tears under control.

"You already owe your life to Phillip." Mattie nodded toward the newcomer. "Of course, if you want to double your debt, then, by all means, run off and find Maleen." When Cutter relaxed but still refused the tea, Mattie relented. "It's almost sunrise. Everything is settling down now. I'll see if I can find the chieftess."

"Thank you, Mattie," Cutter said as she headed for the door. "Hey, Mat?" he called to her. When she turned back around to look at him, he asked, "Did he really save my life, or are you trying to get me to like him?" Mattie shook her head and walked out the door, unable to smile.

"You don't have to like me," Phillip said from the bedside of another patient. "You only have to listen to my instructions."

Mattie returned a few minutes later with Maleen behind her. Maleen's eyes were unfocused and had dark shadows under them.

"I'm here, Love." She took Cutter's hand, cautious of the bandages which wrapped the burns.

Cutter looked at his mother briefly, hoping she understood that he needed his wife more than he needed his mother.

Giving her daughter-in-law a quick hug and patting her son's leg, Lady DeLean quietly busied herself, helping make other patients more comfortable.

"I never doubted you'd be here." Cutter kept his expression neutral and tried not to wince when Maleen sat on the edge of the bed, but she knew him too well for him to be able to hide how much pain he was in.

"I wanted to be here when you woke up. To be the one to tell you..."

Cutter could see the anguish in her eyes, which shone with unshed tears.

"But I hear they made you Chief, you must have been busy."

"We'll see what happens when everything settles down. Right now, I think people are just glad they're not the ones having to organize...all this." Her cheek twitched in a failed attempt to smile. It was no surprise that she found it impossible. The circumstances of her appointment to the position were too much. This was exactly the reason why being named Heir was supposed to be a celebration. When the time came for the heir to become chief, circumstances often prevented celebrating.

"What about Asher?"

"My only rival, and he was the first one to call me Chieftess." She shrugged, one corner of her mouth turning upward, a little closer to the smile he loved so much.

"Oh, then we should celebrate." Cutter touched her face lightly with his hand. Even that small movement caused him pain.

"Oh, sure, let's go dancing." Maleen laughed, though her smile still didn't reach her eyes.

"First you have to convince your physician friend to let me out of this bed."

"I'll get right to it." Maleen laughed again, adjusting the sling on her shoulder. "Sounds like a fine plan."

Considering how exhausted she looked, it was no surprise she needed the release of laughter, even if it was a forced laugh at a poorly delivered joke.

"So, is it true?" Cutter asked, sobering. "My father? Uncle Brice? Not one of the council members...?"

"Just Noture. He was with me. We had just walked out of here when..." Her voice betrayed her as she cleared her throat. "When I saw you thrown back from the explosion, I was so frightened. You didn't move. For a moment, I didn't even think about the council. All I could see was you lying there."

Maleen was unable to stop the tears from flowing freely. Cutter reached out to her. Despite the pain it caused him, he had to hold her, if even for a moment. He'd only seen her cry a few times in all the years he'd known her. Despite his own sorrow, he wanted nothing more than to reassure her that everything would be all right. Maleen melted into his embrace.

"I'm sorry," she said between sobs. "My mind is telling me to pull myself together but—"

"Shh," Cutter assured her. "It's all right to cry." His words of affirmation would mean little to this woman who prided herself in having emotional control.

After a moment, Phillip touched Maleen's arm. "He needs to rest." He gently removed Cutter's arm from around the disheveled woman. "And frankly, so do you. After your recent blood loss, you shouldn't be exerting yourself."

"I have to arrange for the burials." Maleen wiped her eyes. "I hope no one else sees this. It would be better to be thought cold and unfeeling, than overly emotional."

"Matter of opinion," Cutter assured her.

Maleen shook her head. "Someone has to provide stability."

"Let someone else plan the burials," Phillip insisted. "You look like you're ready to collapse."

"I'll get by." Maleen gently touched Cutter's hand again. "You rest. I'll be back soon." She stood up and wavered on her feet.

Cutter grabbed her hand but didn't have the strength to make her stay. "Please rest," he said softly. "If you're ill, who leads?"

Phillip held a mug out to her. "What would look worse? Resting when you need it, or passing out in front of everyone?"

"I said I'll get by." Her voice wasn't nearly as assertive as Cutter expected.

"I made it weak," Phillip said. "You'll be awake and rested in no time."

Maleen stared at the mug in Phillip's hand. She nodded and Mattie unrolled a mat next to Cutter's bed. Maleen sat down and drank from the mug. It took only a moment for the fast-acting sedative to take effect.

"Your turn." Mattie held up another mug. Seeing Maleen in peaceful rest, Cutter took it and rested.

***

By the time Maleen awoke from her thessel-induced sleep, Cutter was already sitting up in bed.

"Hey, sleepyhead, it's about time," he said, weakly.

Out the window, the sun was high. It was nearly midday. How long had they let her sleep? She stood up and glared at Phillip. "A light dose?"

"It was no more than I'd give someone with a broken bone." Phillip looked up from the parchments he'd been writing on. "Your body did the rest."

"How could you let me sleep so long?" She looked from him to Cutter to Mattie.

The small amount of thessel she'd consumed was only enough to put most people out for an hour or so, if at all. Even with her vulnerability, they could have woken her up long ago. Instead, she'd been sleeping since dawn. While she'd been here, sleeping the entire morning away, who was outside organizing what was left of their warriors? Asher? That would not look good to the few supporters she may have had. But whether they thought she was qualified or not—whether *she* thought she was qualified or not—Chief Rabe had chosen her over Asher.

"I need to get out there and assess the state of things." She took a deep breath.

"I should check your bandage first," Phillip said.

"I don't have time for this!" Maleen cringed at the volume of her voice. Phillip was only trying to help, but she was out of patience for anyone trying to delay her from doing a job she had no idea how to do. She lowered her volume slightly, but her tone wasn't any gentler. "I need to go do the job Chief Rabe entrusted me to do."

"I thought I heard an angry woman in here."

Maleen spun around at the sound of Asher's voice. How long had he been standing there?

Asher may not have been surprised by her outburst, but there were plenty of other people trying to rest in the infirmary. Maleen took a calming breath. "What's been happening this morning?"

"I want you to know that everything I've done this morning has been in the name of our new chief," Asher said softly, but firmly. "I may not see things from a woman's perspective, but I know *you* well enough." He sat on the edge of Cutter's bed but quickly stood when Cutter winced at the movement. "I arranged a mass burial, including a monument to the lives lost. These men devoted their lives to each other, I thought it only fitting they be buried together. The monument will contain all their names."

Asher's tone was even and steady. Maleen admired his strength. He held himself so poised, even in the wake of such tragedy. He had lost his father and his uncle. But everyone was missing someone today; brothers, fathers, husbands, and sons—and their chief.

"One of us should say a few words," Asher continued. "I will if you want, but I think it would be more fitting if you do. Either way, I plan to withdraw any claim to the chief's seat I may have had."

"You're giving it up?" The surprise in Cutter's voice reflected Maleen's shock. "Without knowing the council's selection?"

"Last night reinforced what I already knew about the kind of leader Maleen will be." He turned to Maleen, looking her in the eye. "I had forgotten how strong you are. Had that been my Denetra lying there, bruised, burned, and bleeding, I'm not sure I would've had the presence of mind to organize as quickly and as fully as you did. Thanks to you, we didn't lose any other buildings in the fire. The injured were cared for, the only fatalities were those in the hall. Jewel was caught before she could escape." He nodded toward Phillip. "And you didn't let friendship interfere with duty. No," he finished with a defeated sigh, "I can't compare with such competent leadership. Nor would I want to."

"I don't know what to say." Maleen held out her hand, humbled by the fact that he saw the same strength in her that she admired in him. He apparently had more confidence in her than she had in herself. "I'll be forever grateful to you."

Asher grasped her forearm and pulled her close, turning the handshake into a brotherly hug. "You deserve it. Cousin? Chieftess? What am I supposed to call you now?" He broke the somber mood with his usual jovial tone, albeit somewhat forced. "Now, since you're awake, if your husband can spare you, we have work to do." He gestured for her to lead the way out the door.

"Go." Cutter smiled, weakly. "I'll be right here when you get back." He squeezed her hand lightly.

"Before you go, my friend..." Mattie took her hand and led her to a side room. Hastily, she unwound Maleen's braid and brushed out the knots created from the long night and the long nap. She then braided it again, an act which would be impossible for Maleen to do with one arm. "You're no longer just a warrior," Mattie reminded her. "Every time you go into public, you have an image to maintain. You should always *look* composed, even if life is chaotic."

"Thanks, Mattie." Maleen smiled. "Surrounded by men, I suppose ladylike composure is easy to forget."

"Then I'll make it my job to remind you." Mattie gave her a quick hug. Growing up, most of Maleen's friends had been boys, being that there were few other girls in training, and none her age. But, while they had never been that close, the physician's daughter had always been available whenever Maleen had needed another girl to talk to.

Leaving the hut with Asher, Maleen noticed the guard detail she had ordered the previous night was missing. Only a lone guard stood on duty.

"I guess Cutter trusts Phillip now," Asher answered in response to her questioning look. "He dismissed all but the one guard and, acting on your behalf, I concurred. Noture isn't too happy with us, which could be a problem since he's technically second-in-command as the ranking warrior. But without Phillip's help, we would have several more dead, Cutter included. We're not ready to trust him with garrison secrets or anything else, but I think he's harmless. Unlike our friend in here." He stopped in front of the hut which had doubled as a prison for the last several hours. One of the guards nodded acknowledgment and opened the door for them.

Maleen took a steadying breath before walking inside.

"So, the mighty Chief of Acora humbles herself to visit me." Jewel's tone and the sneer on her face were full of malice.

The woman matched Maleen's five feet plus ten inches. Jewel had more bulk, but Maleen was not intimidated. She firmly believed speed won over strength, providing the weaker opponent was fast enough to avoid grappling. Even now with her injured arm, she had no doubt Asher would not allow Jewel to get away with anything.

Maleen envisioned planting her foot into Jewel's face. She could practically feel the satisfaction of scraping her smug sneer off with her boot as if it were a pile of graebig dung. But attacking a prisoner was *not* respectable behavior for one in her position.

Not giving Jewel the satisfaction of seeing her true feelings, Maleen asked the only question she could think to ask. "Why?"

"Why what?" Jewel sat casually, but her voice was full of open hostility. "Why try to destroy our enemy from the inside? Why, in one fell swoop, take out every veteran warrior you have? Or why lie about who I am, get the enemy to trust me by sleeping with every man in the garrison, and learn all their tactics and battle plans?" She paused. "Oh wait... That last one wasn't me." With a milder expression, Jewel may have been a pretty woman, beautiful even, but hatred and malice distorted her features. She appeared beautiful only to those like Lenet, who hated as much as she did.

"There were children injured in your explosion." Maleen kept her tone carefully controlled.

"Ah, yes. Collateral damage." Jewel's voice held no remorse.

For a moment, Maleen could do nothing but stare at the callous woman in front of her. She knew why Jewel hated her, and she knew the history of the feud between the tribes, but why could they not let their grandparents' and great-grandparents' war lie in the past?

"Phillip says you approached him before, about leaving your garrison, but I'm guessing your reason was false."

"Fanton asked me to test Phillip's loyalty." Jewel shrugged it off. "If he hadn't been so careful the first time I went to him and had offered to help me, he would've been tried for treason. But he wouldn't help me. I doubt he would have lifted a finger for anyone but you. And his desire for you compelled him to betray the family who'd taken him in."

Maleen got the impression Jewel hated Phillip as much as she hated her. As close as Jewel was to Fanton's family, it didn't come as a surprise. Realizing Phillip had been set up, relief flooded Maleen that he'd chosen to come to Acora, even after her assurance that no one would know he'd helped her.

"Even if he hadn't come with us, Lenet would have known he helped you, and he would have been executed." Jewel's face showed no remorse for the family who would turn on one of their own. "*You* should've known better than to think I would help you. Of course, when we left Kelvia, I didn't know you were going to be named Chief Heir. When we found out, I sent Sampton on the roof, in case the explosion made you Chief instead of a corpse." She jerked her head in Asher's direction. "He was supposed to take both of you out if you weren't in the hall."

It made sense. No chief, no heir to take his place. Even if Cutter had been in a condition to take over, he was no leader, a fact that was well known and would be exploited by those who would seek to seize power. The internal conflict would have left them vulnerable to attack from the outside, such as from their northern neighbors.

"Well, Sampton missed. Twice. And paid dearly for it," Asher spoke up, sounding undisturbed by Jewel's revelation.

"Shame, too. I've never seen him miss." Jewel shrugged. "He's as good as your lady here."

Maleen's face flushed. Sampton's first arrow had only missed because she'd moved at the last moment. As for the second—she owed Asher a great debt she'd yet to thank him for.

She was getting nowhere with Jewel. Turning to go, Maleen paused at the door when the dark voice behind her said, "Oh, and Maleen, I *have* admitted I was sent by the leadership of the Kelvia tribe, so I expect to be treated as a political prisoner, and I expect to have a representative from *my* tribal leadership present the next time you wish to speak to me." With that, Maleen stepped outside, not allowing Jewel to see the rage that burned through her.

Maleen practically ran to the training yard. Despite her wounded arm, every target dummy in the training yard felt the wrath of her good arm, as well as both feet. She finally let her unrestrained anger loose. Thus far, she'd felt hurt, grief, and confusion; but now her rage burned as hot as the previous night's fire.

The deaths were senseless. The feud with Kelvia was senseless. Cutter lying in a bed with a concussion, broken ribs, and more stitches than she could count was senseless. The pain in her arm, and the inability to use it, only added to her frustration and rage. On top of all that, *she* was the one to decide what to do next for the garrison, and for the tribe.

Maleen would also be the one who had to approach the Kelvian leadership about the sabotage because the saboteur claimed to have been sent by them. The day she'd left Kelvia, Maleen had avoided admitting to Fanton that she'd been sent by her leadership. If she had made that confession, it was likely Fanton would have disregarded it and the *Code of Conduct* he was sworn to uphold. He would have executed her without contacting Chief Rabe.

But Maleen was Acoran. Acorans displayed honor, regardless of how their neighbors acted. She wouldn't deal with Fanton, however. A messenger would have to be sent to Kelvia Proper. Chief Tyndall needed to know what was going on in his territory and at his border. Maybe he already did. Jewel had said it was her leadership who sent her. That could easily extend past Fanton to Tyndall. She needed to question Jewel again, but according to inter-tribal law, Jewel had the right to demand the Kelvian leadership be present, and she'd made that demand clear.

Maleen could only hope Tyndall wasn't a participant in these events. She knew nothing more about the Kelvian chief than his name. She'd have to ask Phillip for advice on the best way to approach his uncle.

One small grace was that the day was half over and there had been no sign of the planned attack. Still, she could not allow the garrison to relax its guard.

With sore limbs and no resolution, Maleen walked out of the training yard to see Asher waiting for her.

"Done with your tantrum?" he asked.

"Are you following me?" she asked. Her jaw was tight and her voice demanding. Even as she asked, she knew Asher didn't deserve her hostility.

"Just thought I'd make sure you didn't go back and use Jewel's face for kicking practice."

"I've got a little more self-control than that." Maleen rubbed her forehead.

"I know. But you usually have more self-control than to throw temper tantrums in the training yard." Asher knew her better than her brother, maybe even better than her husband. "Are you all right?"

His concern was genuine. She was trying to be strong amidst the tragedy, and it was in his nature to do whatever he could to help her.

Instead of answering his question, Maleen simply said, "Memorial service this evening, meeting in the morning. Every warrior who's of age is invited." She turned and headed back to the infirmary. Pausing for a moment, she turned back around to Asher. "I need your help to draft a letter to Chief Tyndall."

"And one to circulate through the tribe. People need to know Rabe's gone, and they need to know who his chosen successor is."

CHAPTER 6

28th of 10th Lunar, 521 AC
Acora, Northern Garrison

"Warriors, come to order, please." Maleen's voice rang clear and strong across the dining hall. She showed no trace of the tears shed at the previous night's memorial, and no trace of the emotional turmoil raging through her.

She needed to be strong for her people. So much had happened in such a short time. When Chief Rabe had nominated her for his heir, she'd been confident. She'd thought she'd have his guidance while she learned to be Chief. And she thought he'd be there to support her against the bigotry which was bound to come. But now he was dead. With that grief came insecurity and something she could admit to no one. Fear.

Standing behind a hastily constructed podium, she began. "Three days ago, Chief Rabe named me as his intended chief heir. No one could imagine I would be taking his place so soon." She took a deep breath. "No, not taking his place...filling his position. No one can replace a great leader such as him. He strove for peace while preparing for battle, and somehow managed to find the balance. He was a good father, not just to his son, but to every one of the hopeful young warriors who left their families to train here. Many of us looked to him as a father when our own were far away.

"He was a wise enough leader to see potential in people," Maleen continued, wishing she'd had this much emotional control at the memorial the previous day, and wondering how these men perceived that display.

"Eleven years ago, he saw a skinny little girl in the training ring knock herself in the head with her own staff. He didn't laugh at her. He didn't patronize her with false encouragement. He didn't scorn her. He helped her up from the ground, wiped her tears of frustration, and reminded her that Lady Warriors are held to a higher standard of emotional control."

Throughout the room, young men Maleen had trained with nodded. They'd seen her grow from a crying ten-year-old girl into a woman who pushed all emotions away, only allowing those closest to her to see them. "Then he showed her once again, the proper stance and the proper grip. It wasn't a one-time conversation. He took a personal interest in the young girl's training. Physical, emotional, and mental. I'm sure you know I'm that girl. I tell you this to point out what kind of man selected me to be his successor. I will never replace him, but if you will allow it, I'll do my best to lead you with the same honor, the same passion, and hopefully, with a little practice, the same wisdom as Chief Rabe did."

Maleen sat next to Cutter as Asher stood up before anyone had time to react. Noture shifted in his seat and crossed his arms. Despite his unease about what Asher might say, Maleen was confident he would concede. Considering the split in the council, he had every right to stand up and ask the warriors to follow traditional succession. But he had said he'd support her, and he had never lied to her before. Maleen didn't believe he would lie to her now.

"Some of you have reminded me that my father's dying act was to convince the warriors' council I should be Chief Heir," he began. "I have to admit, my wife agrees with you. However, I would remind her, and all of you, Chief Rabe's final wish was that Maleen succeed him."

A gasp was heard here and there through the room. From the angry expressions of some, Maleen could tell who would not respond well to what was coming.

"I was in the council room for the debate," Asher continued. "I went in with the opinion that I should be Chief. Yet every quality my father listed for why I should be selected, I knew Maleen possessed as well. In some cases, more than me." A few heads nodded, a few shook forcefully with clenched jaws. Most sat still, listening intently. "The council was split. They took a vote. But we will never know the outcome of that vote. Those men died—" His voice cracked with emotion "—believing in what we have here in Acora. However they voted, each one of them did what he thought was best for our tribe, and I must do the same. In the hours following the tragedy, Maleen proved why she is the best choice."

As he spoke, leaning heavily on the podium, Asher gave no indication of the fondness he felt for his friend. His tone was only professional admiration. "'She lacks experience,' some would say. Don't we all? Every veteran warrior we had in the Northern Garrison was in the hall, save one. 'She's not Rabe's blood,' others would say, but he raised her from that skinny ten-year-old girl we all made fun of—" The corner of his mouth twitched a little "—to one who risked life and limb, in the most literal sense, for this tribe. There is only one more argument we cannot dance around. She is female. To that, I would answer—so what? Your mothers, sisters, and wives are female. Does that make them less Acoran? Does it make them less passionate about doing what's best for this tribe? Does it make them less intelligent or less honorable? Now, I ask you to join me in supporting Maleen, new Chieftess of the Acora tribe. I am rescinding any claim I may have had to the chief's seat."

The response to Asher's speech touched Maleen's spirit. Amid the cheers and shouts of assent, she heard her name repeated over and over by those who would support her. The cheer grew loud enough to drown out any who may have voiced a protest, but two warriors stood and left the room. Those two would not be the only dissenters, but the vast majority were willing to give Maleen the chance to prove herself.

Cutter reached over and took her hand. His face beamed, as proud as if the cheers were for him. Together they stood, Cutter moving slowly.

"Thank you for your faith in me," Maleen said when the clamor died down. "Today, emotions are running high. I recognize it may not be the best time to make such a monumental decision without the input from the warriors in the Southern Garrison." What she was about to do had already met with approval from her husband, brother, uncle, and the friend who'd already become a close advisor. "I would like to make a proposal to you. You have given me your approval. Now, when matters are settled here, I will make the trip south and seek the same confirmation from the rest of our warriors. By confirming me, before Equin, we will also be able to attend the Equin Chiefs' Council to have it confirmed there, and so be recognized across Chalent."

"Excellent speech." The familiar, jeering voice overshadowed the cheers. The clamor died down immediately. "If you are the acting chief, then I suppose it's to you I should be making my demand for the release of my tribesmen." The sound of Lenet's taunting voice whisked away any peace Maleen had, replaced by cold fingers wrapped around her heart.

As he made his way to the front with two Kelvian warriors flanking him, Lenet sneered at Maleen. Two young Acoran warriors followed his two warriors.

"So, acting Chief?" Lenet's eyes flickered to Cutter and back to Maleen. "Who did you have to sleep with to get *that* job?"

Tian moved forward, but Maleen held up a hand. He wouldn't win against Lenet, and no doubt these two warriors were not the only ones he'd brought with him.

"How did you get in here?" she demanded.

"You ought not to leave children at the watchtowers." He referred to the older adolescent students and young warriors assigned to guard duty during the meeting.

"Sorry, ma'am," one of the Acoran youths said, twisting his grip around the staff in his hand. "He hit the watchtower guards with darts. They never sounded an alarm. Someone came over the wall and unbarred the gate. By the time we knew what was happening…"

"He brought a hundred Kelvians into the garrison," the other young man finished.

Lenet handed his staff to one of his warriors and stood with his arms crossed, legs taking a wide stance. His voice lost all traces of mockery. "I demand the release of Jewel and Sampton."

"Sampton is dead. Jewel is being held as a political prisoner for the death of forty-four Acoran warriors." Maleen gripped the side of the podium. She would not allow her temper to rise, nor would she let Lenet see her hands shake. But if he did have a hundred warriors with him, there was much reason for caution and concern.

"Only forty-four? My sources said there were forty-five in your council." Lenet's lack of surprise confirmed Jewel's claim about being sent by her tribal leadership. If Lenet had known the intended extent of the destruction, then so had Fanton, and maybe Tyndall.

"You missed me, Lenet." Noture stepped beside his niece, jaw muscles tight.

"It's a pity." Lenet pretended shame. "Oh, well. You will release Jewel to me."

"No, I won't. She will remain where she is." Maleen kept her voice even and firm. If Lenet thought he could come in here and bully her in *her* garrison, in front of her warriors...

"Then I claim the right of Tamal." Only Lenet's arrogance allowed him to make the challenge with such calm poise.

"You can't do that!" Asher's voice rose in pitch and volume, as other warriors throughout the room voiced their outrage. "Tamal is reserved for chiefs."

"One of them killed my father on the day of their escape. That makes *me* the chief." Lenet's eyes narrowed.

Maleen's chest constricted. Dealing with Fanton as Sub-chief would have been bad enough, but if Noture's arrow had killed him, Lenet would be even more difficult.

"The sub-chief of a province. That hardly qualifies you for the Tamal." Noture said, showing no remorse for the death of Fanton.

Lenet's face changed from scorn to a sarcastic grin. "And being 'Acting Chief' hardly qualifies her to hold my tribesman." He gave a disgusted snort as he pointed a finger at Maleen. "You can agree to the match, or my one hundred warriors can burn what's left of your garrison to the ground. You have thirty minutes."

He turned on his heels to walk out, his two warriors following. Stopping at the door, he glared at Phillip, who stood near it. Phillip braced himself but did not flinch.

Lenet only growled, "You have no right to wear that." He shoved a finger forcefully at Phillip's family crest and left the hall.

Maleen called for silence and the hall quieted. "Prepare for a fight. Lenet is not to be trusted." The well-trained Acoran warriors in the room dispersed to prepare for battle. The unit commanders were gone, but each man looked to the sub-commanders or whomever in their unit had the most experience. Maleen was left standing in the front of the dining hall with only those closest to her.

"He can't be serious about a Tamal match." Phillip stood, mouth gaping.

"Have you never met Lenet?" Maleen asked. "He doesn't joke, and he doesn't fight fair."

"He knows about your injury. He was there when it happened."

"Makes no difference." Maleen stood still while Noture removed the sling from her shoulder.

"You can't honestly think you're going against him with one arm?"

"I have no choice," Maleen snapped, taking the staff Tian held out to her. As she warmed up, every movement of her right arm sent intense pain through it. The days of inactivity had caused more stiffness than she would have expected. "At least I can use it, thanks to you."

"Cutter, you have to talk some sense into your wife."

"The goal of Tamal is to incapacitate, not kill," Cutter said. "She's ambidextrous. If she can swing hard enough with her left hand, she has a chance of beating him." Despite his confident words, his concern was evidenced by his tone.

"No, she doesn't." Phillip looked back at Maleen. "Lenet is a brutal opponent. I know how good you were before the injury, but even then Lenet would have laid you out." When no one would look him in the eye, he tried one last time. "You can't beat him, and he'll kill you. He cares nothing for rules."

"We'll be right by the ring. He won't have a chance to take it that far," Noture said. "She has no other choice." He caught the staff Maleen brought around behind her trying to stretch out her shoulder. "Insist on hand-to-hand," he said.

"You can't be serious." Maleen jerked the staff back.

Noture grabbed it again. "Do that with your right hand."

As Maleen tried to comply, pain shot down her arm and up her neck. She wouldn't have been able to take the staff from a child. She nodded slowly.

"Hand-to-hand." *I'm not winning this fight either way.* She sat down in the nearest chair, the thought hitting her hard.

"Give him Jewel without a fight," Phillip said softly. "And go to Tyndall to have her tried. I don't know if he'll concede. It'll likely depend on who asks, and how you ask. One does *not* go to the Chief of Kelvia and make demands. But she killed a tribal chief. You don't have to fight Lenet for her."

The others stared at him. Maleen was the only one not surprised by his suggestion.

"Not an option." She shook her head sternly. "To give her up without being forced to do so is to allow Lenet to bully us. We're weak enough as a tribe already. We can't give Kelvians, or anyone else, any reason to perceive any more weakness. Lenet will certainly take advantage of it." She stood up and straightened her vest. "We can't fight them. It'll take several days to get reinforcements from the Southern Garrison. We have less than fifty warriors here. We have civilians, including children, to protect. I won't ask my warriors to pay such a heavy price."

Giving in to Lenet's demand would not reflect well with the other tribes on her administration. Often, peace was kept only because chiefs respected the strength of other chiefs. If Acora gave in to Lenet, Kelvia wouldn't be the only tribe to take advantage of the weakness.

"You're all going to let her do this?" Phillip was getting nowhere trying to convince Maleen. "She's your wife. Your sister. Your niece. Your friend." Phillip pointed to each of the men in turn. When they refused to answer the charge, he turned to leave.

"Where are you going?" Maleen called after him.

"To get the infirmary ready for another surgery when you rip your shoulder open on this foolishness," he called back.

"Phillip."

He turned back around.

Maleen took a deep breath. "Find Lady DeLean. I need the two of you to prepare civilians to evacuate if necessary. Have wagons ready with supplies. Move those from the infirmary to the wagons."

Phillip nodded and walked outside, unescorted for the first time.

Maleen resumed her stretches, taking the full half hour to buy Phillip time.

Lenet's numbers had not been exaggerated. As Maleen exited the hall, all around her were the men, and a few women, among whom she'd spent the past year. She'd kept the women at a distance, despite training side by side with them, and she had used the men.

All of them looked at her with the same hatred she saw in Lenet. Several wore no vest. Among those were the three she'd come to respect very nearly as friends. One looked hurt. The other two looked angry. They, along with the rest of the regiment she had trained with, were here for their test.

The only one not holding a staff was Lenet's sister, Kayla. There were more than two Kelvians for every warrior in Acoran colors. The older students were a credit to their training, standing among the grown men, but even if they were counted, the Acorans were still massively outnumbered.

"Do this quickly," Noture advised, following her into the ring. "Don't give him time to take advantage."

Maleen nodded. He often coached her through tournament matches, but that was after having watched opponents long enough to find their weaknesses.

"He fights dirty. Expect tricks." Noture had beaten Lenet in the ring at an Equin Festival a few years before, but there were more unofficial rules of honor in a tournament. Other than that, Maleen had only her own knowledge of Lenet's abilities to draw from. She'd never faced him in the training ring, but she *had* watched him.

As Maleen entered the warriors' ring, she tossed her staff aside, held her right arm close to her body, and raised her left fist. Lenet made a show of tossing his own staff aside and of taking his right arm and placing it behind his back.

"Can't have everyone thinking I'm taking advantage of an injured opponent." His smirk was back as he made a mockery of her injury.

"Even if he fights with one hand, which I doubt he will, he still doesn't have the pain you do," Noture pointed out quietly from behind her.

"I'll manage," Maleen answered him. Looking around at the spectators, she saw Cutter sitting nearby. As she caught his eye, he gave her a reassuring nod. His concern was evident, but he knew she had to do this. All around, Kelvian and Acoran warriors stood, each silently daring the other to make a move. The Kelvians watched Lenet, the Acorans watched the Kelvians.

Looking at Lenet's arrogant sneer, Maleen commented, "I can't help but notice you hide your right hand. How unfortunate for me, I know you're left-handed."

"And since you're ambidextrous, we shall be even." He took his stance with an ugly laugh. "Shall we?"

"Terms first," Noture said, stepping between the opponents.

"Simple. When I win, my warriors and I leave *with* Jewel."

"If you lose?" Noture refused to move.

"Ha! To her?" His superior attitude gave the Kelvians reason to laugh.

Lenet had never seen Maleen's full potential in the practice ring, because while in Kelvia, she had never demonstrated it. She had seen his, however, when he'd sought to discipline a disorderly warrior in front of the trainees. It had taken less than a minute, and the trainees were left to wonder if the man was still breathing when he was carried off to the infirmary. Even with two good arms and a staff, Maleen seriously doubted her ability to beat him, but she could not let him see her doubts.

"If you lose," Maleen spoke up, "you leave here, with your warriors, but not Jewel. Send a representative if you like, but we try her as we see fit." She could only hope if she *did* win, he would adhere to the terms, but from what she knew of him, it seemed as unlikely as her chances of victory. At least when she lost, she'd still have her honor intact. Whereas

Lenet's would suffer for even making this challenge to an injured opponent.

"Very well," Lenet answered, waving away the answer as a trivial matter.

"Both sides agree to the terms?" Noture still stood between them, delaying as long as possible. When they both nodded, there was nothing more he could do. He stepped out of the ring. "Begin," he called.

Maleen's first swing came hard and fast. It wasn't her regular technique, but Lenet had seen her train. He would know she rarely took the opening move. By taking it now, she hoped to catch him off guard. She didn't. Lenet ducked her fist, and as he straightened, he slapped her with an open palm.

Maleen recovered quickly enough to block the next series of strikes. She couldn't keep up with him much longer. The pain in her shoulder slowed her down and even with one hand, Lenet's strength far outmatched hers.

Around the ring they went. Lenet kept his word about only using one hand, most of the time. It was a game to him. If he wanted the match to be over, it would have been—in a matter of seconds. Lenet's greatest weakness was his overconfidence, but Maleen couldn't find a way to exploit it. He knew hers was a recent injury, a fact he repeatedly took advantage of. Blow after blow, Maleen blocked his attempts at hitting her shoulder. She had to block and dodge so much that she had no chance to swing offensively.

At last, Lenet sensed her fatigue, and he was done playing. He swung full strength for her face. She ducked, but in the maneuver, her guard to her right side was down, only for a moment. That moment was all Lenet needed. His left hook hit her injured shoulder. The force and the pain of the blow sent Maleen reeling to the ground. Not letting up, Lenet delivered a punch to her temple that left her sprawled in the dirt, looking up at him. Making his point, Lenet placed a foot in the center of her chest.

"Enough!" Through the fog of the blow to the head, Maleen heard Noture's voice. "You've won your counterfeit Tamal. Take your tribesman and go."

"I'll wait right here for her." Lenet applied a little more pressure to make his point.

With blurred vision, Maleen saw men go off in the direction of the hut holding Jewel, returning with the bound woman a minute later.

"Hello, my dear." Lenet's snarl turned to a smile at the sight of her. "I trust they've treated you well?"

"Better than Sampton," Jewel said, eyeing Maleen on the ground.

"Cut her bonds," Lenet snapped. "And give her a staff."

Asher looked at Maleen. Despite Lenet's ruthlessness, she was not willing to break the terms of the match. At her nod, Asher complied.

"Now get out." Maleen's voice was hoarse as she tried to shove Lenet's foot away. But her strength was gone, a fact which delighted both Lenet and Jewel.

"In due time." He sneered, taking a step back, allowing her to sit up.

Lenet's strongest men, two of whom she'd recently manipulated, were positioned strategically behind her own. Tian and Noture stood with staffs ready. Asher, having handed his staff to Jewel, stood, fist clenched. All three were well aware of the Kelvians standing behind them.

"We agreed to terms." Maleen stood. She wavered, faint and woozy. She stared down Lenet. Had she won, he would not have honored the terms; but he had won, getting Lenet what he wanted. Yet his men stood ready to attack. That realization didn't surprise her.

"*You* are hardly in any position to enforce those terms." He gave a hand signal to his warriors and chaos ensued. Being the warriors they were, Maleen's men expected the attack. Her brother, uncle, and cousin all turned to face off with the men who would have attacked from behind, each one getting the first swing on the Kelvian behind him. Two youths helped Cutter into the nearest hut, coming back outside to stand guard. That was the last thing Maleen saw.

CHAPTER 7

Maleen woke to the swaying motions of a closed wagon. The movement and the dizziness from the blows to her head made her stomach turn.

Cutter opened the back of the wagon. "She's coming around," he said to someone she couldn't see.

"We'll be at the cutoff in ten minutes. We'll stop then. Unless the chieftess has other instructions." Asher's voice was tight.

Cutter came back to her side and winced as he sat beside her. "We're quite a pair, aren't we?" He brushed her hair from her face. Even that light touch set Maleen's ears ringing.

Maleen lay still for a moment, squeezing her eyes shut a few times, trying to clear her blurred vision. "What happened?" she asked as her mind began to work again.

"What's the last thing you remember?" Lady DeLean asked from near the door of the wagon.

"Lenet gave some kind of signal but Noture, Asher, and Tian were ready for the attack. I saw some boys helping Cutter. That's it."

"Lenet blindsided you." Cutter's tone went from being sharp with anger to being soft with love and concern. "He hit you when you weren't looking. Tian, Asher, and Noture were all engaged with Lenet's men. Phillip was right. He would have killed you if it weren't for Janter."

"Janter?" She knew the name as one who had graduated not long before she left for Kelvia. He was young but was well on his way to becoming an Elite.

"After you went down, he jumped in the ring and stopped Lenet from killing you. He held him off long enough for Denetra and Mattie to get you into a wagon."

"He saved my life."

"And gave his," Cutter finished. "He was no match for Lenet's rage, skill, and raw power. Janter fell like a true Acoran warrior." He stared at empty space for a moment. "I should have been the one to protect you."

Maleen understood what it cost Cutter's warrior's ego to have watched the events from the window. He'd been safely tucked away while another gave his life for her. In his current condition, there was nothing he could have done to save his wife or anyone else.

"I saw it coming." Maleen rubbed her temples, which only served to make her headache worse. "We should have been ready."

"Noture and Asher saw it, too," Cutter assured her. "And we *were* ready. It was no accident they knew Lenet's men were there behind them. It was no accident those boys were there to help me. Your forward-thinking ensured these wagons were hitched to teams and were ready with supplies and the civilians, including the younger students, before the match started. No one expected you to win with a bad arm, and no one expected Lenet to leave peaceably either way."

"At least he didn't get everything he wanted," she said quietly, realizing that freeing Jewel wasn't his only goal. He also wanted to make her pay for the death of his father and the personal embarrassment he experienced in having spent so much effort trying to get the attention of a spy. With the number of men Lenet had, he could have come in at any time and taken Jewel by force. The only reason he challenged her was so he could kill her in front of his men—and hers.

"No chief can anticipate every possible outcome." Cutter took her hand. "That's why a good chief keeps others around who think differently. You don't think my father knew everything?"

"He sure appeared to, at least about people. He knew whom to trust, whom to watch. When to be hard and when to be merciful."

"Not intuitively." Cutter nodded his head toward his mother, who chuckled softly. "My mother had that influence on him. He'd usually think the worst of people, and she'd encourage him to give them the benefit of the doubt. Others he would trust, but somehow, she always knew better. They'd go round and round, no one outside the family would even know they were fighting. Mother usually won, and she was usually right. Why do you think he endured the criticism from the Chiefs' Council about his closest advisor being a female? He knew she'd always help him to stay on the right path."

He smiled at Lady DeLean then back at Maleen. "That's why it's so important for you to surround yourself with men like Noture, who has experience and doesn't trust easily. Tian, who would protect his little sister from anything at any cost. And Asher, who knows how you think even better than I do and...who can take command when you can't."

"With the four of you by my side, I can't lose." Maleen smiled and took his hand.

"Five." He smiled slyly. "If you want to keep Phillip around, at least you'll have someone to fix you up when things don't go as planned."

"So now we trust him?" She smiled back.

"After today?" He nodded.

Lady DeLean said what her son's pride would not let him say. "He was instrumental in making sure the children and their mothers got out of the garrison to this caravan safely, along with the injured who were still in the infirmary. We were ready to go before you ever stepped into the ring. Whether Cutter likes him or not, the young man has leadership ability, and he has heart."

"I still don't like him much," Cutter added. "But he has started to earn my trust...and Noture's."

"Asher," Tian called from outside, near the wagon. "This is it."

"All halt," Asher called from only a few feet away. The door to the wagon opened to his concerned face. "Chieftess, we have to get out and walk."

Sitting up, Maleen's head spun, and her vision closed in momentarily. Steadying herself, she asked, "What's happening, Asher?"

"We were outnumbered. There was no winning. Most of the warriors stayed behind to give us time to leave. We can assume when Lenet discovers you're not among them, they'll follow this caravan. We have to make sure they find no warriors among the civilians, or the caravan is in danger. We're taking a back trail, on foot."

Maleen stood unsteadily. Lady DeLean raised a hand to help her. When Maleen tried to take a step out the door, she would have fallen if Asher hadn't caught her. As he set her on the ground, her legs refused to hold her. Asher swept her up like a child.

"Tian, help your sister." He handed her off to him like a parent.

Tian carried her away from the road, up an embankment to a cave. Setting her gently on the ground inside, he said, "The plan is to leave the caravan at the cutoff. This cave is a good place to wait for a day or two to make sure we're not being followed."

"The cutoff? You mean the shortcut to Elm Village?"

"We're going home, Maleen." Tian nodded. "Glad you're thinking clearly enough to understand what's going on."

Suddenly everything was too much. Her chief dead. Her warriors sacrificed in a battle she could not join. Then the thought of seeing her father, stepmother, and half-siblings for the first time in two years left Maleen in an emotional upheaval. Tears pooled in her eyes and streaked down her cheeks. *For the love of Chalent!* She swiped at her eyes, desperately willing the tears to stop. She'd done far too much crying since returning to Acora.

"I won't tell." Tian sighed and squeezed her good shoulder.

Others joined the siblings shortly. Those closest to Maleen remained with her. Cutter sat next to Maleen, putting an arm around her. As Maleen leaned into him, he flinched, and she started to sit up. He held her tighter than she would have expected with his broken ribs.

There were also ten young warriors from the garrison with them. Maleen hoped they would have no reason to need them.

"The caravan is off," Asher said. "Montea is taking the lead."

Maleen nodded. Montea was Asher's mother-in-law and, more importantly, the head of the support staff. As a respected leader among the civilians, she was well-suited for leading a caravan. Lady DeLean would be the only one to outrank Montea if she chose to exhibit authority. Considering Montea had been widowed for nearly ten years, she would be able to sympathize with the other women, without being as distracted by fresh grief. Maleen's eyes filled and threatened to spill over again. *Focus!* She wanted to scream at herself, but she kept quiet and looked at Asher.

Asher continued, either unaware or choosing to ignore Maleen's emotional state, "They're taking the main road to Elm Village. Montea and Denetra will make sure they get there. Hopefully, Lenet won't harass them when he sees we're not there, but if he does, I have no doubt they can handle it. Denetra can even lie to voyants. I don't think even Lenet would get violent with a bunch of women, children, and old men."

He nodded to Cutter. "Your mother will be just another woman in the caravan. She took off her marriage armlet and family crest. They'll have no reason to suspect she's the chief's mother-in-law. They are also sending riders south, by two different routes, to try to intercept the contingent we requested from the Southern Garrison. We want them to meet us in Elm Village." He looked around the cave. "Kelvians will be patrolling the road for a while, and combing the woods, but hopefully they don't know about the cutoff and have no idea where we're going."

***

For two days Phillip waited with the Acorans in and around the cave. Cold rations and water sustained them. Maleen slept more than not. Phillip pointed out that a concussion wasn't something to take lightly and insisted that she use thessel to rest. Having full confidence in the men who surrounded her, Maleen consented, drinking a weak version of the cold tea a couple of times a day. The rest had done her good. Her complaints of fatigue and headache had lessened, and her balance had improved.

"We've had no sign of Kelvians," Asher said after dark the second day. "Tomorrow we head to Elm Village for some real rest." He looked at Maleen for her consent. When she nodded, Cutter followed Asher outside, where everyone but Maleen and Phillip had migrated, to make sure they understood they would be leaving at first light.

"That doesn't bother you at all?" Phillip asked Maleen after they were out of earshot. "The way Asher takes charge, makes a decision, and *then* asks you?"

"It doesn't bother me a bit." Maleen shook her head. "He's a capable leader. Between the concussion and the thessel, I haven't been able to think straight most of these two days. It's comforting to know there's someone I trust able to step in."

"Wouldn't you trust Noture more?" In Kelvia, what Asher was doing would certainly have been suspicious. Kelvians were known for such tactics. The fact that the same family had led the tribe for three generations belied the previous four hundred years of Kelvian history.

"Asher and I grew up in the same garrison since we were ten years old. We've trained together, learned strategy together. We also think alike. He knows me better than anyone, even Tian and Cutter. If he wanted my job, he'd have taken it already. He would've had plenty of support back in the garrison if he hadn't conceded."

Phillip took a breath, about to respond, then blew it out. His cheeks grew warm as he realized how unwise it would be to speak. He'd made the mistake of insulting a chief's family member before, in Kelvia. Best not repeat that mistake here, where he had few allies and even fewer true friends. But he couldn't dismiss his unease at Asher's actions.

It was another moment of silence before Phillip spoke again. "I wish you'd told me months ago you were engaged."

"I couldn't do that without explaining a lot more. A couple of times I considered telling you everything, especially when I figured out why the crass talk about me bothered you so much."

"But you couldn't trust anyone." A pang shot through him. He was used to being mistrusted, but not by those he considered friends.

"Don't think that. I knew Liften, Cantel, and probably even Piel would have turned me in. It wouldn't have mattered how close we were. But not you. I simply wasn't willing to put you in a position to choose between a friend and your tribe. I hated to leave without saying goodbye, but I couldn't put that on you. I only asked for your help when I couldn't see any other way." They sat quietly for a minute before Maleen spoke again. "I never used you for information, and I tried to be careful not to give you the wrong idea."

"You didn't," he assured her. *But even when a fellow knows he doesn't have a chance, it doesn't keep him from wishing.* There was still one question he needed to ask but had to wait until there was no one else near enough to hear it. "Why is it your friendship with Asher doesn't bother your husband, but ours does?"

"Give him time," she assured him. "He's known Asher his entire life. They're family. We were friends long before Cutter saw me as anything more than an arrogant child. You're making progress toward trust with him. He left us alone together, didn't he?"

Phillip wondered if maybe Cutter's dislike for him had nothing to do with the fact that he was a male friend to Cutter's wife. Loyalty was a vital part of life in any tribe. While he'd done it for a noble cause, the fact remained that Phillip had been, not only a deserter to his garrison, but a traitor to his tribe, or at least to his province. Regardless of his motives, it was a fact that would not be easily forgotten by any of their companions.

***

Early the next morning, the troop left the cave, keeping a careful eye out for not only Kelvians but anyone who might report their presence for a profit.

"Doesn't look like anyone's used this trail for a long time," Maleen commented, picking her way carefully down the steep bank of a ravine.

"I haven't been home the entire time you've been gone." Tian offered her a hand to steady her balance. She shoved it away.

"Me either," Noture said. "I didn't care to lie to your parents about why you haven't visited or written, and I couldn't tell them the truth, so I avoided the village altogether."

Maleen watched as Cutter winced each time his feet slid on the loose gravel. He depended on the young men to help him, but Maleen wondered if the walk was too much for him.

"You need to take it easy," Tian warned after the third slip.

"Tell that to your sister." Cutter nodded in Maleen's direction. "In her condition, she shouldn't be overdoing it."

"I'm fine," Maleen said, hoping they didn't notice how tired she was becoming. Home was so close, then she could rest.

"I stopped trying to tell that woman what to do a long time ago." Tian laughed, though he didn't fool her for a second. "Phillip tried to get her to slow down." He raised his voice and turned in her direction. "But she's stubborn."

Maleen snorted and started up the embankment on the other side of the ravine.

"One of the things I love about her. No one gets to push her around." Cutter winced again.

Maleen hurried ahead, groaning silently when Tian and Phillip kept up with her. They weren't going to give her any space until they were convinced she was taking care of herself.

At the top of the embankment, Maleen sat down to wait for Cutter and the two warriors helping him. As much as she wanted to get home, it was a relief to sit for a moment. But she wasn't about to let Tian or Phillip know it.

"Maleen," Tian said, "we need to slow down."

You mean I *need to slow down.* "I'm fine."

"I'm concerned about Cutter," Phillip spoke up, watching him struggle up the slope. "He keeps pushing himself and won't let the other men help him as much as he should. Perhaps you could stay with him? You know him better than anyone else. You'll let me know if he's in too much pain?"

If she stayed in the back of the group with Cutter, she wouldn't be the one scouting ahead, trying to keep track of the rough trail. The trip would be much easier on her. But more than that, she shared their concern for Cutter. Maybe if she slowed down, he would too.

When they resumed their trek, Maleen took Phillip's advice and stayed in the back of the group.

Night fell before they could reach Elm Village, and Maleen gave orders to set up camp. They were only a couple of hours away, even at their slowed pace, but the rough trail would be too treacherous to navigate in the dark.

"We'll still arrive before the caravan," Noture pointed out.

Maleen pushed back her frustration. They'd still beat the caravan, but they'd been traveling too slow. Without her and Cutter's injuries, they should have already arrived. Out here in the wild, she felt exposed, and judging from his tense posture, Noture felt the same way. There was nothing to be done about it. Tomorrow she'd be home.

***

After a cold breakfast the next morning, they were on their way again. Two hours later saw them at the border of Elm Village, greeted by a look-out who recognized Noture. Looking from him to Maleen and Tian, his eyes went wide.

"Oh my." He sighed. "Little Maleen, all grown up, and still the image of your father thirty years ago. Though quite a bit prettier. That must come from your mother's side."

"Thank you, Quinton." Maleen smiled at her father's longtime friend. "We've come with urgent news from the garrison. Will you ask my father and the other elders to call a meeting for the village? Everyone should hear this."

"Of course, my dear." The older man called another to take his post and led the way into the village. Maleen could see from the way he kept looking at her that he wished to ask about her sling and the yellowed bruises on her face and arms. He kept glancing at Noture, no doubt wondering why Noture wasn't in charge of the entourage, but Quinton kept his questions to himself.

"Lesney is in the fields this morning. Not even being in her eighth month can keep your mother away from her crops." He smiled. "I'll gather those in the village while you surprise her." He led the warriors to the center of the village, leaving Maleen with only Phillip—who'd wisely removed his jacket with Kelvian colors, and three of the young warriors.

They seemed to have decided among themselves which of them were on duty at any given time to protect her and to help Cutter.

Coming to the edge of the field where many villagers stooped over the seeds they planted, Maleen spotted the familiar face she sought. With the pregnant woman were two small girls, six and four years old. At the sight of them, Maleen felt a hint of joy she hadn't experienced since the explosion.

"Mother," she called loudly.

The woman straightened up, brushing her brown hair out of her eyes. She looked intently at her stepdaughter's face. "Maleen? My sweet Maleen?" She ran to embrace her. When Maleen winced at the touch, Lesney drew back and looked again, this time seeing the sling and the bruised face. "What happened to you?" Lesney asked, running her hand down Maleen's arm.

"It's a long story, Mother," Maleen said quietly. "I don't want to tell it twice." Louder, for all to hear, she called, "Come, all the adults are gathering at the meeting hall, by request of the Chief of Acora." Maleen put her hand up to forestall the flood of questions. "Everything will be explained. Please, honor us with your attendance in the meeting hall."

Parents handed farming implements to children while adolescents begged to be included with the adults. Many of the oldest among the adolescents, joined their parents. Younger adolescents and smaller children, including Maleen's sisters, Mya and Dara, were instructed to continue the planting.

Approaching the main village, Maleen took the time to look around. It looked similar to when she had left. Wooden huts dotted the hillside. The small trees she'd climbed as a child were no longer small, towering over the homes. Her grandmother's hut was occupied by someone else but still had a flower garden circling the front porch. The home where she had spent the first ten years of her life had been extended to accommodate a growing family. When she and Tian had left, it had been just their parents and the two of them. Eleven years later, there were four more, with another only a month away. Some things were vastly different, yet it was still home.

When they entered the meeting hall, Sonley, Maleen's father, was in no mood for friendly greetings. "What is going on, girl?" he asked his eldest daughter, handing his youngest son to Lesney. "Tian and Noture won't give me an answer. They said to wait for you. We don't hear from you for a year, then you show up *leading* an entourage from the chief?"

"A year?" Maleen startled. "You didn't get my message from a few days ago?"

"The last letter we received from you said you were engaged to Chief Rabe's son. We knew I couldn't make the trip, but your mother sent a gown for the wedding. Since then, all we've heard is your brother apologizing for you and promising you would write as soon as you could."

"I couldn't send personal messages." She could no longer take the time to enjoy her visit. Maleen hurried to the podium at the front of the room. "Everyone listen, please." Maleen tried to quiet the hall.

"If they didn't get your messages, they may have been intercepted," Asher warned, behind her.

"I realize that," she whispered back harshly, covering her near panic with anger.

Lenet may not have waited until Jewel and Sampton found an opportunity for sabotage before sending men into Acora. Accosting expediated couriers would certainly be an efficient way of getting information. The second message had been a copy meant to circulate among all the villages and towns, announcing the death of Chief Rabe, and the appointment of his heir. She'd asked the messenger to start by heading south out of the garrison. There would only be one village on the route before he should have arrived in Elm.

Cutter stood up, hiding the pain the exertion cost him after the long walk the previous day. He stood at the podium, picked up the round stone gavel, and pounded its base several times until the room quieted. He'd only been in this village twice, but there would be a few who knew who he was. He was no diplomat, but his position required him to try.

"I am Cutter, only son of Chief Rabe," he said when the room was quiet. "My father was murdered a few nights past." In the shocked outburst of the crowd, Cutter waited. Rabe had been well loved throughout the tribe, and this village was full of retired warriors who'd given years of their youth to following him and serving the tribe.

Cutter raised a hand and waited for the clamor to die down. He had to be sure his next words were not lost "But it was not before he nominated a chief heir. He knew I had neither the leadership skills nor the ambition to follow in his footsteps, but he wished the chief's seat to remain with his posterity. Therefore, the day I asked this fine young Lady Warrior"—he gestured to Maleen— "to be my wife, he chose to break with tradition and planned to appoint the first Lady Chief of any tribe that I know of." He waited for the murmur to die down again.

"Not knowing Chief Rabe's plan or that she was being tested, she spent the next several months proving to the council that she was worthy of the appointment, acting with honor and fulfilling her duty to her tribe and to her chief. Being from this village, many of you may still see the ten-year-old girl who left for the garrison eleven years ago. But I assure you, she has grown into a fine young woman, as strong and intelligent as she is beautiful. Now I ask you, if you held my father in a place of honor, hear the words of his chosen successor." He nodded to Maleen and sat down.

"You're all my friends and family," Maleen began, standing at the podium. "I've only been back a few times since my uncle convinced my father to allow me to train at the garrison, but I'm still the daughter of Sonley. I still hold to the honor and integrity he taught me as a child."

Having finished laying the foundation of trust Cutter started for her, she told the story of the past few days.

The room fell quiet, heavy with deep sorrow as she paid honor to the lives lost. When she finished, many women wept openly. Men who had fought side by side with those council members cleared their throats, blinked rapidly, or coughed into their hands, all trying to hide the heavy emotions of lost comrades.

Maleen continued with the story of the counterfeit Tamal match, and of Lenet's betrayal of the terms. She told of the warriors who stayed behind so the civilians could escape the garrison and of their bravery in helping the new tribal leadership to escape as well.

"It was our intent to come here, to rest and recuperate from our wounds," she said, finishing her story. "But now that is not possible. I sent my parents a letter on the evening of my wedding. It was sent by expediated courier before the massacre. My parents never received it. There may be any number of reasons the courier never made it to Elm Village, but if it was intercepted by Kelvians, then we may have unwittingly put this village in danger."

"Why would the Kelvians care about our village?" a man spoke up. "The only warriors we have here are old and disabled. We have no more fight in us." Several middle-aged men puffed their chests out a little in objection to that observation.

"Lenet, and the entire leadership of Kelvia, are well known for grudges and vengeance. I infiltrated their Western Province. Noture inadvertently killed the Sub-chief. These are not offenses Lenet will forgive. If he knows this is our home village, he will come here. Now you, as a village, must make a choice. We've sent word to the Southern Garrison for reinforcements to meet us here, but they may not arrive before Lenet does." The caravan would be another day, but if Lenet headed here on graebigs, even on the main road he could be here much sooner.

"My men and I can leave. We will not ask you to risk your lives for us," Maleen continued. "You'll be able to honestly tell Lenet you don't know where we are. The risk is that, even if he believes you, he may use this village as hostages to draw us out. After all, three of us were born here." She nodded to Tian and Noture. "If we leave, there is the risk that you will be overrun, and we do not wish to leave you defenseless. We have the six of us and ten young warriors. It's not much defense if Lenet brings the same number here as he did into the garrison, but it may be better than no protection. We leave the choice in your hands."

"I choose neither," a voice called from the back. "We won't send Sonley's daughter away to be chased down by a madman. Nor will we ask you and your men to fight and die to protect us. We will hide you."

"Lenet's sister is a powerful voyant," Maleen warned. "She came with him to the garrison. If he brings her here, you won't be able to lie to him."

"I'll take the risk," the same voice called. "And I will fight if necessary."

"As will I." The response echoed throughout the room.

Maleen fought against the emotions that welled up inside her. She had not known whether the villagers would ask them to leave or ask them to stay and defend them. But she had not expected them to offer a place to hide. As Chief, she should have been protecting her people, not the other way around.

"As with any choice of this magnitude, we need an Advocate of Dissent." Sonley stood up. "Who will speak against my daughter?"

It had always been the village's way. When Sonley requested an Advocate, he was reinforcing what all those present knew about the kind of man he was. He would die to protect his family, but if it involved the entire village, they must all have a say, and they must make sure all options were heard.

"I will speak." An old man stood up. "Do not take this as dishonor, Chieftess. It is our way."

"You are a wise man, sir." Maleen did not remember the baker's name, but she remembered the sweet rolls he used to slip her when her mother wasn't looking. "Please, speak. None will hold it against you."

"Another option, should the son of Fanton come here, is to turn this woman over to him." A cry went up through the room. He continued anyway, "She speaks correctly when she says Lenet will hold us to get to her. Is that what you want for your children and your grandchildren?"

As he spoke, a young man rushed in and whispered something to a man in the back of the room.

"The choice must be made now," he called out. "The lookouts have reported a band of twenty warriors in Kelvian colors a mile away on the main road."

"Well then," the baker said, "now that my job as Advocate is done—" He smiled at Maleen "—I vote we hide the chieftess and her elect. If these young men won't be recognized, then they should change into farmers' garb and mingle within the village."

From the cry that went up, it was clear that most agreed. Anyone who might have disagreed was drowned out.

This isn't the way the Advocate of Dissent is supposed to work! There should have been more discussion. The Advocate should have stood his ground and given anyone who agreed with the stance he had taken a chance to speak. Maleen pushed aside her pointless objection. There was no time.

"This way, Madam." A woman led them off to a stairway. The second floor of the meeting hall was a storage room. "These crates are empty. If you hear someone coming up the stairs, pull the lids over and they'll never know you're there." She opened a window that overlooked the main road into the village.

From the window, Maleen could see the children who had stayed in the field brought back to their parents. Maleen's sister Mya held tightly to Dara's hand as the younger girl tried to pull away. Maleen's ten young warriors were ushered into huts and emerged again in farmers' clothing. Lesney gathered all the warriors' vestments and brought them to the storage room.

"Mother." Maleen took Lesney's hand. "I can't ask you to do this."

"I promised your first mother I'd look after you and your brother...and your father. At the time, I had no idea that meant I'd become your step-mother. Letting you two go to the garrison was the most difficult thing I've ever had to do, but your uncle was right. It was the right thing. Now look at you." She touched a bruise on Maleen's face then the marriage armlet with Chief Rabe's family crest. "Your father is as esteemed now as he ever was as a warrior. There isn't a man in this village who wouldn't lay down his life for him or for his children. Many of them *owe* their lives to him."

"But Father's health..."

"Has been deteriorating." Lesney nodded, her shoulders drooped. "After five years, he's never recovered from that fall. He's not young. He's as proud as can be that he can still father a seventh child." She rubbed her extended belly, smiling just a little. "I think the disability would have been easier to bear if it happened in battle, rather than a careless fall. If this one time he can be a warrior again, and lead men in battle again, and in doing so he saves the lives of two of his children and his brother, then so be it.

Come what may." She turned to go, pausing long enough to lay a hand on Noture's arm, then Tian's. "Stay out of sight of the window."

Tian put an arm around Maleen. Each knew the other's thoughts because they were also their own. Fear for their father, guilt over bringing this danger to their home village, pride in knowing their father was held in such high esteem that the entire village would consent to protect his grown children.

It wasn't long before they heard a familiar voice holding a more diplomatic tone than the usual arrogant one. Maleen sat under the window where she could hear every word.

CHAPTER 8

"I'm looking for a woman," Lenet said. "She infiltrated Kelvia's Western Garrison, stole our secrets, and then she and an accomplice killed my father, Sub-chief Fanton, as they escaped. She then fled to the Acoran garrison where she had previously seduced your chief's son."

Seduced? Maleen looked at Cutter and, despite the dire situation, she saw humor in his eyes.

"When your chief sought to make her his heir, those who rightly opposed a female heir were massacred and the chief with them." Lenet paused. "That's right, your chief is dead, and his assassin is trying to take his seat. She placed the blame for the massacre on two of my tribesmen who were visiting your garrison at the time. One they killed, the other they imprisoned.

"When I went to her to lobby for the release of my tribesman, she challenged me to a Tamal match. Never mind she is a usurper and I am only a sub-chief, I accepted her challenge. I won the Tamal, yet instead of honoring the terms, she ordered her warriors to attack mine. In the midst of the melee, she and a small band of conspirators escaped. It is that band of renegades we now search for."

"We're a small farming village, Sub-chief. Why come here?" Quinton's voice was strong and confident.

"I understand this woman comes from this village. We thought she might seek refuge among her kinsmen," Lenet said.

Maleen leaned her head against the wall and closed her eyes, breathing deeply, trying to keep the anxiety at bay. For one who didn't know Lenet, his diplomatic tone was respectable. If Maleen hadn't had her father's reputation to back up her claim, there may have been many who would have believed him.

"This Lady Warrior? Does she have a name?" someone asked.

"Maleen, daughter of Sonley. Her accomplice is Noture, brother to the same."

Maleen's apprehension grew at the confirmation that Lenet knew who her family was.

"Sonley's daughter?" A new voice spoke up. Maleen looked between Noture and Tian. They both recognized Sonley's voice. "She left our village more than ten years ago, along with her brother. She's only been back a handful of times since. I often hear her mother complain she rarely even writes a letter." Sonley spoke deliberately. Everything he said was the truth. He'd heeded her warning about the voyant.

"We intercepted a letter she sent here recently," Lenet said. "I'd like to deliver it to her parents. Where are Sonley and Lesney?"

"I saw Lesney in the field this morning. Sonley is an old man. He can often be found in his hut." Sonley's words were still true. Maleen hoped that if Kayla were out there, she wouldn't be able to read him.

Maleen caught sight of Noture's tight-lipped smile.

"Who do you think taught me?" he asked quietly.

Maleen wished she'd been able to learn the skill of deceiving voyants.

She hoped that Lenet wouldn't notice the family resemblance between the man he spoke to and the woman he sought. Sonley's facial hair and graying head would help hide the resemblance.

"He can't be too old." Jewel's voice held none of the diplomacy of Lenet's. Maleen had never heard her speak civilly to anyone who did not hold a higher rank. There was no reason to think she'd be any different here. "His daughter can't be much over twenty and his brother not even forty."

"Sonley's a good twenty years older than his brother." Sonley continued to speak of himself in the third person. "Strong man, fathered children well into his fifties. But he's an old warrior. He suffered an injury a few years back, never fully recovered. It made him old before his time."

"Search the village. I want to know if Maleen is here," Lenet called to his men, finished with diplomacy.

"Now wait just a minute!" From Sonley's angry tone, Maleen could easily imagine her father's face turning red. "I told you, we've rarely seen her since she left as a child."

"You there, boy," Kayla's condescending voice called out. "Do you know which hut we're looking for?"

"Sonley's and Lesney's, ma'am," Maleen heard her brother, Oblam, say. "Which one is it?"

"My mother wants me in the fields. I ought not to take the time to show you."

Maleen beamed with pride at her little brother. He'd learned well, young as he was.

"The boy is a voyant," Kayla called out, without indicating whether he'd been truthful or not. Noture, Maleen, and Tian all looked at each other, mouths open. No one in their family had ever shown potential for voyancey, and to Maleen's knowledge, neither had anyone from Lesney's family.

"We've no voyants in our village." Sonley's surprise sounded genuine.

"Perhaps you do and never knew it, old man," Jewel said with impatience.

"My parents don't even know, ma'am," Oblam said. "It's an ability that scares people. I've kept it to myself since I discovered it."

"Never mind that," Lenet said, undaunted at finding a child who could read emotions. "Where will I find Maleen and her collaborators?" He would not be oblivious to the evasive answers he was being given. The only reason they would have to avoid a straight answer was if they were hiding something and knew he had a voyant with him.

"They're not here," a shaky voice spoke up. "Please, move on, maybe they headed to the Southern Garrison."

"Now that's the lie I've been waiting for," Kayla said. "I told you, all it would take was one frightened person to open their mouth."

"They're here," Lenet called to his men. "Burn the village until you find them."

Burn a civilian village? Maleen couldn't allow that to happen.

"No!" She stood before the open window, seeing that Lenet brought only a quarter of the number of men he'd brought to the garrison, most of them still on their mounts. "Leave them out of this. This is between you and me." Both anger and dread coursed through her, fighting for dominance. She should have run. By allowing the villagers to help her, she had guaranteed bloodshed.

Next to Lenet, Commander Rundel sat on his graebig, his bow in his hand. It was likely only Noture's presence next to her, with his own bow visible, that prevented Rundel from drawing it.

"When Rabe sent you to spy on my garrison and you killed my father, he made it between Acorans and Kelvians, not you and me," Lenet called. "But if you, your uncle, and the Kelvian traitor will give yourselves up, we'll leave the village."

"Don't trust him," Asher said. Tian and Cutter muttered agreement.

Maleen would do whatever it took to protect the village and knew Noture felt the same. But surrendering to Lenet in no way guaranteed the village would be safe.

"As soon as you're in custody, he'll pull the same stunt as in the garrison," Tian gave voice to Maleen's thoughts. "And the tribe will be chief-less five minutes later."

Before Maleen had time to respond either way to Lenet's bargain, Sonley used the staff he'd been leaning on to forcefully dismount the nearest Kelvian. Many older and retired warriors may have populated the village, but they had superior numbers. The moment Sonley swung, the village erupted in fierce combat. Seeing the villagers fighting along with her young warriors, giving all they had against the Kelvians, Maleen turned toward the stairs, reaching for the sling once more, three warriors on her heels.

"Maleen!" Phillip called after her. "You're not ready for this."

"Look after Cutter, Physician," she called back. "And let me do my job."

Grabbing her good arm before she could leave the room, Tian echoed the warning. "Tear open that shoulder and it'll never heal."

"Lucky you. Maybe then you'll be able to outshoot me," Maleen said. She turned to go, but her brother didn't release her arm.

"Not this time," he said, in an uncharacteristic moment of assertiveness. "This time we do have a choice. You can't fight with one arm. The Tamal match proved that." He waved Noture and Asher toward the door. Both men headed down the stairs, apparently in full agreement. If Tian hadn't stopped her, it was likely one of them would have. "Make sure she stays here," Tian ordered Phillip as he released her, closing the door behind him.

"Not a chance." Maleen made a move to follow. She was a warrior. She was the chief! Chiefs led from the front. They did not hide in storage rooms when their warriors went into battle.

Phillip stepped between Maleen and the door.

"He's right. This time you *do* have a choice." As Maleen made a move to push by Phillip, he moved with surprising speed. Grabbing her good arm, he spun her around, her back to him, with her arm pinned between them.

"Let go of me!" she yelled. Instead of complying Phillip reached both arms around her. Gripping one wrist with the other hand, he locked his grip around her.

***

Cutter clenched his fist. Every part of him wanted to lay Phillip out. Every part of him except the part which wanted Maleen safe. If she hadn't been injured, she would have been able to break Phillip's grip and drop him with relative ease. Phillip looked like a strong man, but he had no technique. Cutter could think of three different holds which would have been effective without hurting her. Phillip had only his strength to depend on.

Maleen planted her foot on the wall and pushed off, forcing Phillip back several feet. He tripped, but still held his grip. As Maleen landed on top of him, she landed with the full force of her falling weight on his chest. Despite the loud grunt he let out, Phillip hung on.

Under any other circumstances, *no* injury would have kept Cutter still while someone manhandled his wife, but for her own safety, Maleen needed to stay here. Cutter didn't have the strength to force the issue, nor would he have had the heart to handle her so roughly, and she wouldn't stay voluntarily. That only left Phillip.

"Calm down, love." Cutter knelt next to them. "He's right. You can't go out there."

At last, Maleen stopped struggling against Phillip. He released her, and both stood up. Cutter saw anger flash in Maleen's eye but didn't have time to warn Phillip before she turned and hit him in the jaw. Undaunted, Phillip returned with a punch of his own.

Cutter moved forward. *That* he would not tolerate, no matter what his condition. He would burst stitches before he'd let Phillip swing again. But there was no need for Cutter to step in. Phillip stood straight, arms down, leaving himself open to her retaliation if she had chosen to do so. The physician had no fighting technique. The only reason he had been able to land a blow was because Maleen had not been prepared. Any of her sparring partners would not have hesitated, particularly when she swung first.

Cutter had watched her grow up in the garrison, learning the lesson that if she wore the colors, she should expect to be treated like any man, including being hit with a closed fist. There was a time, when she'd only been Tian's little sister, he had even found amusement watching his cousin teach her such lessons. She'd been hit many times, much harder, by men who knew how to land a punch in the most effective way, but it was the fact the blow came from Phillip which seemed to have caught her off guard. When Maleen did not strike back, Cutter gritted his teeth at the trust she had in the physician.

"If you can't fight me, how are you going to go out there and fight trained warriors?" Phillip asked solemnly.

"I will not allow another to fight my battles as long as I'm able." She backed toward the door as she rubbed her jaw. While her attention was on Phillip, Cutter silently moved to stand in front of it.

"That's the issue." Phillip took a step toward her. "You're not able. Why do you think your brother said to keep you here? Why do you think your husband allowed me to do what I just did? You *were* able. No one questions that. Hopefully, in another couple of months, you will be able again—but *not* now. Don't let your pride and a misplaced sense of honor increase the chances of your injury being permanent or worse, getting you killed."

Maleen turned to run out the door, only to run into Cutter's sizable form leaning against it. "You know I belong out there," Maleen said, looking up at him.

"Not this time." Cutter echoed the sentiment of the other men as he brushed a piece of loose hair from her face. He didn't like doing this to her, but it was for her own safety.

"Not you too?" Maleen made a move to push past him, reaching for the door handle.

Cutter stood firm, though he flinched at the pain her push caused him.

"I need to be out there." Maleen's temper was at an end. She could have pushed harder to leave the room, and she might have been successful, but with Cutter's injuries, and his refusal to move from the doorway, she couldn't leave without causing him excessive pain.

"I'm not moving," he said resolutely. "You may as well watch the battle from the window because if you go out there, so do I." Going out into the battle would mean his death, and Maleen knew it. She knew him well enough not to doubt he would go if it meant staying by her side.

Maleen backed away from the door, looking from Cutter to Phillip, giving them both a pained look. The expression of hurt he saw stabbed at Cutter's heart and his conscience, but he would not move. Had she been thinking straight, she'd have agreed with them.

Phillip took a step toward her. "What happens if Acora loses their chief again? Asher conceded. How many will follow him without question? Cutter admits to not being a leader or wanting the position. You haven't produced an heir through lineage. So, what happens to Acora if you go out there and die?"

Maleen didn't answer right away. She was considering her answer carefully, her face one of stone.

"I can tell you what would happen in Kelvia," Phillip finished. "We'd have a civil war."

Cutter hated to agree with anything the Kelvian physician said, but he wasn't far off. War would be an extreme they would never reach, but with Lenet stirring up chaos, the tribe needed unity, not infighting.

"Tell me he's wrong." Cutter touched her bruised cheek.

Her stubborn pride didn't allow Maleen to say anything, but exhaling slowly, she resigned herself to watching from the window.

***

Noture struck a Kelvian about to swing toward a young villager. Never in the twenty years he'd worn a vest had he imagined he would be fighting a battle in his home village. The children and most of the women had cleared the area, ducking into huts, watching their men fight from the windows. Most of the village men were middle-aged or older, slowing them down. It was only their numbers that kept the Kelvians from over-running them.

As Noture fought, he was aware of his brother nearby. Sonley had taken the first swing, but Noture wished his elder brother had gone inside with Lesney and the children. As the Kelvian in front of him fell, Noture headed to where Sonley fought with a Kelvian half his age. Intercepted before he got there, Noture could do nothing for him.

There had been a time when Sonley would have put down any opponent. He was a champion in the Equin games, and any Acoran warrior would have been happy to have him by his side in battle. At fifty years of age, however, it had all caught up to him. A hip injury had laid him up for months, and even then, he hadn't fully recovered.

Finishing off another opponent, Noture looked up in time to see Sonley fall. Even after he was on the ground, the Kelvian took one last swing.

Noture pushed back his sorrow and rage. He had to concentrate on the battle, not on one fallen warrior, even if that warrior had raised him from adolescence.

Lenet's men slowed down, and Lenet seemed to realize they could not overcome so many opponents. He called his warriors into retreat. As Kelvians hauled unconscious comrades onto their beasts, the villagers let them go. Noture hurried to kneel by where his brother lay. Seeing no movement in his chest, Noture reached with a shaky hand to feel for a pulse. Nothing.

Why did you have to do that? Noture asked silently. He knew the answer. There was no way Sonley would have allowed his daughter or his brother to surrender to Lenet. No one else in this village could have led the charge as effectively as Sonley. If he had gone inside to hide from the battle, more than half of the villagers would have followed his example.

"We will be back, *Chieftess*." Lenet spat the last word like profanity as he looked up at the window where Maleen stood. With one last vile look distorting his features, Lenet rode off.

Lesney ran out of her hut and dropped to her knees, next to her husband. Her sobs made it clear she already knew her new status as a widow.

"Lesney…" Noture didn't know what to say. She had every right to hate him. To hate her stepchildren. To yell and rail against them. To condemn them for coming here. Instead, she squeezed his hand.

"It's not your fault," Lesney said through her tears, as Tian joined them. Moments later, Maleen knelt with them as well.

"Do you want us to pursue?" one of the young warriors asked.

"No." Maleen's voice was steady. But she only fooled those who did not know her well. "Everyone is too spent." The young warrior nodded and walked away. Maleen looked back down at her father. "I should have been out here, fighting alongside him, not hiding in a storage room while he gave his life." Her voice broke. Only a little.

"He got to be a warrior one last time." Lesney wiped away her tears. "Not only did he fell a Kelvian or two, but he did it for a greater cause than ever before. You had no way of knowing. It's not your fault."

Maleen nodded, expression of stone, lips tight.

A Lady Warrior is held to a higher standard of emotional control, Noture heard Rabe's voice from many years ago. If he could go back, Noture would have a few words to say to Rabe for putting that in Maleen's head. Rabe had no idea the emotional damage he'd done with that statement.

Two men in green vests lay dead. The retreating Kelvians had not taken the time to retrieve the corpses. Five villagers lay among them, two very young.

Swallowing back her emotions, Maleen stood up. "They will all be given an honorable burial."

"Let the village elders see to it," Lesney pleaded, looking up from her husband's body. "You have to go."

"And leave you with this mess?" She indicated where Phillip knelt next to a fallen man, setting a bone.

"If you're here when they regroup and come back, we won't be able to hold them off again. If you are killed, then these men...and boys...died for nothing." To the families of these heroes, the significance of their deaths would not be forgotten. But no amount of honor given to them would bring them back. "Take Oblam with you. If he truly has voyant abilities, he will be a great asset to you."

Noture understood the battle raging inside his sister-in-law. Lesney's face was blank; only her eyes gave evidence of her emotion. She'd just lost her husband. An incredibly dangerous man was hunting her eldest two children. Now she was sending her third child, the first from her womb, with them into danger.

"You all need to come," Asher spoke up. "You, your children, and any other relatives you may have. Don't leave anyone here who Lenet can use to draw Maleen out of hiding."

"He's right, Lesney." Quinton sighed sadly. The murmur of the gathering crowd concurred. "Take your children, keep them safe. You will be protecting them and this village."

Noture heard the sorrow in Quinton's voice. "It will be safer for everyone if our family leaves," he agreed.

CHAPTER 9

Half an hour later, funeral pyres were ready and Maleen was prepared to go. The generous villagers supplied them liberally. With four children and a pregnant woman to look after, they would have to travel even slower. Leaving the young warriors behind would mean less defense for the travelers, but more for the village. And the smaller the group, the easier to hide.

"The Southern Garrison?" Cutter asked.

Maleen nodded. "I promised the northern warriors I'd seek approval from the south. Only the timeframe has changed. Chief Tyndall needs to know what's going on here. Lenet may have intercepted the message I sent about Jewel. I'll send one more message. If we don't hear from him, then I want to go into Kelvia and make a personal appeal and ask Tyndall to remove Lenet as sub-chief."

"Equin is too far away to do it in front of the other chiefs," Tian pointed out.

"Think Tyndall will do it? Without being pressured?" Asher looked at Phillip.

Phillip could only shrug. The rivalry between the tribes went back several generations, perhaps as far back as the formation of the tribes. There was no record of why it had begun, and no one knew how to end it.

"Tyndall's a hard man," Phillip said. "But Lenet's actions reflect on the honor of all Kelvia. Tyndall must do *something* to save face with the other chiefs."

"First," Maleen sighed, "we speak with the warriors in the south. Then we figure out how to get to Kelvia without running into Lenet's men.

"We'll have to stay off the main road and the frequently used trails." Asher drew a rough map in the dirt. "The trick will be intercepting the contingent coming up from the south, so they don't end up here."

"I'll send a couple of the men along the road," Maleen said. "On graebigs so they meet them as far south as possible. We," she pointed to what would have shown up as mountains on a real map, "can stay out of sight by moving through the Border Mountains."

"Lenet only brought a fraction of his warriors with him here." Asher stared at the dirt map. "The rest are likely scattered all over Acora by now."

"The trails through those mountains are rough and narrow. Graebigs won't make it." Tian looked at Lesney. "Mother, can you make it on foot?"

"I'll have to." She smiled and patted her stepson's hand.

"I'm also worried about Cutter," Phillip spoke up. "We may be risking too much if we hurry through the mountains."

"Don't worry about me," Cutter said. "If a pregnant woman can make it, so can I."

"She doesn't have—"

"So, we take it slow." Maleen cut off Phillip's objections. "On the main road, it would take about four days to get to the Southern Garrison on foot. Through the mountains, we can expect at least twice that. We have more than enough supplies," she asserted. She added a dot to Asher's map. "There's a village right before the garrison for Mother and the little ones. Providing they have a midwife, there's no need for them to come to the garrison with us."

Phillip opened his mouth and shut it again, biting back whatever he would have said. If Maleen wasn't still angry with him for keeping her inside during the fight, she may have pitied him.

Asher scattered the dirt over his map as Quinton approached.

"When Lenet comes back—" Asher started.

"We'll tell him we have no idea where you are or where you're going," Quinton said, as he sighed with deep regret.

"A caravan should be showing up in another day or two. Can you help them? They've suffered a lot of loss." Maleen cleared the lump that stubbornly appeared in her throat. She would grieve later when she had time to be alone.

Quinton nodded. Taking her hand, he said, "I'm not too keen on this female chief business, but if it is to happen, the daughter of Sonley does honor to the tribe. For Sonley and for Chief Rabe, we will accept Rabe's choice." He stood straighter. "And I have influence in many of the villages around here. Your story will be told, hopefully before Fanton's son can spread his lies."

"Thank you, my friend. You do a great service to the families of Rabe and Sonley." Maleen gave him a small smile.

"Or perhaps now, the families of Cutter and Tian?" He turned to the two men. "May you each earn the right to lead your families." He turned and went to join the rest of the villagers at the funeral site.

As the band departed, Maleen turned to take one last look at her home, wondering if she would ever see it again. Departing while the village was empty ensured no one would be able to tell Lenet which direction they went. He might assume they were going south, but without knowing for certain, hopefully he'd keep his men scattered all over Acora until she could send them all back over the border.

She'd sent another message to Kelvia proper. The expediated courier should only take two days to arrive, then three days to get to the Southern Garrison with a reply—providing he could get a fresh mount at regular intervals. If she didn't hear from Tyndall shortly, she'd have to go to Kelvia to make a personal appeal. Once the chief of all Kelvia heard the true sequence of events, she could only hope he would act without pressure from the other chiefs—and she could only hope he was not a participant in the attack on Acora. If he were, it could very well mean none of them would return from Kelvia.

As they stopped for a short rest, after half a day's hike into the foot-hills east of Elm Village, Oblam spoke up rather shyly, "I think we need to change plans."

The adults looked at him in confusion. "Speak up, boy," Noture encouraged him.

"I saw Galino listening when you were making plans. He said he didn't hear anything, but he was lying. He's going to try to sell the information to that man."

Asher swore. "He's going to get his family killed is what he's going to do."

Noture looked at Oblam curiously. "How do you know what he's going to do with the information?"

"I don't know." The boy shrugged. "I just do. Same as I knew that when Maleen stood at the window, yelling at that Kelvian, everyone was ready to fight, especially Father."

"Oblam did insist I take the little ones inside, right before Sonley took that first swing," Lesney said, nodding. "How did you know to do that?"

"Sometimes I know what grownups are going to do because of how they feel."

"You know how grownups feel?" Noture asked.

"Sure, Father was relieved when he took that first swing. It's the first time he felt needed in a really, really long time. He didn't expect to walk away from the fight himself." Oblam spoke quieter, looking at the ground. "But he wanted to protect people."

"Oblam, how do I feel right now?" Noture asked him.

"Anxious, like all our lives are in your hands. But Maleen feels the same way. Why do you both feel that way?"

Avoiding the question, Maleen sat next to him. "Okay, little brother, if you're so smart, why can I still do this?" She reached out to tickle his side. Oblam scooted away before she could touch him.

"I'm too old for that. I'm old enough for warrior's training," he insisted.

"So you are," Cutter said. Four of the five warriors present had all begun training at Oblam's age. "When this is all over, I'll see what I can do. I think I have some pull with the chief." He smiled at Maleen, but she only gave him an angry look. His face fell. "Even if she is mad at me right now."

"Maleen doesn't want me to go to training. She's worried about me." Oblam hung his head.

Maleen looked at her brother's hopeful eyes and a stab of guilt went through her. She pushed it down, following years of training that had become like instinct. Oblam's eyes changed from hopeful to wounded. Could he sense her trying to push away her emotions? Why would that make him sad? He didn't think it was *him* she was trying to push away?

She crouched down to look him straight on.

"I'm not saying you can't join the training. You're right, I don't want you to. I'd be worried about losing you. But I won't stop you. You believe me, right?"

"I believe you. But you're hoping Mother will stop me."

Maleen smiled, looking up at Lesney in time to see her try to hide a smile. "The first rule of being a voyant is to keep quiet about other people's emotions unless it's necessary to reveal them." She reached over to ruffle his hair, but he moved too quickly. She cocked her head and looked at the boy for a moment. "You know what I'm going to do before I do it, don't you?"

"I know as soon as you feel it." He looked around at the adults. "Why does that worry you?"

"A conversation for another time," Noture said. "Right now, we have to make some new plans. I, for one, am convinced if Oblam says we'll be sold out, then we will be."

"We need to move from the rough trails to no trails." Maleen stood up. "If it takes longer, so be it. We need to make sure Mother doesn't overdo it." *Or Cutter.* But she wouldn't stab at his ego by saying it aloud no matter how angry she was with him.

"There's a storm coming. We need to find shelter. We'll head deeper into the mountains tomorrow, then head south," Maleen instructed, hoping the rain would start soon, and be heavy enough to wash away any tracks they may have left.

***

That evening everyone huddled in a single hastily built shelter, trying to stay dry. Phillip removed Maleen's sling and inspected the wound under the bandages.

"No infection." He looked satisfied with his work. "I don't want you to try to move it yourself yet. There's no additional damage from the Tamal, but it needs a little longer."

Maleen nodded. The pain had to show on her face as he prodded, and she wished everyone wasn't staring at her.

Finished with his inspection, Phillip replaced the sling and moved aside so Cutter could sit next to her. Instead of accepting his closeness, she crawled out of the shelter and walked a little way in the rain.

Cutter followed her out "You haven't said two words to me," he said once they were out of earshot of the shelter.

"My father died in battle today, and I had to stay away and watch it. Like a coward. What do you want me to say?" She made no effort to hide her fury.

"It's not about what I want you to say. It's about what you *should* say as the chief."

Maleen looked away, unable to meet the censure in Cutter's face.

"I can tell you what my father would have said. He had to stay in the garrison while other warriors fought for him. Had to stay behind while *you* infiltrated Kelvia—knowing what it did to me and how it made me feel—and choose to act against his personal feelings for the good of the whole tribe."

She whirled to face him, face hot with anger. "You don't understand! That was my father!"

"And I haven't lost my father?" he asked quietly. "With the inability to do anything about it?"

Maleen bit back her angry retort. He was right. They'd both suffered loss. But as Chief, she was expected to be there, to lead from the front... Wasn't she? Cutter had to understand why she was so angry with him and Phillip.

"You'll face any opponent in battle or in the ring, but when it comes to confronting emotions, you run away like a coward." Cutter's tone was as gentle as the hands he put on her shoulders. It was the truth in his words that hurt. "You know I'm right. You have to swallow your pride long enough to admit it." Cutter really did know her well.

"You know as well as I do that a warrior is held to a higher standard. Especially Lady Warriors. Because women are so often perceived as being emotional, we have to work extra hard to overcompensate. Your father taught me that."

"My father was wrong," Cutter said, his voice slightly more forceful. "Not about most things. But about the emotional control he insisted on you and the other Lady Warriors exhibiting. Our emotions are what make us human. They're what make people willing to follow a leader, what make a leader great. Anyone who knew my father knew he cared deeply about the people around him, and about protecting the tribe. You're no less a leader than he was. Being a woman doesn't exempt you from the right to feel. Don't you see that? Or can't you think beyond your own internal battle about being the perfect warrior?"

"I'm thinking just fine!"

"Are you? Then why don't you share with me exactly what it is you're thinking. And for once in your life, tell me what you're *feeling*."

"You know me better than that." Maleen pulled away and turned her back to him.

He grabbed her good arm and spun her around to face him. His eyes widened a little at the sight of her tears.

She hurriedly wiped them away.

"Talk to me," he said softly. "Stop cramming it all down inside."

"You want me to say it out loud?" she seethed. "You want me to say how helpless I feel right now? How my shoulder has forced me to be weak? How every time I try to show that I'm fit to be Chief, as I promised the tribe, all of you stop me? Tell me I can't do it? Like I'm doing it wrong?" She looked up at the clouded night sky, took a deep breath, and squeezed her eyes shut. When she opened them again, Cutter was standing close. "How you seem to have a very different idea of what being a chief looks like."

Cutter put both arms around her. "We can't support a dead chief," he said softly.

***

The next morning, the sun shone brightly on the wet surroundings. As they threw off their furs, the travelers each grabbed their vestments. The warriors put on their vests, trimmed with purple. Phillip reached for his physician's jacket.

He stared at it for a moment. The green trim had been removed and, in its place, sewn, however poorly, purple trim. Phillip looked up at Maleen. She nodded to him, packing away her spare vest that was missing its trim. By putting on the jacket, he indicated he accepted her wordless apology and her offer of an official position as an Acoran physician, never mind the fact that the sewing looked like it was done by a woman with one arm and no domestic skills.

It had to have taken every ounce of humility she could muster for Maleen to forgive him and Cutter for their actions the previous day. He still stood by his actions, but it hadn't been easy. Apparently, Cutter had been able to talk sense into her last night.

Emerging from the shelter, Cutter already stood outside. He glanced at the jacket and nodded. Not exactly an offer of friendship, but at least it was one of acceptance. Perhaps there *was* hope of making a home in Acora.

CHAPTER 10

11th of 11th Lunar 521 AC
Border Mountains, Southern Acora

"I have a present for you," Cutter told Maleen at breakfast nearly a week later. He reached behind a nearby rock and pulled out her bow along with a new quiver full of arrows. "You probably shouldn't start shooting yet, but since Phillip took the stitches out a couple of days ago, I thought you should walk into the garrison armed, whether it's this evening or tomorrow."

She gasped and reached for the quiver. "It's beautiful." The artwork etched into the treated leather on the quiver astonished her. She'd seen him making the arrows. He was a skilled fletcher and had been teaching the children the steps involved in making arrows, but she had no idea when he'd worked on the quiver. "Thank you."

As she leaned over to kiss him, Oblam yelled, "Mother, make them stop kissing!" The adults all laughed as she kissed him anyway.

"Today, *I* bring back supper," Maleen announced after breakfast as Phillip checked the healing progress one last time and tossed aside the sling.

"Don't expect too much," Phillip warned. "You've been out of practice for weeks now. You'll be lucky to pull the bow far enough to fire an arrow." He lowered his voice. "This sort of injury takes time to heal, and if you push too hard, you may not recover full function. Please, listen to your body and take it easy for just a little while longer."

"I understand the risk, but I have to at least try." She squeezed his hand. He would not understand, but hopefully he wouldn't push the issue.

"Now onto you, my friend." Phillip gestured and Cutter stepped in closer.

"My ribs feel so much better," Cutter said as Philip's fingers probed them. He flinched as Phillip pushed but covered it up with his usual warrior's bravado.

Phillip stepped back, shaking his head. "You're still healing. You need to take it easy."

Cutter's eyes narrowed and Maleen wondered if she should step in. She didn't want to interfere with Cutter's health. But couldn't Phillip see how his words stung the fierce warrior? Cutter hated having his activities restricted and was chafing under the physician's instructions.

Not that I've been any better, Maleen thought.

Phillip sighed. "I know this is hard for you. I don't want to tell someone I respect that he has to hold back. Please believe me when I tell you it will be worth it."

Cutter stalked off rather than respond.

Maleen shook her head. Rather than develop the common ground they'd found before, both men seemed set on escalating the tension between them.

Oblam's gift wasn't helping any.

Since it was no longer a secret, he was stretching it, seeing how far it could go. He'd started with the children, revealing that six-year-old Mya despised looking like her sisters and wanted to cut her hair, just to be different. Four-year-old Dara was frightened of everything. And two-year-old Nolel hated camping out.

After Mya punched him for having a big mouth, Oblam had turned his attention to the adults. When he revealed that Noture felt a desire for a family of his own, Noture had responded in surprise that Oblam had been able to get past the guard he usually kept up to keep voyants out of his head. Most of Oblam's observations were small matters, but it had happened so frequently over the past week it left every adult wishing they could keep their emotions to themselves, not to mention the mess it made of the unresolved issues between them.

Maleen thanked Phillip again and collected her bow and quiver. She needed space. By tomorrow afternoon, they'd reach Oak Village. From there, it was only a couple of hours to the Southern Garrison. She needed time to collect herself. Time to think.

Away from the camp, it was peaceful. The winter air was colder in the mountains than at home, but a single layer of thick fur was enough to keep warm. They'd probably see snow up north if they ended up in Kelvia. But here, the air was crisp and clear. Lalot birds were singing high in the evergreens. Their bright song matched their green and yellow plumage. It was a sound rarely heard close to camp with all the noise of children and arguing adults.

With the stitches out of her arm and without the limited mobility of the sling, it was time to evaluate her training needs herself. Knowing she needed to get back into practice with her bow, she set up a target.

The first time she tried to pull the string back, the truth in Phillip's words fully dawned on her. The pain was so great she couldn't pull it back far enough to release the arrow. Steeling herself against the pain, she yanked the string back and released. Her arrow went wild, and she bit back the vulgarity on the tip of her tongue.

After a time of frustratingly unfruitful target practice, Maleen got the distinct impression she wasn't alone. Peering over a steep bluff she saw two men in warriors' garb, trimmed with Kelvian green. Below her, a few feet from the men, Oblam hunched behind a boulder.

Stay hidden, little brother. Maleen hoped he could sense his perilous position. Oblam looked in her direction and moved a hand slightly. He knew she was there. It was then she realized Oblam had warned her. He had sent her that feeling of not being alone, knowing she was nearby.

The two men walked along, giving no indication they knew two Acorans hid nearby. Oblam turned quickly in Maleen's direction. For an instant, she saw herself through his eyes. Behind her! She spun around in time to avoid being grabbed by a third Kelvian.

"Up here," he called to the other two. "I found me a pretty Acoran."

Dropping her bow, Maleen grabbed a dead tree branch.

"Pretty little thing thinks she can use a staff." His ugly laugh carried to the other men on their way up the steep incline.

With three blows, Maleen demonstrated that even out of practice, she could make her tribe proud. One Kelvian unconscious, she turned back to the bluff. One of the men was halfway up. The other, whom she recognized, was still farther behind.

Call Tian, she willed to Oblam, hoping he sensed her plea, but not daring to call to him aloud. If he could warn her without giving up his hiding spot, hopefully he could communicate their peril to their elder brother, as well. Dropping the makeshift staff, she picked up her bow again. Drawing an arrow from the quiver, she pulled the string, ignoring the intense pain shooting through her.

"That's far enough," she bluffed. If the Kelvian recognized her, hopefully he'd also recognize the skill she'd previously demonstrated. She held her hands steady, giving no indication of the pain or the fear-fueled adrenaline running through her. She was frightened not so much for her-self, but for the innocent child at the bottom of the bluff. "Who are you and what do you want?"

"We're looking for some outlaws," one man said. Both of them slowed their ascent, only inching forward.

"Three Kelvians looking for an outlaw, in Acoran territory?"

"Being as Rabe's been dead for a little while, we didn't think he'd mind."

"What about his successor?" Maleen asked. "Think she'd mind?" Thankfully, they were too far away to recognize her, and the fur she wore covered the family crest on her vest.

"She's the outlaw we're looking for. Her and her accomplices who killed our sub-chief." They continued their subtle advancement. "Chief Lenet has declared her an outlaw being that she's responsible for his father's death."

"*Sub*-chief Lenet needs to get his facts straight," Tian said, stepping out from the woods behind her. Wearing no fur, his vest was clearly visible, though his crest wasn't likely to be recognizable to the Kelvians. "And he needs to stay on his side of the border."

Maleen let out a sigh of relief as she released the tension on the bow, resisting the urge to rub her shoulder.

"Get your friend and get out." Tian gestured with the staff in his hand.

As one of the men approached their unconscious comrade, Oblam yelled from his hiding spot, "Maleen, look out!" The warning came in time for Maleen to see the knife come at her. She shifted, deflecting the knife, and put her elbow in the nose of the assailant. He dropped the knife and grabbed his broken nose.

"Maleen?" The third man recognized her as he neared the top. "Nice to see you again," he sneered. He had reason to be furious. How many evenings had she listened to him brag about his part in the leadership's plans? His efforts to impress her had only given her information to use against his tribe.

"Hoya. Why am I not surprised to see you here in Acora?" Their camp wouldn't be safe for long, and Maleen called to Oblam, "Oblam, tell the others we're leaving. Now!" The boy hurried from his hiding spot toward the camp.

"Too late." Hoya reached to his side and took hold of the horn that hung there. Hoya ducked behind a boulder to avoid the arrow Maleen drew. Neither Maleen nor Tian could reach him in time to keep him from blowing the horn. The sound reverberated off the cliffs. Not taking the time to dispatch the Kelvians, Maleen and Tian hurried off in the direction of their camp.

"We can't lead them to the others." Tian changed directions, pushing through heavy underbrush. Maleen followed his lead. When they came to the edge of a clearing, Tian asked, "How are your climbing skills?" He cupped his hands together at the base of a large tree.

"Out of practice." Maleen used his boost to reach the first branch.

"Not a sound," he warned. "The tribe needs a chief." Instead of following her up the tree, he ran across the clearing and ducked into the underbrush.

Maleen climbed until she was well hidden in the branches of the tree, ignoring the complaints from the muscles in her arm. It wasn't long before more Kelvians stormed into the clearing.

Not much for stealth, Maleen thought, daring to peer through the branches. Three Kelvians, all different than the first ones they had encountered.

One without a vest stooped down where Maleen and Tian had emerged from the trees. Maleen knew him. In a drunken stupor, Piel had tried to get too close one night. He'd learned his lesson and never tried that again. And, to her knowledge, he'd never drank again, either.

"Two sets of prints." Piel crossed to the tree Maleen sat in. "The smaller set stops here." He looked up. One of his companions drew his bow, aiming it into the tree. "Why don't you come down, Maleen? Make this easy," he called. "Chasing you around Acora could drive a man back to drinking. You *do* realize you are about to help me earn my colors?"

Maleen's heart beat wildly, but from the direction of the archer's aim, it appeared he couldn't see her. But they knew she was there. Slowly, without making a sound, she reached for her bow and nocked an arrow. She would only have one shot then they would know where she was. She couldn't trust her aim. Target practice that morning proved it would take some time to return...if it returned.

An arrow flew from the bushes where Tian was hiding. The Kelvian with the drawn bow fell, his arrow flying wildly. Relieved, Maleen scanned the bushes, trying to see any trace of Tian, glad when she couldn't. If she couldn't see him from up here, the Kelvians wouldn't be able to see him from the ground.

A second arrow flew and hit a second man. Piel raised a reed to his mouth. His dart flew to the origin point of the arrows. Maleen heard her brother cry out as the dart found its mark.

"I've got another one for you, Maleen," Piel called up the tree.

Instead of raising the reed to loose another dart, however, he reached for his horn. Even if she could have climbed down from the tree quickly enough, he would have been a worthy opponent, particularly with her recent injury. She did not know if she could take him. She had to take the chance—or face an unknown number of Kelvians...alone. Her arrow found its target for the first time that day. Piel would never wear a vest.

Climbing down from the tree, Maleen stepped over the bodies of the fallen enemy. She couldn't look down at Piel's face. She had to concentrate on survival. She ran to the spot where her brother lay and pulled the blow dart from his leg, thankful it wasn't big enough to do any real damage. Tian's breathing was regular, but he didn't move.

Thessel-tipped. She couldn't move him, but the footprints in the clearing would lead any other Kelvians to this exact spot. They should have considered that when they chose their hiding places. It was a foolish mistake both were too smart to have made.

The tribe needs a chief. Tian's warning echoed in her head.

But I need my big brother. Before Maleen could decide what to do, she heard someone in the underbrush. They hadn't come through the clearing, so they hadn't seen the footprints. Slow enough not to make a sound, Maleen drew her bow again. She crouched low, next to Tian's still form, aiming in the direction of the movement. Whoever was there was much better at stealth than the last trio. There were two, maybe three people. In the thick brush, it would be easy for them to pass within a few feet and never know the Acorans were there. The rustling, however, told her they were heading for this exact spot. After a long moment, Maleen saw a face through the thick foliage.

"Oblam!" She released the tension on her bow as he and Noture came into view.

Oblam put a finger to his lips. "There's two people close by," he whispered. "Their feelings are really hostile." They sat silently, keeping vigil for half an hour before Oblam announced, "They're gone."

"You could sense how many people were out there?" Maleen asked.

Oblam nodded.

"He also knew where to find you and that something happened to Tian," Noture said.

"I'm glad you're on our side." Maleen smiled at her young brother. He didn't return the smile. He sat staring at Tian, tears forming.

"I could sense both of you. You were scared, but he was even more, then he was…not angry but resolute, I think."

"That's a very grown-up word," Maleen commended him. "And yes, he was willing to protect his little sister, whatever the cost to himself."

"But then I couldn't sense him anymore, and you got more scared." The boy was in tears.

"It's okay, Oblam." Maleen realized the source of his dismay. "He's only unconscious." She held up the dart. "Thessel-tipped. Like when a physician needs a patient to sleep and they won't, or can't, drink the tea. Kelvians use it on blow darts to incapacitate an enemy. All we have to do is wait a little while longer for it to wear off, then he'll be fine."

"So, he's not dead?" Oblam wiped away tears.

"No, sweetheart." She pulled the boy to her lap, despite his size. "He's not dead. If you sensed my fear when he went down, then it's because from where I was hiding, I couldn't see him." She pointed out the rise and fall of Tian's chest--though it was slow, it was steady—and she showed the boy how to check for a heartbeat.

Though still clinging to his elder sister, the boy's tears ceased. "Mother's scared," he whispered.

"Are there others with her?"

"Just Cutter, Phillip, and Asher. They're packing up camp. I think I may have sent my fears to her. She's scared for the little ones, and us."

"We'll get them to a village safely," Noture promised. "We shouldn't be more than a day from Oak Village. Probably less."

Oblam took a deep breath and stood, wandering into the clearing.

"Where are you going, boy?" Noture tried to keep his voice down.

"No one's around," Oblam said confidently. A little quieter he added, "No one alive, anyway." For a moment he stood by the bodies of the fallen Kelvians. Maleen and Noture looked at each other, not sure how to help him. Maleen got up and stood beside him. She placed her hand on his shoulder.

Mother wouldn't like this, but if the boy were going to be a warrior, he couldn't be sheltered from death. As his sister, it wasn't her place to decide what to shelter him from, but it was too late to go back now. She'd been older than Oblam the first time she had seen a dead man. At twelve years of age, she and her classmates had attended the funeral of a fallen warrior at the insistence of the commander of her training unit. Three years later was the first time she'd seen someone lying dead with an arrow in his chest.

Oblam was only ten. A week ago, he'd seen his father and others killed by enemy warriors. Now, he saw the outcome of the violent lives his elder siblings sometimes had to lead.

"His name was Piel." She indicated the only Kelvian whose name she knew. The only other time she'd needed to take a life, she had not known the man's name. Knowing, not only Piel's name but many other details about him, made his death even more difficult.

"We have to remember the enemy has a name. Every time we fire an arrow at someone, it's someone's son, brother, father, or friend. We can't let the enemy become faceless. It may make what we must do easier. But killing should never be easy."

"He was your friend." Oblam's voice was barely a whisper.

Maleen swallowed past the lump in her throat. When had she started considering Piel her friend? Him, Cantel, and Liften. She had used the warriors. She had only been close to Phillip. But those three... How many times had their jokes and banter gotten her through a tough day? Their friendships reminding her that not all Kelvians were of the same cast as Lenet?

"Yes. He was my friend," she finally said. "Until he found out I wasn't who he thought I was." The memory of them in the Acoran garrison hit her hard. Cantel had shown the same hard, angry look as Piel, while Liften had looked hurt. If she ran into Cantel and Liften, she wasn't sure she would be able to kill them too.

"They were going to hurt you," he said softly. "You had to do it."

"Yes, Oblam, we did. As warriors, we do what we must do to protect the tribe first, weaker members of the tribe second, and ourselves last. I never like to aim my bow at a person, no matter who they are. But sometimes it becomes necessary. Though it makes me sad, I do what I must.

Being a marksman, I've caused many injuries without taking lives, but even that is, and should be, difficult."

Oblam nodded. Maleen was proud of the maturity he displayed in handling the situation.

"You're the chief. Protecting you *is* protecting the tribe." He leaned over and picked up Piel's dart-blowing reed and a pouch containing more darts and several thessel leaves.

"That's why Tian gave away his hiding place to protect me. He'd do it for any one of us but protecting me has become a priority for him."

"And for Cutter, and Asher, and Uncle Noture." Oblam paused. "And for me." He walked back to the thicket, darts and blowing reed in hand.

Maleen stared after him, wide-eyed. His resolve frightened her. He was too young to fight fully grown men. He'd barely begun his training. Up until now, he'd been the son of a retired warrior turned farmer. If Father had raised the younger ones as he had her and Tian, Oblam would be able to handle a staff by now, but their father had been ailing, and their mother didn't wish to have a third garrison warrior. To protect his chief and sister was too much responsibility for a child. Maleen hoped their mother wouldn't allow him to return to the garrison with them for training, at least not yet. Perhaps he'd be more prepared in a couple of years...or at least she would be.

Tian did not share Maleen's vulnerability to thessel, and only a short time later, the foursome returned to the camp where the others were waiting. They deliberately made enough noise to not appear to be sneaking up on the camp. Asher and Cutter both had arrows aimed at the spot where they emerged from the woods. Seeing who was approaching, they lowered their bows. Lesney ran over and threw her arms around Tian.

Cutter approached Maleen and lifted her chin so he could see her eyes. "What's wrong?"

She just shook her head. If she tried to explain it, she'd lose control of her emotions. She was already on the edge. She started to walk past him.

Cutter caught her hand. "You had to kill?"

"Yes," she said quietly. "Someone I knew."

He put his arms around her. "It's all right to cry."

"No, it's not." She blinked hard. "Not for me."

"Especially for you," he said into her hair.

Fat tears fell. A few at first. Then they came faster. Unbidden. Unwanted. But once they started, there was no stopping them.

Maleen sobbed. Out in the clearing she had held together, but in the comfort of Cutter's arms, she was able to release her sorrow at having taken a life and having been a part of two other deaths. No one outside of this group would ever see her break down and express such deep emotions, but those here understood her. None of them would judge her for being emotional.

"Oblam was right," Noture reported. "He knew where to find them, and he knew where the enemy was." The past week should have begun to accustom everyone to Oblam's newfound abilities, but they still marveled. Noture sat next to Lesney as she tied a bedroll to a pack. "I want to take the boy with us when we leave you in the next village. To the southern garrison, to Kelvia, then back to the garrison for proper training."

"I thought you would." She smiled sadly and nodded her consent. Looking at the ground, she added, "His father would be proud."

Maleen said nothing. As Chief, she couldn't refuse a willing candidate for training, no matter what her personal feelings were. She was surprised at how easily Lesney agreed.

"Ready?" Cutter drew back from Maleen, caressed her face, and reached for his pack. "We should be going. It's already midday and we still need to avoid the main roads. Oblam, you'll let us know if there are people nearby?"

"Yes, sir." The boy nodded somberly.

Maleen took a quick look around. The fire had been put out with dirt and still smoldered. They left nothing behind which would indicate who had occupied the camp, but if the Kelvians found it, they would assume it was the correct one, and the warm pit would indicate how long ago they abandoned it, but it was better than the smoke that water would create.

As they began their trek on the narrow trail, Oblam dragged his feet, then absently kicked a small stone along the trail until it landed to the side. He didn't seem to have the energy to retrieve it and dragged his feet again.

Maleen walked beside Phillip. "We had to... We killed three Kelvians," she said sadly. "I knew one of them. Piel is dead."

"You did what you had to," Phillip reminded her. "Piel heard my lectures about crossing the border without just cause, but he chose to stay loyal to Fanton and Lenet. That's not your fault. He could have made a fine warrior if he'd had a better sub-chief to serve under."

Maleen moved on to explain to her mother about Oblam's most recent experience with death.

"That explains his somber mood." Lesney sighed sadly as Oblam found another stone to start kicking. "It's the second time he's seen death in a month. I wish I could have protected him for a little while longer from the harsher realities. He's so sensitive to the people around him. He always has been. Now I suppose we know why."

Maleen nodded and filled Lesney in on what happened earlier. "I've never even heard of a voyant projecting emotions to others, much less their vision. He's an extremely gifted boy." Maleen hesitated. "But he is only a boy." She had no right to interfere in her mother's decision to allow Oblam to train, but she couldn't let the moment pass without expressing her apprehension.

"He's the same age you were when you and Tian left for the garrison," Lesney reminded her. "I didn't think either of you were ready, but Noture and your father thought otherwise."

"I suppose so, but we'd already been training with Father."

"I've already told him he can go," Lesney said with regret in her voice. "I know your father would have let him. I couldn't say no. He says he has to. He's taken it upon himself to protect his chief."

Maleen was unsure how she felt about her contingent of bodyguards. A chief was a warrior. She would never convince the others to relax their guard over her, but the boy...

"He's too young for such a responsibility."

"I don't think we could keep him from it if we tried."

CHAPTER 11

That night the party made a cold camp amidst the tall evergreens. There would be no fires in the dark, not when their pursuers could be nearby. While the adults discussed plans for the following day, Oblam took out his new weapon. He cleaned the tips of the darts carefully. Then he set up a target to practice with the dart-blower.

"I'm not sure that's a warrior's weapon." Maleen sighed, watching him. She'd heard several Kelvians warriors bragging about their victories with them. Dishonorable victories by Acoran standards. "But after what he saw today, I'm not sure I want to push the bow on him."

"The lethality of your bow depends on your marksmanship," Phillip said. "With good aim, you can incapacitate. With bad aim, you miss or kill. The thessel-tipped darts Kelvians use only need to hit a target to incapacitate. The dishonor comes when they kill an unconscious opponent." His sigh of regret told the story of how many times he'd seen that happen. "Not all Kelvians behave like that, but the few who do give us all a bad name."

"It's no more dishonorable to blow a dart than to shoot an arrow," Noture said. "I'd say let him keep it. I'll still teach him to use a staff. But the bow can wait until he starts formal training in the garrison this fall."

Piel had tried to teach her to use a dart-blower in the Kelvian garrison.

"Dart-blowers are a *Kelvian* weapon," Maleen said.

Phillip stiffened slightly.

"And Simoten and several other tribes," Noture scolded.

Maleen said nothing.

His target practice finished, Oblam came and sat between his mother and Maleen.

"Hit anything?" Maleen asked, trying to make up for her harsh words.

"Better than you and your arrows this morning," he teased.

"Oh? And how long were you watching me before we ran into those Kelvians?"

"The entire time." His childlike giggle spread to the others.

"You're slipping," Asher teased Maleen. "I sent him after you the second you left camp this morning, and you never even knew you were being followed?"

Oblam laughed with Asher, some of his good humor returning after the long day. In the lull of the conversation, Oblam yawned.

"Oblam," Noture said, "part of being a warrior is knowing when your body needs rest. No one is going to tell you when to go to bed anymore."

At first, Oblam looked proud to be treated like a grownup. When he saw Noture's stare, however, he seemed to realize that, in all reality, he was being sent to bed.

"I think I'll go get some sleep." He stood, kissed his mother, and ducked into the shelter he was sharing with the little ones. "Don't talk about me until morning," Oblam called from his bedroll. The adults laughed and followed his example. Noture took the first watch and everyone else headed to their beds.

***

As she had so many times in the past week, Maleen lay awake late into the night, every sound in the woods startling her. She'd insisted that without the sling and stitches, she take a turn at keeping watch for the first time since they left the garrison. When it had been her turn, she'd drawn her bow twice, only to see a nocturnal creature scurrying away at her sudden movement. It was several hours past midnight when Asher relieved her, yet she had still lain awake, jumping at every sound. She scolded herself for being too emotional about the current situation, escalated by the previous day's encounter.

When at last she drifted off to sleep in the early hours of the morning, Maleen dreamt of the man she'd killed. In the dream, everyone blamed her for the deaths of Piel and his two companions. She tried to tell them she had no choice, but they wouldn't listen. Throughout the dream, Oblam's face stared silently, questioning her.

When Maleen woke up, the sun was barely peeking over the horizon, coloring everything a soft gray. Cutter had the final watch of the night, so he was already awake. In the predawn light, he had dug a small pit and within it, he built a small fire that would not produce enough smoke or light to be seen from any distance. Maleen breathed in the fresh morning air.

Cutter handed her a warm cup of fentel. "You were restless last night."

"Couldn't sleep." She sat down on a log and sipped the warm drink. "When I did, I just had nightmares." She stared at the steam coming off her mug. "I hate not being in control of my emotions."

Cutter put his arm around her. "You're not the only emotional one around here. After everything that's happened, we're all on edge. I'm wondering if Oblam is projecting his fears in his sleep. I dreamt about the men you and Tian faced yesterday. I wasn't even there, but in the dream, I saw their faces, clear as day. Not the normal images you see in a dream that you can't identify later. Somehow I knew it was the men you encountered...and everyone blamed you for their deaths."

The similarities between Cutter's dream and her own were unsettling. "Think he blames me for the death of those men?"

Cutter shrugged. "More likely he's afraid others will blame you. He seemed to understand it all yesterday."

"You're talking about me again," Oblam said from behind them.

"Sorry, little brother." Maleen patted the spot on the log next to her. He sat down. "It's difficult not to. Your gift is still so new to all of us."

"Did you have a bad dream last night?" Cutter asked.

Oblam nodded.

"Will you tell us about it?"

Oblam hesitated before answering. "I kept seeing the faces of those men Maleen and Tian killed yesterday. Everyone blamed her. I tried to tell them it wasn't her fault, but they wouldn't listen."

"Are you afraid people will blame me for the death of those Kelvians?" Maleen asked gently.

The boy nodded. "I know it's not your fault. You didn't have any other choice, but other people can't sense what I can."

"Listen to me." Maleen looked him in the eye. "Those were Kelvian warriors on Acoran land. Tian and I only did what had to be done to protect ourselves. If roles were reversed, Kelvians wouldn't hesitate to kill Acoran warriors just for being on the wrong side of the border. No Acoran is going to blame me."

"But the Kelvians might."

"The Kelvians may use this as an excuse to continue the feud, but even they know better. For Lenet to make a charge with the other chiefs, he'd have to admit he sent men into Acora to find us. The other chiefs won't like that. Everyone should be staying on their own side of the border and take intertribal matters to the Chiefs' Council."

Breaking the somber mood, Cutter handed a mug to Oblam. "Here, a warrior's morning drink."

"Really?" He took the mug of fentel.

Cutter laughed at the face Oblam made at the first taste. "Diluted, unsweetened, and cold."

"Why you rotten..." Oblam's cheerful voice carried as he ran forward to tackle his brother-in-law.

"Whoa there, boy. I'm getting better, but I'm not there yet." Cutter held him back until Oblam's knees went weak from laughing. "Now, Asher over there, he's fit as can be." He pointed to the sleepy man emerging from the shelters.

"Not before my morning cup." Asher held up a hand to stop the mock attack. "I promise to show you some moves later."

"Here you go." Oblam picked up the mug he had set down. Asher took a drink and instantly looked for someplace to spit it out.

"On second thought, maybe I'll show you now." Asher ran after the laughing boy, who allowed himself to be caught and tickled.

The boy's laughter stopped. He froze in the middle of a bear hug from Asher. "They're coming!" His eyes went wide with terror.

"Who?" Asher released him.

"Kelvians, I think. They're looking for us, and they're definitely *not* friendly. They're still quite a ways away, but they found our trail from yesterday."

"Everybody up," Maleen said, kicking dirt over the fire. "We're going. Now! Mother, get the little ones, let's move. Leave everything but water and weapons. We'll reach Oak Village before midday."

How far "quite a ways away" was to a child was unpredictable. They had no time to waste. In less than five minutes the party set out, little ones wailing at being awakened so early. In an effort to quiet them, two of the men lifted the smallest two to their shoulders.

The trail was well-marked and easy to follow. It was also hard-packed, so they would not leave obvious footprints, though if the pursuers found their camp, they could take a good guess at which direction to go.

After half an hour, Oblam reported, "They found our camp."

"And they're not traveling with little children," Lesney pointed out, breathlessly. The trail may have been easy, but the pace Maleen set was not.

"We should be close to the village by now." Maleen couldn't slow down. Her family was depending on her to keep them safe. It may not be safe in a strange village, but they were still in Acora. It would be safer than out here in the wild with Kelvians on their tail, and no chance of reaching the garrison in time.

Another half an hour of rushed travel and Oblam reported, "We have to hide. Now!"

Noture took command. "Into the tree, Oblam. You too, Maleen."

Maleen hesitated. She should be by the side of her warriors.

"Don't fight in front of the boy if you don't have to," Noture instructed quietly. "He'll try to protect you, and he's too young. You need to get more practice in before you're ready for combat."

What he said made sense, but it wasn't the only reason for sending her into hiding. He was being overprotective. Again.

"I may not be where I was, but I *can* shoot again," she said.

"Then shoot from up there." Noture pointed.

"Let's go, Chieftess." Oblam pulled her to the low starting branch and climbed.

Maleen hesitated but followed him up.

Cutter handed her the two smaller girls, Dara and Mya, but refused to follow them, despite Phillip's insistence. Maleen and Oblam showed the girls where to put their hands and feet on each branch, climbing as high as they dared.

When Dara started crying, Maleen tried to reassure her, "Big sister is here, I'm not going to let anything happen to you." Maleen hoped she would be able to keep that promise. The child nodded and wiped her eyes. From her perch, Maleen saw Lesney crouch in the creek bed with the smallest child, two-year-old Nolel. When the fighting started, hopefully Lesney would be able to sneak away up the creek with him, without being seen. The men chose their hiding positions. They would have the element of surprise and would use it to their full advantage.

"Oblam, can you tell how many there are?" Maleen asked.

"Five."

Maleen's five men all had bows, though she doubted Phillip would fire his at all, much less at his former tribesmen. Maleen had hers as well, though she still couldn't trust her aim. Her staff lay on the ground, inconspicuous at the base of the tree. If they were discovered, they'd have a chance, but only if she could hit her target.

A few feet above her, Oblam took the darts out of his pouch. Taking one thessel leaf, he folded it several times before piercing it with the tip of each dart. Maleen wasn't sure if it would deliver enough thessel to be effective. Physicians usually crushed the leaves to get an extract, but at least he was thinking.

He was a brave boy.

"Your first dart could give away our position," she cautioned.

"I know, Chieftess."

"Are you sure you can hit your target?"

"Yes, Chieftess."

"Be careful up there, Oblam."

"Maleen, please. Let me do this." His tone contained none of the childlike qualities an average ten-year-old's should have had. "I can protect my sisters *and* my chief."

"I know you can." *But you shouldn't have to.*

"Shh—they're coming."

The pursuers gave no indication they knew how close they were to their quarry. Their voices were low but audible. From where she sat in the tree, Maleen could see three men and two women on foot. The trail was too narrow for graebigs. With great effort, Maleen tried to hide the emotions she felt when she recognized Lenet, Kayla, and Jewel, along with two other warriors she knew from the Kelvian garrison. The last thing Oblam needed was to sense her fear, or her hatred, but her efforts were likely futile.

Would Kayla be able to sense them, the way Oblam could? She had recognized Oblam as a voyant upon one meeting with him, but she hadn't realized Maleen had been hiding in the storage room in Elm Village. It was common knowledge that the better a voyant knew a person, the harder it was to hide. This would be Maleen's third encounter with Kayla, who had a reputation for being a strong voyant. As easy as she was to read, Maleen feared Kayla would know where she was, putting Oblam and the girls in danger.

"Let me take the first shot," Oblam whispered. She knew he meant well. The dead men he'd seen the previous day had left an impression on him. Their faces haunted him, and he preferred an alternative to bloodshed. He wasn't old enough to understand that Lenet would continue to pursue them until he was dead...or she was.

"No, Oblam. We don't even know if it's enough thessel to work," she whispered desperately. "If they don't know we're here, we'll let them pass."

Below them, Maleen watched Kayla stop ten yards from the tree. She looked around, expectantly. Those with her drew arrows from quivers.

Maleen's throat constricted. She breathed deeply and deliberately, knowing a fight was likely inevitable.

"What is it?" Lenet asked hopefully.

"Someone's here." Kayla looked up to where thick branches obscured her view of Oblam. "You there, in the tree, what are you doing up there?" she called.

Maleen thought about responding but, from previous experience, knew she couldn't lie to Kayla. Even if she could, Lenet and Jewel would be sure to recognize her voice.

"I'm frightened," Oblam responded to Kayla's question, sounding younger than usual. "I have my sister with me. We heard there were Kelvian warriors coming through, and so we hid." His words were true. Though he said sister instead of sisters, Maleen hoped Kayla couldn't sense his avoidance, but it was a mistake that could easily cost them.

"Who told you we were coming?"

"A boy in the last group who passed."

"Who was in that group?"

"Two women, a few men, some children."

"One of the women, was she pregnant?"

"Yes."

"The other one, what did she look like?"

"Young, thin, red hair, but not bright, kind of a brownish red." He gave a vague description of Maleen. "And the others called her 'Chieftess.'"

"Why would they call her that?" Kayla called. Was she testing his truthfulness?

"She was their leader, I suppose. She *really* didn't like being told what to do by the men with her."

Kayla made a motion with her hand, but Oblam's dart found its mark before any of her companions could respond. The warrior next to Kayla stumbled only a moment before he dropped. A second dart barely missed a Kelvian with an arrow trained on Oblam's voice.

Without hesitating, Maleen shot. Her aim was off only a little and the arrow pierced the fleshy part of his arm. Despite the danger he still posed, she was glad Oblam hadn't witnessed another kill.

"Maleen, I know it's you up there," Kayla sneered. "You have to control those emotions if you're going to hide from me. Even the boy does better than you." She turned, looking into the grove of trees on the other side of the trail. "And honestly, Phillip, I know you too well for you to even *think* of hiding from me."

Phillip emerged, and Kayla's eyes widened at the sight of his physician's garb in Acoran colors.

"I don't understand what my aunt saw in you."

Eyeing the bow he held at his side, Lenet said, "Honestly? For an Acoran woman, you pick up a bow?"

"I said I'd never pick up a weapon for a senseless fight," Phillip said firmly. "Protecting the innocent is hardly senseless."

"You're forgetting, *cousin*"—Kayla's voice grew menacing as she pointed into the tree— "that woman is hardly innocent. She killed my father, your uncle and chief. Now you pick up a weapon to defend her?"

"Get some dry wood," Lenet said, never taking his eyes off Phillip. "We'll see if a little smoke brings them down."

Fearing for the children, Maleen swung to the ground. She drew her bow on Lenet. "What do you want?" she demanded.

"Why do you ask stupid questions? I want you both dead," Lenet jeered. "Who's in that tree?"

"Just a boy who found a non-lethal way to protect his chief."

"Don't you think I found out who your family is?" Lenet wore an arrogant grin. "Let's see, your father was one of the casualties of our last encounter, your mother—or stepmother rather—is pregnant, and your little brother is the voyant we encountered before. He's in the tree, I suppose? And I believe the man said there were three smaller children related to you, as well. Where do you suppose they are?" He glanced at the tree.

"You should be more concerned about where her *elder* brother is, Lenet." Tian stepped out of his hiding place, bow drawn. Asher, Noture, and Cutter joined them, surrounding the Kelvians.

"Sweet sentiment." Lenet snarled, undaunted by the Acorans, despite the fact that one of his warriors was unconscious and another had an arrow in his arm, leaving the Kelvians outnumbered, even discounting Phillip. "But *my* dear sister is the strongest voyant alive. Not only did she know when we were approaching your position and how many of you there are, but she is able to shield the presence of companions from other voyants."

Maleen turned quickly, scanning the area, bow still drawn. The tension hurt her arm, but she couldn't let down her guard.

"Oh, don't worry, they're out there. Kayla's made sure your little voyant can't sense where or how many of them there are."

Maleen desperately hoped he was bluffing. Oblam's next dart found its mark in Kayla's neck.

"No!" Oblam yelled, even before Kayla hit the ground. "She was hiding more than twenty." As Oblam swung down from the tree, Lenet gave a call. The hiding men appeared from the bend in the road behind them.

"See what I mean?" Lenet spun his staff, ready.

Maleen released her arrow as Lenet dove to the side and she missed. Looping the bow across her back, she tucked her toe under the staff she'd been standing behind. Catching it in midair, she swung around to the nearest of the warriors, knowing better than to go straight for Lenet. Asher and Noture were the only ones with a chance of beating him, and only if they were able to go one-on-one with him. The bedlam began, but the small band of five, plus the boy, was no match for the band of twenty.

From her peripheral, Maleen saw Phillip step away from the fray. Kelvians may not always act with honor, but they were taught to avoid non-combatants in the middle of a battle, particularly one wearing a physician's jacket. But he was smart to move away before Lenet's men decided they hated him more than they cared about intertribal law.

Maleen soon found herself facing off with Jewel. The larger woman was fast and strong. Maleen was faster. As Maleen used that speed to her advantage, the Kelvian woman was soon out of breath, but Maleen didn't stop. She couldn't stop.

"You're too soft to win," Jewel hissed.

"Better soft than a coldhearted killer."

"You think we didn't find Piel and the others?" Jewel circled her prey. "He was supposed to be your friend."

Maleen stepped in a careful circle, never taking her eyes off Jewel. "Piel gave up our friendship when he came into Acora."

Jewel gave one final thrust. She left herself open. Before Maleen could exploit it, she found herself grabbed from behind, a strong arm closing around her throat. The flexed muscle cut off her air and lifted her feet off the ground. She dropped her staff and kicked at Jewel while she struggled to free herself from her large assailant. Unable to pull in air, her face went numb, her hearing dulled, and after a long moment of helplessness, darkness closed in.

***

Cutter saw the large Kelvian grab Maleen. This time he *would* do something. Another Kelvian stepped in front of him, and Cutter swung. The man parried his blow and brought his staff around to hit Cutter in the side. Fire exploded in his ribs, from his side to his sternum. Ignoring the pain, Cutter punched the assailant, who went down.

Five steps closer to Maleen, another person stepped up. This one was female. A student, judging from the fact that she wore no vest. She was small—how could she possibly think she could stand up to him?

As he felt a staff connect with the back of his shoulder, Cutter realized the young woman had only been a distraction. Turning to face the new assailant, Cutter ducked his next blow. Both the man and the woman came at him.

Cutter never liked to hit a woman, but if she were in this battle, it couldn't be helped. Cutter punched her across the face, sending her to the ground.

Turning back to the man, Cutter saw another group approaching. They couldn't manage the enemies they had! The newcomers didn't wear vests. As one took on the assailant in front of Cutter, he noticed the man's family crest was trimmed in purple. They were Acorans.

Relieved of that opponent, Cutter turned again to the last place he had seen Maleen. At that moment, an exceptionally large newcomer hit the man who held her in a stranglehold. When the man released his hold to defend himself, Maleen crumpled to the ground. Cutter stumbled over to her.

"Maleen?" He shook her shoulder, dread sinking into his being.

"Wake up, love. I need you here." His chest tightened as he watched her chest rise and fall in quick succession. She was alive. He would make sure she stayed that way. He stood up, ready to swing at anyone who came near. Ten yards away, Noture fought hand-to-hand with the man responsible for the entire mess. They were a good match, but Noture prevailed. Lenet went down. Noture probably would have killed him, but another Kelvian attacked, drawing Noture's attention away from Lenet.

Jewel knelt next to Lenet. She looked up and called the Kelvians into retreat, ordering a couple of men to help their fallen leader. Cutter reached down, trying to get Maleen's bow from her back, but the fire in his chest burned, and he sat heavily beside her.

The Kelvians retreated the way they had come. One picked up the red-headed voyant woman. The other unconscious ones were left where they lay. The villagers followed those retreating just long enough to make sure they were gone.

Maleen was breathing, but still unconscious. How long had she been without oxygen when he hadn't been able to get to her? He had promised to always be there for her. He'd failed her and, if she died, he'd have failed the tribe.

"The village is two minutes away." A large man put a hand on Cutter's shoulder. "My mother is a healer, and your physician is already there."

Cutter reached under Maleen to pick her up. He would usually have been able to carry her with only moderate effort. But at this point, he couldn't even lift her. Fire burned in his chest and abdomen as he stood up and stumbled.

"I'll get her." The man lifted Maleen gently. Two others took Cutter's arms and he leaned heavily on them.

"Thank you," Cutter said.

The man nodded. "We should move quickly."

"Dara? Mya? Come on down," Noture called up the tree where the girls remained unharmed. "Where's Oblam?"

"Oblam?" Cutter called, looking around him. "Come on out. The fighting's done."

Oblam trotted out from the trees, his eyes full of tears. "Is she...?" He couldn't finish the question as he stared at his sister's limp form in the stranger's arms.

"She's alive," the man assured him. "At the moment."

CHAPTER 12

Maleen gasped as she sat up abruptly. The pounding in her head made her regret her quick movement.

"Careful, my dear," an old woman's gentle voice said. "You must have an awful headache. My son says it was quite a brute who had you in his grip."

"Who are you?" Maleen asked hoarsely, accepting the cup of water someone handed her.

"My name is Tyana. I am the village healer." As she spoke, the woman shuffled around, checking on other injured people around the room.

Maleen occupied the only couch. She didn't recognize the injured people sitting in chairs and laying on mats on the floor.

"Nothing like the fine physician you have with you, but I do what I can. You are in Oak Village."

The woman would have been tall if she were not hunched with age. Her dark brown eyes were set deep in the wrinkles of light brown skin. Her gray hair fell in waves down the middle of her back.

"My family?"

"Your mother says everyone is accounted for." She handed Maleen a root of some sort. "Chew this. It'll help with the headache. Your husband warned me not to give you thessel."

"I need to see them."

Tyana looked at her and pointed to the root. Maleen sighed and chewed it slowly. It tasted bitter, but almost immediately her headache began to subside.

"How did you find us?" she finally asked.

"All will be answered," she said with a wave of her hand. "But your mother and the others will want to see you first."

Maleen followed Tyana to another room, warmed by a fireplace and lit with a lamp in each corner. Cutter stopped pacing and hurried to embrace her. Sitting near the fireplace were Mya and Dara. Noture, Tian, and Asher came to their feet when she walked in. Noture let out a long breath.

Phillip stood near a bed where Lesney lay, a pained expression on her face. After a moment she relaxed.

"Mother?" Maleen knelt beside the bed.

"It seems I exerted myself too much. The baby isn't going to wait another month." She smiled. "Don't look so concerned, I'm not the first woman to give birth, and it's only a little early. Everything is progressing normally." She touched Maleen's cheek. "Or have you forgotten your mother was a midwife long before she was a mother?"

"Not to mention she's done this for herself four times already." Noture stood behind Maleen and put a hand on her shoulder.

Across the room, the old woman stooped down to put logs in the hearth. "It'll be a while still, but it'll be today."

"Let me do that." Cutter turned. He was unsteady for a moment then knelt to help her.

"You, young man, need to sit and be still. I'm not a helpless old woman. Old, maybe. But never helpless."

"I'm fine," Cutter insisted, picking up a log to add to the fire. Tyana grabbed it and slapped his hand away.

"Don't try lying to this old voyant." Tyana waved the log in his face. "When all other things fade, that is what voyants depend on. Our ability increases with age."

"You're a voy—?" Lesney's question cut off as another contraction hit.

"Yes, it's how I knew you desperately needed help when you arrived." She turned to Maleen. "It is also how I know your mother has not told all there is to tell." She raised an eyebrow. Maleen looked away rather than answer.

"Everyone out," Tyana announced loudly as she stood. "Physician, see to your patient. My granddaughter, Grata, is a midwife. She'll be nearby if you need her." The old woman led everyone outside. Only Phillip and a young woman remained with Lesney.

"She's supposed to have another month," Tian said once outside, his voice revealing his concern.

"She's strong," Tyana said.

"She's also forty years old."

"Yes, your mother is strong, too, but I was referring to the child. As strong as her big sister, perhaps?" She paused, looking closely at Tian. "What is it that really has you concerned?"

"Our first mother died when she was born." He nodded toward Maleen. "I don't remember her, but when each of them came along..." He ruffled Mya's hair. "Guess I'm a worrier."

"You're the eldest. Your duty is to worry about your family. The more it grows, the more you worry," Tyana said.

"He does worry too much," Mya said, straightening her hair.

"Please, Madam Tyana, tell me what happened." Maleen sat on the porch next to Cutter. Mya climbed on her lap, curling up. Maleen held her tightly, stroking her soft hair, thankful for the group's safety.

"I saw the physician and Lesney crest the ridge. I could sense the trouble and sent for my son. He led our villagers to help." Tyana waved her hand to indicate the people moving about the village.

Oak Village was similar to Elm. Huts dotted the clearing. Though smaller than Elm, the village was more secure, being deeper in the woods, surrounded by mountains. A large building stood in the center, just as the meeting hall did in Elm. Apparently, they used their seclusion to train warriors apart from the garrison. That wasn't unheard of in any territory. In fact, Chief Rabe had encouraged it. If a village had to send for aid every time a threat appeared, it could be torn apart before help arrived.

"How can we thank you?" Had the village warriors not arrived when they did, she would be dead and, likely, so would her companions—maybe even the children.

"Well, you can start by telling me what your mother and physician left out. They didn't tell all there was to tell, and neither has anyone else.

You wear warrior's garb yet travel with children and a pregnant woman. Stranger yet, the men defer to a woman?"

"I am grateful for your help, Tyana." Maleen's heart skipped and her mouth went dry. "We were on our way here to leave my mother and the children while the rest of us continue our mission. But it's too dangerous to tell you everything."

"Dangerous to whom? This village or you?"

The wise woman was reading her. Maleen couldn't help but wonder if perhaps Tyana guessed the truth.

"For you." Her partial truth would be evident to the old woman. Maleen added, "And until I discuss things with Oblam, maybe for us. It's difficult to know whom to trust. Oblam is a voyant. When he is here, we'll see."

"An honest answer." Tyana patted her hand.

A few moments later Oblam came running up the porch steps, followed by an exceptionally tall, well-built, middle-aged man, huffing behind him trying to keep up.

"Oblam." Maleen gathered him into her arms as best she could with Mya still on her lap. "Where have you been?"

"Javon was showing me the village." Oblam looked at the floor.

"He needed a distraction." The man put a hand on the boy's shoulder.

"I thought you were...I thought... It's my fault. That Kelvian voyant wouldn't have known you were there if I wasn't with you." Oblam swiped at the tears on his face.

Maleen handed Mya to Cutter and pulled Oblam to her. Looking him in the eye, she said, "Listen to me. It wasn't your fault. They knew we were close by. You were able to confuse Kayla. She only knew who we were because, even though she was talking to you, she was reading me. I've never been able to hide anything from voyants."

"It wasn't just the two of you." Cutter put a hand on the boy's shoulder. "Phillip is her cousin. She's known him too long for him to hide from her. Even if she hadn't sensed you, or read Maleen, she'd have known Phillip was there."

Maleen hugged her younger brother. "The next time you stop sensing the presence of someone you care about, you can't immediately assume the worst. You will only make rash choices if you think those close to you are dead. Do you hear me, Oblam?"

"Yes, Chieftess," Oblam said the title quietly, but there was no doubt both Tyana and Javon heard.

"Ah. I thought so," Tyana said softly. "Go and say hello to your mother, young man. But only stay as long as the physician says it's all right."

"Yes, ma'am," Oblam said, hurrying through the door she indicated.

"Thank you for doing what you could," Maleen said to Javon, who stood only a few inches shy of seven feet. He shared his mother's brown eyes and skin. His black hair was sprinkled with strands of gray.

"It was my pleasure, Madam." He nodded in respect. From the lack of questions, Maleen guessed that news from the Northern Garrison had reached this far. Good. Then the commander of the Southern Garrison would be expecting her.

"We need people to know that Chief Rabe is dead and who his chosen successor is, but at the moment it would be too dangerous if certain people—like the group you chased off—were to know *where* I am."

"Don't say anything to anyone," Tyana said to her son.

Javon nodded and turned to go. Turning back to Maleen, he asked, "The brute strangling you, did he know who you are?"

"Yes, he did." Maleen nodded.

Understanding the implications, Javon turned and walked away. "All right, gentlemen, those Kelvians aren't going to like being embarrassed by a bunch of villagers, let's make sure we're ready when they get here."

"Are they coming for us?" Oblam emerged from the hut.

"Most likely." The old woman sighed. "But with three voyants in the village, they won't sneak up on us, will they?"

"No, ma'am," Oblam said, standing straight with his chin up.

"Three? Your son?" Maleen asked.

Tyana nodded. "But not his daughter. Sometimes these things skip generations." She turned to Oblam. "And you, young man," she went on, putting a bony finger in his face, "have a rare gift. Only once have I seen one so young be so strong. Someday you will even be able to tell if those you love are dead or unconscious. Until then, your sister is right, always assume the best, but be ready for the worst. Someday you may even be able to serve as your sister's Grand Voyant."

***

The sound of a baby's wail woke Maleen from her fitful sleep. A new sister, if Oblam was correct. The cry lasted only a minute before quieting. Maleen turned to look at Cutter, sleeping beside her. Someday it would be their turn.

For an hour or more, Maleen laid awake staring at the ceiling. Even here, in the security of the visitor's hut in a village, she'd slept sparingly. Cutter's even breathing beside her told her he finally slept. Throughout the night he'd been restless, each movement causing him pain. Maleen remained still, afraid to disturb him. He needed rest. The fight had been too much for him, though he wouldn't admit it to anyone, not even her.

Nights like this, when she lay awake, remembering events and her part in them, Maleen often wondered how Rabe could have had the confidence in her to make her his successor. It wasn't that she didn't think a woman could be qualified but, after a fight like yesterday's, she seriously doubted if *she* were qualified. The men around her were completely committed to her, yet Maleen had done nothing to deserve their loyalty. Sometimes she wondered if the tribe would have been better off if Asher had not conceded.

But Rabe had chosen her. She had to remember that. The memory of the pride on his face as he made the announcement reaffirmed Maleen's commitment. She had to do this.

Dawn hadn't yet broken when Maleen heard a quiet voice. "Chieftess," Javon's deep voice said from outside the open window, "my mother would like to speak to you." Maleen quietly crept out of bed.

"You must go, early this morning," the old healer reported. "We will care for the little ones as your mother recovers, but the enemy must not find you here. The children will blend in with other families if the Kelvians come, and I can hide two or three from other voyants, but not all of you."

"Madam Tyana, I can't thank you enough for the help you've given us. We'll be gone before dawn," Maleen assured her.

"You must take the boy with you. He has a great gift. You will need it. His dedication to you goes well beyond his years. Something few people know about voyants is we can often sense each other before we can sense non-voyants. If Fanton's son has a voyant with him, the boy may be able to tell you when he's nearby. Your mother is feeding the baby. Be sure to bid her farewell and get her consent to take the boy."

The party prepared to leave the still-sleeping village, supplied with provisions offered by Tyana and Javon. Though they wouldn't be needed, to refuse them would be to let the village know their destination was nearby, confirming anyone's suspicions they were headed to the garrison.

"Go quickly, Chieftess," Tyana said. "The village will be awake soon. No one here should know which way you went."

The sky was just starting to light as they stepped out of the village. Dawn was coming, but they could be halfway to the garrison before the sun rose fully.

And hopefully before the rain starts. Maleen took a deep breath of the damp air. She loved the fragrance the woods gave off before a rainstorm but walking in the rain wasn't her idea of a good start. She'd look like a drowned rodent by the time she met the southern warriors. But the clouds didn't look promising.

In the trees, birds called to one another, screaming warnings of the coming storm. She couldn't identify the bird. Not a lalot. Maybe some sort that preferred life closer to the sea.

Over the next hour, Maleen walked slowly. She couldn't let her rush to get to the garrison have a negative effect on Cutter's health. He'd overworked himself in yesterday's fight. He wasn't even near ready for combat, but considering how outnumbered they'd been, he'd had no choice. Maleen understood that. But watching him wince every time his foot slid on the loose dirt, or he stumbled over even the smallest of rocks in the path, she wished he'd hidden instead of fought.

She sat down to rest and grabbed Cutter's hand, insisting that he sit next to her.

"Everyone needs to stop looking at me like they think I'm going to break in half," Cutter muttered near her ear.

"I'm sorry, love," Maleen stroked his hand with her thumb. "We're worried. You can't blame us for that."

"Staring and startling every time I flinch isn't going to make me any better."

He had a point, but Maleen wasn't sure she would be able to stop demonstrating her worry for him.

"How much farther?" Oblam asked. His voice had the tiny whine of a tired child, trying to be mature.

"Another hour of this downhill stuff?" Tian shrugged.

"A little longer," Cutter said. "If we were traveling at a regular pace we'd be halfway there by now, but we're traveling too slow. You'll know we're almost there when you can smell the sea." He stood up and started walking again.

Maleen looked at Noture. The concern on his face matched her own.

"Let him set the pace," Phillip said quietly. "Unless he sets it too fast."

Maleen nodded. If anyone else set the pace, he'd push himself to keep up, and wouldn't let the rest of them know when he needed a break.

The next time Cutter sat down, Oblam sat nearby, giggling.

"What's so funny?" Asher asked.

"I can sense Tyana." He laughed louder.

The adults were instantly on alert. "Where?"

"Back in the village."

"We've traveled more than three miles already. How is that possible?" Noture asked.

"Two powerful voyants?" Asher said. "I suppose anything is possible."

Maleen hoped that piece of information also meant that Lenet hadn't been to the village yet.

"Tyana's making silly faces at Jillian." Oblam giggled again.

Once again, the adults around him sat dumbfounded at the boy's gift. Noture chuckled and stood up to lead the way as they continued on.

Twice more over the next two hours, Cutter sat down. Relieved he was taking care of himself without their insistence, Maleen stood behind him and squeezed his shoulders. She wouldn't say anything. Nothing would make Cutter feel any better about his inability to make the trek at a reasonable pace.

Gradually, the land around them changed, going from hard-packed dirt surrounded by evergreens to soft sand, where only small plants would grow. Coming over a rise, Maleen smelled it. The unmistakable scent of the ocean. The garrison wasn't far. She'd not been here often, but she remembered being able to get a glimpse of the sea from the watchtower on the southern gate.

"Ready?" Noture asked as they came into view of the front gate.

"You know the commander?" Maleen didn't answer his question.

"Met him. A long time ago. He probably won't remember me. If he does, I'm just Sonely's little brother. Everyone with any rank knew your father."

"Is it as bad as being *his* younger cousin?" Asher asked, poking Cutter in the ribs.

Cutter flinched at the touch.

"Sorry," Asher said.

"Would you get serious?" Maleen glared at him.

"Would you not be cranky as you're about to meet your second-in-command?" Asher returned. "At least until you assign a new commander in the Northern Garrison."

A new commander. Because Commander Nell had been in the council hall. Maleen took a deep breath and started down the last hill toward the garrison. She could do this. She *had* to do this.

All five men stood half a step behind her as she waved to the man on the watchtower. He wouldn't know her, but they wore vests. That was enough to let them in. Then many would recognize Cutter and maybe Asher, or at least their crests.

The watchman yelled something to men on the ground inside, and the gate opened. The man who met them took one look at Cutter and ordered a boy nearby to find Commander Lutin. Without a word, he indicated they should follow him to the commander's office.

Commander Lutin came to his feet as they entered. He looked at

Cutter's crest, then Maleen's. His scowl was evidence of his feelings as the others took up positions in deference to her. Cutter stood slightly behind her, but at her left shoulder. Asher stood at her right. Had they done that on purpose? Giving Asher the higher honored position? Phillip stood near the door with Oblam, a hand on his shoulder, indicating he should be still and quiet. Noture and Tian stood to the side, arms crossed, stance wide, looking every bit the bodyguards they seemed to think they were.

In addition to the commander, three southern warriors stood in the room. One was a young man, not yet in adulthood. Another was a woman, about Noture's age, maybe slightly older. Her family crest matched Commander Lutin's. Considering the age and resemblance, more likely his unmarried daughter than his wife.

The woman smiled slightly as she looked at each of them in turn. "Noture. It's been a long time."

"Too long, Sasha." Noture's face seemed to soften a little bit. Or perhaps Maleen imagined it.

The third warrior, Maleen recognized. She'd trained with Gavin, years before. He'd also know Asher as a fellow classmate, Noture as the instructor for their first year of training, and Cutter as the instructor for their last.

"Commander Lutin?" Maleen nodded at him. "I am Maleen, Daughter of Sonley, Daughter-in-law-and successor to the late Chief Rabe."

"We've received your latest message," Lutin said. "We've been expecting you."

"We had slower travel due to injuries. But we're here now."

"So you are. How do you wish to proceed?" He waved a hand toward two chairs across from the desk he sat behind.

Maleen sat. Asher still stood behind her, but Cutter sat next to her. Good. Not only did he need to rest, but she needed him as close to her side as possible. "I believe that to have my warriors' support on the battlefield, I first need it in the council hall. I want to call a meeting. Explain our firsthand account. Then ask the southern warriors to follow me as the northern warriors did."

"And you expect they'll be happy to do so?"

"I expect that those who know me can vouch for my abilities on the battlefield and off." She resisted the urge to look at Gavin. "And that those who knew Chief Rabe would know he wouldn't have chosen me lightly. He expected the best from his warriors and would expect more from his heir."

"How many of my warriors know you?" Lutin glanced at Gavin, then back to her.

"Two or three whom I graduated with. A few others a year or two ahead or behind me."

"I can vouch for her, Commander," Gavin grinned sideways. "Though in all our sparring matches, I never thought it would come down to this."

"*All* your sparring matches?" Cutter snorted. "I never put you together in the ring until the last few months. And that was because you both needed some humility beat into you."

"It didn't work." Asher snickered.

Neither Commander Lutin nor Sasha looked amused. The young man standing in the corner covered his mouth to hide his grin. Maleen didn't crack a smile but glanced at Gavin. "Thank you for your support, Gavin, but when it comes to the bare bones of the matter, it's important that the warriors see me as one Chief Rabe thought was the best choice. Not the person who knocked a man twice her size on his derriere."

"I seem to remember that happening the other way around." Gavin tapped his chin like he was thinking hard.

"You're both wrong." Cutter chuckled. "I remember calling the match before one of you seriously hurt the other. You were too big, and she was too mad at you."

"Gentlemen?" Maleen shook her head. First, they had work to do. They'd have time to reminisce later. She wondered if Gavin would volunteer to be one of the replacements they'd need in the Northern Garrison.

"It's still early," Commander Lutin said. "The letter you sent, about Chief Rabe... It's been circulated. Everyone knows what happened and who you are. Maybe we should schedule the meeting for after the mid-day meal? That would give you a chance to make your presence known around here?"

"An excellent idea, Commander." Maleen stood and offered her hand. Lutin's handshake was firm, but his expression was not friendly.

She left the room with the others right behind her. Both of Lutin's men followed them out, but Sasha stayed inside.

"I don't think my grandfather likes the situation you're putting him in," the young man said once the door had closed behind them.

"Delv!" Gavin barked. "Don't you have somewhere to be?"

"Yes, sir," Delv muttered and walked off.

"He'll be able to take his grandfather's place someday." Gavin watched him go. "If he gets rid of that attitude."

"Want to specify what situation he thinks I put Commander Lutin in?" Maleen asked.

Gavin shook his head. "Not really."

"All right. How about you do it anyway."

Gavin looked at her and chuckled. "Bossy as ever."

"As hot-headed as ever, too," Tian chuckled. "You may want to do what she says."

Maleen rolled her eyes. "Spit it out, Gavin."

"Lutin is..." He stopped. "He trained with Commander Nell."

"So?" Phillip asked.

Maleen had forgotten for a moment that Phillip and Oblam were there. That was just like Phillip—fade into the background while hearing and analyzing every word that was said.

Gavin looked around, then back at Noture. "I had an instructor once who told me never to badmouth a leader in public. Come on."

Maleen followed him across the courtyard, reminding herself that he wasn't the same ill-tempered, aggressive youth he had been any more than she was the hot-headed, arrogant girl he'd remember.

"Sorry." Gavin opened the door to a small hut. "My wife is out of the garrison with the children, visiting her mother. My hospitality may be a little lacking."

Maleen took a seat without waiting to be asked. "What's the issue, Gavin?"

"You know how commander Nell felt about Lady Warriors?"

"Yes. His wife had been one and when she fell in battle, he became opposed to us. That's why I'm the only Lady Warrior in the Northern Garrison. Everyone else has gotten sent down here or to the outposts."

"Lutin hates that they always get sent down here. He shields his daughter as if she were untrained, though I've seen what she can do when necessity calls for it."

Noture stood by the door, still on alert. "When we trained together, she'd never have accepted special treatment from anyone. Not even her father."

"Things change." Gavin shrugged. "My point is that his... not really chauvinism, like Nell, but certainly protectiveness over the ladies has spread to some of the warriors. I know it infuriates some of them, others enjoy the special treatment. But my point is that I don't know how easy it will be to convince the warriors to follow a woman." He sat down heavily. "Please know that *I*, for one, know better."

Maleen took a deep breath. "Thanks for the warning. I better go start meeting these men and figure out the best way to convince them I can do this."

"I think for most, it's not a matter of whether or not you can, but whether or not you *should*."

Apparently, there would be some discussion before she would ask for their support. By giving men like Lutin a chance to air their grievances, perhaps they could be convinced that their complaints were invalid. She didn't hold out much hope for this to be unanimous, but perhaps seeing they were in the minority would convince them to remain quiet—*if* they were the minority.

***

"Commander Lutin." Maleen approached him as the warriors gathered in the meeting hall. "Would you moderate today's meeting?"

"Why me?" Commander Lutin asked.

"Because to ask any of them," she explained, nodding to her advisors, "would be to invite the accusation of bias." And hopefully, letting Lutin act as the leader here would give off the impression that she didn't intend to make monumental changes to the current leadership.

"All right," he agreed. "If you're ready to start?"

Maleen nodded and took a seat in the front row, on the end of the semicircle. She would allow warriors with the biggest egos to claim those in the middle. Cutter and Noture sat on either side of her, Asher and Tian directly behind. As much as she appreciated Phillip's support, this was not a meeting she could invite him to.

"Gentlemen, Ladies, come to order." Lutin stood at the podium. "I expect you all to conduct yourselves in a manner advantageous to this council." A murmur of agreement went through them. "You have all been made aware that before he died, Chief Rabe appointed his daughter-in-law as his heir. When he died, the warriors of the Northern Garrison voted to allow her the position of acting Chief."

"Without consulting us," someone called out.

"Immediately after the massacre, bringing stability couldn't be delayed for the time it took to get word down here and wait until you responded," Noture said. For the moment, Maleen would let him respond for her. Otherwise, the same answer from her could easily be interpreted as becoming defensive and making excuses.

"Instead, you came under attack from Kelvian forces. Again," the same man replied. "From her own account, it seems the Kelvians were hostile because of *her* actions."

Cutter raised his voice. "Actions she was ordered to take from Chief Rabe and the former council."

"The fact remains she antagonized Fanton."

Maleen stood up. This wasn't supposed to be a debate about her mission to Kelvia. "My time in Kelvia has no bearing on this meeting. When I returned home, I answered to the council at that time. Commander Brice himself commended my actions, and we all know how he felt about me personally."

A man next to the first objector stood up. Maleen didn't remember his name, but she remembered him from his time in the Northern Garrison.

He and Cutter had never gotten along and had come to blows twice. Once was over comments about her.

"Commander Brice believed you married into the family to acquire the chief's seat." His voice rose, calm and clear. "Many of us wonder if, perhaps, he was correct."

Cutter jumped up, fist curled. From behind them, Asher jumped up and caught his arm before Cutter could lunge forward.

"Are you so blind you can't see that? If it hadn't been you, it would have been your cousin." The dissenter looked pleased with the discord he had sown.

Maleen stole a look at Asher. His fist clenched almost as tightly as his jaw.

"Enough," Lutin called from the podium. "We are not here to discuss the way it came about. Only whether or not we believe this woman will make a good chief."

Cutter shrugged off Asher's hand which prevented him from smashing his fist through the man's face and sat down.

Maleen gave him a small smile and sat next to him. She appreciated his support, and his defense of her honor, but his temper was not going to help her.

Noture stood up. "When Kelvians attacked the Northern Garrison, she went one-on-one with Fanton's son to try to bring peace. She almost died for it. There was no making peace with Lenet." He growled at the name. "Her kindness and diplomacy make people want to follow her. Ask any warrior who knows her. The only ones who will not vouch for her are the ones who have an issue, not with the warrior, but with the woman. Acora should be long past that by now. Rabe strove to be an example to other tribes. So now, let's prove it. A woman is as capable of leading us as she is to fight beside us."

Maleen reached over and squeezed Cutter's hand. Diplomacy was not usually one of Noture's strengths, but he'd spoken well.

"The strength to lead and the strength to fight are not the same things," someone spoke up. His voice was not argumentative. Simply thoughtful. "It's a different kind of strength."

"There was a time when Rabe could beat any man in this room. She may be good, but she's not that good," the first of the two loud men called out.

"There was a time, maybe," Gavin agreed. "But as all men do, he aged. So, when that time came and went, did you ask him to step down? Of course not. The chief needs to be a strong warrior. But not necessarily *the* strongest."

"She is nursing an injury at the moment," another familiar warrior said. "But when she is fully healed, I dare any of you to step in the ring with her. Ninety percent of us would not be walking away victorious."

Maleen grinned. That was the kind of support she needed—men outside of her elect who weren't afraid to admit she was better than them.

For half an hour, discussion went around the room. Most comments and questions were stated calmly. Occasionally, one of the two loud ones would speak up, but it didn't take long to notice they were outnumbered. A few who didn't know Maleen wanted to postpone the vote until she was able to prove to them she was as good a fighter and as intelligent a leader as the others claimed her to be. The largest complaint was not that the men took issue with following a woman, but rather how it would affect their image with the other tribes. Apart from Timend, they were all far more patriarchal than Acora. Strength was more than just an image to maintain for the sake of their collective egos. Appearing weak was dangerous.

"Why can we not select Rabe's son as Chief?" someone suggested. "Many chiefs have had their wives as their advisors over the years, Rabe included. It would allow Rabe's chosen successor to lead, but by proxy through Rabe's son."

"What do you say to that?" another asked Maleen and Cutter.

"It's not even been an hour since you've seen my temper." Cutter glared at the two troublemakers. "Yet you still believe that's a better solution? Yes, I could lead you, and depend on my wife's wisdom, strategy, and everything else that makes her an excellent chief. But what does that say to our Lady Warriors? They can fight and die by our side, but if they want to lead us, they must hide behind a man? It does them an injustice, and it does nothing for the future generations of Lady Warriors who only wish to be given the same chances as the men." He looked at Maleen, who was surprised, not by his support, but by the diplomacy in his answer. "I'll do it if you wish, but I don't think it's a proper solution."

"Didn't Chief Rabe have any other kin?" a man asked. "I believe he had a brother, did he not? And that brother had a son."

Asher stood up. "He did. But that is irrelevant. Chief Rabe chose Maleen. Not me. I say we are here to decide if Rabe's choice of Heir was the correct one, *not* to find a replacement if she is not. This vote must be based on her ability to lead, and our respect for Rabe's ability to choose the most competent successor. Not on whether or not someone else is able to lead."

There was scarcely any discussion after that. Maleen left the vote in the hands of Commander Lutin, leaving the hall with Cutter, Tian, and Noture who wouldn't be participating in the vote.

It was only a few minutes before Maleen was called back into the council hall.

"Lady Maleen," Commander Lutin began solemnly, "you are aware of the controversy we have had. Your opponents made no secret about their thoughts on the matter, nor have your supporters. The vote was simply a 'yes' or 'no' as to whether we wished to honor Chief Rabe's choice and confirm you as our chief. Every person here was given a stone to use to vote." Lutin removed a cloth from two jars. One was nearly full of stones, the other held only a few. When Lutin turned the jars around, Maleen could see the writing on the sides. The fuller one said "Yes," while the other one said "No."

"I have not yet voted." Lutin made a show of dropping his stone into the fuller jar. "Congratulations, Chieftess." He held out his hand to her amidst the cheers of most of the gathering.

"Thank you, all." Maleen turned to the gathering. "I know this was a difficult choice. I hope that as time passes you will see it was the correct one."

***

Two days passed with no response to the messages Maleen had sent to Kelvia. That could mean two different things. Either Lenet's men covered enough of Acora to accost expediated couriers and the message never reached Chief Tyndall, or Tyndall didn't respond because he was involved in Lenet's actions. Maleen wasn't sure which would be worse.

On the afternoon of the third day, Maleen sat with her advisors, Commander Lutin, his daughter, and his grandson. Sasha and Delv seemed to be acting as Lutin's advisors, though he hadn't given either the title of Commander. Probably because Delv was too young, and Sasha would have been the first woman to wear the title. If she proved to be as good as Noture remembered her being, Maleen would suggest that Lutin rectify that.

Maleen studied Lutin carefully. She felt sympathy for the man. One of his sons had been in the council hall. He'd lost the other, Delv's father, fifteen years before. Sasha was the only one he had left. But it was no reason to shelter her. At least he hadn't pushed her to marry. Even in Acora, there were few single women Sasha's age, and far too many arranged—or at least pressured—marriages.

"How long will you wait to hear from Tyndall before you assume he's not going to answer?" Lutin asked.

"One more day." Maleen didn't look at her advisors. She needed to appear strong, even when she didn't feel confident. If they disagreed with her, they'd let her know, but not in front of Lutin. "Then we go make a personal appeal."

Lutin nodded slowly. "How long after that do I wait before sending a full legion into Kelvia if you don't return?"

"You think Chief Tyndall is a part of the massacre?"

"I wouldn't put anything past any Kelvian." Lutin glanced at Phillip then back to Maleen.

"I disagree." Phillip had enough tact not to acknowledge Lutin's silent accusation. "Tyndall is a hard man, but he's not a murderer. His biggest mistake was giving Fanton autonomy over Western Kelvia. But I genuinely believe when he hears of Lenet's actions, he'll rectify it."

"Is that an opinion of a nephew wanting to think the best of his uncle?" Cutter asked. Maleen thought there was a hint of hostility in his voice, but he'd not come to her with any complaints of mistrust. He trusted her judgment regarding Phillip.

"Not at all," Phillip replied without a trace of emotion. "Tyndall barely regarded me as family, particularly since my mother died. Adopted children are not always accepted by the entire family. But I do know him well enough to know what to expect."

"I trust Phillip's assessment," Maleen said. "Regardless, we have to do something. We cannot allow Lenet's crimes to go unpunished. If we wait until Equin to make a charge, it makes Tyndall look bad to the Council. That is not the way to gain his support."

Lutin nodded. "Let Sasha know what supplies you need. She acts as the Lady of the Garrison."

A warrior who acted as the mediator between the support staff and the Commander? Maleen opted not to comment. She did not want to interfere with the way Lutin ran his garrison, even if it wasn't the way they did things in the north.

"Thank you for your support, Commander." Maleen stood up. Her men followed suit.

"I'm going to get some rest." Cutter kissed her cheek and walked out the door.

Instead of following, Maleen sat back down. "Commander, I'm not waiting one more day. I'm leaving first thing in the morning. Before Cutter is awake."

Behind her, a relieved sigh came from Phillip.

"He's worse off than he'll let on?" Lutin asked.

Maleen nodded. "He can't go to Kelvia with us." Guilt tightened her chest. She'd never lied to Cutter before.

"Are you taking the boy with you or do you want us to send him back to his mother?"

She didn't like the idea of taking Oblam into Kelvia any more than she wanted to take Cutter. But they'd need him along the road. "I'll be taking him. We need a voyant."

"Will you stop at the Northern Garrison?"

Maleen had to stop and think. Would that be best? She needed to know what kind of mess Lenet had left behind.

"I don't think that would be the wisest thing to do," Noture said. "We need to stay off the main roads to keep hidden. Lenet likely has someone watching the garrison. He'll know when you're there."

"The contingent you called for two weeks ago can be made ready in less than a day," Lutin said. "Gavin volunteered to lead it. I suggest you head to Kelvia, keeping out of sight from Fanton's son, if he's still in Acora. Gavin can lead a third of our southern warriors to the Northern Garrison, and either request more, or send some home, depending on what he finds when he gets there."

Lutin was a smart man. Maleen's first instinct was to agree with him, though what she really wanted to do was find out how many people survived the attack on the garrison.

"I'll let you know by this evening," she promised. This time when she stood, she headed out of the office and to her guest quarters.

In the bedroom, Cutter was lying down. He sat up to greet her and grimaced.

"Why don't you ask the garrison physician for some thessel for pain relief?" Maleen took his hand.

"Don't need it," he said.

Maleen stared at him, lips pursed. "You're as bad as me." She tried to chuckle.

"No one is as bad a patient as you." He put an arm around her.

She wanted to melt into him, to let him soothe away all the worry, all the guilt of what she planned to do the next morning. But she was afraid to lean on him at all. He was in so much pain. "Shall we ask Phillip which of us is worse?"

Cutter chuckled and took a shaky breath.

"If you're not going to let Phillip check you, at least go see the garrison physician," she pleaded. "You need to be able to rest." *And be sleeping too deeply to hear me leave in the morning.*

"If it'll make you happy." He stood and reached for her hand.

She gave him a small smile. "It would make me very happy." Whatever reason he needed to give himself for asking for help was all right with her.

***

17th of 11th Lunar, 521
Southern Garrison, Acora

The next morning Maleen slipped quietly out of bed, careful not to disturb Cutter. After consulting with Phillip, the garrison physician had promised to do everything he could to keep Cutter in the garrison.

Please take care of yourself. I did it because I love you.
-M

She left the note on the lampstand, resisting the urge to kiss him goodbye. He wasn't going to be happy. If she didn't do this quickly, she was going to let guilt endanger her husband.

When Maleen stepped out the door Tian, Asher, Noture, Phillip, and Oblam stood waiting. She put a finger to her lips and silently closed the door behind her.

Lutin and Sasha saw them out the front gate, with enough supplies to get them to Kelvia.

As they began the day's trek, everyone seemed to sense Maleen's dark mood.

"You did what you had to do," Tian reminded her after an hour of walking in silence. "He overdid it. You don't have to be a voyant to know how much pain he was in."

"He's going to be mad," Oblam spoke up. "But don't worry, he'll probably blame Phillip." The boy giggled.

"I never even suggested it," Phillip defended himself. He looked at the ground, the corner of his mouth turned up. "But you're probably right."

"I wouldn't want to be you when we get back. He hits harder than anyone I know." Asher gave an exaggerated sigh, patting Phillip on the back.

"Somebody better tell him the truth, before I end up with a busted jaw!" Phillip looked at Maleen.

"You'd have suggested it if I'd asked," Maleen said. She'd done what was best. She hoped Cutter would be able to see that.

***

The company traveled all day through the Border Mountains. The sky was overcast but looked like it would hold its rain—hopefully until they were out of the area. Hills became mountains, and they continued northward. Winter was well underway, but snow was rare this far south. Maleen doubted they'd be so lucky when they reached Kelvia. They stopped only for a short rest at midday but hurried on their way to cover as much ground as possible.

Evening came and they found shelter in a cave.

As she lay on her bedroll that night, alone, Maleen could see Cutter's smiling face. She wiped away a tear as her longing for him got the best of her. *I am a warrior. Chieftess of Acora. I will not be overcome with emotion*, she scolded herself. *Lady Warriors are held to a higher standard of emotional control.* Was this how Asher felt, having to leave his wife behind when they left the caravan, heading away from the garrison? Emotional control be hanged. Maleen let a few tears slip as she fell into a restless sleep.

***

The company got an early start the next morning and every morning for the next week. Exhausted from poor sleep and emotional turmoil, each day Maleen pushed it aside and led the way up the trail. She and the other adults constantly checked with Oblam about people in the area. Occasionally, he sensed someone, but never anyone with any hostility in their emotions. All the same, they avoided people whenever they could. They made much better time without having to worry about Cutter or Lesney, and the sixth evening after leaving the Southern Garrison they approached the last town before crossing the border.

Mulberry was a large and rather unfriendly town, wedged in the valley between tall mountain peaks. Finding the inn, Noture got them two private rooms.

"A nice supper for a change?" Asher asked. "Anyone care to join me?"

"No discussion of anything in the dining room," Noture instructed. "We can't take a chance of being overheard."

"Yes, Uncle." Tian rolled his eyes at the obvious statement.

"Yes, Uncle," Asher echoed and dodged the fist that came in his direction from Tian.

"He's not *your* uncle." Oblam laughed.

"Oh, yeah? Well, what if I want to claim him?" Asher bent down to Oblam's eye level. "I need someone to keep me in line."

Instead of responding to Asher, Oblam froze where he was.

"What is it, Oblam?" Maleen asked. His expression set everyone on edge.

"She's here!" The boy ran to the window and flung open the shutters. Down below, entering the building across the road, was Lenet's sister, Kayla. She turned around in the doorway, looking down the street.

Maleen yanked the shutters closed.

Oblam rummaged desperately through his pack. Finding his pouch, he grabbed a dart and a leaf and jabbed himself in the arm. Missing the bed, he fell to the floor, unconscious.

"Oblam, what did you do?" Maleen knelt by his side.

"Hopefully, he kept Kayla from sensing him." Noture nodded his approval. "Good boy."

"Will she sense the two of you?" Tian asked, looking between Maleen and Phillip.

"She'd have sensed another voyant without trying," Phillip said. "But hopefully not us *if* she's not actively looking."

If she *was* actively looking, it meant someone had reported their presence to Lenet. That was a frightening possibility.

No one went down to supper that evening, and they still took turns keeping watch all night.

CHAPTER 13

Oblam was still drowsy early the next morning as the company emerged quietly from their rooms. "Apparently, your vulnerability to thessel runs in the family," Tian said to Maleen as he picked the boy up. "Glad it skipped me."

"His small size doesn't help, either," Maleen said.

In the dining hall, a few guests lingered from the previous night. One man, smelling too much of cheap ale, didn't seem to realize the night had passed and it was morning.

"Hey, beautiful." He grabbed Maleen's arm. "I've got ten dener that says I can give you a night to remember."

Pulling away from him, Maleen grabbed his arm and twisted it in such a way that his shoulder nearly dislocated. "And I have three men here who will relieve you of more than your currency if you touch me again."

The proprietor was quick to step in. "All right, no more ale for you," he said to the man. "Get home to your wife before she comes looking for you—again. Everyone else, unless you're ordering breakfast, get out," he said with a good-natured laugh, then turned to Maleen. "My apologies for my friend's lack of manners, madam. Now, what can I get you for breakfast?"

"We won't be staying, sir." Maleen watched the drunk leave, rubbing his shoulder and grumbling something about uppity females. "We've a long way to travel today."

"Ah, well." The proprietor reached behind a counter to grab an already-prepared basket. "Here are some sweets for the boy's breakfast."

The man put it in her hands and, moving closer, said, "Pleasant travels, Chieftess."

Maleen looked around, wide-eyed. The dining room had cleared out, so no one was around to overhear. "How did you—?"

"I packed fruit and pastries in the basket for the road, but will you have a cup of fentel before you leave?" The man ushered them all to a corner table. He brought cups of fentel along with a cup of juice for Oblam. Oblam's eyes were barely open as he reached for the mug. Maleen wished he were awake enough to read the man.

The man sat down to join them in a fashion which would look like a friendly gesture if anyone walked in. "I'm Brock."

"How did you know?" Maleen repeated.

"News travels fast," Brock said. "We received word of what happened at the garrison. Kelvian warriors have been in and out of every Acoran village from border to border looking for you. They're spreading a different story than the one we originally heard."

Maleen tried to hide her dread. To the general population, it would look like she had disappeared to protect her own hide. She didn't have time to explain her reasoning to Brock, and she couldn't trust him with their plans for the next few days.

"How did you know who I am?" Maleen stared him in the face, daring him to lie to her.

"Apart from the fact that a limited number of Acoran women wear a warrior's vest?" He pointed to the previous chief's crest on her vest as well as Asher's, and Sonley's family crest on Noture's and Tian's. "I saw those when you walked in last night. I wasn't always an innkeeper. I used to fight with your father. Word has it the daughter of Sonley has gone into hiding. The family resemblance is uncanny." He looked at Noture. "I don't imagine you'd remember me. You couldn't have been older than twelve when I retired, but now you look exactly as I remember Sonley looking over twenty years ago. You *must* be the ambitious little brother he was so proud of. And you three, same eyes, same hair, same face. There's no doubt you are Sonley's children. I had no idea he had one so young. I heard Talora died not long after he retired."

"When I was born," Maleen filled in. "He later remarried. His youngest child was born a few days ago."

"He must be proud." Seeing the long faces, the innkeeper closed his eyes for a moment. "Did he go as a warrior?"

"Yes, saving the lives of his family." Maleen tried not to allow emotion in her voice but wasn't entirely successful. When this was all over, *then* she would grieve the loss of her father. Privately.

"Good. Now you must go. There are Kelvians in town. They came in here for supper last night. They seemed to dislike the soup for some reason." He chuckled. "Perhaps it might have something to do with my wife spilling it on the one who acted like the leader. They're not likely to come back, but you need to go before they're moving about the town." He stood up as a customer walked in. "Pleasant journeys, travelers," he said cheerfully. In a sleight of hand gesture, the innkeeper handed Noture back the currency he'd paid for the rooms, winking at Maleen. He turned to his customer. "Now, my good man, what can I get for you?"

The band stepped outside into the sunrise. "He wanted to help." Oblam rubbed his eyes and yawned, awake enough to answer the question everyone wished to ask, but no one had.

That was the last word spoken until the group was a half hour into the woods, staying on the back trails rather than risking the main roads. Knowing where at least part of Lenet's party was, a weight lifted from Maleen's shoulders. If the Kelvians were in Mulberry, they were not harassing the citizens of Oak Village, nor the Southern Garrison. Half a mile out of town, the weight was back. It was selfish to think of Oak's safety before Mulberry's, simply because her family was there. But Mulberry was large, she reasoned. They would not tolerate a band of Kelvians starting trouble.

Yes. She breathed easier. *It's better that they're in Mulberry.*

"We should be nearing the border in half an hour or so." Asher climbed down from a tree. "I can see the watchtower at the main road."

"Can I have the sweets now?" Oblam asked.

Maleen smiled at him. Despite all he'd been through with them, he was still a ten-year-old child.

"Sure." She handed him the basket, but instead of digging into the pastries, Oblam dug to the bottom of the basket. Maleen watched him curiously.

"I know he hid something…" Oblam mumbled, then pulled out a leather chip and examined it. "It almost looks like a dener."

"It almost is." Phillip took the currency and examined it. "It's a Kelvian homer. Worth about the same on the other side of the border."

"There's a bunch of them in here."

Phillip looked into the basket. "Three months of living wages, at least."

"Time to be Kelvian, I suppose." Asher held his currency pouch open and waited for everyone to empty their own into it. He stood by a big boulder on the side of the trail which would be easy to identify later, counted off fifty paces away from the trail, dug a hole, and buried the lot. Each warrior removed the vestments indicating they were Acorans and buried those as well. Asher scattered leaves and a few inconspicuous branches over the fresh dirt.

Without the vestments and her husband's family crest, Maleen felt vulnerable. She sat on a rock, knees pulled to her chest, twirling the hair at the end of her braid, trying to hide her feelings. Realizing she looked more like an insecure little girl than the leader of a tribe, she stood up, blinking back the tears which threatened to betray her emotional state.

The men knew her too well for her to succeed at hiding her feelings, but none of them said a word to her about it as they devoured the contents of the basket, eating while they discussed the next step. If they followed the trail around the bend, it would meet the main road. If they continued due north, there would be no trail.

"The watchtower guards will be looking for us if we follow the main road," Noture warned.

"But if anyone sees us crossing the border on rough terrain, we'll look suspicious no matter who we are," Asher said. "We have no idea how frequently the border is patrolled."

"I think all we need is a good explanation for why we were in Acora, and where we're going in Kelvia. It's not as if they'll be expecting us to sneak *into* enemy territory… Is it?" Tian asked.

"That innkeeper knew where we were headed," Oblam pointed out, holding up the Kelvian currency.

Everyone was quiet for a moment.

"So, we continue to avoid the main road," Maleen said.

"Got it." Asher's cheerful voice urged everyone to get moving. "Oblam, we're counting on you to let us know when people are nearby."

"Don't put that on the boy," Noture hissed in his ear.

"I failed at that before." Oblam looked at the ground. "I thought there were only five. There were more than twenty, and I didn't realize how close they were until it was too late."

"It's okay." Maleen's heart ached with sympathy for him. She bent down to his level. "That wasn't your fault. You're just learning to use your ability. You do your best and we'll face what comes, together." She gave him a hug.

"Yes, Chieftess." He looked up and nodded. "You lead the way. I'll tell you if people are coming."

"Okay, little brother." Tian swung him upside down, before righting him again. "Shall we be going?"

Crossing the border proved less difficult than any of them imagined. The terrain was rough, but it meant they were less likely to encounter other people. Oblam's high energy kept the group moving quickly. He and Asher raced each other. Asher tried unsuccessfully to goad Maleen into joining them. Half an hour later, they were in Kelvian territory.

There was no change in the rocky terrain. The only indicator they were crossing the border were wooden signs, nailed to a line of trees. The signs were worn by years of weather until they were unreadable, but years ago, someone had wanted people to know when they crossed into Kelvia.

"How far to the Central Garrison?" Maleen asked Phillip.

"Forty miles or so, if I remember my geography lessons correctly," Phillip said. "I haven't been here for five years, since before my mother died. I do remember it's all mountains that get taller and steeper. Several of them are dormant or extinct volcanoes. Volcanic glass is one of the resources that make Kelvia so wealthy."

"Villages?" Asher asked.

Phillip shrugged. "I don't remember that much detail. We never went on foot, so the trip took a day from the Western Garrison. We never stopped in villages."

As they walked around boulder after boulder, Oblam chewed his lip in thought. "Phillip?" he spoke up. "Your adopted mother was Lenet's aunt, right?"

"Yes. It's the only reason Fanton didn't discharge me from the garrison a long time ago."

"And Fanton was Chief Tyndall's brother?"

"Yes, both Fanton and Tyndall are my adoptive uncles," Phillip answered Oblam's unasked question.

"That's how we get in." Oblam looked up, smiling, proud of his deduction. "You are visiting your uncle. Nothing to it."

"Were it only that simple," Phillip said, shaking his head. "They've certainly gotten word that Fanton is dead and who is responsible. Lenet would have made my change of loyalties known as well. He's always hated me, even when we were adolescents. This treason makes that hatred legitimate."

"But you can still be loyal to Kelvia, just not Fanton's branch of the family."

Maleen envied the boy's optimism, even if it was born of ignorance. "Oh, to be ten again," she mused.

"You wouldn't want to be ten again." Asher smirked. "String Head." He used the nickname he'd tormented her with when she'd first come to the garrison as a child.

"Oh, String Head, is it?" She laughed. "Perhaps I'll run and tell my big brother you're picking on me." Maleen clearly remembered her ten-year-old self, stringy hair and all, running to eleven-year-old Tian, who had always been happy to shut the other boys up for her, especially Asher.

"I was so furious when I found out about that," Noture said.

"She was the only girl in the training unit," Asher said. "It was bound to happen."

"Not about the teasing, that was just you being children. I was furious because the student I had recruited was acting so...spinelessly. It made me look bad as the recruiter and your training commander." Noture looked at Maleen. "Remember what I told you that day I found out why Tian was getting into fights?" He chuckled.

"You said 'I will not have a student who asks others to fight her battles.' You threatened to send me home in front of the entire unit."

"And I meant it. No one could ever accuse me of playing favorites, not even with the two of you. Now look where you are," Noture marveled. "Can you imagine if I had sent you home?"

"The next time I called you 'String Head,' you gave me a bloody nose," Asher said, reminding her of the event which had begun their friendship all those years ago.

"And I couldn't have been prouder," Noture said.

"You knew about that?" Asher asked. "I never told any adult why I had a bloody nose that day."

"I watched the whole affair from the dining hall patio." Noture laughed.

"She gave you a bloody nose and you let her get away with it?" Phillip asked Asher, laughing. "Difficult to believe you'd have let her get away with anything, even as children."

"He didn't hit her back because I was standing right behind him," Tian stated. "Of course, I was still bigger than him back then." The entire company laughed.

"Now, here you all are, fighting battles for me," Maleen said seriously, breaking the light mood. "I can't help but think if I were male, you wouldn't be quite so protective." The surrounding silence confirmed her fears as they all sat down to rest for a moment.

"Father always taught us to watch out for the girls, to not let them get bullied by boys who were stronger," Oblam defended.

"Unless she swings first or steps in the ring, you will show your sister the respect due her as a lady, and the protection due her by simply being your sister." Tian crossed one arm over his chest and stroked an imaginary beard, in imitation of their father.

"And you, young lady," Oblam lowered his voice and shook a finger in

Maleen's direction, "will act with honor and dignity for the bereavement of the tribe."

"Betterment of the tribe," Maleen corrected, laughing at her brothers, then sighed. She'd heard both statements many times. No doubt Mya and even Dara had as well.

"I'm sure you did a fine job, Oblam, but the girls in the village are *not* Lady Warriors. Even Dara and Mya need someone to look out for them, at least until they follow us to the garrison, but a warrior must be allowed to fight, female or not," Maleen said.

"But your typical Lady Warrior isn't our chief," Tian said slowly. "Yes, perhaps we protect you more, but not because you're not capable. If something happens to you, the entire tribe suffers for it. We lost our chief recently. All family connections aside, we can't let that happen again. That's why we must keep you safe, even if it means stepping on your warrior's pride a little."

"Speak for yourself," Asher said. "I do it because if I let anything happen to you, I have to deal with your brothers and uncle, not to mention Cutter, and who needs that hassle?"

"Besides," Tian joined in the teasing, "if anything happened to you, we'd have to deal with Watchtower here as Chief." Tian used the nickname Asher had been stuck with during his adolescent years.

Asher took a mock swing, but Tian easily avoided it.

"You're all children," Noture said, shaking his head, standing up to continue the journey. As they resumed their walk, he put an arm around his niece. "There's a big difference between *asking* someone to fight your battles and allowing those who care about you to protect you."

"I know." She shrugged. "But—"

"But nothing," he said firmly. "We're glad to do it. This isn't *just* a job." He gave her a squeeze and kissed her head before releasing her. Maleen thought on her family's words as they walked. Noture and Tian made sense. The chief should be protected. When she became a warrior, she had taken an oath to protect the tribe. Protecting the tribe meant protecting the leader of the tribe. But since the chief was also a warrior, it hadn't occurred to her to think about that much. She realized that she had never seen Rabe go on a mission or even lead a patrol the way the other council members did. If that was the case, had she been too sensitive when Cutter and the others, even Phillip, had tried to protect her?

No, she decided. Phillip had no reason to protect her as a chief. He wasn't even part of the tribe when he'd barred her inside at Elm Village... But he had acted similarly to protect Cutter, because of Cutter's injuries.

So, if Phillip was acting as a physician worried about a patient, something she'd seen plenty of during her time in Kelvia, his protectiveness made sense. And if what Noture and Tian were saying was correct, maybe she had overreacted. Maybe years of feeling as though she'd always had to prove herself because she was a woman in an occupation made up of mostly men had colored her perception of what her allies were doing.

It was certainly something to think about.

***

Late in the evening, the band met up with the main road. They all agreed they were far enough from the border that, without their Acoran colors and family crests, the main roads would be relatively safe, and much faster. No one here would recognize them, at least not until they were close enough to the garrison for someone to recognize Phillip.

As they made camp that night, Noture turned to Maleen. "Have you given any more thought as to how we get an audience with Tyndall?"

"I like Oblam's plan," Maleen said. Everyone stared at her wide-eyed, as if she had lost her mind. "Think about it. No one will recognize the rest of us. How else do we get in?"

"You can tell them who you are," Tian said slowly.

"Sure, they'll let us in then," Asher said, "and instead of an audience with Tyndall, we get an audience with a prison cell or the wrong end of an arrow shaft. We still have no idea if Tyndall participated with the Western Province. Even if he didn't, Lenet's version of events has certainly made its way up here."

"Then we risk a message getting to Lenet before we can even *see* Tyndall," Maleen added. "He seems to have messengers all over

Acora. No doubt he has them in Kelvia, too—even in his uncle's garrison."

"Phillip?" Noture looked at him. "It would be you who is taking the risk."

Phillip nodded slowly. "With Oblam there to warn me before I get a knife in the back? I will do this for you, Chieftess."

***

At dusk the next day, the party passed a town. Stopping on the outskirts, they made camp early. "Time to see if these *homers* are real." Asher took a pouch of the currency and headed for the town.

"Nothing too frilly!" Maleen called after him.

"Plain and boring. Got it." Asher waved.

"You want dry rations again, or you want to help me catch some supper?" Tian asked Phillip as he tied a bone hook to the end of a string fastened to the tip of a long pole.

"I'm in for some fish." Phillip followed him to the water's edge.

Maleen silently went about gathering firewood, amassing a much larger stack than they'd need. She had to do something to keep busy. Noture kept looking at her as if he wanted to say something but never did. He never had been particularly good at finding that perfect thing to say.

By the time Asher returned, Phillip and Tian had caught a nice string of small fish, cleaned them, and laid them over the fire. They were in Kelvia. If anyone came by their camp, she'd have to be the one serving the fish. Kelvian men expected it. She hoped no one would come along, though the thought of spilling a plate of fish in Asher's lap was amusing.

Asher interrupted her thoughts, handing her a package. She unwrapped it and held up a blue dress. It was a beautiful shade. Nearly matched her eyes. He'd left out the frills, but it still would have been better as a dull gray. She didn't want to stand out at all. Nothing about her said Kelvian. A pretty dress was the last thing she needed.

Along with the dress, a matching blue headscarf fell out of the package. Smart. Her hair would give her away to anyone who'd been given a description of her. This would hide most of it.

"It's confirmed," Asher said. "Both sides of the story have made it up this far. Warriors are keeping a close look out for us. It's a good thing we didn't cross the border at the road."

CHAPTER 14

After lying awake for hours, Maleen got up, wrapped herself tightly in a fur, and took a short walk away from the camp. The cloudless sky, full of stars, and the cold air did more to wake her up than to make her tired.

"When was the last time you slept a full night?" Phillip's voice startled her.

"Oh, I don't know. Maybe back in that cave. When I had a concussion. Out here, I can't sleep more than a couple of hours at a time."

"It shows," Phillip said. There was only concern in his voice. No condemnation. "You need to sleep before you see Tyndall tomorrow."

"I'm fine," she snapped.

"No, you're not. You've been short-tempered lately, and a bit clumsy. Even Oblam has noticed it."

"Sorry if I haven't met your expectations of a good traveling companion," she retorted, with more hostility than she intended.

"Thanks for proving my point." Phillip raised an eyebrow. "I think we should sleep in tomorrow and get a late start. Make sure everyone is well-rested. We need to be ready..." His voice trailed off.

"We need to be ready to fight our way out of Tyndall's garrison if need be?" Maleen finished what Phillip wouldn't say.

"You've been exhausted since we left the woods before Oak Village. You need rest."

Some of the tension left her shoulders as the urge to object to Phillip lessened. His observations were correct, as usual. The lack of sleep weighed heavily on her mood and her physical performance. Phillip always put his patients first. And she'd been a terrible patient.

"When this is all over, and I can go home to Cutter and my garrison, then maybe I'll sleep." Maleen went back to the fire, where Asher was keeping watch. "I'll take the next watch. I can't sleep anyway," she told him.

"Again?"

"Don't start."

"Sorry." He held up a mug of fentel and another with water that had a green tint to it. "Clear your head or get some rest." He held out the green drink. "I suggest resting."

Maleen stared at the two cups. He was right, as usual. But she hated the way thessel made her feel after she woke up.

Maleen became aware of Phillip, standing behind her. "I can't sleep, Physician. Your harassment isn't going to make me tired."

"It's weak." Phillip nodded at the cup. "I thought about dosing the fentel, but...I'd rather you voluntarily rested."

"Asher would probably let you do it, too." She grabbed the thessel tea. Asher only chuckled in response.

"Goodnight, Chieftess." Phillip went off to his bed.

"I suggested it," Asher said after he was gone, tossing the contents of the other mug into the bushes. "You need sleep. I'll take an extra watch."

Maleen finally consented and took the mug to her bedroll. She sipped it slowly, more grateful for friends who watched out for her than annoyed at bodyguards she didn't want.

***

Maleen woke late in the morning to the sound of Noture's angry voice yelling at Phillip. *Good, he's mad enough for the both of us,* she thought, trying to clear her head. Why had she agreed to it?

"She needed rest," Phillip said defensively. "Warrior or not, Chief or not. She's a human being and humans need rest. I didn't make it strong, and she didn't drink it all. Even with her vulnerability, we should be able to be on our way by midday. It's only another hour or so to the garrison."

"Half the day is gone already. We need to get this done. With the information Asher got last night, we can be certain we're being hunted even on this side of the border. What kind of strategy is that?" Noture kicked dirt over the fire, though it did more to demonstrate his mood than to put the fire out.

"Leave him alone, Noture." Asher came to Phillip's defense. "I talked her into it. I won't apologize for it."

"All this fighting for what?" Maleen joined the men. "What's done is done. Let's pack up and move."

***

Less than an hour after leaving their camp, Phillip stood looking at his mother's birthplace. He hadn't realized how much he missed his homeland until they'd crossed the border. Though he grew up in Western Kelvia, the Central Garrison held many happy memories because his mother had been so excited whenever they visited. This would likely be the last time he would be allowed to set foot inside...if they lived through this visit.

A watchman in the tower issued a challenge as they approached. "Who's there? State your name and your business."

"I am Phillip—son of Tamar and Kel, sister and brother-in-law to Chief Tyndall. I wish to speak to my uncle."

"Tamar's son? To my knowledge we haven't heard from you in some time," the man on the tower said. "Do you have proof of your identity?"

"If memory serves, my uncle always employs a Grand Voyant. Have her question me if you like."

"Very well. You and your companions will leave your weapons at the gate." He called instructions to the men at the gate to open it and escort the band inside.

"My sister walks with a limp," Tian said. "May she bring a staff to lean on?"

"Very well." The watchman on the ground looked her up and down.

Always thinking, Phillip thought, as Maleen leaned on the staff. He'd seen her fight enough to know she relied more on speed than strength. Her staff was an important asset. If they had to fight their way out of the garrison, she would need it. With her shoulder mostly healed, she could swing and block as hard and as accurately as ever, though occasionally he caught a grimace of pain.

The Acorans were shown to a grand stone building. Phillip had been in garrisons in nearly every tribe on Chalent. Most were built from wood, like the Acoran garrison. The walls were wood, the buildings were wood. It was the most plentiful and easiest building material, no matter what part of the continent a tribe was on. Here the only wood was the gate and the doors and shutters on each building. Everything else was made from stone.

The size was enormous. It would easily fit two of the Western Garrison inside. The smallest building here was larger than the largest one in the Acoran garrison. In the center was the biggest one. Once inside, they were shown to a room that could only be described as a throne room. As a child, he'd often wondered if a builder from long ago had envisioned himself a king, like in the stories his mother had read to him.

From another chamber, a man entered the room with a girl of about seventeen. She was beautiful, with black hair worn in a long braid and light brown, flawless skin. The girl carried herself with an air of confidence that belied her age and her size. Despite being several years older than Oblam, she wasn't much taller than him. She had a green scarf draped over her shoulders.

"A voyant," Oblam warned.

"Not the one I was expecting," Phillip said. He recognized the girl, but she'd only been a child last time he was here. At the time, the adolescent Kayla had taken joy in taunting the young girl. Phillip had overheard rumors about her parentage that had given Kayla cause to despise her.

Phillip had not known the girl was a voyant the last time he'd seen her. The Grand Voyant he'd been expecting was an older, rather rude lady. He wondered if the older woman had done something to be replaced by this young girl or if she had retired.

"Speak your piece quickly, son of Tamar," the man said, gruffly.

"I have a message for my uncle," Phillip said, hoping he sounded more confident than he felt. "I don't know who you are, but I know you are not him."

"I'm the commander of this garrison. Chief Tyndall is out on urgent business." The man huffed. "You will leave the message with me."

"No, sir, I will not. When will he return?"

"He will not tell you, Hathon," the girl interjected. "He is determined to give his message only to Tyndall."

Hathon? The son of the previous garrison commander. Phillip should have recognized him. He really had been gone too long.

"All right," Hathon replied. "Then you leave me with no choice. Phillip, adopted son of the chief's sister, I charge you with treason, based on your abandonment of the Western Garrison." As guards poured in to surround the visitors, he added, "Did you think we wouldn't have heard of your defection by now?"

"I thought you might have." Phillip didn't flinch. "But I bring a message from the Chieftess of the Acora tribe."

Hathon raised up a hand and the guards held back. "Speak your message," he demanded.

"To none other than Tyndall."

"And these with you? Who are they?"

"Friends."

Hathon looked at the girl. "Well?"

"They keep their secret to remain safe. There is no deceit, except the woman's staff. She has no limp."

"Excuse my sister. She needed reassurance." Tian took Maleen's staff and handed it to a guard. "The ruse was my idea."

As she gave up the staff, Maleen straightened her posture and held her chin up, but only for a moment. Dropping her gaze to the floor, she let her shoulders slump a little, looking meek, if not a bit timid.

Much better. Phillip hoped only the voyant would see through her act.

"When will Tyndall return?" Phillip asked again.

"By this evening. Be warned, he brings warriors from the garrison *you* forsook." Looking at the guards, he instructed, "Show them to quarters. Don't bother with hospitality."

They were shown to a room with only a single cot and a chair. As the bolt on the outside of the door slid into place, Maleen sat in the chair with her head in her hands. "If he's bringing warriors from the Western Garrison..."

"Then you *might* be recognized," Phillip said. "If you are, then you may have to appeal to Tyndall directly, without my introduction to soften matters."

"Until then, I still think this commoner act is our best bet," Noture said. "The western warriors may not be in the hall when we're summoned."

"But I can't lie to the Grand Voyant." Maleen shook her head. "She'll see right through me the moment I say *anything*, maybe before."

"She already did," Oblam said. "She just didn't say anything."

"You're sure?"

Oblam nodded. "She doesn't know who you are, but she knows it's an act. And she knows I'm a voyant and didn't tell the commander."

"Why would she do that?" Maleen asked.

"For me," Phillip said. "My father saved her life years ago. Lenet and some other boys came close to killing her when they tossed a nest of fire beetles on her. They claimed they didn't know she was allergic to them and had only been playing around. If another visiting boy and I hadn't happened by when we did, or if my father hadn't been as skilled a physician as he was, she would have died. Maybe this is her way of repaying a debt."

"Then we may be able to get the entire story into the open before they realize we brought the chieftess to their doorstep," Noture said.

***

Time stretched on. Maleen paced in the small area. She sat. She stood up and paced again. Maybe she should have told them who she was, at least then— No. Commander Hathon wasn't likely to treat her any better.

At last, they heard the scraping sound of a bolt being slid out of place. Everyone stood as the door opened to a small gathering of guards.

"Only the defector," one said. "The others are to remain here. If he only wishes to deliver a message, he doesn't need help from Acorans."

"She is the one with the message." Phillip inclined his head to Maleen. "I'm only here to escort her safely into the garrison."

"Safely?" the man scoffed. He looked at Maleen and laughed. "You should choose your companions more carefully."

Maleen said nothing. She had to play the part of the silent female for only a little while longer.

The guard shoved Phillip out the door and grabbed Maleen by the arm, tighter than necessary. She resisted the urge to break free from his grip and break his arm in the process.

Walking through the corridors, Maleen took a deep breath of fresh air every time they passed a window. The room had been stuffy, and she'd spent a couple of hours in there. Outside, dusk had fallen, bringing a chill. Soon, someone would come along and close all those shutters.

They stepped back into the great hall. The Kelvian chief sat on the raised platform. To the side, Rundel, commander of the Western Garrison, sat at the table, next to Hathon. Phillip muttered something Maleen didn't catch as they entered the room. Commander Rundel stood abruptly when he saw Phillip and Maleen.

"Relax, Rundel," Chief Tyndall said from his raised platform. "My nephew is harmless." Tyndall may have seen Phillip as harmless, but the scowl on his face indicated he had heard of Phillip's defection and was not likely to forgive it.

"But the-the w-woman," he stammered, red-faced.

Looking at the warriors who stood near the platform, Maleen recognized too many of them. Her heart pounded wildly. Any acting would be pointless.

"Phillip, who have you brought into my stronghold?" Tyndall demanded.

"Uncle, in the name of my mother, Tamar, I beg you to hear this woman out."

"Who is she?" he demanded, standing up. Tyndall appeared to be about fifty. His hair was mostly gray, as was the two-day stubble on his chin. His dark eyes were set in a mildly wrinkled face. But he appeared strong. His countenance alone was enough to let those around him know he meant business. He was six feet tall, with a muscular build from years of fighting.

Maleen took a step away from the guard. Head high, she declared, "I am Maleen, Chieftess of the Acora tribe, the final request from the great Rabe of Acora." Her voice rang across the room, filled with authority. Her name meant little here, but she hoped Rabe's would carry some weight.

At her words, Rundel waved to the guards. Even if she had her staff, she would be no match for the four Kelvian warriors who surrounded her and Phillip. Several more were positioned around the room. She allowed herself to be bound, offering no resistance.

Maleen looked up to see a look of distaste cross the face of the Grand Voyant. On a hunch, Maleen squared her shoulders and met Tyndall's eyes, hoping the voyant held some sway and had the courage to speak up.

"Is justice gone from Kelvia?" Maleen asked.

"What did you say, woman?" Tyndall asked.

"Is justice gone from this territory? Will I be arrested for coming before you, unarmed, to speak my piece?"

"She's right, Chief," the voyant said boldly. "This woman has risked everything coming here. Will you not hear her out?"

"What does this female know of justice?" Rundel asked Tyndall, indicating Maleen. "Have you already forgotten she killed your brother?"

"I did not," Maleen said firmly, but not any louder than was necessary. "But I was partly responsible." Her voice was steady, holding no trace of fear—not because she had none, but because she would not let the Kelvians see it. In truth, she barely held her terror at bay as her heart thudded and she had to remind herself to breathe.

"Explain," Tyndall ordered.

"It is a story which must be told from the beginning, sir," Phillip spoke for her. "I ask in the name of my mother, Tamar, that you hear it from start to finish before pronouncing judgment."

"Who do you think you are to invoke the name of my dead sister?" Tyndall's tone was dark, and his face twisted.

Phillip didn't flinch. "I am her son, whom she loved as though I had been born of her womb."

"The one weakness of a great woman," Commander Rundel said from the side.

"Perhaps," Phillip conceded, "but will you hear the tale?" He stared at Tyndall, not wavering.

"Very well," Tyndall growled. He sat, arms crossed and jaw set.

Maleen had to tell every detail. If she left anything out, particularly those details which wouldn't put her in a good light, the Grand Voyant would sense deception.

"Grand Voyant," she asked before beginning, "what is your name?"

"I am Tara."

"Well, Tara, I trust you will tell your chief of my truthfulness?"

"It is why I'm here."

"Begin your tale, woman," Tyndall ordered.

It was no mere oversight that the bonds tying her hands were not removed. If this failed, Maleen hoped the others wouldn't blame Phillip. He'd done what he could. With the way he spoke to Tyndall, he'd put himself at significant risk.

"I became an Acoran warrior at the age of fifteen. I stood equal to any other Acoran warrior. Mostly we kept the peace. Sometimes we resolved border skirmishes with a neighboring tribe."

"Namely Kelvia?" Tyndall interrupted.

"Yes. Over the past few years, the Western Province of your tribe invaded more frequently. Fanton was testing us. Two years ago, the situation worsened dramatically. They set ambushes on our roads, raided our villages, and even attacked our garrison." At Phillip's suggestion, she would tell the events with the assumption that Tyndall knew nothing about them. There would be no mistaking the narrative for accusations against him.

"You're saying all this occurred without my knowledge?" Tyndall gripped the arms of his chair. "That is quite an accusation to make against my brother."

"You have a vast territory. You cannot possibly know all that goes on. No one questions the wisdom you showed when you divided it into provinces, only the choice of Fanton as sub-chief. If we were to fight off what was becoming an increasingly dangerous threat, we needed to know their tactics. About a year ago, I became engaged to Chief Rabe's son. At the time, unbeknownst to him or me, Chief Rabe resolved to make me his chief heir. Being female, he needed to prove to the council I was the right choice for the future leader of our tribe.

"Without knowing why I was chosen, he sent me to infiltrate the Western Garrison. I did this by participating in your Equin festival events at a nearby village. I was aware that, while in Acora we recruit young then train, in Kelvia you find promising warriors from the games. To this knowledge, I added a bit of feminine persuasion, and Lenet recruited me."

Maleen continued the story of how she had obtained information from Kelvian warriors, how she'd worked hard to earn trust, but then claimed nerves when tested. Then she arrived at the part that involved her failed escape. She mentioned her injury and explained that Phillip chose to help because Fanton wasn't about to allow a fair trial. She told about Jewel's and Sampton's aid, and about the pursuit when one who'd been sent to her aid fired the arrow in the dark which had killed Sub-chief Fanton.

"He fired it, in the dark, in my defense. He did not seek out your brother to kill him, and only knew it was a pursuer who was crossing the border, not who he was."

"Who was the archer?" Tara asked, apparently sensing missing information.

"Irrelevant to my story." Lenet knew Noture's identity, but if Maleen could keep it from Tyndall, she would.

"Is he one of the companions you have brought to my stronghold?" Tyndall's eyes narrowed as he glared at Phillip.

"His identity is irrelevant to my story," Maleen repeated.

"He is one of them," Tara told Tyndall. "But it's not Phillip."

"Which one?" Tyndall demanded.

"Ask them if you wish," Maleen said firmly. "I will not betray him to you." She glared at the voyant.

"She won't tell you," Tara said with certainty.

Maleen was thankful Noture wasn't in the room. Even though he could lie to voyants, *her* emotions would certainly have given him away to Tara.

"Finish your tale, woman," Tyndall growled. No doubt he intended to question her companions later, with the Grand Voyant by his side.

Maleen continued, including the events which followed the escape.

"Jewel?" Tyndall stopped her when she told of the explosion. "Daughter of Simon, the alchemist?"

Maleen looked at Phillip. She had no idea who Jewel's father was.

"Yes," Phillip said. "She stayed on in the garrison when Lenet expelled Simon."

"She is engaged to my nephew, is she not?"

"I do not know how far their relationship goes," Phillip said. "Neither cared to keep me in their confidence."

Tyndall nodded, more in acknowledgment than in the belief that Simon's daughter killed so many. "Continue."

Maleen told about Lenet's interruption of their meeting and of his Tamal challenge.

"Lenet challenged you to Tamal?" The chief pounded his fist on the arm of his chair, his nostrils flaring. His fury was no longer directed solely at Maleen. "Surely you know he had no such authority. That is *my* right. Not his."

"My warriors were decimated by the explosion. We had less than half the number of warriors Lenet brought into my garrison. I had no choice if we were to have peace."

"You fought him? With a stitched shoulder?"

"Yes. And, as expected, I lost." Maleen took no pleasure in telling Tyndall of the dishonor that followed the match. The slight shake of his head told her he didn't believe her. She pushed through, despite her fear. Even if Tian, Asher, and Oblam were released, both Noture and Phillip would be dead with her if she could not convince Tyndall of the truth.

Tyndall finally looked at Tara. Tara confirmed Maleen's truthfulness, and Maleen breathed a sigh of relief. Whatever Tyndall's judgment, at least he knew the truth.

"He would have killed an opponent after a Tamal match?"

Maleen nodded. "But for the actions of my tribesmen and Phillip, I would be dead. If we hadn't left the garrison when we did, it's likely that not only would I have been among the dead, but also my husband and the only other living relative Rabe had. With no chief and no heir, Lenet would have been responsible for untold chaos in Acora."

During Maleen's story, Rundel had visibly become more uncomfortable.

"Commander Rundel, what did you have to do with this?" Tyndall demanded.

"I followed my sub-chief. I did my duty to avenge your brother." Rundel shifted in his seat. His agitation increased every time Tara looked at him.

Knowing Rundel's involvement in the other events, Maleen continued. "My story is not done, Chief." She proceeded to tell of the attack on her home village, looking pointedly at Rundel.

"We were searching for an outlaw," he defended.

"Outside of your territory and by threatening to burn a village!" Maleen raised her voice, only enough to make her point. "Among the dead was my father." Maleen tried to keep her voice steady. Better anger than sorrow, but she didn't want Tyndall to think she directed her anger at him. "And two young boys, barely into adolescence."

She then continued to the battle near Oak Village. "That time we were spared only because of the actions of a nearby village." She hesitated. Seeing the questioning look on the Grand Voyant's face, Maleen added, "Had they been a moment later I would, once again, have been the victim of Lenet's hate." Maleen despised admitting she and her men hadn't been strong enough, but it was the truth.

"You're telling me my nephew ordered the death of a chief?" Tyndall's red-faced expression was one of both sorrow and anger.

"Lenet sought an enemy in her own territory. When he found her, he ordered a murderer executed." Rundel slammed his fist on the table in front of him.

"He should have come to me, and I would have gone to the Chiefs' Council!" Tyndall yelled.

"She hasn't even been confirmed by her tribe, much less by the Council." Rundel stood. His disregard for Tyndall's elevated position did little to help his defense.

"Enough!" Tyndall thundered, glowering at Rundel until the man sat back down. Tyndall turned to Maleen. "I received word from Lenet as he traveled in your territory, Lady Maleen," he said solemnly. "I was informed that my nephew crossed the border trying to catch his father's murderer. He failed to tell me the details of his father's death or of his pursuit."

"Now that you know?" Phillip dared to ask.

Looking at Maleen and pointing to Phillip, Tyndall warned her, "I would not have this traitor speak for you. It does not help your case." Looking up to the guards, he called, "Return them to their companions. Treat her as a dignitary, not a prisoner. I will consider the matter tonight."

A young guard took Maleen's arm, leading her to larger quarters. He was rough when he untied her hands. Turning around to face him, ready to give him a piece of her mind, Maleen recognized the tall, dark-skinned young man from the Western Garrison.

"Tyree?" Maleen said, dryly. "Nice to see you again."

"Wish I-I could say the s-s-same. But I don't usually as-associate w-with bed warmers."

"So you call me that. But if I remember correctly, you were the one to brag about your conquest," she reminded him. The young man had been the first one she'd tried to get information from. "I could have revealed nothing happened. That after so many mugs of ale, you fell off your stool, and I helped you to your bunk in the warrior's barracks, then I went to mine in the trainee's barracks. Instead, I let you spread your wild tales."

"To your own b-benefit," he stuttered. "I was so w-wasted I didn't remember anything the next day. My peers assumed what happened, and I l-l-let them. When you didn't correct the story, I thought it was correct."

Maleen raised an eyebrow at him. "I didn't know that. But it wouldn't have changed anything. If you were in the hall a minute ago, then you know what my motives were, and you know I needed the reputation among your warriors. You were only the first. Things like that happened all the time. But, despite the rumors, I was never with any man in your garrison—not one of the warriors, not Phillip, not Lenet—no one.

"Once I had a reputation, none of your fellow warriors would admit he wasn't able to convince me to go to bed with him. The more they tried to impress me, the more information I was able to glean." Before he closed the door, she added, "To your credit, even drunk off your stool, you never gave up any useful information. It almost made me reconsider my methods."

Tyree shut the door, sliding a bar in place. *So much for being a dignitary,* she thought. Tyree had originally appeared to be an easy target. It had been easy to get his attention. He was eager to make the acquaintance of a lady who didn't ridicule his stutter. He'd even been a good conversationalist once he drank enough to overcome his nervousness, but every time she prompted him to brag about plans for an upcoming battle, he would change the subject. After the single encounter, he'd never approached her again. And having had better results with others, she'd never encouraged him to.

She had not known he didn't remember anything the next day.

CHAPTER 15

Almost immediately after Tyree left, the door opened again and a steward brought a meal, enough for several people. A moment later, Maleen was relieved to see that when the men were escorted into the room, Phillip was with them.

"Phillip says Tyndall heard the whole story?" Noture asked.

"Every word." She nodded. "By the time I was finished, he was ready to destroy Commander Rundel for just being with Lenet," she said between bites. At least the cook seemed to have gotten the message they were dignitaries. She didn't think the roasted meat and well-seasoned vegetables were normal fare for prisoners.

"We're not in the clear yet," Noture warned. "If he sides with us, he'll face some harsh criticism for going against his own in favor of outsiders."

"Let's hope Tyndall is willing to bear the weight of that criticism to do what's right," Maleen said. The guards at the side of the room stiffened. Maleen ignored them. She didn't care what they thought of their chief or of her. After supper, the men were escorted to other rooms.

Tyree and another guard stood in the doorway of her quarters. Tyree informed her, "We've been instructed to take you for more questioning."

"Lead the way." She gestured to Tyree. He led. The other guard followed closely behind, as though expecting she'd not cooperate. His caginess put Maleen on edge. As they turned down another corridor, she asked, "What else does Tyndall still need to know to make a judgment?"

"It's not the chief who summoned you," Tyree said, over his shoulder. "It's C-Commander R-Rundel."

Maleen stopped dead in her tracks. "I won't speak to Rundel without Tyndall present."

"In this garrison, you'll do as you're told." The other guard grabbed her arm, trying to force her down the hallway.

If this short, stout man was trying to force the issue by himself, he'd not heard of her skill.

"Remove your hand, Kelvian," she ordered as she slid from his grip. "I am Chieftess of Acora, and I will *not* be manhandled."

As he tried to grab her again, Tyree stepped in, "This is n-n-not what the ch-ch-ch-chief meant by treating them as dignitaries."

"The commander wishes to speak to her." The other put a finger in his face, "Do your duty, or leave it to another."

"My first duty is to my *chief*." Tyree was several inches taller and a couple of decades younger than his tribesman. He took a step between him and Maleen, glaring down at the man. "And the chief gave an order as to how she was to be treated."

The shorter man threw a quick punch that sent Tyree reeling. By the time he reached for Maleen again, she was ready for him. Deflecting his hand, she slammed her palm into the man's sternum, sending him into the wall, knocking the wind out of him. The commotion brought several more guards running from around the next corner.

"Rundel wants to speak with her in the garden. Make sure she gets there," the breathless guard commanded. He kicked Tyree, who was trying to regain his footing, toppling him over again.

Maleen found herself grabbed from several angles and pinned, face to the wall, by strong hands and heavy bodies. These men were prepared, carrying rope with them. Rundel knew she would not come quietly. Her hands were once again secured behind her. The ropes dug painfully into her wrists.

"Tyree! You have to—" A hand clasped over her mouth. As the hand pulled away, someone secured a gag. Her legs still free, Maleen struck out, knocking one Kelvian back, only to have him replaced by another. Two large Kelvians, one on each side, dragged her, struggling, down the corridor, a third Kelvian following. As they exited the building, into a garden, two guards held her while the other found Rundel.

Out here in the isolation of the large garden, no one would hear her, even if she were able to scream. The walls of the building were thick, the wall around the garden was high, and the roof was covered in glass panels. If Rundel was going through this much trouble to speak to her without Tyndall present, this was not about questioning her. In Tyndall's hall, he'd been agitated but hid behind the excuse of following his sub-chief. If Rundel still intended to remain loyal to Lenet, even after witnessing Tyndall's anger, then her life was in imminent danger, and her companions were behind a locked door.

Pushing away the threat of overpowering fear, Maleen struggled uselessly against the bindings. Lashing out with her foot, she struck the guard's kneecap, knocking him off balance. He regained his footing and grabbed her from behind. The last guard stood in front of her. She backed up hard, knocking the first into the wall. He still didn't let go, and she picked both feet up and kicked the other in the gut. She brought her heel down hard on the first man's foot. He wavered and Maleen backed into the wall again, this time ramming the back of her head into the man's nose at the same time. He couldn't hold his grip as he wheezed, and blood poured from his nose.

Running through the dimly lit garden, desperate for a place to hide, Maleen outran her pursuers and ducked behind a large planter. Kelvians ran past, yelling at one another to find her. In the dark, another figure moved along the wall. Tyree had recovered from his bout with his tribesman and crept through the garden, no doubt looking for her without giving away his position. He had tried to bring her to Rundel, but not in the same manner as the other guards. He'd probably only been doing as ordered, but Tyndall's order overruled Rundel's when he realized the truth of what was happening.

Knowing Tyree was her best bet, Maleen looked to where the other guards had run, spread throughout the garden. Before she could leave her hiding place, however, she felt someone touch her from behind. Spinning around, preparing for another round with the Kelvians, she met with a fist. Cantel, a Kelvian warrior who'd only been a trainee when she left their garrison, stood over her. No doubt he'd earned his colors in the attack on Acora.

Sprawled on the ground, hands still bound, gag still in place, she looked up at Cantel, flushed with anger that her former friend would take such a dishonorable swing.

"Don't look at me like that. You've had that coming for a long time," he snarled. He grabbed her arm and pulled her to her feet. "We trusted you. We trained beside you. Piel stopped drinking because of the lesson you taught him."

Maleen wondered if Cantel knew his friend was dead by her hand. If she had not been gagged, she would have informed him, and threatened him with the same fate, without letting him see how heartbroken it made her.

"And the whole time you were a *friggin* Acoran?" He expressed his anger with another blow to her cheek that sent her to the ground again. She kicked his feet out from under him and aimed another kick for his face, but he rolled out of the way. He stood back up and kicked her in the ribs. "She's here!" he called to the other Kelvians.

The first Kelvian to respond was Tara, the Grand Voyant from Tyndall's hall. She carried a staff in each hand. Dropping one, she swung the other at Cantel's head, ensuring he couldn't kick Maleen, or call the others again. Indicating Maleen should remain still, Tara knelt beside her and cut the rope.

Maleen ripped the gag from her mouth. "I must see Tyndall, unless he's the one who orchestrated this," she said breathlessly, pressing a hand to her sore ribs.

"Tyndall had nothing to do with planning your murder," Tara whispered. "He is a hard man, but an honorable one." Sheathing her knife, Tara handed the longer of the staffs to Maleen. Her own was a foot shorter. She helped the Acoran chieftess to her feet. "Trust no one but Tyree. He's the one who called me." She pointed to the gate, exiting to the courtyard, about fifty yards away. "We go that way."

"I won't leave without my companions," Maleen insisted, shaking her head.

"You misunderstand," Tara corrected her. "I'm not helping you escape the garrison. Tyndall is in the courtyard."

She sprinted in the direction of the gate, Maleen on her heels. Halfway there, Rundel's men intercepted them. Tara's staff tore through the first Kelvian's staff and connected with the second. Hearing someone behind her, Maleen turned in time to duck the blow from Commander Rundel. Desperately, the two women fought, holding off three Kelvian guards and the commander.

Tyree put down a fourth guard and came running in their direction.

Tara yelled at him, "Find Tyndall. Now!" The young warrior ran through the gate before anyone could stop him.

Maleen was impressed by Tara's handling of the staff. Her small stature made her a smaller target, a trait she exploited. Her shorter staff gave her a shorter reach, which she made up for by moving closer to her opponents, often keeping them off guard. Despite how well she fought, Maleen couldn't help but wonder if they were not overrun because Rundel's men were afraid of the repercussions of injuring Tyndall's Grand Voyant. The three grunts seemed to be holding back. Rundel, on the other hand, did not.

After several minutes, more Kelvian warriors entered the garden, a red-faced Tyndall and a nervous Tyree among them. The newcomers subdued Rundel and his accomplices.

"Rundel, explain yourself," Tyndall demanded, a vein pulsing in his neck.

"I wished to ask the woman a few questions of my own," Rundel defended. "She refused to come with the guards, they had to use force, but your little voyant there interfered."

Winded, but still standing, Maleen offered her staff to one of the guards who'd come in with Tyndall. She didn't intend to go anywhere. Trying would be futile, even if her shoulder could handle it.

"I don't trust Rundel," she said.

"Nor do I," Tara interjected. When Tyndall looked at her, she added,

"He has a murderous intent toward the chieftess. I sensed something troubling from him in the hall when he accused her of your brother's death, but I couldn't figure out what."

Tyndall turned back to Rundel, too enraged to speak.

Rundel began stammering. "You listen to that voyant too much, Tyndall. She's only a child, but she knows that, for whatever reason, you will believe anything she says."

Tyndall shot Rundel a look Maleen couldn't read. It appeared he'd crossed the line when he insulted the chief's Grand Voyant.

Instead of continuing his bluster, Rundel tried to excuse his behavior. "I was trying to allow you to save face with the Council. You couldn't avenge your brother without looking bad to them, but you must remember this female is responsible for Fanton's death." He looked from Tyndall to Maleen, the hate obvious in his eyes. "Fanton must be avenged, for the honor of Kelvia!"

"It wasn't your choice to make," Tyndall growled. "Arrest them."

"Revenge isn't the only thing he wants," Tara said. "He's hiding something else." Tara glared at Rundel. He refused to meet her eye but glowered at Tyree.

Maleen looked from Tara to Tyree. "Thank you," she said. Tyree had made the honorable choice, though he had as much reason to hate her as Rundel and Cantel did, perhaps even more.

"M-my duty is to my chief," Tyree said, refusing to take her offered hand.

As the Kelvians not involved in the plot took away Rundel and his collaborators, Tyndall turned abruptly to the building. "Tara, bring the woman."

Though a moment ago they'd been allies, Tara set her jaw and visually insisted Maleen follow Tyndall. For one so young and so small, Tara was certainly resolute. Maleen offered no resistance as they followed Tyndall into the building. "A Grand Voyant *and* a Lady Warrior," Maleen commented to the girl. "It's a rare combination."

Tara was in no mood for conversation, even if it was offered as a compliment. Maleen followed Tyndall down the same corridors Rundel's men had taken her through earlier. He stopped at the room that Maleen's companions were sharing for the night. The guard at the door slid the bar and opened the door.

Every man in the room was on alert. Oblam must have known something was amiss, but with stone walls and a thick door, they'd been helpless to do anything about it. As Tyndall entered the room, each man stood expectantly. When she entered behind him, they could see her bruised face, torn clothes, and disheveled hair. She held up a hand to forestall the angry, and probably violent, outburst that would come from Noture.

"I want to know which one of you killed my brother," Tyndall demanded.

At first, all four men stared back at him as he looked at each of them in turn. Tara stepped up to each one, searching for something. Maleen didn't know if their silence to an inquiry they knew the answer to could be mistaken for guilt. Noture wouldn't want any of them accused.

"This one." Tara indicated Noture.

Noture gave her a questioning look. He sighed. "Yes. I shot an arrow in the dark at an unknown assailant, in defense of my tribesman."

"What else?" Tara asked.

"What do you mean 'what else'?" Noture looked down at the girl.

Maleen closed her eyes and took a deep breath, realizing Oblam wasn't the only voyant who could read Noture against his wishes.

"It was dark," Noture said. "I didn't even know it was Fanton, or that I had killed him until Lenet showed up in Acora claiming to be the new sub-chief."

"There is still something he's not telling us," Tara said.

Noture could have made a claim to the chief's family. If Tyndall were as honorable as Tara said, it could make all the difference as to whether Tyndall made a judgment himself or went to the other chiefs to make a judgment. Yet Noture remained quiet, not wanting to cause more issues for Maleen or to give Tyndall more cause to make a charge against *her*.

"You are a strong voyant," Maleen answered for him, knowing he would not speak up. "Noture can often hide his intent from voyants. What he is trying to conceal is that he is my uncle." Looking at her companions, she indicated both Tara and Tyree. "These two Kelvian warriors saved my life tonight. We hide nothing from them."

Tara was satisfied with Maleen's answer and told Tyndall so. Tyndall stared hard into the face of the man who confessed to killing his younger brother.

"From what your niece has told me," he said, shoulders slumped, "it seems my brother got what was coming to him. I thought if I looked into the face of his killer, I might feel sorry for Fanton. But I can't." He squared his shoulders and turned to leave. "Follow me, all of you."

Around every corner of the building was another pair of guards. Each came to attention when Tyndall passed. Entering a study, Tyndall ordered the nearest guard, "Call a scribe." When the scribe arrived, Tyndall dictated an edict to him.

> *To all the provinces of Kelvia and all tribes across Chalent,*
>
> *From Tyndall, Chief of Kelvia,*
>
> *On this day I do hereby declare Lenet, son of Fanton, brother to the Chief of Kelvia, to be an outlaw. The Western Province of Kelvia is to be dissolved, its members incorporated into Kelvia Proper.*
>
> *Lenet is hereby removed from any claim to the chief's family. Any tribe or province who finds him may do as they see fit with him and any co-conspirators.*

Tyndall handed Maleen the first copy he signed. "I will send copies throughout Kelvia," he promised. "The last I heard, he was in Acora. Do with him as you see fit."

There was no forgiveness in Tyndall's look or tone. Maleen understood that to forgive the infiltration of the Western Garrison, much less the death of his brother, would have been, to Kelvians, a weakness Tyndall refused to show.

Honor, however, dictated that Lenet be dealt with. His dishonorable conduct, compounded by Rundel, who was loyal to him, reflected on the tribe, and upon the chief's family. With both anger and sadness on his face, Tyndall dismissed them. Guards escorted them back to quarters, but the door was not secured.

***

The following morning, after being served breakfast, Maleen prepared to leave Kelvia with the declaration about Lenet in her hand. Her shoulder ached from events the previous night, but Phillip could find no additional damage. He'd done well when he repaired it, but she'd still be experiencing pain for some time. Maybe forever.

She and the men with her stepped out of the building into a bright winter sun. Snow had fallen overnight, and the glare was blinding.

"Lady Maleen," the Grand Voyant, Tara, called to her as they were retrieving their weapons from the guardsman at the gate. "Chief Tyndall wishes to speak to you before you leave. Bring Phillip and one advisor."

Noture handed his knife and staff to Tian.

"Asher." Maleen glanced at Noture. "Sorry, Uncle. She said an advisor, not a bodyguard. If he wants to make a charge against our physician, my garrison commander should be there with me."

"Garrison Commander?" Tian balked. "He's twenty-one years old."

Asher grinned and clapped Tian on the shoulder. He leaned over and in a mock whisper close to Tian's ear he said, "So is she." He handed his knife to Noture and followed Maleen and Phillip back into the building.

Maleen stole a glance at Phillip. Calm and collected, no one would know he could be about to face sentencing for treason.

"You can't endanger a truce between Acora and Kelvia for one person," Phillip said.

Her head knew he was correct, but her heart feared for her friend, and she strained for any alternative to allowing Tyndall to take Phillip from them.

They followed Tara to the same office they'd been in the previous evening. Not exactly an official setting for having someone extradited. Of course, they were in Kelvia. Tyndall didn't need to extradite Phillip. All he had to do was not allow him to leave.

Tyndall sat behind his desk and when they entered, Tara moved to stand behind him.

"Not the first advice I'd planned to give you for being chief, but you should have asked to bring the boy." Tyndall looked only at her, not at her companions. "You should go nowhere without a Grand Voyant."

"I'll be sure to remember the tip," Maleen said. "What would have been your first advice?"

"To garner as much support in the Chiefs' Council as you can."

"The Council is still two months away." It seemed that as soon as one problem was solved, another showed itself. She still needed the Chiefs' Council to confirm her. Confirmation would usually have been a simple matter. Debates sometimes happened when heirs were chosen, but by the time a chief died or retired, it followed that the heir would become the new chief. Because of the timing of her selection and Rabe's death, Maleen had never been confirmed as Heir by the Chiefs' Council.

"Though Lenet has been disowned, he will still hold some support from chiefs who would have preferred that his father was the Kelvian chief rather than me."

Maleen schooled her expression. She'd never been privy to the politics surrounding the Council. No doubt it would have been one of the first issues Rabe would have instructed her on. "Suggestions for dealing with them?"

Tyndall handed her a piece of paper. "I suggest you don't wait two months to have the Council confirm you."

"Correct me if I'm wrong, but doesn't that *have* to take place at Equin?"

"It has to take place at a Chiefs' Council meeting. Not necessarily at Equin." He indicated the paper.

Maleen glanced down.

To all tribal chiefs across Chalent
From Tyndall, Chief of Kelvia
1st of 12th Lunar, 521

Your presence is requested at an emergency convergence of the Chiefs'
Council. Urgent business, which cannot wait until Equin is to be discussed.

The meeting will take place on the 15th of 12th Lunar at the Central
Garrison of Kelvia.

"Emergency Council?" Maleen looked up at Tyndall. "You feel that
strongly about not waiting?"

"As you get to know the other chiefs, there are a few things you
will learn about their personalities. The first is that many of them are
chauvinistic."

"I've seen that even as a warrior." Maleen chuckled a little. "Not as
much within Acora, but any time I've had dealings with those outside, it
was as Cutter's betrothed when everyone thought he was next in line, not
in an official capacity. Visiting chiefs and others rarely saw me as equal,
even when I wore a vest to those gatherings."

"Don't expect it to get better." He sighed. "Now, not only are you not
going to be seen as an equal, but there will be resentment that you sit in
our meetings as if you are one of us. Because after this emergency meeting
you will be. Now, the way I see it, by not telling the chiefs what the
emergency Council is about, a few of them won't bother to show up."

"Not bother to show up to an emergency meeting?"

Tyndall chuckled. "Equin is only two months away. Surely anything
pressing can wait that long. For those who have far to travel, I'm asking
them to take a week-long trip, each way. Then, since Kelvia will be
hosting the Equin festival, they must make the trip again for the regular
Council. Coland won't show up. If I know Wan, neither will Simot,
though they're much closer. And if you're lucky, Braven will use the
winter weather as an excuse for Randor not to come."

The three most chauvinistic tribes on Chalent. "You'd do this for me?"
Maleen sensed there was probably an ulterior motive. "Why?"

"New chiefs are not the only ones who need to garner support," he
said simply. "The time will come when favors get called in."

In other words, she would owe him. At least he was upfront about it.

"I will see you in two weeks." Turning to Phillip, Tyndall added, "I now have *no* nephews. I never want to see *you* in my garrison or in Kelvia, again."

Phillip nodded. Maleen saw the look of hurt mixed with relief on Phillip's face. Though he was loyal to her, he was still Kelvian. But Tyndall had every right to charge Phillip with treason, an executable offense. Banishment was a lenient sentence.

Tyndall waved his hand toward the door. "Borrow mounts to ride home. You're a chief now. Act like it."

CHAPTER 16

Six hours after leaving Tyndall, the company approached the Acoran Northern Garrison. It was eerily quiet. The smell of burnt wood permeated the air.

"Something's wrong," Maleen said, as a watchman she didn't recognize waved at her from the tower. It took longer than it should have for the front gate to open. Cutter stepped out with Gavin and several other warriors. Maleen slipped off her graebig and into Cutter's arms.

"You're a foolish woman," he whispered, holding her tight. Even in his hurt and anger, he would never say such a thing in the hearing of others. "How could you leave like that?"

"You know why I did it."

"That doesn't mean I have to like it." When he pulled back from her, his face was red, and anger flashed in his eyes. Maleen had never seen him this angry. His focus flickered to someone standing behind her. "Physician," he called.

As Phillip turned to answer his call, Cutter punched him in the face as hard as he'd ever hit any man. Phillip lay sprawled on the ground as Maleen stood gaping at Cutter.

Warriors who'd come out of the gate with him stared wide-eyed, but no one said a word. One knelt by Phillip, while others took the graebigs inside the gate.

Maleen was at a loss for what to say to Cutter. He really had thought leaving him behind was Phillip's idea. Just like Oblam had warned.

"Discuss it later," Gavin said, looking between Phillip's prone form and Cutter. "Before you come inside, you need to see something." Gavin's words were as ominous as his tone.

"What is going on, Gavin?"

Gavin didn't answer but turned the corner around the side of the garrison and stopped.

There, in the graveyard, stood the monument to the massacred council, but it was the sight of a second wooden monument that brought Maleen to her knees. The mass grave was twice its former size. From the second monument, Maleen read the names. Theon, the first person to save her life when they'd only been adolescents. Tobal, Blane, Elam, name after name, the names of nearly every young man she'd graduated with years before, young men who had been brothers. Younger men, boys really, who had recently graduated and many yet to do so. Older men who had fought for Acora for more years than Maleen had known them. More names, representing more men who had given their lives in the face of Lenet's treachery. Fifty-three names in all, thirty-two warriors and twenty-one of the older students. Below the list of names was the inscription:

FOR THEIR CHIEF AND FOR THEIR TRIBE

"Did none make it out?" she asked quietly.

"We buried the dead when we arrived." Gavin's voice cracked. "I didn't have a roster, but there were no survivors inside the garrison when we got here."

Cutter laid his hand on his wife's head as she knelt by the monument and wept.

She wept for the lives lost. She wept for the wives without husbands. She wept for the children without fathers, for the mothers without sons. Had she not been pulled out, there would have been nothing she could have done for them. It didn't seem right that they died while she lived, just because a young man felt compelled to protect his chief. The same act that took her from the garrison in time to save her life also saved the lives of those who'd gone with her. Her husband, brother, uncle, and best friend lived while so many others lost husbands, brothers, uncles, and friends.

Not knowing how long she'd been kneeling there, Maleen stood up, wiped her eyes, and lifted her chin.

Cutter embraced her tightly. He made no effort to hide his own tears. "This is how a chief grieves. You wouldn't be human otherwise."

How well he knew the difficulty she had in letting others see her emotions. After a moment she pulled back and turned to face Gavin. "How bad is the damage?"

He closed his eyes and slowly shook his head.

Not waiting for him to collect himself enough to answer, Maleen walked briskly back to the front gate and stepped inside.

The sight was beyond anything she could have expected. Every building in the garrison had been burned to the ground.

***

That evening, Maleen, Cutter, and Noture wandered through the destruction. The light of their lamp gave an eerie glow to the remains. How thankful she was that Gavin had arrived first and taken care of the dead. She would not have been able to handle walking in and finding the bodies of her comrades—the bodies of her friends.

It was a peculiar feeling to be home, yet not be home. The student's barracks where Maleen spent five years, the warriors' barracks she'd lived in as the only Lady Warrior for another five years, the private quarters Cutter had built for the two of them, all gone. Only piles of ash and rubble told the story of where they once stood.

Though it had been a month, the smell of burnt wood still permeated the place. Ash and tiny flecks of char blew around in the light breeze.

A month ago, she hadn't considered that Lenet would do anything but chase her. But staring at what remained of her home, Maleen found she wasn't surprised by the devastation. Lenet wouldn't have had enough men to hold the garrison and hunt for her. Destroying it was, to a man like Lenet, the better option.

In several places, the wooden walls surrounding the installation were blackened, where a burning building had been close. Someone had gone through a great deal of effort to ensure the garrison walls did not burn down.

"Lenet is making a statement," Noture pointed out. "To wipe out any trace of the garrison would have been too easy. By leaving the empty walls standing, he's leaving a warning to anyone who dares to cross him. An empty monument."

Maleen didn't have time to brood. She needed to take decisive action but wasn't sure how. This was why a good chief kept wise advisors.

She called those men closest to her, along with Gavin to a structure that had been set up as a command tent. Cutter was still in a rotten mood as they all sat down on logs set around a large stump.

Phillip sat as far from Cutter as possible, his eye and cheek a hideous shade of purple. She'd have to clear the air between them as soon as possible.

"If Kayla senses Oblam nearby, it won't be long before Lenet knows we're back in Acora," Asher said, glancing sideways at his cousin.

"The boy has been through enough," Maleen said. "I'm sending him to Mother as soon as she decides where she wants to settle."

"You can't do that to him." Noture sat forward on his log-chair, palms flat on the stump.

"I can and I will." Maleen frowned at him. She was stepping over the line between Chief and family, perhaps even acting out of emotion. At the moment, she didn't care. Oblam had acted bravely, but he wasn't ready for the violence that surrounded garrison life. He needed the safety and security of a village, and he needed his mother's arms, not his sister's battles.

Cutter stood up, his seat rolling back to the edge of the tent. "The boy isn't our main concern. We need to find the madman, whatever it takes, preferably before he has a chance to disrupt the emergency Council." He stormed from the tent, leaving the others to stare after him.

"He's been like that since you left," Gavin said, sending Maleen a knowing look. "I don't blame him. I wouldn't have responded any differently." Gavin glanced at Phillip, then back to Maleen.

Asher groaned. "Of all the times to be a stubborn, hot-headed—"

Maleen didn't stick around to hear the rest of what Asher thought about his cousin's behavior. She followed Cutter outside. "Cutter!" she called after him. "Wait, please." She caught up to him before he walked out the gate and put a hand on his shoulder.

"He doesn't understand our ways. Why is he even in that meeting?" Cutter turned to her. He grabbed her arms, his eyes pleading with her to understand his anger.

"Who?" She didn't like the look on his face. He was not quick-tempered, but when he *did* lose his temper...Phillip's face was a minor example of what he was capable of.

"Phillip. He thought it was perfectly acceptable to leave your husband behind while you went off to risk your life. If anything had happened to you, and I wasn't there..." He gently touched the bruise Cantel had left on her cheek.

"I had Noture, Tian, and Asher. All great warriors and good friends and...and none of them are recovering from broken ribs and internal injury." She put a hand on his chest and blinked back the tears that threatened her composure.

"He had no right!"

"Stop, Cutter! Phillip had nothing to do with it. He didn't even know I was going to sneak off until I told Lutin," Maleen confessed, unable to control the tears streaming down her face. "It was my idea. I didn't ask anyone's opinion about it. Just me. If you're angry with anyone, it should be me." Her voice was quiet as she swiped at her eyes.

Cutter's eyes went wide with hurt. He grabbed her hand and pulled her out the gate, far enough into the woods that the watchtower guard would not be able to see them.

Maleen sat on a log and waited for him to speak his mind.

Cutter sat next to her. Then he stood up, looking down at her. He opened his mouth and shut it again, pacing a few yards.

Still, she waited.

Cutter stopped his pacing and stood in front of her. "Do you have any idea how badly I want to shake you right now?" He ran a hand through his hair.

Maleen said nothing. Cutter would never lay a hand on her no matter how angry she'd made him.

"When I woke up, and you were gone, I felt so helpless. I'm your partner, your friend. I'm supposed to be there for you, no matter what. But all I could do was wait, wondering if…" His voice trailed off and he fell silent, too overcome for words. Cutter sat next to her.

"You've watched me ride out of the garrison many times before."

"This time I didn't get to watch you ride out, to kiss you good-bye, to—"

Maleen cut him off. "How many times have you kept me from the fight in the past month? Because I was injured and vulnerable? Because your duty to the tribe, which trumps all else, meant protecting me?" It was hard for Maleen to admit, but she was beginning to see that Asher, Noture, and Cutter were all in the right to protect her.

"Before my father died, we were just warriors, we didn't have a choice," Cutter said. "We went where we were sent. Now, we—*you*—have a choice. You shouldn't have gone without me."

"I'm just as capable now as I was then." Maleen bit back a much angrier retort.

"I know—" he yelled, then stopped and took a deep breath. He lowered his voice. "I know that. That's not what this is about." He stood up and paced again.

"You have to trust I can make the right choices about what chances to take." Maleen stood and took his hand. "You want to protect me. That's not a bad thing for a warrior or a husband. I know it's been hard, but I finally see that sometimes, I have to let you. Even though it's hard on the warrior in me to do it."

She chewed her lip. "I need you to trust that I can protect my warriors. Even you. I'm sorry for the fight we had in Elm when you kept me from the battle. I wasn't ready for it, and you weren't ready for what-ever fight we could have been facing in Kelvia. Seeing how badly it's hurt you, I'm sorry that I went behind your back, instead of having an honest conversation with you." She put her arms around him.

Cutter returned the embrace. "Thank you," was all he said.

Something between them shifted into place. At last, they'd reached an understanding. Maleen buried her face in his chest, inhaling the scent of him. How she'd missed it. "I love you."

"And I love you," he returned before tilting her face to his and giving her kisses that started tender, gentle, and chaste but gave a hint that they wouldn't stay that way.

***

The next morning, Maleen came from the tent that served as her private quarters feeling better than she had in a long time. She was with her husband again. She was in warrior's garb again, with no more skirt getting in her way. She'd even managed to get a full night's sleep. Only a part of the threat had been neutralized, but this morning Maleen felt, for the first time in far too long, as though everything was going to be all right. As long as she had Cutter and the others, she could actually pull off being Chief.

Cutter emerged from the tent right behind her. She watched him from the corner of her eye, looking for any sign that the previous night's activities had been a mistake. He was still in a lot of pain, but if she'd added to it, he wasn't likely to let her know. They made their way, hand in hand, to the command tent where the others were already waiting.

With Gavin was the man from Oak Village who'd led the rescue and chased off the Kelvians. His tall, intimidating form was impossible to forget.

"Javon?" Maleen shook his hand.

"Forgive me if I'm overstepping bounds," Gavin said. "But I thought you could use a voyant, and probably wouldn't want to use the boy."

Maleen looked around the tent. She trusted everyone here, why would she need a voyant?

"Having one of us around is a good habit," Javon said. "And you can decide if you trust me long before you need a Grand Voyant at the Chiefs' Council."

"You saved our lives," Maleen said. "Trust is not an issue." She hoped he believed her. She laughed to herself; of course he believed her. He was a voyant.

Phillip was the last one to enter the meeting room, looking unsure of whether he had a right to be there.

Maleen waved him to a seat. It wasn't quite the warrior's council Rabe had to advise him, but it was a start. She took a deep breath. "Lenet has hunted us long enough. Now it's our turn."

"When word gets out that he's been disowned and declared an outlaw, most of those warriors will hightail it back to Kelvia," Asher pointed out. "Those who don't will be considered nothing more than mercenaries"

"How many would you count on being loyal to Lenet?" Cutter asked.

"Only those he paid." Maleen looked at Phillip.

He nodded. "There were several warriors from the Western Garrison who were only there because of promised payment, beyond the regular stipend. Those might stay with him if he manages to find a way to keep paying, but few others will. Most Kelvians have enough honor to follow only a duly appointed leader."

"What about Kayla?" Asher asked, looking at Maleen. "How well did you get to know her in their garrison?"

"I left as much space between her and me as I could. I can't even get a partial truth past Winloen. Kayla's twice as strong. There's no way she wouldn't have seen right through me at the first conversation."

"Do you think she'll stay loyal to Lenet?" Asher looked at Phillip.

"She's her mother's daughter," he said with a scowl. Funny, he'd said something similar about Lenet, not that long ago. "She'll go where she thinks the power is. If she stays, we'll know she thinks there's a chance for Lenet to regain some sort of position. Otherwise, she'll go crying home to Tyndall. But...he is her brother. They've always been inseparable, more so since their mother died. She may go back to Tyndall, but as an informant for Lenet."

"If she clashes with that young Grand Voyant and starts telling Tyndall lies…" Maleen took a deep breath.

"Kayla's not our main concern right now," Cutter reminded them. "How do we find Lenet?"

"We hunt from one end of the territory to the other."

"If I may, Chieftess?" Javon spoke for the first time. "Perhaps it's time you act as a chief, instead of a warrior."

Maleen stared at him. "Chiefs *lead* men into battle, they don't just send them."

"But you're not going into battle. At least not yet," he reminded her. "Send men to search the territory. But you stay here until the emergency Council."

"And hope he comes to us?" Maleen asked.

Javon nodded. "If scouts can find him, it makes your trip to Kelvia in two weeks that much safer. Even if they don't, they ought to begin recruiting. Acoran law states each village should be sending at least two able-bodied fighters in the event of a territory-wide emergency. Considering the number of warriors lost, I think this qualifies."

"Thoughts?" Maleen asked. She was not ready to leave the chase in someone else's hands.

"I know how badly you want to give chase," Noture said with a gentler tone than she'd heard him use in a long time. "But you know Javon makes a lot of sense. Commander Nell, Chief Rabe, and Brice are all gone, and all the unit commanders are gone. We need you here, not out in the field. We need to be ready. Not just for Lenet, but for whatever could come our way from Kelvia if Kayla overshadows Tyndall's Grand Voyant."

"And Oblam?" Tian asked.

"You're both too protective," Noture said. "Your attention will be divided. That can't be good for you or for the garrison."

Maleen bit the inside of her cheek to avoid a snide remark about Noture's protectiveness. He made a good point, even if he was equally guilty.

"We stay in the garrison for now. I'll send Oblam to Mother as soon as it's safe to travel."

"Or," Tian said, "when the support staff returns, invite Mother to bring the little ones here."

That was a possibility to consider at a later time. Maleen stood up. She wasn't fully convinced staying put was the best plan, but she would be foolish to seek advice from the more experienced Javon and Noture, then ignore it when they agreed with one another.

As the small council dispersed, Cutter spoke up. "Phillip?"

"Yes?" he answered, keeping his distance this time.

"It's come to my attention that you were not responsible for my exclusion from Kelvia. I wish to apologize for assuming it was you who orchestrated it when you arrived yesterday." He indicated Phillip's dark bruise and swollen cheek.

Did Phillip understand what it cost the warrior's ego to admit a mistake? Apparently, he did. Phillip did not hesitate to offer his hand to seal their truce, once again.

"I only hope you didn't hit the real offender so hard." Phillip looked at Maleen, cloaking the seriousness of his inquiry with a chuckle.

Cutter shook his head. "She's too fast, and until my ribs heal a little more, she'll probably hit harder." The two men laughed together for the first time. Maleen joined them.

***

Throughout the day, the sound of hammers and stone axes echoed through the garrison. The warriors who'd come up with Gavin had wasted no time beginning to rebuild. The gate opened to a team of graebigs dragging a heavy log. Another team dragged a bundle of much smaller ones. The larger log would be cut down to size to make anything from furniture to firewood. The smaller logs would rebuild the walls of each building. It would take many more loads, but she had instructed that the barracks be the first building rebuilt. Then the other living quarters. Then the structures that made a garrison a home and a fortress.

Maleen supervised the work, and occasionally helped lift a heavy load, or held something still while someone hammered or lashed it in place.

She ignored the glares she received from Phillip. Her shoulder ached, but she needed to use it if she expected it to get stronger.

Amid conversations, Maleen heard many low voices crack with emotion as they discussed the men who had died. All the warriors from the Southern Garrison and the outposts knew warriors from the Northern Garrison. Not a single one of them was able to say he didn't recognize a name on one, or both, of the monuments. The sounds of mourning would be repeated when the civilians returned. They, too, lost loved ones —brothers, fathers, husbands, and sons.

Around dusk, Maleen wandered to the graveyard. Several young men knelt by the mass grave. Not wanting to intrude on their grief, Maleen turned to go.

"What are we doing about this?" One man's voice stopped her.

Maleen turned back around. He stood, facing her. These young men had lost so much, even before they were old enough to be considered men. Though they wore vests, being under twenty, they had not even had a vote for the new chief.

Maleen did not answer at first. She stared at the monument and read the names all over again. "Who did you lose?" she asked him.

"Father and grandfather died with the council. Then a brother." He pointed to one monument then the other. "So, what are we going to do about this?" All the men had come to their feet and stood staring at her.

"We're going to find the pair who did this." Maleen lifted her chin. "And I'm going to fire the arrow to execute them myself. If Kelvia harbors them, despite the declaration from Tyndall, we will respond accordingly."

A silent moment passed. She could see the contemplation on each face as they looked at each other, then back to her.

"Then we will stand beside our new chief." Only one spoke, but the others nodded in agreement.

CHAPTER 17

A week after returning home, Maleen sat in her newly erected office with Cutter and Asher discussing how to balance strength between the two garrisons. They could keep both near full strength with the help of the villagers. But few villagers wished to commit permanently to the garrisons. They would be rotated, each village providing enough support for three months at a time to make sure both garrisons were well manned without drawing manpower from the outposts. Gavin requested a permanent transfer to the Northern Garrison, lending his support to his former classmate. He directed much of the work of rebuilding. Maleen considered leaving him in charge when she and Asher went to the emergency Council meeting in another week.

Asher was in the middle of drafting a letter to the Kelvian leadership that if Jewel returned to Kelvia, they wanted the woman extradited.

"We found him." Noture barged into the office. "Commander Revere's patrol sent a message back. Fifteen men, all wearing Kelvian colors, but looking ragged."

"You're sure it's him?" Cutter stood up.

"Not too many red-headed men in Acora. Much less wearing green and leading raids."

"I'll get a unit together." Cutter headed to the door, Asher on his heels.

"No." Maleen stood up, stopping them in their tracks. "I'll lead it."

Cutter opened his mouth and closed it again. As Maleen went out the door, she brushed a hand on his arm.

"It's still too soon."

Thankfully, he didn't argue with her. It was still her job to keep her warriors safe, and until Phillip said he was ready, she was going to continue to keep Cutter out of the fighting as much as possible. Neither he nor Asher said anything to her about leading the mission. They knew that if there was a chance of catching Lenet, she had to do this herself.

The messenger from the patrol led the chieftess and twenty-five warriors out of the garrison, riding south for nearly an hour. When they met up with the unit on patrol, Commander Revere nodded, a look of approval at seeing the chieftess with the reinforcements.

"They're packing. They may know we're out here and watching." He led the way to a bluff that overlooked a camp. Amid the camp was a man, too far away to see his face, but he had red hair and the right build. He and all the men around him wore vests, trimmed in green. A moment of watching revealed a woman among them. Blonde hair. She stood close to the man...intimately close. Jewel.

"Noture, take a quarter of the men around to the south of them. Asher, east. Revere, west." Between those she brought and the patrol unit, there were fifty warriors. If they could get in position, they could overwhelm Lenet, coming at him from four sides.

Five minutes later, before the others had time to get in position, the outlaws mounted graebigs.

"We have to go now!" One of Maleen's men held up a horn.

"Sound it," Maleen called, leading the charge from the north as the horn sounded.

By the time they got to the bottom of the bluff, Lenet's troupe was gone, leaving a clear trail to the west. How close had Revere been to getting into position? When a group of Acoran warriors joined hers, and Revere rode up next to her, she knew they had not been close enough.

The two groups pursued, but the other two would be too far away to catch up unless she could slow Lenet down. With only twenty-five of them, it wouldn't be overwhelming, but they still outnumbered the outlaws.

She pushed her beast harder as she saw the dust the outlaws kicked up. Their mounts were tired after the hour-long ride from the garrison. Could they really catch them? Rounding another bend, the road stretched on for a good distance, but no one was in sight.

"Where'd they go?" Revere slowed his graebig.

"There!" Maleen pointed to large prints the beasts had left in the mud, leading to a grove of trees.

Maleen led the way. As they entered the woods, Revere rode next to her.

"Keep your eyes open." As Maleen gave the warning, movement above caught her attention. At the same moment, something heavy fell from the branches, knocking her from her mount. It took only a second to realize it was Lenet. They were both on the ground, but he had been prepared for the fall, she had not.

Thanking her quick reflexes, Maleen rolled to the side before he could hit her. The sounds of the fight going on around her faded as she stood, face-to-face with Lenet.

"It's about time you found us," he snarled.

"If you wanted to go to prison, you could have come closer to the garrison." She watched closely, looking for any movement that would telegraph when he would strike.

"You're a fool to come yourself." He lunged at her, fist flying.

Maleen ducked and maneuvered around him.

"Fast as ever." Lenet circled her. "But you're no hand-to-hand fighter."

He was right. Her staff was on her graebig's saddle. They had Lenet's men outnumbered, but could she avoid him long enough to get help? He was as fast as she was.

She nearly avoided Lenet's next strike, but he grazed her upper left arm. She returned with a punch to his ribs that didn't faze him.

She needed to stall. "Don't you think you're overreacting a bit to a woman not returning your attention?"

"You're more arrogant than I thought if you still think that's all this is." He brought his foot up and caught Maleen in the chest. She staggered backward but didn't fall.

A quick glance around and she saw Revere put down a Kelvian. He picked up the fallen man's staff and tossed it in her direction before engaging another man.

The staff landed a few feet from them. Lenet's eyes went to it, then back to her. At the same moment she dove for it, Lenet moved. Maleen grabbed it first, and as she rolled to her feet, she hit Lenet twice.

"You still can't beat me," Lenet said, carefully stepping out of her striking range.

Movement to the side caught her eye and Maleen dove out of the way as a graebig trampled the spot where she had been standing.

"Half our men are down!" Jewel said from the back of the mount. "Finish this another time."

Maleen sprang to her feet, sprinting at the graebig. By the time she swung at Jewel, Lenet had mounted behind her, and they rode off. Frantically looking around her, Maleen grabbed another mount and pursued. Those few seconds were enough to give Lenet and Jewel a head start.

Another graebig came alongside her. "Trying to go off by yourself?" Revere called, keeping pace.

"Care to join me?"

"Your uncle would never forgive me if I didn't."

Fifteen minutes into the pursuit, Maleen's graebig slowed and refused to be goaded into picking up its pace again.

"Son of a troll!" Maleen swore.

"We've cut down the size of his force," Revere said as they rode much slower back to the site of the battle. "We'll find him again."

He sounded like Asher. Maleen felt nowhere near as optimistic, despite the skill of the trackers they sent to follow his trail.

CHAPTER 18

13th of 12th Lunar
Northern Garrison, Acora

Maleen sought out Noture to make final plans for the emergency Chiefs' Council in another few days. He stood in the training yard with his students—recently returned with the civilians—standing erect, in four neat rows. Tirzah, the schoolteacher, stood next to him, arms crossed, looking completely out of place in her dress with her long hair flowing loose over her shoulders.

"What class was it they were being disruptive in?" Noture asked, not realizing Maleen had come to stand behind him and Tirzah. A few of the students stood taller and held their heads a little higher when they saw her.

"Government," Tirzah said. "With an emergency Council called this close to Equin, I thought a review in world politics was in order."

"I see. How do you explain your behavior in the classroom?" Noture waited for an answer for a full minute before anyone spoke up.

"It's boring. Why do we care how other tribes run their governments?" one of the students called from the second row.

"Yeah!" another said. "Acora is anonymous."

"The word is autonomous," Tirzah snapped.

"Autonomy only goes so far," Noture said. "For example, in a few days, our chief must get the other chiefs to confirm her position."

"My father said you all did that already."

"Acoran warriors agree to follow her," Noture said. "But that doesn't mean other tribes will acknowledge that she's in charge here."

Some of the older students looked from Noture to Maleen. She put her finger to her lips and pointed to Noture. They returned their attention to him.

"Who cares?" the same boy asked.

"You should," Noture said, his voice firm.

"Why?"

"You're an archer. Where do you get your arrowheads?"

"My father buys them. Or I get them from you when we practice making arrows."

"And where do your father and I get them from?"

The boy shrugged.

"They're made from obsidian. How many volcanoes do we have in Acora?"

No one answered.

"Apparently, they pay attention in geography class about as well as government," Tirzah said.

"None," a girl in the back row spoke up.

"Correct," Noture said. "We trade with Portdill for them. What kind of wood makes the best staff?"

"Panapus," a student called out.

"Only grows in the tropics. Anyone enjoy shellfish? The arctic region has the best. All kinds of materials, foods, medicine. They come from all regions across Chalent. Now imagine our leaders said they don't care what the other chiefs think. We're going to skip Equin this year. Lady Maleen doesn't get confirmed. What happens?"

"Dismissed from the Chiefs' Council." The girl in the back row looked from Noture to Maleen and back again as she answered.

At least someone paid attention in class.

"Correct. And any tribe which does not participate in the Council no longer participates in trade. No more obsidian, no more panapus wood. Acorans who make their living trading graebigs and bovines suddenly have a much smaller market."

"But why is it set up that way?"

"Not being allowed to trade is only the punishment for not participating. The whole point of the Council is so that leaders of each tribe can come together and help one another keep the peace. For example, if Timend and Portdill have a disagreement they can go to war, or they can both tell their side to the Council. What the Council decides is binding."

"But why do they care who our chief is, so long as she participates in the Council?"

The older students waited eagerly for Noture's answer, while the younger ones shifted their weight, looking like they'd rather be anywhere else.

"That's a good question," Noture said. "I'm afraid I don't have an answer for you."

"What if she goes to the Council but they don't confirm her?"

"It won't come to that," Noture said.

"But what if it did?"

When Noture didn't answer, Tirzah did. "She'll have to step down, or Acora will be dismissed from the Council."

Several pairs of eyes darted from Tirzah and Noture to Maleen. Enough to make Noture turn to see what drew their attention.

"Like I said, it won't come to that." He spoke more to Maleen than to the students.

"But you'd step down?" the girl asked, looking at Maleen. "Let a group of men take it all away just because you're a woman?"

"Yes," Maleen finally spoke up. "I wouldn't be much of a chief if I let my desire to be here and my desire for an egalitarian society have such a detrimental effect on the entire tribe."

***

"You need a Grand Voyant," Tian said. "And you need your garrison commander."

"I need Cutter," Maleen said firmly. "And don't pretend you trust Javon completely. At least if I depend on Tara, she's already proven herself loyal to Tyndall."

Tian and Noture had both expressed concern over how easily she trusted Javon. But he had saved their lives.

"You can't look to the Kelvian Grand Voyant every time you need to know if someone is telling the truth," Asher said. "But in this instance, I think I have a solution."

"She only gets two advisors with her," Cutter said. "The Chiefs' Council has been run the same way for as long as it's been overseeing Chalent."

"Every ten-year-old school child knows that." Asher rolled his eyes. "I'm suggesting she take you and Javon."

"You're going to wait outside the Council room?" Maleen asked. He was one she was sure she would take.

"No, I'll wait in Acora." He laughed at everyone's expression. "Consider this. Don't give the other chiefs a reminder that there is another option. Maybe they know Uncle Rabe has another living relative other than Cutter, maybe they don't. But let's not remind them of it."

"Then I choose Cutter and Noture. I don't need a voyant." She hoped her tone was firm enough that none of them would argue with her.

"Sure you can keep quiet, Uncle?" Tian asked. "Advisors aren't allowed to say anything to the Council. What do you do when someone insults her? Because they will."

"I'll manage." Noture sat with his arm crossed. He looked satisfied with the solution. He was probably glad to be going, and glad she didn't choose to take the untested voyant.

"What I need to know are unspoken rules," Maleen said. "I don't want to accidentally insult someone."

"Sorry, I was never invited to join Rabe there," Noture said. "It's a place for commanders and Grand Voyants, not longtime friends."

Cutter took her hand. "Nervous?"

"Why would I be nervous?" Maleen squeezed his hand. "I'll be in a foreign place, doing something I've never been trained to do, to try to convince a bunch of men I don't know that I'm as good as they are."

"You *are* as good as they are." Cuter kissed the back of her hand.

Yes, she absolutely *had* to have him by her side.

***

15th of 12th Lunar, 521
Central Garrison, Kelvia

"Ready for this?" Cutter asked as he held the door open.

"Does it matter if I'm ready?" Maleen entered Tyndall's grand hall, now converted to a Council room. She took a seat at the large round table between two empty chairs. Cutter and Noture took the two chairs behind her.

Across the table sat Bontel, Chief of Timend. She'd met him before, but for the rest of the chiefs, she'd memorized their names and would know them by the color of their vests and, hopefully, their family crests. Three men in grey vests entered. The one who sat at the table must be Chief Ricmond of Portdill. Chief Bontel looked surprised to see him.

She was certain she could count on Bontel to vote in her favor, but she had no idea of the gender politics in Portdill. How many other chiefs would show up? There was no law that required them to be here. Only that the decisions made were as binding as if they took place at Equin.

The next trio to enter wore red vests. Maleen's confidence fell. Chief Wan of Simot would never consent to his nearest neighbor being led by a woman. Tyndall hadn't expected him to show up, though his travel time was not much more than Maleen's. Two on her side, one against, and she had no idea of the fourth. Or any idea of what would happen if the vote were a tie.

"Who are you?" Chief Wan demanded, a question which echoed in the expressions of the others, though not as harshly.

"I am Chief Rabe's successor," she replied calmly.

"I thought the stories were exaggerated," another chief said, shuffling into the room with Tyndall. Orange vest—Chief Garret of Fleat. The two men with him resembled him, though younger. One was around Maleen's age, the other closer to her father's. Their family crests were identical. Three generations, yet the older one did not retire. Perhaps in their culture, it wouldn't have been surprising.

"What stories would those be?" Maleen folded her hands on the table, looking him in the eye as he lowered himself into a seat. She hadn't even been sure her notice had reached the other chiefs. Even if it had, all it said was that Rabe was dead and Maleen was acting as the chief until her confirmation by the Council. She wasn't obligated to tell them the circumstances of his death, nor was Tyndall obligated to inform them of why he called this meeting.

"Stories that Rabe was taken in by a female who killed him."

Maleen's confidence fell again. Two for, two against, one unknown. No tie.

"Gentlemen," Chief Tyndall said. "We will wait until all the chiefs have arrived."

In deference to the host, Maleen said nothing. She would get her chance. It would be better to let Tyndall make the introductions anyway.

"Jev?" Tyndall looked at the man in the grey-trimmed vest.

"My father is ill. Nothing serious, but he has given me his approval to sit in his stead." The man handed Tyndall a sealed parchment.

Tyndall nodded. "Welcome to the Council."

So, not Chief Ricmond. His son, Jev. Maleen would have to look up laws regarding heirs taking their chief's place. Apparently, it was allowed.

Ten minutes of silence passed.

Bontel shifted in his seat and looked at Maleen. "I assure you, madam, we are not always this unfriendly. It's simply that Tyndall has called us away from our work without telling us what the emergency is. I'm sure you can see how that would weigh on anyone's mood."

Behind Tyndall, Tara and Hathon sat as his advisors. In addition to her Grand Voyant scarf, Tara now wore a green-trimmed vest. Maleen briefly wondered what battle test she had passed to earn Kelvian warrior status. Perhaps her part in defeating Rundel had been enough.

"Gentlemen, Lady Maleen. Welcome to my home," Tyndall stood up. "I think we can assume the others are not coming. That is unfortunate. They are not going to like missing today's vote. The issue at hand is the security of one of our tribes." He glanced at Maleen, then around the table. "The point of the Chiefs' Council is to ensure security and peace between tribes. Recent events in Acora have caused unrest that will spill to other tribes if we do not take decisive action now, rather than letting it sit unsettled for another month and a half. I will let Lady Maleen explain to you what has happened, but know that she has my support."

Wan stood up, straightening his red-trimmed vest. "Rabe's murderer cannot take his place." He sat back down, not looking at Maleen.

"I can only guess what twisted version of events you've heard," Maleen said, "but I did not kill my father-in-law, and I did not marry into the family with the expectation that—"

"Lady Maleen." Tyndall put up a hand to stop her as he stood up. "Gentlemen, I will explain the role my former family played in those events in due time. Just know that I hold no animosity toward Acora for them. That being said, I must insist you listen to her side before assuming the misinformation which has apparently crossed the borders has any truth in it. Lady Maleen, please, begin at the start." He sat down.

Maleen rose to her feet. With a steady voice, she started at the beginning, explaining why Lenet hated her. None of the chiefs would have been happy to have a spy in their midst, but only a couple could honestly say they wouldn't consider sending one if the circumstances called for it. She explained that when she returned home, she married the man she loved, without regard to his status as the chief's son. Muttering and disbelieving huffs sounded like they came from one of Wan's advisors when she claimed she'd been as surprised as everyone else when Rabe named her as his heir.

"We have heard of the massacre," Bontel said. "But the story was that it was caused by a usurper. A good lesson in not believing rumors."

"I did not kill my chief," she said. "Lenet sent saboteurs. One of them is dead. The other is hiding with Lenet."

Another murmur surrounded the red vests.

"Ask your voyants." Maleen allowed a bit of forcefulness into her voice, but she did not yell.

Even after conversing with his Grand Voyant, Chief Wan still clenched his jaw and shook his head.

"But you admit, you instigated hostilities between your tribes," Garret said.

"Hostilities between our tribes have been going on since before *I* was born," Tyndall said. "You can hardly blame her for that."

"You would support this female?" Wan growled.

"After the steps she took to make peace? Yes, I do."

Jev gasped in surprise. Few people would have believed peace between Acora and Kelvia was possible.

"We should not be discussing this without Lenet here to tell his side," Garret said.

"If he'd come to me, he would have had his chance." Tyndall slapped the table. "I trust the word of my Grand Voyant. She says Lady Maleen tells the truth. My question to you is, do you trust yours?"

"Very well. If Tyndall holds nothing against her, neither can we," Bontel pointed out. "I think we should vote to confirm her."

Maleen gave him a nod of thanks.

"Not yet," Jev said. "There are other matters to consider."

"Such as?" Maleen asked, knowing what he would say.

"A weak chief is a hazard to peace within a tribe, and between the tribes. A chief must be able to put down any resistance to his leadership."

"My warriors' council supports me. That alone makes a chief strong." *And I can beat any man in the room except the two sitting behind me.* Bragging would not help her, especially if they called on her to prove it. Her arm wasn't quite ready for that yet.

Bontel spoke without rising to his feet. "If her council supports her, according to the laws of her tribe, that's all she needs. What right do we have to say no to that? I move we vote."

What right, indeed. That was her sticking point. She had only to insist to the chiefs that she'd been selected according to the laws of her tribe. Autonomy dictated she should be chief.

Her confidence deflated as soon as Wan spoke. "A female is too emotional for such a responsibility. It is in their nature. They need those emotions as they bear and nurture children. *That* is their responsibility.

It has been since the beginning of Chalent. Giving a woman political responsibility not only allows emotions into politics, but also encourages them not to take their responsibility of motherhood seriously."

"You speak of runaway emotions, Chief Wan. But as I recall, it was you who made a scene when a woman sat at this table." Bontel's mouth twitched just a little. "And, despite your accusations, *she* stayed surprisingly calm."

Wan's face turned nearly as red as his vest as he glared at Bontel.

Maleen wanted to shake Wan. His generalized statements about motherhood didn't apply to her. He did not know the extent of her emotional control, and *no one* knew how badly she wished to continue her predecessor's bloodline. Not even Cutter knew that. Though he likely shared the sentiment, they'd never discussed it. It simply hadn't happened yet.

"A few of us use our wives as advisors, Wan. Perhaps overall they are more in tune with their emotions, but it is to their benefit and ours. What my wife's sensitivity to social overtones adds to my tribal management is invaluable. Your accusation of being overly emotional has no bases when applied to this one woman. If you bothered to listen to anything she just said, you'd have heard of her recent loss. Loss that would have most men in tears. Yet she is calm and in control. Tyndall, call for the vote."

"We cannot make this a binding vote with so few chiefs here," Jev said. "Five are missing and only one sent a proxy. If you had informed them of why you called this meeting, they would have been here, including my father. We should wait for Equin to finalize whether we choose to confirm her or not.

"The other chiefs were given a chance," Tyndall said. "Clearly, if a matter is important enough for a chief to call an emergency Council, then it's important enough for their attention. If they couldn't see fit to make the time to attend, that is their problem."

"My father has trusted me to represent him and the interest of Portdill. But I do not know how he would vote on this."

"As a proxy, you must take your best guess," Garret said. "Or you vote by what you believe to be right. But it is no reason to delay the vote."

"Agreed." Tyndall stood up. "Acora needs our assistance in bringing stability to their territory. Lady Maleen needs the authority to try former Kelvians within her borders. Her warriors support her. If you agree that this is all she needs, vote yes. Bontel?"

"Yes."

"Wan?"

"No."

"Garret?"

"Abstain."

Maleen hoped that would work in her favor, but she still didn't know what would happen if the vote were a tie.

"Jev, standing in proxy for Ricmond?"

"I cannot, in good conscience, vote for a woman without knowing how my father would have voted. I vote no."

"I vote yes," Tyndall said, glaring at Tolly. "Will you really make us drag this on for a month and a half? Think of what the instability would do to any tribe."

"Very well." Garret stood up. "I do not approve of a Lady Chief. Particularly one who isn't even a blood relation to her predecessor. But what I disapprove of even more is this Council's interference in what is obviously an internal affair. If the Acorans wish to weaken the house of Rabe in this manner, that is their business. I vote in favor of confirmation. Good day, gentlemen."

Maleen held her head high as she walked out of the Council room.

It was done.

Her installation was complete.

No one could undo it.

CHAPTER 19

7th of 13th Lunar, 521 AC
Acora, Northern Garrison

Maleen walked into the tent serving as an infirmary. She had been too busy in the past three weeks to check on Phillip and see how he was settling in to life as an Acoran. "How is Theon?" She asked, peeking at the sleeping babe in the cradle near the door.

"Much better," Phillip said. "His fever is gone. I'm going to let his mother take him home, as soon as they have a home."

"Barracks are done. Next project will be the private quarters."

"How much priority does a garrison widow have among so many families?" His voice held a hint of tenderness as he looked at the mother, sleeping in a chair next to the cradle.

"Brendla's husband is a hero, same as all the others who gave their lives. We treat the widows of heroes accordingly. Those with children will have priority."

Phillip nodded his approval.

A loud horn blast sounded from the main gate. Maleen ran outside, her heart in her throat. Had he finally come?

The man on the watchtower yelled to the ground. "Twenty riders coming! Kelvian colors! A man in the lead, flanked by two females. One has bright red hair!"

Kayla! If it was Lenet, the other female would certainly be Jewel. But he wouldn't dare bring only twenty men.

Warriors grabbed weapons, women took children to the large tent serving as a dining hall, where it would only take a few guards to keep them all safe, and commanders yelled instructions to students. Since they were still young and inexperienced, Noture sent his students to the dining hall with the women and the garrison children.

The speed in which the garrison had been put on alert made all the drills over the past weeks worth the effort. Slinging her bow over her shoulder, Maleen climbed the ladder to the watchtower. The riders were led, not by Lenet, but by Tyndall. Riding with him were Kayla and Tara.

So, Kayla has abandoned her brother, or at least made it look like it. Maleen was now concerned about what lies Kayla may have been telling Tyndall. Would Tyndall believe his Grand Voyant over his own niece? It gave her a little reassurance that Tara still wore a green scarf, while Kayla did not.

Attached to Tyndall's mount was a long pole. From it hung a green banner with the outline of two hands, held up in peace. The Banner of Diplomacy did little to settle Maleen's nerves.

Seeing the chieftess on the watchtower as he approached the garrison gate, Tyndall called to her, "Chieftess, my warriors are apprehensive about my visit. Will you allow them to remain out here, while we speak in private?"

"They may." Despite his previous help, Maleen still didn't completely trust the Kelvian chief, and now he wished to bring Kayla into her garrison. "But any who *do* enter with you must lay down their weapons first."

"You have your orders," Tyndall called to his men. The men assembled into neat lines. They didn't relax, but they did not take an aggressive stance.

"Commander?" Maleen called to the ground where Asher waited.

"I'm on it," he called back. Asher opened the gate and, as Tyndall entered, Asher led thirty men out of the garrison to ensure the Kelvians waited for Tyndall peaceably.

Maleen climbed down from the tower to greet Tyndall and the three who entered with him, ordering the gate closed behind them. Kayla never carried a weapon, other than her mind and ruthless cunning, but Tara and Tyree handed bow, staff, and knife to a boy who stood ready to take care of their mounts. No one dishonored Tyndall by requesting his weapon. If the chieftess wanted him disarmed, she would be the one to make the request.

"You have me at a disadvantage, Tyndall," Maleen addressed the other chief. "You bring two voyants, while I have none here."

"Call the boy if you like," Tyndall offered.

"He's not in the garrison." Apparently, Javon had chosen a poor time to take Oblam on a fishing excursion. She would have preferred to have Javon sit in on this meeting.

"Kayla will remain out here," Tyndall said as they crossed the courtyard to the chief's office, ignoring the heated look Kayla gave him.

"Phillip?" Maleen said. "I know how you feel about your cousin, but I need someone who knows her."

"I won't let her out of my sight." Phillip and Kayla glared at each other as Tyndall followed Maleen into her office.

"She is my niece," Tyndall said. "My only living relative, unless you still count Lenet or your physician, but she isn't to be trusted any more than they are."

Cutter, Noture, Tara, and Tyree entered the office with the chiefs. Both Acoran men showed Tyndall enough respect to remove their knives, as his companions had been required to do, leaving only Tyndall and Maleen with any sort of weapon in the meeting. Not that either Cutter or Noture would need them, nor would Tyree.

"Make your point, Tyndall," Noture said as they all sat.

Tyndall shot him a look that would have made a lesser man cower. "My nephew is giving Kelvians a bad name. It's widespread knowledge by now that he's been disowned and declared an outlaw, yet he still raids in Kelvian colors and wears my family crest. It's not just in Acora either. He's crossed into Simot and Timend as well."

"We get the reports." Maleen nodded. "We send men after him, and every time he slips away."

"He's a smart man. Even in his hatred for you, he doesn't come here. What if I told you I can flush him from hiding?" Tyndall paused. "When I get home, I'm going to announce a pardon."

"What?" The table shook as Noture stood up abruptly. "He'll come out of hiding then, to be sure, but as a Kelvian and a member of the chief's family. He'll gather warriors again."

"There is much unrest in my house." Tyndall put up a hand. "Factions fighting amongst themselves. In the past month, there have been two assassination attempts on my life, and one on Tara's because she saw them coming." He nodded to Tyree. "I've had to assign a bodyguard to her, even within the garrison. I intend to announce Lenet is not only pardoned but also my chief heir."

"You can't be serious." Maleen looked from Tara to Tyndall. Had they lost their minds?

"I'm not young. To the masses, it will look as though I'm naming an heir for fear of dying without one, because if I do, Kelvia will be plunged into a civil war. But you'll notice I'm making this pronouncement right before Equin. I fully expect there to be resistance to it in the Chiefs' Council."

"I'll be the first to resist!" Maleen was adamant. There was no way she would allow such a decree to go unchallenged.

"Don't make a complaint to the Council. You do not have enough support from the other chiefs. Considering your history with Lenet, they will dismiss you as being too emotional." Tyndall shook his head.

"I will not sit by and allow—"

"Do not make a complaint." Tyndall cut her off. "Issue a Tamal challenge."

"You're going to make an announcement you know will be challenged by Tamal?" Cutter asked. "What sense does that make?"

"It will force Lenet's hand," Tara said. "He won't allow the match to happen if he can help it."

"And, when he tries to stop it," Tyndall said, "we will have him caught in the midst of a crime."

"By 'try to stop it' you mean his crime will be trying to kill Maleen," Cutter growled. "Again."

"Try, yes." Tyndall nodded. "Kelvia is hosting the Council this year. You will be in my territory. Lenet will not be expecting Kelvians to help you, but they will. Even the factions who would usurp me will not want any blood relation of mine named Heir."

"I cannot issue a Tamal challenge to a man thirty years older than I am."

"I'm going to do this," Tyndall warned. "If you don't issue the challenge, he will be my heir. None of the other chiefs will have the courage to cross Kelvia, except maybe Bontel. Even if they did, you would have the best chance of drawing Lenet out before the match."

"If you're wrong, and he doesn't try to stop it? Or if he tries something but we can't prove it's him?" Maleen asked. "Tara will know Lenet's intent, but she won't be able to testify about it in court."

"Then we fight the Tamal." Tyndall stood to leave. "I will not throw the match, and I'm not as feeble as my age suggests. You not only have the best chance at drawing Lenet out, but also of winning a Tamal match *if* it goes that far."

Everyone stood with Tyndall and followed him out of the hut. He strode to his waiting mount. Kayla mounted her graebig next to Tyndall, questioning him angrily about why she'd been excluded from the meeting. His response was lost in the wind.

"He doesn't trust her," Tara said, "but she will know there is a plot as soon as Tyndall announces the pardon."

From her mount, Kayla shot Maleen an unreadable look.

"What was that?" Maleen asked Tara.

"She already knows something is going on. She'll be as aware as I am that you don't like it, but you don't feel you have any other choice."

"Any way you can keep her from reading me at Equin?"

"That's an ability few voyants have." Tara shook her head.

"Will she warn Lenet?" Maleen asked.

"Tyndall will not allow her to leave the garrison without a warrior he trusts," Tara said. "Those are few. It's why she's here, instead of leaving her in the garrison. Her messages are monitored, and she knows it. Both those she receives and those she sends, so she will not be able to warn Lenet until the pardon is announced and Lenet comes to the garrison. There is much unrest in Kelvia. I only hope Chief Tyndall's new wife can give him a real heir before it's too late, otherwise his house will be lost, and we *will* have a civil war." Tara strode to her own graebig and mounted with more grace than would be expected of anyone as small as she.

Having said nothing the entire time, Tyree only gave Maleen a quick glare before following Tara.

"Good day, Chieftess of Acora," Tyndall called a formal farewell, and the four rode from the garrison.

Maleen watched them go and took a deep breath. Three weeks, then she would fight another Tamal. This one would be a legitimate one, fought in front of the Chiefs' Council. The terms would have to be honored, but what did it say about her that she would challenge a man more than twice her age, in response to the first major decision before the Council since her confirmation?

"It says how opposed you are to this pardon," Noture said when Maleen expressed her concern to her advisors. "And even more so to Lenet being named Heir."

"I don't entirely trust Tyndall," Asher said. "How do we know he will adhere to the terms if the match is fought?"

"The chiefs have too much respect for the Tamal. It was begun so that two chiefs could settle differences without their warriors spilling one another's blood. The terms will be enforced," Maleen said confidently.

"I'm more concerned with before the match." Cutter reached for Maleen's hand. "The whole point is to use Maleen as bait to lure Lenet out of hiding. But we all know he won't show up and announce 'Here I am. I'm going to kill you now.' He'll be underhanded and sneaky, probably hire assassins. I don't like the whole plan."

"I'll invite Javon and Oblam. Javon is experienced and Oblam is still young enough to tag along with his big sister, unnoticed."

"He won't be allowed in the Council meetings until he's sixteen," Noture reminded her.

"But he'll know the intent of every man who goes in and out, Lenet included."

"If Lenet doesn't disappear the second Kayla warns him," Tian said.

"No." Phillip chewed his lip. "He won't need Kayla's warning. He'll know there's something going on, but he won't be able to pass up this opportunity. If he can stop the match that's supposed to prevent him from being Heir...I doubt Tyndall will live long past the Chiefs' Council that confirms him."

***

24th of 13th Lunar, 521
Kelvia, outside the Central Garrison

"The man's a fool if he didn't think I'd see through him," Lenet growled.

"If you knew it was a trap, what are you doing here?" Kayla hissed.

"The chance to legitimately become Chief? I can't give that up. Whatever they're plotting, I'll be ready. When *that woman* tries to spring her trap, I'm going to kill her."

"Equin is four days away. How are you going to avoid Tara that long?" Jewel asked. "She may already know you're here."

Lenet shot his new wife a disgusted look. She needed to stop doubting him. She'd been questioning him more and more since he gave her the marriage armlet. But he'd had to. She'd wanted his commitment for a long time, and he couldn't afford to lose her loyalty. She was good at what she did, and he couldn't threaten her with turning her in. He wasn't completely heartless where she was concerned.

"Tara will know my intent the second I'm in the same room with her. So...I make sure she can't tell anyone." The thought of finally being rid of the little thorn that had haunted his family for years gave him some satisfaction.

"You can't kill her," Kayla warned. "Tyndall doesn't trust me, he'll get another voyant from somewhere else."

So much for that little bit of satisfaction. "You can shield me from her?" Lenet asked.

"Not for an entire day, much less the entire festival." Kayla chewed her lip. "Even I'm not that good."

Lenet let a smile creep across his face. "Shield me just long enough to have a talk with our small friend."

"She'll call Tyree," Jewel said. "They've got some kind of emotional bond."

"I can block that," Kayla said.

"Which tower is guarded by someone we trust?" Lenet asked.

"Western gate. That's how I got out without being reported," Kayla said.

"Jewel, stay out here until the festival starts."

"But—"

"Don't argue with me, woman." He pointed a finger in her face. "I'll be back tonight. In the morning, I'll walk in the front gate. When the festival starts and the crowds are thick enough to hide, you can come in."

"You should come with him, now." Kayla grinned at Jewel. "Hathon wouldn't let the holiday stop him from extraditing your hide to Acora."

"Stop it," Lenet ordered. Both ladies would follow him anywhere, but their bickering was going to make him crazy. "Kayla, let's go." He headed to the west gate. When he saw who was on the tower, he smirked. "Are you going to marry him?"

"Are you going to give him a promotion when you're Chief?"

"No."

"Then no." She grinned. "Doesn't mean I can't enjoy him."

A little sneer made its way to his face. His sister certainly knew how to use a man to her advantage. Their father wouldn't have liked her behavior. The old man deserved the grave he rotted in. Diplomacy had never served Kelvia well. Strength and intelligence were what it took to lead. Jewel was the strongest woman he knew, and Kayla was the smartest. They both made him a better leader.

Once inside the garrison, Lenet and Kayla made their way to the main building. The place was dark. Few torches still burned and avoiding the light was an easy thing.

"Ground floor, south side," Kayla said. "Tyndall's in the corner room, she's three windows down. Tyree's in the next one."

"Ground floor? She's moved up in the world," he snarled. He really hated that girl. He'd have enjoyed killing her more than just threatening her, but that would have to wait.

As silently as possible, he slipped a stiff piece of leather between the shutters, lifting the inside latch. If Kayla could do what she said she could, Tara would never sense him coming. This would be easy...providing she slept alone.

Peeking into the dark room, he saw a single form on the bed. *Hmph.* Naturally, Tyree was too straight-edged to sleep with her before she hit the age of maturity. That made Lenet's task easier.

He pulled himself over the window ledge, dropping silently to the floor below. Tara didn't move. She lay on her back, long hair spread over the pillow. Silently he moved to the bed. If Kayla couldn't block her connection to Tyree, he'd have to kill them both. Tyree wouldn't be as easily intimidated as the girl, and if he had to kill Tyree, Tara wouldn't keep quiet about who killed her man.

Hoping Kayla was as good as she claimed, Lenet pulled two handkerchiefs from his pocket. He rammed one into her mouth and by the time she opened her eyes and tried to push him away, he had the other halfway around her head to tie it securely. Her muffled scream barely reached his ears. There was no chance anyone else heard it. Tara reached to pull it off and Lenet grabbed both her hands, yanking her off the bead, pinning her arms behind her with one hand, and wrapping his other arm around her neck.

He could feel her strength drain away as the lack of oxygen drained every ounce of adrenaline. Just a moment longer, and he wouldn't have to worry about her interference ever again. But Kayla was right. Who knew what voyant Tyndall would find to take her place? Not everyone could be as easily intimidated as this girl. As Tara lost consciousness, Lenet released her, letting her limp body fall to the floor.

He uncoiled the rope at his side and tied her hands together, securing the other end to the leg of the bed.

Tara moaned and opened her eyes. Just a slit at first. He waited for her to get enough air for her dizziness to pass and to look him in the face. A smirk turned into a full grin on his face as her eyes focused on him. The terror he saw in those eyes only emboldened him. With Kayla's shield, Tara would have no idea that he didn't plan to kill her.

Lenet stood up, towering over the girl. How did this weak child ever manage to earn a vest? Favoritism, no doubt.

From the floor, Tara kicked him in the shin. Her bare feet did nothing to him, but he drew back a foot anyway. He kicked her in the stomach. As much as he'd have liked to have bloodied her face, any visible bruises would leave questions to be answered.

"Good evening, little one." He crouched next to her.

Her eyes unfocused for a moment. When she focused on him again, her eyes were wide and her breath shaky.

"What's wrong? Can't find stutter boy?"

Tara tried to move away from him. She scooted away but could only move a few inches.

"When I come in the gate tomorrow, you will convince Tyndall that every word I say is true. I don't know how that Acoran woman got her lies past you, but I am innocent of everything she accused me of. Think you can do that, little one?"

Tara didn't nod or shake her head.

"You can do this for me," Lenet said, "or you'll die. And not quickly. All your secrets will come out in the open. Everyone will know who you *really* are."

Her eyes narrowed. Did she actually have the nerve to be angry? Lenet grabbed her hair and jerked her head back. Eyeing her bare neck, he wanted to choke her to unconsciousness. But his fingers would leave marks. He eyed her scarf, hanging on a hook on the other side of the room. It would be soft enough. But nothing was within reach that wouldn't leave a mark.

He pulled his knife from his belt. Her eyes went wide again as he touched it to her neck.

"Tyndall will believe every word I say. He'll believe that all I want is for our family to continue in the chief's seat, and neither I nor Jewel were responsible for what happened in Acora. You convince him of that, and you'll live." *For another few days.* "Do we have an understanding?"

Tara nodded. Lenet had no way of knowing if she meant it. "First sign of betrayal, I kill you and your bodyguard." He cut the rope and dragged Tara to her feet. He spun her around, holding her back to him. Her head barely came to his chest.

He looped one arm around her neck, and locked the other one behind her, in just the right position to cut off blood flow to the brain.

It took only a few seconds for Tara to go limp again. Satisfied he could release her without her sounding a warning, he laid her on the bed and ungagged her. Unless she spoke up, no one would be the wiser. He'd have to make sure his threats stayed fresh in her mind. This wouldn't be the last time he paid her a midnight visit. Silently, he slipped back out the window to where Kayla was waiting.

"She won't say a word."

CHAPTER 20

Three weeks after Tyndall's visit, Maleen sat on her mount ready to start the six-hour ride to the Equin Festival in Kelvia. She would be surrounded by the five men she'd come to depend on more than she would ever have expected. Noture sat on his graebig, his impatience showing in the way he shifted in his saddle and wrapped and unwrapped the reins around his hand.

They waited for the other men to say their goodbyes. Mattie, the physician's assistant, looked uncomfortable as she watched Tian check the straps to his graebig's saddle. It was the third time he had checked them.

"Why doesn't he ask if he can court her?" Maleen asked Cutter as they watched Mattie's hurt expression when he mounted without saying anything to her.

"Some warriors aren't made for marriage," Noture spoke up.

"Like you?" Cutter chuckled at him.

"Like me." Noture sighed. "Sure."

"She loves him. He's gotta know that." Maleen sighed. "And I know my brother well enough to be fairly confident he feels the same."

"None of our business," Noture reminded her.

"Yeah, yeah." Cutter smirked.

"I want to see him happy," Maleen said. "Mattie's a sweet woman. She's honorable. She'd—"

"Give you lots of nieces and nephews to teach." Cutter laughed.

Maleen shrugged. The thought had crossed her mind.

A hoot of laughter came from the stabling area. Javon swung Oblam high in the air before sitting him on the graebig. He had been wonderful to the boy over the past two months. Lesney had sent word that she'd be in the garrison as soon as it was deemed safe to travel with small children. Meanwhile, Javon had unofficially taken Oblam under his wing. He gave him lessons on using his voyancey, and on keeping quiet about what he read. He made sure he kept up his studies with the other children in the garrison classroom. And he brought him books that would point him in the direction of studying medicine, since that seemed to be where his interests were heading.

Maleen hoped Javon would choose to stay in the garrison perma-nently. The others were right when they said she needed a Grand Voyant, and Oblam wasn't old enough. She wouldn't ask him yet. For the time being, she still wanted Cutter and Noture with her in the Council meet-ings, even if it meant depending on Tyndall's voyant.

Asher kissed his wife, Denetra, one last time and mounted his beast.

"You'll keep him safe?" Denetra looked at Maleen.

"You know I will." Maleen grinned at her as Asher snorted behind her. "If he'd listen to me once in a while, it'd be easier."

Denetra gave a half smile and turned to walk away. She wasn't the easiest person to deal with, but at least she seemed to have accepted Asher's position.

"Phillip," Maleen nodded to him as he rode up beside them, preparing to leave. "No one is going to blame you if you don't come. Kelvia is not the safest place for you."

"I have to make things right. If that means risking Tyndall seeing me in Kelvia, so be it." As determined as he was, Maleen wasn't going to try to deter him any more than she already had over the past three weeks.

"We'll watch his back," Cutter said. "I'm the only one who gets to hit him."

Maleen had to hide a grin at the wink he gave her.

This was it. Maleen turned her graebig toward the gate. In front of her, Tian rode with Phillip. Behind her, Asher rode with several other warriors. To her left was Noture. Then, to her right, there was Cutter, her beloved. He was a tribute to the chief's family. A strong warrior, though still healing from his wounds.

Several of her elite warriors, who knew nothing of what was to happen, accompanied them only because they wished to participate in the Equin games in Kelvia. Some of them even brought their families. She had thought about forbidding it. But these warriors were on leave. They had a right to spend the holiday as they pleased. They only traveled together for the sake of numbers and, once they arrived at the festival, as a show of strength.

They made camp that night, far enough from the Kelvian garrison to not be accused of requesting early entry, but close enough to arrive before many of the other chiefs who had farther to travel.

"I'm taking the first watch," Noture said as he walked away from the campfire.

"Wake me for the second," Maleen called after him.

"Not happening." Asher sat down next to her.

Maleen groaned. A part of her wished they would just let her be Chief and a warrior, but she was the only one who could draw Lenet from hiding, and if the plan failed, she was the only one to challenge Tyndall with the Tamal. If they were ambushed before reaching Tyndall's stronghold, it would be difficult to point the blame to Lenet.

Maleen did not like being manipulated by Tyndall. This was his plan, and he was going to pull it off in a way that manipulated her into doing what he wanted. He was going to do it, however, whether she consented or not. Tyndall knew Maleen couldn't refuse. To refuse to cooperate would cause great harm to both Kelvia and Acora.

Knowing that Lenet was going to be in plain sight in the Kelvian garrison, a part of her wished they could behave more like Simotens. The Chief of Simot was reported to have had more than one adversary assassinated, and they were not always internal conflicts. That kind of behavior, however, was unacceptable for Acorans. An adversary had to be dealt with honorably, no matter who he was, or what he'd done. If she ever behaved in such a dishonorable manner, Asher, Lutin, and the outpost commanders could, and should, remove her from the Chief's seat.

***

1st Day, Equin 522
Central Garrison, Kelvia

The next morning, crowds were thick as they neared the Kelvian Central Garrison. In this crowd, it would be difficult to see someone draw a knife or blow a dart. As they passed one camp, two children ran after a ball in the road. At another roadside camp, two men had gotten an early start on the celebration and their drunken voices carried as they shouted vulgarities at one another. One man took a swing at the other and Tian had to pull up abruptly to prevent his graebig from stomping the man's head as he fell in the road. Feeling vulnerable each time they needed to stop, everyone was on edge by the time they arrived at the festival.

The festive atmosphere of the Equin celebration was apparent long before they reached the Kelvian garrison. Friendly tribes greeted each other with banter and mock punches. Rival tribes avoided one another for the sake of peace. Warriors intermingled with merchant caravans and other civilians, buying trinkets for loved ones and sampling foods from other places.

One performer twirled sticks with fire on the end while another performed pyrotechnics. Amid the flames he conjured, images of the explosion in Acora came to mind, but Maleen pushed them away.

As they drew nearer to the host garrison, there were more warriors from every tribe, but fewer civilians. This one time, the garrison's main gate stood open during the day. No challenge was issued from the watchtowers. Chiefs, warriors, merchants, and merrymakers all streamed in and out. It would be this way until nightfall on each of the next three days. Phillip wisely opted to stay out of the garrison, not wanting to make life more difficult for Maleen, and not wanting to risk defying Tyndall's order to stay out. He risked enough just entering Kelvia.

As Maleen entered the garrison, the others pulled back only enough to allow their chieftess the honor of riding in first. Coming with a full contingent of warriors was a show of strength every chief used every year, but as it was at the emergency Council, only two companions would be allowed into the main building to enjoy the hospitality of the host tribe. The others would compete here, in the courtyard, but would have to vacate the garrison by nightfall.

Kelvian stable hands took Maleen's mount, along with Noture's and Cutter's to the stables. Only those staying in the garrison could stable their graebigs there.

In the huge courtyard, rings had been set up for the staff and hand-to-hand tournaments. Her companions would miss not competing, but while there was any possibility of a confrontation with Lenet, they needed to make sure they were not worn down from a tournament.

Maleen stepped into the main building with Noture and Cutter.

"Welcome, Lady Maleen." Tyndall greeted his guests with Lenet and Tara standing by his side.

"Sir." She nodded to Tyndall and Tara. Maleen stiffened, seeing Lenet. He glared at Tara, and the girl shifted her weight and looked at the ground. If she was going to work at Tyndall's side, Tara needed to do a better job of hiding her emotions.

Maleen gave Lenet only a glance. He looked back at her, eyes filled with hate, unmatched by anything Maleen had ever seen. At the sight of him, the two men with her tensed.

"Why all the hard looks?" Lenet's arrogance chafed. To the credit of both men, neither Cutter nor Noture reacted. For the moment, Lenet was protected on account of being a member of the chief's family. "I hope you'll enjoy your stay." Lenet's smirk belied his words.

"I'm sure I'll be more comfortable than on my last visit." Maleen looked at Tyndall.

"Rundel was imprisoned for his crime," Tyndall assured her.

"Imprisoned? Rundel should have been hung from the gate by his toes," Noture muttered, as they followed a steward to prepared quarters.

Late that afternoon, Maleen stood watching the staff tournament.

She stood alone, deliberately giving an assassin the opportunity to strike. Knowing her men were nearby, and that both Javon and Oblam were reading the crowd, did little to calm her nerves. Why couldn't Tyndall have scheduled the first meeting for earlier in the day? Because they wanted it to look like this was any other festival. Chiefs and their heirs often competed in these tournaments. Maleen caught a glimpse of Tian through the crowd. He tapped his nose, then the back of his head, giving her the hand signal to look behind her. Before she could turn around, Maleen heard an insincere, sugary voice that made her skin crawl.

"I suppose since you were confirmed last month, you don't feel the need to demonstrate your strength?" Kayla drawled.

Maleen didn't look at her, resisting the urge to slap the false smile she knew Kayla would be wearing.

"My activities are my own business," Maleen replied, her outward calm giving no indication of how she genuinely felt about the woman standing behind her, though no doubt Kayla knew the extent of her unvoiced hostility.

"Where is that attractive husband of yours?"

"He's around." Maleen refused to be baited. To attack a member of the chief's family during a festival would not bode well for her support in the Council. "As are my brother and uncle."

"And I suppose the boy and that old giant of a man are about the grounds somewhere?" Her tone held a slight hint of a threat as Kayla pointed out that Maleen had been watched coming into the garrison, and those watching did not know who Javon was.

Not taking her eyes off the match, Maleen answered, "If I were you, I'd be more concerned about where your kin are than mine."

Kayla scoffed. "*My* cousin doesn't have the nerve to show his face in this garrison. Not that he's much safer outside."

"I was referring to Lenet and you know it." Maleen applauded the end of the round, which advanced one of her warriors into the finals. "After all, the first chance Lenet gets, he'll betray Tyndall." She looked back at the redheaded woman before moving off to congratulate him. "And you."

As Maleen merged into the crowd, someone grabbed her arm, making her jump. Asher. She breathed a sigh of relief.

"You're standing awfully close to a known enemy." He leaned close to her ear.

"A knife in the back from Kayla? I don't think so." Maleen let him lead her to a less crowded area. "With all these people around, only a trained assassin would dare. I'm counting on all of you to spot him before I do." Maleen paused for a moment. "There are bigger threats than Kayla. I saw Jewel in the crowd earlier."

"Did she see you?" Asher asked, looking around quickly.

"She made sure I knew she did, but Oblam said he only sensed hate, not a murderous intent."

"Maybe she doesn't know what's going to happen at the meeting tonight."

"Lenet doesn't know we know Tyndall's going to name him. Maybe he didn't tell her so she wouldn't give it away to Oblam or any other voyant."

"Didn't Commander Hathon promise you that she'd be arrested?" Asher asked. "Tyndall may have one less Kelvian on his side than he thought."

"She tinted her hair and is growing it out. Without vestments, no one in the Central Garrison is likely to recognize her."

"Tyree would," he reminded her. "And he can't be the only one from the Western Garrison here and still loyal to Tyndall."

"He may be." Maleen sighed, hoping she hadn't misjudged Tyree. "Jewel made sure I saw the marriage armlet she wore. It had Tyndall's family crest that Lenet still wears."

"So, she got him after all." Asher laughed.

"Her armlet is nothing but a yoke," Maleen said. "She has no hope of power on her own. She puts up with his mistreatment so she can be somebody. Lenet wouldn't know how to love. Not for real."

"Those two deserve each other," Asher said, still chuckling.

Maleen saw nothing humorous. If Lenet *did* marry Jewel, and he *did* win the chief heir position, there would be no diplomatic way to have the woman extradited for her crimes against Acora.

CHAPTER 21

The first afternoon of the festival went by without incident. That evening Maleen caught another glimpse of Jewel as they entered the dining hall where a banquet had been prepared for those staying in the garrison. Though Jewel hadn't entered the competition, she carried a staff with her. Maleen wondered if Jewel was trying to make her nervous, to remind her of what she was capable of.

When Maleen reported Jewel's presence to Commander Hathon, he guaranteed her he would instruct his men to keep an eye out. Oblam had been close enough to confirm he meant what he said, but Jewel was smart enough not to be spotted by Hathon's men, at least not until Lenet's position was official. As Maleen entered the banquet hall, despite the woman outside, Maleen knew she was safe. In this room, though some of those present had opposed her the previous month, none would resort to murder—except Lenet. If he did it here, he'd make it look like an accident. She'd never see it coming no matter how vigilant she was.

After the guests were seated, Tyndall entered with his escorts. Tara walked on one side, and slightly behind Tyndall. Lenet walked on the other, directly next to him, wordlessly declaring himself equal to his chief. Lenet's imposing figure made Tara look even smaller, but Maleen understood firsthand what the girl could do. After greeting his guests, Tyndall approached the only three empty seats in the hall, directly across from Maleen.

Maleen's nerves were already on edge and now she had to sit and eat, looking into the face of her enemy. She wondered if the steward who'd seated them had something against her—or worked for someone who did—arranging the seating on purpose.

Shifting uncomfortably, Tara attempted small talk. "We missed you in the staff tournament today. I thought for sure you'd enter"

"I was on the sidelines, watching the competitions. I'll be in the archery contest tomorrow afternoon." Maleen wouldn't take her feelings about Lenet out on his tribesman. "But I chose not to compete in the staff tournament."

"After your shoulder injury, you can still shoot straight?" Lenet's snide remark earned him a glare from Tyndall.

"We'll see tomorrow," Maleen said. Entering the contest was an automatic response, but she hadn't had the time to test her skills over the past few weeks.

"Too bad about the staff tournament. Tara nearly made it to the semifinals," Lenet pointed out.

"I saw," Maleen said. "It took one of my best warriors to eliminate her." *Why won't he just sit quietly and let the rest of us do the same?*

"Too many men hesitate because I'm female," Tara added.

Anyone who did not know Lenet would have thought this to be normal dinner conversation. It rattled Maleen's already frayed nerves, and Lenet seemed to know it.

"Now if Tara would learn to use a full-size staff, then she'd have greater reach and would likely do much better," Lenet added.

"When you learn to use a staff a foot taller than you, then you can tell me how to fight." Tara bristled under his criticism.

"I'm just saying you've compensated for your small stature, instead of overcoming it. With the right training, you may even give Maleen here a good fight. *If* she's not afraid to compete next year."

"My lack of participation bothers you?" Maleen's rising temper was evident in her voice.

Cutter put a hand on her arm. The look Tyndall gave her across the table sent the same message. *Pull it together.*

"If you gave as good a showing as I'd expect you to, I could have faced off with *you* in the semifinals instead of some underaged welp." He spoke as if it were the most natural thing in the world. "We could have settled everything in a single match."

"I have better things to do than get my skull bashed in." Maleen threw her napkin on her plate, stood up, and stormed out.

As she left the hall, she heard Lenet raise his voice, loud enough for the entire hall to hear, "You see how she insults us, even in our own home? Emotional as always."

***

"That was not wise," Noture warned her later. "It made you look emotional and did nothing for your support. I don't think I've seen you that short-tempered in an awfully long time."

Maleen knew there had to be a balance between concealing her emotions, as she had been taught by Rabe, and letting them show to the point of seeming emotional, but she couldn't find it.

"I couldn't sit near that man another minute." Maleen shook her head. Though it sometimes took significant effort, she usually kept her temper under control. Under the circumstances, however, she couldn't seem to think straight where Lenet was concerned. "To sit there, talking about the competitions like...like...like everything that happened because of him was nothing... I couldn't do it."

They were on the way to the meeting hall for the first session of the Chiefs' Council. Not for the first time, Maleen wondered if she had made the right choice of advisors. As badly as she wanted both Noture and Cutter with her, she needed to know what each of the chiefs was feeling. She also needed to know if her outburst had affected what little support she had.

Being slightly anxious all afternoon had turned to major apprehension since supper. It wasn't limited to internal emotions, either. While she was jumpy, short-tempered, and couldn't concentrate, she also had a headache and stomach pains that wouldn't go away. A part of her was thankful she could blame her emotional response to the situation on a physical ailment. Even if she didn't know what that ailment was.

As chiefs and their companions gathered in Tyndall's great hall, each nodded to one another. While receiving hard looks from several other chiefs, Bontel, who'd been one of Maleen's supporters, stopped to speak with her.

"You should have broken a plate over his head." He'd been near enough at supper to have heard the entire exchange.

"Oh, yes." Maleen smiled at him. "It may have made *me* feel better but would have looked even worse than my little temper tantrum."

"Everyone knows he deserves it, and worse," Bontel said. "They're just afraid to cross Tyndall by banning him from this hall." He sighed. "But if Lenet crosses into Timend again, after his pardon, *I* will make a charge against Tyndall. I trust I'll have your support?"

Maleen nodded, then added thoughtfully, "But not until others have decided whether to support you or not. I wouldn't want anyone to choose not to support you because they don't want to agree with me."

"I hadn't considered that. Wise thought. Thank you." Bontel nodded to her.

As Bontel went to take his seat with his wife and Grand Voyant, Maleen resisted the urge to inform him that Tyndall wasn't as committed to his nephew as he'd made everyone believe. At least she hoped not. There was still a chance that Tyndall wasn't to be trusted.

Not being experienced enough to sort through the emotions of the large crowd, and not being well acquainted with Tyndall, Oblam would have had to get close to the Kelvian chief to read him. He had not been able to. And anyone with any deceit on their mind was smart enough to avoid a voyant as experienced as Javon. Though Javon wore no scarf and they'd told no one he was a voyant, Kayla certainly could have informed Tyndall. But Maleen trusted Tara and believed she would inform her if Tyndall were deceitful.

Noture had warned her against trusting so easily. He'd said that saving her life from Rundel, in no way indicated that Tara and Tyree were trustworthy. Javon had concurred with Noture, though he'd originally earned her trust the same way. Maleen, however, continued to insist Tara could be trusted.

The hall soon filled up. This time all ten chiefs sat at the large round table. Chief Ricmond looked a little pale, but he sat at the table with his son behind him. Apparently, he really had been ill, not avoiding the emergency Council. In addition to those who had been at the emergency Council, there was Chief Tolly of Gantin wearing a yellow-trimmed vest, Majet of Barnet in teal, Braven of Randor in brown, and the one who had traveled the farthest, but looked none the worse for wear, Zan of Coland in a black-trimmed vest. Each chief had his two companions behind him, most heirs or Grand Voyants, some wives; all advisors. Maleen noted the fact that she was the only chief present without a Grand Voyant as one of her companions. She would rectify it the following year. It was a poor decision to depend on another chief's Grand Voyant. Particularly since Tara didn't seem inclined to even look in her direction. When everyone had arrived, Tyndall stood up.

"Welcome to my home, gentlemen, Lady Maleen. I would like to call this Council meeting for Equin, Year 522 to order. I trust you all received the message regarding what was decided at the emergency Council meeting two months ago. To those of you who did not attend, I'd like to introduce Lady Maleen of Acora."

Maleen nodded to the chiefs, wondering if she should stand.

Chief Braven didn't give her the chance. "You should have waited. We all should have been present."

Garrett snorted. "If you couldn't be bothered to show when an emergency was declared, that is your own fault. I for one do not care to rehash that meeting."

"Agreed," Tyndall said. "Perhaps we were too hasty, but it is done. On a related note, as the first order of business at this meeting, I wish to announce I have chosen a chief heir." He took a deep breath. "You all know my son died several years ago. His mother bore no other children. I have remarried a younger woman, but I'm afraid it is too late to father another child, much less wait for him to grow up. I have only two living relatives. My brother Fanton's children." Maleen wasn't surprised he didn't count Phillip. "It is Fanton's son, Lenet, whom I name my chief heir. I ask now, as is our tradition, that you will confirm him."

"Your nephew is a known outlaw!" Bontel shouted in dismay before Maleen had time to respond.

"Did you not receive my notice that I have issued him a pardon?" Tyndall said. "I sent it three weeks ago."

"I did," Bontel said, glancing at Maleen and back to Tyndall. "That you pardon him is your business as long as he stays in Kelvia, but to make him Chief?"

"It is my choice," Tyndall said calmly, giving no indication of his true intent.

"It is an unacceptable choice." Maleen stood, her voice strong and clear, showing no hint of the storm of anxiety which coursed through her. "This man is responsible for two massacres in Acora and innumerable other crimes, often ending in someone's death."

"That depends on whose version of events you believe." Lenet rose slowly. His voice held no arrogance or hate, his volume only loud enough to be heard clearly throughout the room. He would try to win them over with diplomacy.

"Can't they see through his ruse?" Cutter whispered behind her.

"The voyants will," Noture assured him.

Maleen wondered how Lenet had overlooked that detail.

"I have been informed that some of you have heard from the opposition. I ask you to hear the other side of the story before passing judgment. You would not convict a man without giving him the chance to speak. I only ask for the same opportunity before you deny my right to be named Heir." He waited until the majority of the chiefs gave their consent. "The so-called massacre was committed by a member of my garrison. She was furious about the murder of my father and infiltration of our Western Province. When I went to Acora to retrieve her, to try her as a Kelvian, the woman who, at the time, I thought had killed my father, not only refused to allow it, but she ordered her men to attack my warriors. Knowing this woman as I do, I had made sure to bring enough warriors with me to force her hand. Instead of capitulating when she was outnumbered, however, she and a few others abandoned their post and fled."

Lenet left out the Tamal challenge. Even if he accused her of making the challenge, for him to have accepted it, without being a chief, would have damaged his support. "My men and I fought our way out of the Acoran stronghold and pursued. Remember, I thought this woman had killed my father in Kelvia. Now she had attacked my men when I came to her under a Banner of Diplomacy. While in Acora, I received word that this female had snuck in here and deceived my uncle, even convincing him that one of his loyal officers had betrayed him. When I was declared an outlaw because of her lies, I did what I had to do in order to survive. Even my own sister abandoned me."

"That tribesmen you had come to retrieve?" Maleen asked, her tone dark. "The one you say you intended to try for the massacre? Why does she wear a marriage armlet with your family crest?" Maleen's accusation sent a murmur among the Council.

"You are mistaken," Lenet said, with a much calmer demeanor than Maleen displayed, smart enough not to demonstrate open hostility to her in this room. "I have not seen Jewel since your garrison nearly three months ago. If she escaped, it is on you and those who abandoned your garrison with you."

"He is telling you the truth. He has not seen her." Tara's voice said one thing while her face clearly indicated the opposite. Maleen narrowed her eyes at the girl. She had seen the armlet herself. Why would Tara lie to her in front of the Council? Was she *that* frightened of Lenet?

Addressing the Council once again, Lenet said, "You've heard both sides. Ask your Grand Voyants. Which version of the story is true? Search my emotions—search hers." He sat down abruptly. Maleen slowly sank into her chair, appalled at the bold-faced lies Lenet hoped to pass off with so many voyants in the room. The look Tara gave her across the room was full of remorse. She clearly had not wanted to speak for Lenet. The girl was petrified.

Grand Voyants and chiefs conversed. It was soon apparent the hall was split. "He's paid the voyants," Noture whispered, leaning forward so only Maleen could hear, "or threatened them. Tara included."

"How much were you paid, voyant?" Maleen addressed the Grand Voyant of one of the chiefs who had not attended the emergency

Council. Her accusation sent a wave of alarm through the room. "How much has this murderer paid you to lie to your chief?" she said, standing again. "A month and a half ago, when I told half of you the details of what happened in Acora, there were five voyants in the room, all of whom are here again. Not one of them accused me of deceit. *Now*"— she slammed her fist on the table— "*how much have you been paid*?" Maleen did not yell, often. She found it was often ineffective, but after hearing Lenet's lies, putting the blame on her, she was quickly losing her temper.

"Enough!" Tyndall hit the table. "Never before has this Council interfered in a Chief Heir issue. Confirmation is simply a formality and a tradition."

"Never interfered?" Maleen questioned, a little quieter. *Does Tyndall honestly intend to go through with this?* Surely, he could tell Tara only lied because she was frightened of Lenet. If he *had* believed the lies, the Tamal match would be the only solution to allowing Lenet to gain control of Kelvia. "Never before, except when two of you opposed me and voted to keep me from this seat merely because I'm female. From your attitudes today, I can see there would have been more if you could have been bothered to attend."

"From your outburst today, I can see we were correct," Wan, Chief of Simot remarked.

"My emotional state is not in question here! What is in question is whether or not this predator is worthy of the chief's seat." How could they so blatantly accuse her of being emotional? It wasn't as if men didn't lose their tempers and act emotionally. They just wouldn't admit it.

"Very well," Chief Majet of Barnet said. "We have heard the arguments. We will take a vote."

Maleen had done the math. The four chiefs who had not been at the previous meeting appeared to believe Lenet's lies. And Maleen didn't think there was any way Wan would vote against Lenet, because it would mean supporting her. In fact, Bontel was the only one she knew for certain would vote with her to keep Lenet from being confirmed.

"No!" Maleen yelled. "I claim the right of Tamal to prevent Tyndall from making this man his heir!"

Lenet knocked his chair over as he jumped up. "You have no right!" he yelled, his hatred no longer masked.

"I have every right!" She matched his volume and his fierce look. "So much more than you did the first time you tried to kill me."

"You surely don't mean to claim Tamal against a man twice your age?" Chief Tolly spoke up, his eyes narrowed, and brows pinched together.

"If that is the only way to keep this man from the chief's seat, then so be it." Her face burned and her heart pounded.

"Perhaps it is because you never had the benefit of being mentored by your predecessor, and as this is only your first Council perhaps you are not aware of the way we handle matters of such importance," Chief Wan said harshly. "The Tamal is reserved for only the most extreme circumstances. It has never been used in a chief heir issue. Nor should it."

"Perhaps *you* do not understand what kind of a threat this man poses if he takes leadership of the largest tribe and the largest fighting force on the continent. I know my rights." Maleen stood straighter as she repeated, "I claim the right of Tamal to prevent Tyndall from making this known murderer his heir."

"What have you to say about this, son of Rabe?" Wan addressed Cutter.

"Do not look to him!" Bontel yelled before either Cutter or Maleen could respond. "He is *not* a chief."

Wan did not turn his piercing gaze away from Cutter.

"I think," Cutter answered slowly, without standing up, "you've as much right to ask me that as Maleen would have to ask your wife why you're a graebig's backside. *She* is Chief of Acora. Address her accordingly."

Wan blustered at such an insult. "Are you aware of how this appears, *Lady* Maleen?" he spat out. "You hate this man. You claim he killed your warriors—including your father and father-in-law. You claim he tried to kill you, twice. It looks to me to be nothing more than your personal vengeance. You can't take it out on him, so you take it out on his kinsman."

To the rest of the Council, he said, "Everyone in this room knows she is the strongest staff fighter on this Council and among most, perhaps all, of our heirs. It is certainly not the image we want to give her at the start of her administration. If we allow her to wield that strength now, what's to stop her from doing it every time she is on the losing side of a debate? To call a man who is over fifty years old into the ring is not in the spirit of the Tamal."

"She doesn't need to fight an old man," Lenet called over the uproar the comment caused. "As his chief heir, I hold the right to fight his battle. And I'm one heir she *cannot* defeat."

Maleen's self-assurance plummeted. This was one issue they hadn't anticipated. She could not defeat Lenet in the ring, even if it were a fair fight this time. He'd taken first place in the tournament earlier in the day. She was not *that* good. Fear buzzed through her as she wondered if Tyndall had planned for it to work out this way.

"You are not Heir yet!" Bontel yelled. "You cannot take the match."

"You cannot ask a fifty-year-old man to fight against a young garrison-trained warrior with the benefit of training with two different tribes, and who fights only for vengeance and spite," Lenet yelled. "Female or not, I have seen what she is capable of!" Not being a chief, he shouldn't have had a voice in this room, much less a raised voice to a chief, but no one pointed out that fact.

As the arguments went around the room, Maleen's head began to swim. Anxiety gripped her chest and held tight. The noise of yelling chiefs created pressure on her ears, shooting pain through her temples to the backs of her eyes. Her stomach turned, uncomfortably. *This anxiety will not get the best of me.* Maleen fought for control.

Tyndall stood up, hands raised. "This argument is pointless. I will not have another fight my battles for me so long as I can hold a staff. You worry about my age, perhaps I have slowed a little, but I'm as strong as I ever was. I will fight the Tamal for the right to name my nephew Chief Heir. No vote! Just the Tamal!"

As Tyndall made his declaration, Maleen let out a breath. If Tyndall refused to let Lenet fight, it reassured her that Tyndall was, in fact, on her side.

"No, Uncle. Don't let this female—"

"You will be quiet," Tyndall ordered Lenet.

"It must be a fair match," one of Lenet's supporters spoke up. "Hand-to-hand. No staffs. Her youthful speed versus his masculine strength."

Maleen's confidence began to wane once more. She could beat Tyndall with a staff, there were few men she couldn't; but middle-aged or not, he was a strong man, trained to use that strength. Maleen had trained hand-to-hand. Her technique was close to flawless, but due to her lack of physical strength, it was far from her strong suit. The Council, however, reached a consensus, with only Bontel objecting. If Maleen agreed to hand-to-hand, they would allow the match. The match would determine whether Lenet was eligible for the chief's seat. Maleen had no choice but to agree. The only other option was a vote Lenet would win.

As the Council dispersed for the night, Lenet gave a long ugly look at Maleen. "Tread carefully, Acoran," he said, too quietly for anyone else to hear the implied threat, and he turned to leave the hall.

As Tyndall and Tara passed her on their way out of the room, Tara said softly, "I'll explain later." Then she followed Tyndall out.

***

"Tomorrow, whatever the outcome, this will all be over." Maleen sat between Cutter and Oblam that night at their fire, still feeling ill, but not letting on to anyone else. Oblam knew it. Maleen could tell by the way he kept looking at her.

Cutter and Noture both preferred that she stay within the garrison walls, but it was more likely for an assassin to come out of hiding among the campsites. Out here, she also had the benefit of two trusted voyants, both of whom she knew had not been paid or threatened.

"Why do you have to fight?" Oblam had matured in the past months, but his uncomplicated innocence still couldn't make sense of the violence around him.

"To keep Lenet from being Chief Heir in Kelvia."

"Why can't the chiefs see what kind of man he is?"

"We think he paid some of the Grand Voyants," Cutter said sadly. "To think that even one could be bribed is impossible, yet he got to at least four of them, with currency or with threats. The chiefs depend on them to determine the truth. Even Tara lied in the Council hall."

"Whatever reason the voyants lied, to those chiefs Maleen is the aggressor, not Lenet," Noture pointed out. "Some of the other chiefs will support Lenet, simply because an 'emotional female' opposes him."

"If I lose tomorrow," Maleen said to Tian, "you and Asher need to head back to Acora as quickly as possible. You have to secure the border."

"You want us to leave you here?" Tian's jaw dropped. "Lenet will want to take his anger out on you whether he's confirmed as Heir or not."

"Cutter and Noture will stay with me. It's more important that our warriors know to fortify the garrison and the outposts along the border. I've told Asher to recall those on leave for the festival. We need every available man ready for what will come from Kelvia when Lenet has Tyndall assassinated." She said *when* not *if*.

"It's more important we keep our chief safe," Tian argued.

"You cannot allow your protectiveness for your sister to deter you from your duty as an Acoran warrior," Javon advised. "I'll be staying as well."

"We have a chain of command for a reason." Noture nodded. "Your job is to follow orders. It's Asher's job to question her wisdom, not yours. She *has* issued an order, not asked for advice. You want to question it, go through Asher."

Tian nodded solemnly. Maleen was grateful Javon's and Noture's reprimand had hit the mark. Arguing with her brother was the last thing she wanted to do. But he was one of the few who could get away with arguing with her, so long as it was only this small group who heard it.

Asher came and sat by the fire, breaking the solemn mood. "Okay, Physician, I'll take you up on that compress you offered."

Phillip laughed at him as he reached into his bag.

"What happened?" Maleen asked.

"Nothing," Asher said. But his black eye and the stiffness in his movements betrayed him.

"There was some talk," Tian said.

Asher shot him a look, which Tian ignored.

"Had something to do with the easiest way for a woman to gain a position of power." He stared at the ground and jerked a finger in Asher's direction. "This bozo jumped in rather than let me defend my own sister."

"He'd have squashed you," Asher said.

Maleen stared at the flames. Not exactly a conversation she cared to have in front of Oblam. "Did you win?" She glanced at Asher.

"You have any doubt?" He chuckled.

Phillip used some herbs to make a poultice. With others he made a soothing drink, handing them both to Asher.

"I still have some thessel if you need it," Oblam reported, reaching for his pouch.

"Hold on to it," Phillip said.

Maleen nodded. It was more important that Oblam keep his thessel leaves for defense than for medicine that wasn't completely necessary.

"I need to get to sleep," Maleen stood, not surprised when Cutter and Noture joined her. Of course, they weren't even going to leave her alone long enough for the two-hundred-yard walk back to the garrison gate.

Once inside the building, Noture passed his own room to walk them to theirs. When they went inside, he continued down the hall.

"You know he's going to be pacing out there all night," Cutter said as he shut the door.

"I suppose that should be reassuring," Maleen said as footsteps passed the door going the other way. "Except that I'd rather he be well-rested in the morning."

Cutter took her hand and pulled her to sit next to her on the bed. "It's because he cares."

"I know." She leaned against him. "I'm not going to be able to sleep well, either."

"You're not feeling well." He stroked her hair, murmuring in her ear.

"I'm fine."

"Didn't we agree to be honest about what's going on? And take care of each other?"

Maleen didn't say anything for a moment. Footsteps passed the door again. "I've been having dizzy spells. I don't know what's causing it. Probably just the elevation."

"You didn't have issues with the elevation in the Border Mountains. Did you have problems when you were here last?"

Maleen hesitated.

"Should I ask Javon to question you?" He lifted her chin to make her look at him.

"No. I've never had elevation issues before."

"Have you talked to Phillip?" He still held her chin and stroked her cheek with his thumb.

"No," she admitted.

"So, you plan to get in the ring tomorrow, having dizzy spells, and you haven't talked to a physician? Have I got my facts right?"

Most of them. Maleen nodded. She wouldn't share the extent of how poorly she felt. Supper hadn't settled right, but she didn't want him to worry.

Footsteps sounded again. Glad for the distraction, Maleen went to the door. "Would you get some sleep?"

Noture glared at her. "Cutter still isn't ready for a fight."

"The door bolts from the inside, and we have no window," she said, wondering if Tyndall had assigned them an interior room on purpose. "For anyone to get in, they'd be making plenty of noise to wake you."

Noture said nothing but gave her a sly grin. "What's wrong? Hard to act married when your favorite uncle might overhear?"

Maleen's cheeks grew hot. "Good night." She shut the door hard and slid the bolt. Footsteps faded, and the door next to them opened and closed.

"Look what the steward brought," Cutter pointed to the tray on the table. Two pastries sat there. "When you left before dessert, he offered to bring some. I told him the berry ones were your favorite."

"How can you remember all the little details like that?" She smiled and brought the tray to the bed.

"It's my job to remember." He smiled and picked up the berry one.

He hated berries. Instead of taking a bite, he held it up to her mouth, dabbing a little of the cream on her lips. "When was the last time we were able to sit down and enjoy a quiet treat?"

"I don't know." She grinned, picking up the pudding-filled one and holding it to him. "Probably when we ate a piece of wedding cake in our quarters."

"I don't remember eating that cake." He licked the pudding off and scooted closer to her. "I remember it being there, but I think we had better things to indulge in rather than sweets."

"I thought our indulgence was better than the cake." She took a large bite of the pastry and set the tray aside.

"I know it was." Cutter surged forward, bringing a surprised giggle from her as she fell back on the bed, the weight of him both reassuring and intoxicating.

CHAPTER 22

The next morning, Maleen woke from a nightmare with the world spinning around her. She sat up cautiously.

Cutter's hand gently brushed her shoulder. "Another dizzy spell? I wish you'd talk to Phillip about it."

"After the Tamal." She leaned over to kiss him. "I promise."

"If you're ill, you shouldn't be in the ring," Cutter insisted as they climbed out of bed.

"I'm fine. Stop worrying."

"Tyndall isn't that old, you know," Cutter said as they dressed. "About the same age my father was, and he could still put a warrior in his place when the occasion called for it. And about the same age as Javon. He's not even garrison-trained, yet we've seen what he can still do." He put his arms around her. "I'm worried about you."

"No one else can do this. Everyone knows it's a bad idea to give Lenet a chance at the chief's seat."

"I don't think there's a man in that room who supports Lenet because they think he's right. Every other chief is afraid to challenge Kelvia, or they plain refuse to support you. The lying voyants are just an excuse."

"I've got the best chance of beating Tyndall. I'm the youngest and the fastest. You wouldn't want Garret in there fighting with such an important outcome on the line."

"Garret would have his son fight."

"Well, I don't have a chief heir yet, and I won't be choosing one for some time. Besides, I'm younger and faster than Garret's son."

"But hand-to-hand?" Cutter asked. "I know you're tough enough to take some hard hits, but you can't hit hard enough to be effective against a man his size, with his training. There is a limit to how many hits you *can* take." He held her close, kissing her neck.

"Are you trying to talk me out of this?" She slipped away from his embrace.

"No. I just have this foreboding. I've always been honest with you. You wouldn't want me to stop now?"

"Of course not." She leaned in close to him again, not wanting to be anywhere else.

"So, here's what I really think. I want you to ask the Council for an exception. Ask them to allow me or even Noture to take the match for you." He held up a hand before she could interrupt. "I know you can't do that. But it's what I *want*."

"And any request for a postponement due to illness will be met with suspicion, even by those who might otherwise have supported me."

"I know." He kissed her palm.

"If I win, Lenet will never be eligible for the chief's seat again. Even if Tyndall dies with no heir. If I don't fight, we forfeit, and Tyndall makes Lenet his heir. Lenet will have him killed within days. He'll invade Acora shortly after that. Same consequences if I fight and lose—only then I'll have to drink some of Phillip's thessel-dosed fentel and sleep off the headache for two days." She smiled and leaned forward to kiss Cutter.

He pulled back. "Don't make light of this. Not even Tyndall thought it would go this far. We were all so sure Lenet would make a move as soon as you challenged last night, or even before."

"Think Tyndall will throw the match?" she asked as she pulled her boots on.

"No. He knows you could never accept the victory. Every voyant in the room would know his intent before he did it." He paused. "They would have known his intent as soon as he refused to allow Lenet to take the match for him. As is, they've got to suspect there's something you and he aren't telling them."

"I suppose we can still hope Lenet will strike before breakfast." Maleen wound her hair into a tight braid.

"Oh, not before I've eaten, please," groaned Cutter playfully, reaching for her again. "I need my energy to kick Lenet's tail if he tries to interfere with the match."

***

Maleen felt worse after breakfast than when she'd woken up. She had kept it light, enough for energy but not enough to slow her down. Her stomach objected to even that. Both Cutter and Noture were with her in the arena, set aside for important matches such as this one. In the center of the arena was the ring, around it were rows of seats, each one elevated slightly higher than the one in front of it, ensuring that, even from the back row, spectators could see what was happening.

"My uncle offers that you invite your whole party into the arena." Kayla sneered, approaching Maleen confidently as she tied the leather shin guards in place. "Let your family in to see your humiliation." Kayla walked away with an inviting smile in Cutter's direction, her demeanor unchanged when her flirting was disregarded.

"Someone please remind me why I can't slap her." Maleen watched Kayla stride away.

"Chief Tyndall's family, his garrison, we want to end the feud. Any of this sounding familiar?" Noture said, knocking his knuckles on Maleen's head.

It wasn't jealousy that prompted Maleen to consider violence against the red-headed beauty. Cutter would never even give Kayla a second look. It was the arrogant, prideful way Kayla went about trying to get his attention. That, and Kayla did it to get under her skin.

"I'll go invite your brothers, Javon, and Asher in." Cutter gave her a quick kiss. "Don't start without me." She watched him disappear through the gathering throng.

"It seems my family members are not the only ones invited to witness my humiliation," Maleen commented on the growing crowd, most of them in commoner's clothing. The arena would hold close to three hundred people, and it was quickly filling up.

"Keep your eyes open," Noture said, tying the laces on her bracers securely. "This is Lenet's last chance to stop this match."

"He's seen me train hand-to-hand. He may not feel as though he has to," Maleen said quietly, her nerves threatening to show again. If Lenet was confident in Tyndall's ability to win, he may allow the match. If she lost, he would be Chief Heir. If the match didn't happen because of an attack on one of the combatants, then another chief could still make a challenge. And Bontel probably would. "If I lose…"

"If you're not in a condition to do it, I'll make sure Asher and Tian follow your orders," Noture promised. "Tyndall knows your weak point," he coached, tapping her right shoulder, which still gave her problems, but not enough to affect her performance unless she was careless enough to let it get hit. "Keep your guard up. He's not as quick as you, but he won't need as many good shots to do a lot of damage."

Maleen nodded. She knew these details, but Noture was doing the job she'd given him when she made him an advisor. Noture was, quite possibly, the strongest warrior in Acora. He'd taken first place in the Equin Games' staff tournament two years in a row, proving he was amongst the strongest warriors not just in his tribe, but across Chalent. He'd stopped competing, but if he had slowed down since then, it wasn't enough for anyone to notice. His coaching had benefited her before. Maleen wouldn't ignore it now.

"If the worst happens…" She stared at the ground for a second.

"Asher won't have any resistance." Noture understood what Maleen could not say.

"All the same, I put it in writing. I gave it to Javon. I didn't want Cutter to find it and worry more than he already does." Maleen cleared her throat. She'd tried to convince herself Tyndall was honest, and that an assassin would be spotted before he could strike, but the fear of dying in this ring wouldn't leave her. "Have you seen Tyndall fight?"

"Not recently." Noture shook his head. "The last time I faced him in the Equin games was more than ten years ago. He practically took my head off with a right hook."

"Okay, watch out for the right hook, got it." Maleen stretched her legs. She would need to use her nimble speed if she were to have any chance. "I suppose I should dance around him until he gets tired?"

"Don't joke," Noture said, seriously. "This isn't a random match to show off."

"I know what it is," Maleen said resolutely. She tried not to allow Noture to see her anxiety. He'd be the first person to try to call off the match if he knew she was ill.

It wasn't long before Maleen spotted Oblam leading Asher, Tian, and Javon. The men's eyes scanned every corner of the crowd. They came to the edge of the ring where seats had been reserved for them.

"Phillip chose to stay out of the garrison," Asher informed her. "He sends his best wishes but won't risk Tyndall's wrath."

Maleen nodded. Tyndall had warned him once. The next time Tyndall saw Phillip in Kelvia, much less the garrison, he could charge him with treason. With Lenet in the mix, staying out of the garrison was certainly the wisest choice.

Tian looked around. "Where's Cutter?"

"Didn't he come back in with you?" Maleen asked.

"We haven't seen him. We just got a message from Tyndall inviting us to witness the match."

Oblam sat with a look of concentration that turned to one of distress. Before anyone had time to question him, he jumped up.

"I'll find him." He tore out of the arena, ignoring the complaints of those he bumped on his way out.

"Javon?" Maleen asked.

"I don't know him well enough to find him in a crowd. Sorry."

"Competitors to the ring," someone called from the center of the arena.

"Find Cutter!" Maleen demanded of Tian as she climbed the two steps into the raised ring. From the time they were children, Cutter had always been there, watching her compete. When they were younger, it had been because she'd always competed with or against his cousin, but from the time she was fifteen, she couldn't think of any competition where Cutter had not been there to cheer for her, except when she'd been in the Kelvian garrison.

This match was so much more than a simple competition. She needed Cutter. He was her strength. She could not be Chief without him, and she could not beat Tyndall without him there, cheering her on.

Tian made no move to leave the arena. Maleen realized the choice she had put on him. He could leave to obey his chief or stay nearby to protect his sister. He'd chosen to stay. Maleen understood the choice. If, in fact, Tyndall did intend to make Lenet his heir, and had been misleading them the whole time, then there was a chance Tyndall was as willing as Lenet to fight dirty, whether the Council was present or not.

As people took their seats, Chief Garret of Fleat, the eldest among the chiefs, made the announcement. "The Tamal Challenge was developed, generations ago, to settle arguments between two tribes that could escalate to war. Instead of sending warriors from each side into battle, chiefs have used it, on occasion, for the purpose of saving lives.

"A challenge has been issued before the Council for the first time in nearly fifteen years. It has been issued because there is much discord among the chiefs about Chief Tyndall's choice of Heir. He has chosen his nephew. Chieftess Maleen claims no man pardoned from the crimes *she* accuses him of should ever be allowed the chief's seat. Therefore, she has issued a Tamal challenge. It has been decided they will use hand-to-hand combat. His masculine strength balanced with her youthful grace and speed." He turned to the combatants. "The terms have been set, are you ready?"

Maleen felt another dizzy spell coming on. Her breathing constricted a tiny bit as anxiety took hold. *Not now*, she thought, even while her voice answered affirmatively to the officiator.

"Take your stance." The pair stood in the center of the ring, right hands up, the back of their hands touching. Maleen had never been intimidated facing off with the largest and strongest among Acoran warriors. Tyndall wasn't nearly as large, and he was past the age when most warriors retired. Yet, Maleen couldn't get past the anxiety that was making even steady breathing difficult.

I've never had this much riding on a match before. She tried to convince herself that's all it was. That, and whatever the illness was. She took one last glance at the door. Still no Cutter. This was wrong. They couldn't start yet!

"You're shaking, Chieftess," Tyndall noted in a voice only she could hear.

"Don't worry about me," Maleen replied, willing her hand to stop trembling, lest illness be mistaken for fear. "Let's get this done."

Instead of the command to begin the match, a loud yell came from the back of the crowd. "What kind of treachery is this, Tyndall?" Someone in a blue vest pushed his way through the crowd, carrying a large burden on his shoulders. Several others helped him lower the dead man to the ground. Hearing the murmurs that started circulating and seeing the troubled look on Oblam's face as he reentered the arena, Maleen knew, before seeing his face, that the corpse was her husband.

CHAPTER 23

"He's been stabbed in the back." Chief Bontel stood from where he had been kneeling by Cutter's body. "In your garrison, as you are about to fight his wife in Tamal. So, I'll repeat the question. What kind of treachery is this?"

Maleen's knees went weak. She stood steady only by force of will. Stepping down from the raised ring, she slowly knelt by Cutter's side. Lifeless eyes stared back at her. Eyes that had been filled with so much love, eyes that only that morning were filled with concern. Cutter said he'd had a foreboding about the match. However, neither of them could have imagined *this* turn of events.

"Maleen has many enemies, including many in this arena. How dare you put the blame on my uncle?" Lenet's angry voice sounded far away. As did Bontel's angry reply.

"*Your uncle* would not be my first guess."

As she knelt there, Maleen could not tear her eyes away from the stilled face of her love. A drop fell on Cutter's purple-trimmed vest. She touched her face, surprised to find tears. She could not cry in front of these men! Her heart refused to listen to her head.

She took his limp hand in hers. A hand that would never hold her again. She stared into his face. Eyes that didn't see. A mouth that would never again kiss her, never tell her how much he loved her, never speak up in her defense against critics.

He would never again make love to her. There would be no children. No more arguments about her safety, and no more making up.

Lenet did this. The rock in the pit of her stomach had nothing to do with the illness, as the outrage took hold. He hadn't held the knife, but she had no doubt he'd ordered it. Perhaps it had been Jewel. She wasn't above stabbing a man in the back. Maleen had to put an end to this. She had to prevent Lenet from taking the Kelvian leadership, then she had to have both of them extradited, tried, and executed.

"We will consider continuing this ludicrous Tamal after you have had time to grieve." The officiator laid a hand on Maleen's shoulder.

"No!" She feared for every person close to her. If Lenet was willing to murder her husband, then Tian, Asher, and Noture were in danger. Knowing Lenet, even Oblam was not immune to his rage. And Lenet already wanted Phillip dead. Bringing them all to Kelvia had been a mistake. She had to put an end to this. Today.

She pushed herself back to her feet and turned to Tyndall, who'd come to stand behind her. "Oblam, come here." The arena was quiet as the boy obeyed. "Chief Tyndall, look my brother in the eye and tell me you had nothing to do with this."

Tyndall said somberly, "Lady Maleen, I had nothing to do with your husband's murder. I have heard of no plot against him, or you. We will investigate this. When his murderer is found, there *will* be an execution."

"Oblam, speak up so you can be heard," Maleen told her brother. If Tyndall was lying to her, she wanted everyone in the arena to know it.

"He's being open and honest, sister." Oblam's voice carried throughout the quiet arena.

Maleen dared a look at Lenet. There was no evidence of guilt on Lenet's face. Only a sadistic smirk, daring her to make an accusation when no one would question his alibi. To accuse Lenet here would serve no purpose. He'd been in this arena when the murder took place.

She wiped her eyes and breathed deeply. Cutter was dead, but she could not yet grieve. She was too angry to grieve. If she gave in to grief, emotions would overwhelm her. Love for her husband. Hatred for the one who was responsible. Confusion as to why this was all happening. Guilt over the fact that someone had done it because of their animosity toward her. Sorrow that Chief Rabe's line was gone. Then there was a desire for vengeance which surpassed everything else.

She focused every emotion into a burning desire to beat Tyndall. Then she could have vengeance on Lenet.

"We will continue the Tamal," Maleen said, her eyes now dry and her voice steady. "I will be a chief now, and a wife later." She dismissed Oblam and, climbing the steps again, she took her stance. "He's the only voyant I trust completely," Maleen said to Tyndall as he joined her. She stored away the pang of grief as people respectfully removed Cutter's body from the arena. Voices of the murmuring crowd ran together and Maleen saw everything through vision that came in waves.

"We don't need to do this today," Tyndall said gently. "No one will think less of you. Not a man here would dare call a grieving widow emotional."

"And give him the chance to strike again?" she whispered back. "Who will it be next time? My brothers?"

Tyndall nodded and took his stance.

As surprised as everyone else, the officiator called out the order to begin.

Tyndall looked worried. He warned her in a voice too low for anyone to hear, "Pull yourself together. Use that rage. If you lose this match, I *will* make him my heir. Unless it can be proven."

Maleen's vision continued to waver. Whatever this illness was, it was going to cost her the match if she didn't master it. Each opponent took careful swings, judging the speed and reach of the other. Maleen had greater speed, but Tyndall had a longer reach and greater strength. After several minutes, Maleen struck with a swift kick. Tyndall shook it off and took a swing. Back and forth they went, neither doing any serious damage.

If you lose, I will make him my heir. Tyndall's words stuck in Maleen's mind as she countered Tyndall's swings, avoiding most of them.

She struck and backed away. Punches to his body were a waste of time. She couldn't hit hard enough to have an effect. Her kicks seemed to slow him, but not by much.

Each time she raised her leg to kick, dizziness threatened to take her down faster than Tyndall's counterstrikes. Each wave of dizziness was followed by nausea. She needed a headshot he wasn't ready for. He wouldn't concede the match if he were conscious.

If you lose... Another dizzy spell caused Maleen to stumble. She couldn't help but think Tyndall held back. He should have laid her out when her guard was down.

At last, Maleen went in for a good kick, but it was too slow. Tyndall deflected her foot, and she came in for a cross with her right hand. It was uncontrolled and shoddy, but she was powerless to fix it. Tyndall easily avoided it. The momentum from the swing spun Maleen around with no help from Tyndall. Her swirling vision closed in and as she collapsed, Tyndall caught her on the way to the floor.

"Strike!" Lenet yelled. "Strike now! Why are you hesitating? End this."

"This woman is ill!" Tyndall called, cradling her head in his lap. "Get a physician."

"What are you doing?" Lenet's voice sounded like he was right next to the ring. "Too much rides on this match to go soft."

If you lose this match...

No. I have to get up! I can't lose! Too much rides... She couldn't keep her thoughts coherent. And she couldn't get up.

"Would you have it said your appointment to Chief Heir only happened because of a sick woman?" Tyndall scolded.

"Out of the way." Tian's voice was right next to Lenet's.

"You can't interfere with the match," Lenet growled.

"The match is over," Noture barked. "Chief Garret! Call it."

"What?" An old voice sounded confused. "Oh, yes of course. That's the match." He declined to declare Tyndall the winner.

Tyndall moved aside as Maleen felt herself lifted from the floor.

"I'm here, little sister." Tian's voice was soft and reassuring but only served as a reminder. Cutter was not there.

CHAPTER 24

Maleen woke up to whispers in the room around her.

"She's been having dizzy spells," Oblam said. "I should have told someone."

Maleen wanted to hug him, to reassure him, but she felt that if she moved, she would fall off the bed.

"She told you about them?" Noture asked.

"No, I sensed them," Oblam said sadly. "Cutter knew, and he was worried, but I thought if he didn't think it was serious enough to share with all of you, then I shouldn't either."

The instant Maleen dared to attempt to sit up she regretted it. "Oblam," she said, laying back on the pillow and closing her eyes, fighting off nausea. "You were correct to keep it to yourself. We thought it was just a small matter. I promised Cutter I would see Phillip about it after the match." She swallowed past the lump in her throat.

"How long have you been getting these spells?" a stranger asked. He wore a physician's jacket trimmed in green.

"About the time we got here. Headaches and nausea, too."

"Anything else?"

"Nightmares and anxiety, but I imagine that's because of knowing what Tyndall was going to do in the Chiefs' Council, and what I had to do to prevent it." Maleen draped an arm over her eyes, blocking the lamplight. Her head pounded and her stomach turned. She probably shouldn't have mentioned that she'd known what Tyndall was going to do, but the physician said nothing about it.

The physician nodded. "I'd like everyone to clear the room."

"Why?" Maleen peeked from under her arm and narrowed her eyes. Her mind was still foggy, but for the physician to demand the fighters leave the room was enough to make her suspicious. "Where is *my* physician?"

"I assure you, Madam, I am the most skilled physician you will find in Kelvia. That is why I work in the Central Garrison."

"No offense intended." Maleen tried to sit up again. "But my husband was murdered and there are very few people I trust. I want my own physician. He's somewhere in the camp outside the garrison. I'll not consent to be examined by any other."

Oblam moved slightly. Was the boy restless, or had he given the hand signal to indicate there was a malicious feeling in the room?

"Lady Maleen, perhaps you are unaware of the general sentiment around here about the son of Tamar? He abandoned his post in the Western Garrison. The garrison was left without a physician, and because of that, his sub-chief died while he aided an infiltrator." Quite likely the physician knew the identity of the infiltrator, but he declined to voice that detail.

"I'm well aware of his crimes in Kelvia, but I will see Phillip, even if I have to go outside to do it." She made a move to rise. If this Kelvian had that much animosity toward Phillip, there was no telling how much animosity he felt toward her. She would not trust him.

"Very well." The physician looked at Oblam. "Go and fetch him, boy. But his safety is on all of you."

When Javon nodded to him, Oblam went out to do as bidden.

"If the rest of you will not leave, I will give my diagnosis in front of all of you. Lady Maleen, it is too early to be sure, but I believe that perhaps your husband's family line did not die out with him this morning."

Had she heard correctly? Was her dead husband to be a father? If so, it would have had to be very recent. Less than a month. Too recent for any ill effects to start manifesting. No, she could not trust this man. She would not believe it until Phillip came.

"What?" Javon came to the bedside. "My late wife was—and my daughter *is*—a midwife. My mother is a village healer. When they've consulted with one another, I've had to overhear more about the female body than any man wants to know. I've never heard of pregnancy causing such a reaction in a healthy woman."

"Different women react differently." The physician waved his hand in dismissal. "Hormones can cause anxiety in any woman. Many have the stomach problems she complains of. To have dizziness and nightmares are not unheard of, nor are headaches."

"But it still wouldn't explain why she collapsed," Tian jumped in. "Tyndall never struck her hard enough."

"As I said, it's too soon to be sure, but with everything that has been going on, it's quite likely that her emotional state has affected her physically."

"I will see *my* physician." Maleen tried to get up again, believing it was her physical state that had been affecting her emotionally for the past couple of days.

"I have a question for you." Javon's booming voice caused the pounding in Maleen's head to increase. "Did you send the boy out because you know he is a voyant?"

"How dare you," the physician said, raising his voice. "You imply I would endanger my physician's status? To what end?"

"I meant no disrespect, Physician. I just had to ask the question." Javon sat back in his chair, arms crossed.

"I'm going to help Oblam find Phillip." Tian made a move toward the door.

Unable to clear the fog in her brain, Maleen wondered if Javon suspected the physician of malice or if he was testing him to see if it was known that the large fighter was also a voyant. Not wanting to think about anything, Maleen lay back down and closed her eyes.

***

Every time she woke up, Maleen felt like she was underwater. She felt pressure on her head and her chest, her breathing slightly constricted. Everything was muffled, and nothing made sense. Her vision came in waves. Even inanimate objects appeared to move.

***

"What are you doing here, Acoran sympathizer?"

Why did the physician have to yell?

"I was told she requested me." Phillip was here?

"I already gave my diagnosis."

"Knowing nothing about her health, how can you think you can jump to a conclusion like that?"

"I've been doing this longer than you've been alive."

Maleen wished they'd take their argument outside but didn't have the energy to speak up.

***

"Oblam warned me he was going to lie to you."

"That's exactly what I sensed, but I can't figure out his motives."

"Do you know what's wrong?"

"Not yet."

"Think he knows?"

"Can't ask him without revealing that Javon's a voyant."

What were they talking about? It wasn't making any sense. Nothing was making sense...

***

Noture sat in Maleen's room with Asher when Maleen awoke, looking around wildly. Seeing the panic in her eyes, Noture came to her side.

"What is it?" He sat on the edge of her bed.

"Father!" She grasped the front of his vest. "Father! They've killed Cutter!"

"Maleen, snap out of it, you're babbling." Noture gave her a gentle shake.

"No, Father. They've plotted to destroy us. You have to claim the right of a father. You have to avenge your son-in-law. You have to do it, Father!" She laid her head on Noture's shoulder and wept. Noture looked helplessly at Asher. He would have to wait out the hallucinations.

"She's out of her mind." Asher shook his head. "She looks at you but sees Sonley."

Maleen reached out to Asher. "Rabe! You can do it. Claim the right of both Chief and father. You can make sure Fanton doesn't get away with this!"

Phillip and Oblam entered the room as she made her impassioned plea.

"She's gone hysterical. She's seeing those she lost three months ago!" Noture moved aside to let Phillip get close. "And she thinks Fanton is still the enemy." Concern for his niece was second nature to him, but this was entirely new.

"Stay away from me, Kelvian!" Maleen screamed. As Phillip came close, she scrambled to the far corner of the bed, her shaky, shallow breathing and cold sweat indicating the terror she experienced.

Phillip looked at the others for help. "What happened?"

"She just woke up and started pleading with us to avenge Cutter. But not with us, with Sonley and Rabe," Asher explained.

"Maleen? It's me, your friend, Phillip." He inched slowly toward her.

"Kelvians are responsible for my husband's death!" she yelled and struck out at him, darting to the other side of the room, pushing herself against the wall, putting as much space between herself and Phillip as possible.

"Her emotions are jumbled," Oblam reported. "Hate, revulsion, fear, anger, confusion, I can't make any sense of them."

"Are you two going to stand there gawking and let this man get away with this?" Maleen turned to Phillip and raised her hands in a fighting stance. "I'll do it myself. Come on, Kelvian! Let's see what you can do!" Even in her mental state, Maleen's technique was flawless. Phillip was too slow to respond as she pummeled him. Noture and Asher rushed forward, but not before she landed several good blows. It took both men to restrain her.

"Maleen." Noture slapped her. "What's happening? Can you tell us what's happening?"

Instead of answering, Maleen pulled away from Asher and swung on Noture. Countering each move skillfully, he held back his natural instincts to strike back. Twice he caught hold of her wrist, but both times she squirmed from his grasp and tried to punch him again.

From behind her, Asher grabbed Maleen. Crossing his arms in front of her, he grabbed both of her hands. Maleen struggled and screamed vulgarities at him, but he didn't let go. As good as her fighting technique was, Asher's was better, and he was stronger. At last Maleen, exhausted, collapsed into his arms, cried for a moment, then slept once again.

Noture looked helplessly at his niece. She slept, her face stained from tears, the profanity that was so unlike her rang in his ears. Desperately, he wished there was more he could do for her.

***

After another fitful sleep, Maleen woke up to see Oblam, Javon, and Phillip in the room with her. Phillip had his back to her, mixing herbs at the table.

As she sat up slowly, Javon spoke to Oblam. "Find your uncle." When the boy was gone from the room, Javon approached the bed. "How do you feel?" He gently brushed back loose hair.

"Confused," she confessed. "What happened?"

"How much do you remember?"

"I know we never finished the Tamal. The garrison physician tried to tell me I was pregnant, but Phillip countered that. Other than that, it's just a bunch of nightmarish images, all afternoon."

Javon looked at Phillip, who still stood with his back to them. Sitting on the edge of the bed, he took Maleen's hand. The large man took a deep breath.

What was wrong with him?

"Maleen, the Tamal was two days ago."

"Two days?" Maleen's eyes went wide. "The entire festival is over? They declared Tyndall the winner?"

"No. Asher stood in for you in the Council. Some of the chiefs tried to give Tyndall the victory. Lenet would have had him accept it, but Tyndall refused. He knew he'd not hit you hard enough to have caused you to collapse. He said when you were well, you could fight again. Asher asked me to come to the Council with him since Oblam's not old enough. Tyndall meant what he said."

"Lenet couldn't have liked that." Maleen rubbed her eyes.

"Let's just say, he forgot the respect due to chiefs, until Tyndall threatened to have him removed from the Council room. For now, Lenet's appointment to Chief Heir is up in the air, but the pardon was never contingent on the match, so it still stands."

"And Cutter?"

Javon shook his head. "We've no clues. We were all watching you, so someone took him out instead then disappeared without a hint of who it was." He paused, looking at Phillip again. He wouldn't meet Maleen's eye. "There's something else you need to know. The last two days have been difficult. You'd sleep a while, wake up ill, eat some food, and go back to sleep. This morning you woke up and you were..." He fumbled for the right words.

"You were out of your mind, is what you were." Phillip turned around with a mug of herbs.

"What happened to you?" Maleen gasped at his swollen and bruised face.

"You happened," he said more gently. "This morning you woke up like a madwoman. You thought Noture was Sonley and Asher was Rabe, and you thought I—" He pointed to his face "—was a Kelvian." He shrugged. "Which technically I suppose I still am, no matter what color I wear."

Maleen had dreamt Phillip wore a green jacket, and Chief Rabe and Sonley had refused to do anything about the Kelvian in the room. She'd dreamt that she'd taken her anger out on Phillip because he was the only Kelvian she could get to. It seemed her nightmare had spilled into the waking world.

"I did that?" She sat in disbelief. "To you? One of my dearest friends?"

"This and a few bruised ribs. Nothing that won't heal." He patted her hand and offered the cup, smiling gently. "Then you turned on Noture. Lucky for him, he's faster than I am, and he knows your moves."

"He should, he taught them to me." Maleen looked down at the mug, seeing her hands for the first time. Blood crusted her bruised knuckles.

"Mine, not yours." Phillip dipped a washcloth in the basin and cleaned and wrapped her swollen hands.

"Most of your warriors went home after the festival," Javon said. "Asher sent a message with them, leaving Gavin in charge until you get home. He was instructed to fortify the garrison, and the outposts along the border."

"But Tian and Asher didn't go home." Maleen rubbed her hand over her eyes, trying to overcome the fatigue that still plagued her.

"No. Being that you technically didn't lose the match, Lenet isn't yet Heir. Asher and Tian didn't feel like they were disobeying your orders by staying in Kelvia, and Noture concurred. He knows the two of us can't keep a constant vigil without them. We're not about to trust the Kelvian guards assigned outside your room."

"That makes sense." Maleen nodded. "As much as anything makes sense right now."

"Asher seemed to get some amusement out of leaving Gavin in charge." Javon finished with a questioning look.

"Gavin's a smart man, and as strong as you are. He's completely dedicated to the tribe." Maleen smiled a little. "But in our last year of training, if anyone had said he'd be assisting me, no one would have believed it."

As she drank the warm liquid Phillip gave her, Maleen began to relax.

"The garrison physician isn't happy with me being here. I'm not his favorite person." Phillip sighed. "I countered his diagnoses by telling him I didn't know what was wrong, not a very potent argument."

"But he was lying?" Maleen hadn't dared to hope, but she had to make sure.

Phillip nodded. "Both Javon and Oblam sensed deception. Unless there's something you haven't shared, there's no reason to jump to that conclusion."

"It would have had to have been in the last week or two."

"So, too recent to have any symptoms." Phillip patted her hand.

"And too soon for me to sense another life," Javon said.

"But we didn't want anyone to know that Javon is a voyant, so we couldn't just tell him we knew he was lying. He's been in a time or two, making sure you're resting and eating, but I'm not welcome out there. Tyndall may have forgiven you, but I'm not taking any chances."

"Forgive is a strong word," Maleen said. "I'm not sure that's what Tyndall feels toward me. He can't be happy that I brought his brother's assassin into his garrison and the Council meetings." She paused, looking sadly at Phillip. "I'm sorry. I wasn't thinking clearly when I requested you to come. You should have stayed outside."

"It's all right," Phillip assured her. "I've managed to avoid Tyndall, but I thought Lenet was going to pop a vein when I was shown to this room. It galls him to no end to see me come and go, though I move about the garrison as little as possible."

"He's worried you'll find out what's wrong?"

"That, or he just hates me—maybe both—probably both."

"Definitely both," Javon said. "Now that I've been in the Council meeting with a scarf, Lenet knows I'm a voyant. He's been avoiding me. But apparently, he didn't think to mention it to the physician because he doesn't seem afraid I'll know he's lying."

Maleen sighed and rubbed her eyes again.

"I'll see if I can find you some thessel next time I'm in Merchant's Row," Javon promised Phillip. "Even if you make it weak, it'll help her get some restful sleep, instead of this restlessness, and we'll not be depleting Oblam's supply."

"Just make sure it's not grown here. In the higher elevation, it grows differently. With her vulnerability to it, there's no telling how she would react." He looked up from the bandages he had just finished wrapping. At the same time, Javon, who was the son of a village healer, came to the same conclusion. "How...?"

"The food?" Javon eyed the plate which had been left for Maleen less than half an hour before. "It would explain the hostile feelings the Kelvian physician has every time he comes in to make sure she was eating properly and his agitation when he found out she slept all morning and skipped breakfast."

"Skipping breakfast and not yet having the midday meal would also explain why Maleen is more coherent now than she has been in the last two days," Phillip added. "The headaches, the stomach pains, the restless sleep, all reported side effects of thessel grown in places where the pods freeze in the winter."

"That's enough reason to use it, right there," Javon said. "But I've never heard of it causing hallucinations."

"With her vulnerability to it? Who knows what side effects it would cause," Phillip said.

"Would you two quit speaking in riddles?" Maleen rubbed her temples. They weren't making any sense. "What are you trying to say?"

"I'm trying to say someone has been putting small amounts of high-elevation thessel in your food, probably since you got here and probably in increasing amounts, to make sure you're in no condition to fight. It would explain the illness." Phillip grimaced. "And substance-induced anxiety would explain the lack of emotional control during the festival and Council meeting Noture described. I'll give you one guess at who's behind it."

"But how do we prove it?" Javon asked.

"We question him with only voyants we trust there," Maleen answered. "I can only think of three at present, and one of them I've come to question as of late."

"No one can be convicted based on what a voyant says," Javon reminded her. "And if you want to avoid finishing the Tamal match, we need a conviction, not just accusations to take to the Council."

"Before we make any accusations, we have to test the theory," Phillip said. "I'll bring you some food from the outside camp." He turned to leave. "Don't touch that stuff." Phillip stopped at the doorway. "In your current state, you need a warrior by your side. If someone came, and it was just me with you, I wouldn't be able to protect you, no matter how hard I tried." Phillip left the room.

"I have to give him credit," Javon said. "He knows his limitations and isn't afraid to admit them."

"He's a good friend," Maleen agreed. "And as honorable as any Acoran warrior."

"You're tired again," Javon said.

"Yes, but I'm afraid of the nightmares."

"Takes a mighty big warrior to admit what she's afraid of." Javon sat next to her on the bed.

"I'm also afraid of being Chief without Cutter by my side." Her voice broke. For the first time since Cutter's death, Maleen sobbed. Not the quiet trickle of tears she'd cried when she knelt over her husband's body. Or the frantic tears induced by hallucinations. But true, body-wracking, uncontrollable, soul-cleansing tears.

Between sobs, she said, "I'm afraid of what will happen to the chief's seat now that Rabe's line is gone. I'm afraid of... I'm just afraid."

I'm afraid of not being good enough on my own.

Javon put his arms around Maleen, rocking her gently. "Today you be afraid. Tomorrow, we shall see."

Javon's voice was soothing, and Maleen was near to a peaceful sleep from his gentle rocking when the door creaked open.

"Don't worry, I'm in my right mind," Maleen called to whoever was hesitating behind the door.

Always on the alert, Javon rose to see who it was. The last thing Maleen saw before the third dart hit her was Javon falling on the floor, two darts in his chest. The last lucid thought Maleen had was that she would not be finishing the Tamal.

CHAPTER 25

As Maleen opened her eyes, the room spun around her. She lay still for a minute, waiting for her stomach to settle. Scanning her surroundings, she found herself on the floor of a storage room; a basement, she guessed, observing the coolness of it and the small windows, high on the wall. Judging from the stored tables and chairs, it was located below a dining hall or meeting room. Her hands and feet were bound. As her eyes adjusted to the dim light, she saw Javon nearby, in the same situation, struggling against the strong ropes. Why were they not dead? Perhaps it was another faction, not Lenet, who'd brought them here.

A woman's voice sounded from the shadows. "Tyndall must speak to you."

"Tara?" Maleen was shocked to hear the Grand Voyant's voice. She couldn't always trust her judgment about people, but she'd been so sure Tara was an honorable woman. She'd even trusted that she had a good reason for lying in the Council, but to be here, like this, with Tara standing there, was too much to grasp.

Tara instructed someone to retrieve Tyndall, then approached the secured pair. "I must apologize for the way you were brought here. We needed to get you out of the room with as little commotion and with as few people aware of it as possible. We also had to do it before the next shift came on duty, outside your room. The darts were diluted. You've only been out for about twenty minutes, and we only used the ropes so you will hear Tyndall out before becoming violent. You will be free to go once you have heard what he has to say." Tara said all this calmly, no longer afraid. Perhaps it had been Lenet's presence that caused the young woman to behave as she had, but it didn't explain the current situation.

Maleen looked at Javon. He looked intently at Tara. His flat expression did nothing to alleviate Maleen's fears. A moment later Tyndall entered the room with all the energy of a vegetable slug.

"I told you there is much unrest in Kelvia," he said sadly. "It has come to my attention that there has been a plot to destroy you and me both, and to continue the discord between our tribes. We expected that plot to come in the form of an assassination attempt. It seems we were wrong."

"Phillip thought someone may have been contaminating my food," Maleen answered carefully.

"Yes, that is the report I received from one of my trusted people this morning." He nodded to someone standing in the shadows. Even in the dark, Maleen could see it was Tyree. "Tara was there to reaffirm my faith in him."

"I overheard a member of the kitchen staff talking to the steward who delivered food to your room," Tyree explained. "We don't know the reasoning behind it, but we can all take a guess at who's paying them. I suppose Lenet wanted to make you weak for an attack while making the chief look bad to our people and to the Council."

"But he didn't attack me," Maleen said, stoically. "It was Cutter they assassinated."

"So many are stuck in the belief that females are too emotional," Tara said. "I suppose someone thought by taking such a drastic measure you wouldn't hold yourself together long enough to strike back." Tara hesitated. "We don't know who killed your husband. When Lenet saw him...his shock was almost as great as yours."

"You're telling me Lenet wasn't responsible?" Maleen felt ill. She'd been so sure. Who else would have enough animosity against the Acoran chief's family to resort to murder?

"It may have been one loyal to him, but he didn't know about it," Tara said. "I've known him long enough. There is no way he could deceive me."

"We know that Kayla can hide companions from other voyants." Maleen blinked hard, trying to clear her head and process what Tara was telling her.

"But she hasn't hidden him. If she did, I'd be sensing nothing from him. Like he wasn't even there. But I can sense him. I just don't sense guilt or even satisfaction from him. Someone in that arena knew about it but was not guilty themselves, so we know it was planned. I couldn't sort through all the mixed emotions in the crowd to find out who it was before he disappeared, but it wasn't Lenet...or Kayla. She was surprised as well."

"Why are we here, Tyndall? What purpose does this serve?" Javon spoke up. "I'm sorry, Maleen. I know you need to find out who killed Cutter, but right now there is a more immediate issue to deal with."

"Word of anything that happens here will travel quickly to my other provinces and to the other tribes." Tyndall paused, considering his words carefully. "I must apologize to you, sir," he said to Javon. "My instructions were to take Maleen from her room with her uncle. It is supposed to be to Noture I make this request. *He* has a debt to pay." Tyndall looked back to Maleen. "I would like to invite you and your voyant, since he is the one here, to stay here until you are feeling better. I believe you trust Tara? She will bring you food and water. When you have regained your strength, we will have men ready, then we will leak your whereabouts to Lenet."

"Meanwhile the rest of my party thinks what?" Cognitive thought was still a strain.

"Tara can take a message to them if you'd like, but I would advise against it. If Kayla learns of my deceitfulness to her, she will warn Lenet. She avoids Tara because she can't read her, and Tara is usually with me. But the more people who know where you are now, the more likely Lenet will come before you are ready for him."

"How do you know he will come himself?" Maleen asked. "He hasn't yet."

"When we let him know where you are, we will make sure we have enough men here to subdue however many he sends." Tyndall clenched his fists. "Then we will *make* them tell us who sent them."

Maleen did not like his tone, or what he implied, but if Tara could shield them from Kayla, then the plan might work...if she could trust those around her.

"I don't trust any of your guards at this point." Maleen looked pointedly at Tyree, then back to Tyndall. "Not since they aimed a dart-blower at me. And frankly, considering the ropes, I'm not sure I trust you."

Tyndall nodded to Tara, who knelt and cut Maleen's bonds, then Javon's. Tyree grabbed two staffs that had been leaning against the far wall and set them on the floor next to Maleen.

His hands free, Javon took hold of Tara's arm, staring her in the face, trying to read her. Tyree, the only guard in the room, stepped forward.

Tara put her hand up to stop him. "There's no danger. I sense no hostility from him. And if he grabbed the knife, you couldn't move fast enough anyway."

After a moment Javon released her arm.

"You trusted me at your back once," Tara said to Maleen. "Will you do so again?"

"Yes, Tara. I will." Maleen nodded, willing to trust in her original assessment now that she knew the reasoning behind the abduction, and because they'd been released before she gave Tyndall an answer, though he only had two people to act as guards if she and Javon refused.

"Then trust I can read Tyndall as easily as Oblam reads you. He is doing the only thing he can think of to ensure your safety and put an end to all this."

Ensure her safety...by using her as bait. Again. Maleen looked at Javon for his support. He wasn't one of her warriors, she would not order him to do this with her. And he would tell her if Tyndall or Tara were lying. When he nodded, she looked at Tyndall. "Very well. We will be your bait, but when you send your men in, I expect mine to be with them. And I will be sending them a message."

"If you must." Tyndall nodded.

Tyree went to a storage cabinet. Pens, inkwells, and paper filled one shelf. He brought one of each to Maleen.

Asher,

Do not look for us. Yet.

Have Oblam read Tyree, Tara, and Tyndall as often as possible. You'll know when and where.

Maleen

After the Kelvians were gone, Maleen asked, "Am I mistaken to trust her?"

"Tyndall meant every word he said. The weariness you saw was not an act. He's desperate to end this. The young man who came with them is as easy to read as you are. He has a strong dislike for you, but he is loyal to Tyndall. I'm unconvinced about the young woman, though."

The blood drained from Maleen's face. "You sensed something in her?"

"She's extraordinarily strong. Maybe as strong as Oblam, but with more experience."

"But did you sense deceitfulness from her?"

"No. I sensed nothing at all from her."

***

In the corridor, outside the empty room from which Maleen had been taken, Noture had a guard pinned to the wall. "Where is my niece?"

"I don't know," the guard answered, struggling against the strong man's grip. "I just came on duty. I didn't even realize the room was empty until you came back."

"He's telling the truth," Oblam said. "But he's not so much afraid of you as of someone else when they find out she's gone." To the guard, Oblam asked, "Who are you afraid of? Tyndall? Lenet?" Oblam paused for a moment. "He's one of Lenet's," he finally said.

"A dissident? Well, maybe we should do Tyndall a favor." Noture drew back a fist.

"Hold, Acoran," Tara called, coming down the corridor, Tyree right behind her. "I'm aware of who the dissidents are. Lenet's men and others."

"I suppose you want me to let go of your tribesman?" Noture looked down at Tara.

"I insist on it." Though small in stature, Tara held her back straight and her chin up. Noture, never intimidated by the largest warrior, much less this small, noticeably young woman, made no move to release the restrained man.

Asher put a hand on Noture's arm. "Tyndall's civil unrest is of no concern of ours. It won't help us find Maleen and Javon."

"He's right," Oblam said softly, eyeing Tara. "And if this man doesn't know where they are, Lenet may not either."

Noture released the guard who gladly took his leave, no doubt to report Maleen's absence to Lenet.

Tara watched him go around the corner before speaking to Noture. "Part of our issue is the law forbids a voyant's emotional sight to convict a man, or to remove him from his livelihood. We saw in the Chiefs' Council what can happen if chiefs depend on corrupt voyants." She reached for her pouch—the one that looked exactly like the dart pouch Oblam carried.

Reflexively, Noture grabbed her arm.

"Remove your hand, Acoran," she said coldly. "I have a message for him." She nodded toward Asher. As he withdrew cautiously, she pulled out a piece of paper and handed it to Asher.

Asher took only a second to scan the page. "Do you know where they are?"

Tara nodded. "Your Chief and voyant are both safe but instructed I shouldn't tell you where."

"Oblam?" Noture eyed the young woman suspiciously. Maleen trusted both Tara and Tyree because they'd saved her life. But with all that had happened, any Kelvian could have switched loyalties several times.

"I have spent my entire life building a wall against other voyants," Tara told Oblam. "Behind it is too much pain. Javon couldn't read me. It's why he sent me to you. I'm going to let down a piece of my wall so you will know Lady Maleen is safe. I trust anything you see that is unrelated to our present situation you will keep to yourself."

Oblam nodded. As the two voyants stood eye to eye for a moment, Oblam's winced. "Yes," he finally announced. "They are both safe. Tara can be trusted. She wants Lenet stopped as badly as we do."

"And her bodyguard?" Noture looked at Tyree.

"If I were in your p-p-p-place, I'd be just as suspicious. From what other voyants tell me, I couldn't hide anything from the boy even if I w-w-w-w-wanted to," Tyree admitted.

"He doesn't like us, but he is loyal to Chief Tyndall and Tara." Oblam nodded, confident in his assessment.

"Very well then, young lady." Noture held out his hand to Tara. "You have our trust. Now, I want to know where my niece is."

Tara shook her head. "You will not find out from me. Not yet. She and Javon have both consented to keeping the secret, even from you. But Kayla will know we know if she asks you. Stay away from her. You're good," she told Noture, "but not that good. She's as strong as I am. Every time you get near her, she's that much closer to reading you." Looking at Oblam she added, "Feel free to seek your sister out. If you can find her, so can Kayla. We need to know immediately if I'm not sufficiently hiding her."

As Tara turned and walked away, she called over her shoulder, "Keep the boy away from Kayla until he learns to build a wall of his own."

***

"What do you mean she's gone?" Lenet slammed his hands on the table. "You were supposed to be guarding the room."

"I just came on duty. I was taking over for Duncan." The informant shifted uncomfortably.

"So, Duncan knows where she went, or at least who she left with," Jewel said, putting a hand on Lenet's shoulder. "I'll find out."

"You still need to stay out of sight," Lenet scolded. "She saw your armlet. You never should have let her see you, much less that. I can't afford for you to mess up again."

"It was a stupid mistake," Kayla said from across the room. "Not that I'd be heartbroken to see you get extradited to Acora."

"No one asked you," Jewel hissed.

"Stop it," Lenet ordered. "Right now, we need to figure out where that woman went without incriminating anyone."

"The Grand Voyant knows who your men are," the guard said.

"Of course, she does." Lenet waved away his concern.

"She said so in front of the Acoran. If she said it to him, she's said it to Tyndall."

"I'll deal with her later. It's too late for Tyndall to do anything about it. We've got too many men already in place. Right now, we have to find the Acoran tart."

"Why can't Kayla find her?" Jewel asked.

"That half-sized daughter of shame is hiding her," Kayla said. "She has to be. There's no other explanation."

"Tara can do that?" Jewel questioned.

"Why not? She's stronger than Kayla, and Kayla can do it." Lenet sat down.

"She is not stronger than me," Kayla said through clenched teeth. "She can't see through my shield any more than I can see through hers."

"So how do we find the Acoran tramp?" Jewel set to work massaging the neck muscles that were threatening to give Lenet a monster of a headache.

Kayla stood at the window. "Where are you going?" she muttered under her breath.

Lenet stood and looked out. In the courtyard below, Tara walked casually with Tyree. "How can he be so attached to her?"

"If you weren't so mean to him, maybe he wouldn't have left the Western Garrison." Kayla looked at her brother. "Strong as he is, he'd have been an asset. Almost as much as his father used to be before he was stupid enough to get arrested."

Lenet looked down at his sister. "Never complain about my leadership again," he snarled. "His father was arrested for following my orders."

"Sorry, little brother." Kayla flipped her hair back. "I'm just... That's it." She turned back to the window. Lenet followed her gaze as Tara and Tyree disappeared around the corner of a building.

"What's it?"

"I can't find Maleen because Tara's hiding her. I can't read Tara because she's a graebig's backside. But I can follow Tyree. He's so easy to read it's ridiculous."

"You're not making sense," Jewel complained. "Who cares where Tyree is?"

"No, she's right," Lenet said as Kayla sat down with a concentrated look on her face.

"They're going to the mess hall." Kayla chewed her lip.

"That's helpful."

"Get that woman out of here," Kayla barked.

"Shut it, Jewel," Lenet warned. "Let her concentrate."

"On what?" Jewel rolled her eyes.

"On finding out where Tyree goes that's not likely for a bodyguard to go," Kayla said. "It could be a while, but I bet Tara and Tyree visit her before the night's over. As much as Tyree hates her, I'll know when he's in the same room."

***

As agreed, Tara and Tyree brought food and water to Maleen and Javon that evening. The day of rest without the tainted food had helped Maleen feel better. The dizzy spells were spaced further apart, and the stomach pains were gone. By morning, she'd be ready for a fight.

As Maleen ate, she questioned Tara about the unrest among the Kelvians.

"There are several factions, Lenet's being the strongest and the most dangerous."

"Why does your chief tolerate them?" Javon asked.

"He can't confront one sect without risking that another will strike," she said.

"So, he bides his time, placating each one." Maleen understood.

Tara nodded. "He trusts my judgment, but still has to deal with Kayla. He can't banish her from the garrison without risking that she will raise her own faction, and she has not committed any crime we can prove. For the time being, she's still loyal to Lenet. If he's out of the picture, Kayla will go where she thinks the power is, which isn't likely to be Tyndall. She can't read me and, for now, Lenet *thinks* he's threatened me into silence to avoid Tyndall knowing the extent of his hostility toward him."

"Lenet threatened an adolescent girl a quarter his size?" Javon asked Tara, looking at Tyree.

"Don't blame Tyree," Tara said. "Even bodyguards need sleep. The first night Lenet was back in Kelvia, before he even let Tyndall know he was here, he came in the window of my room. I think Kayla was hiding his presence from me and somehow hindering the emotional connection I usually have with Tyree. Lenet made sure I understood how ruthless he is. He gave me this." She shoved her sleeve up to show them the yellowed bruises on her arm. "Among others."

"What did he want?"

"He tried to force me to convince Tyndall he was innocent of the massacres in Acora, and all he wanted was for their family to continue in the chief's seat. He threatened that if I told Tyndall of his true intent, my death wouldn't be swift, and my past wouldn't be secret. I lied about Jewel in the Council because we want Lenet to think his intimidation has been successful. Whatever he says in Tyndall's hearing, I confirm and tell Tyndall the truth later. When Lenet is ready to strike, he doesn't think we'll be ready for him."

"We hoped making Lenet think she was working for him would keep her safe," Tyree added, but sighed regretfully.

"The night before the meeting started, it was the same thing. I didn't hear him come in, but more surprising was that I didn't sense him, and I couldn't reach out to Tyree again to call him for help." Tara shook her head. Clearly still troubled by the visit, she fidgeted with the neckline of her dress. "This time I was sitting at my desk, debating whether or not to try to get a message to you before you got here, and considering how to word it so you'd know who it was from, without giving it away to anyone who might intercept it."

"You wanted to warn me Lenet was ready for me?" Maleen asked.

Tara nodded. "I was brought back to reality by my scarf tightening around my neck. I couldn't breathe, and there is no way I could match his strength even if I knew he was coming. But he was just trying to scare me. If he wanted to kill me, I'd have been dead the first time. Even if he gave me the chance to yell, the walls are too thick for Tyree to have heard from his room. There was no way for him to know I needed his help."

"Lenet kn-n-nows if he kills her, Tyndall will have to f-f-f-f-find a new Grand Voyant who Lenet hasn't b-been able to get to," Tyree said. "There's no guarantee he'd be able to manipulate whomever Tyndall managed to find. Especially if he w-w-w-went to another tribe." He nodded toward Javon.

"So, I was forced to sit in that chair, with Lenet standing over me, with this scarf getting tighter and I couldn't do a thing about it. Lenet said when you arrived, I was not to speak to you and pointed out if you or Tyndall knew his intent, or that he threatened me, strangulation would be too swift and not painful enough. Before I blacked out, he reminded me again that he knew what I was hiding and threatened everyone I care about." She blushed slightly. "Apparently, he thinks Tyree is more than my bodyguard."

"Are you?" Javon looked at Tyree, eyes narrowed. Tyree was young, but Tara was still an adolescent.

"No," Tyree answered, "Sh-she's like a little sister to a few of the warriors in this garrison, myself included. I've slept on her couch every n-n-n-night since then, so if you hear rumors, you know why. I won't take the chance he'll sneak in again."

"Since then, every time I see Lenet, he fidgets with my voyant's scarf. He's reminding me of that night, and what he can do. Out of the dissenting voyants in the Council, two were paid, the other was threatened. From the fear I sensed from her, Lenet took less care about being subtle with her. He doesn't fear her chief's retribution like he fears Tyndall's."

Maleen nodded, remembering the fear she had in the Kelvian garrison every time she was near him. "I can only guess what form of intimidation he used."

Tara shrugged. "I don't have any family for him to threaten. My parents are dead. I've been raised here since I was ten years old. I'm not attached to any man. Tyndall and Tyree are the closest I have to a father and brother. Lenet wants both of them dead whether I help him or not. Pain is the only thing he has to threaten me with, both physical and emotional. He's quite capable of both."

"So, whatever it is you hide from other voyants, Lenet knows?" Javon probed.

Tara nodded. "So does Kayla."

"And it's bad enough for Lenet to use as blackmail?"

"He can try," Tara stated with a fierceness Maleen had never seen from her. "But I'd let everyone know my secrets before I'd help that man. He just doesn't know me as well as he thinks he does."

"If Tyndall dies in this conflict, I want you both to head south to Acora as fast as you can," Maleen said.

"This is our homeland." Tara waved her hand around. "Our loyalties are here."

"Your life is more important. Anyone loyal to Tyndall will not live much longer than he does. You may not have reached the age of maturity yet, but we both know Lenet does not fight fair. If he knows you didn't do as he ordered, he *will* follow through on his threat, even before he kills Tyndall. And even if he thinks you did follow his orders, when Tyndall is dead, you're one more loose end to tie up. He'll have Kayla. He won't need to go looking for a Grand Voyant."

Maleen looked to where Tyree stood, always alert. He nodded to her unspoken request. He would make sure Tara left Kelvia if necessary. If Tyndall died, Tyree would need to leave Kelvia as well. He'd made his loyalties clear when he sided against Rundel.

"Don't wear your vests or scarf when you cross the border," Maleen warned them. Hostilities between the tribes would resume and rise to new heights the instant Lenet gained control of Kelvia. Few of the warriors at the border outposts would recognize these two as allies. It would be safer for them *not* to be recognized as Kelvians.

CHAPTER 26

Maleen lay awake that night, unable to close her eyes. By the sounds of Javon's soft breathing nearby, he didn't share her inability to sleep. Lenet had no way to find them. There was no reason for either of them to keep watch, yet Maleen was still afraid to sleep. Every time she closed her eyes, she'd see Cutter. She didn't have time to grieve right now. If she wasn't well rested when Lenet came...

Maleen felt for the comfort of her staff. It lay next to her mat, right where she had left it hours ago. Her hearing pricked as she thought she heard something. It was probably early morning by now, but was it time for the kitchen staff to be up and about upstairs?

No. Someone was shuffling through the storage room. Moonlight through the window reflected off red hair and pale skin. The nearly silent figure wasn't alone.

Maleen reached over to wake Javon. She put a finger to her lips. Their eyes were accustomed to the darkness. Hoping those approaching would not have the same benefit, both reached slowly for their staffs.

Lenet had come too soon. They would be on their own.

Maleen was careful to keep her breathing steady and slow. If the intruders believed they were asleep, they would continue to move in slowly. When one of the figures neared her, Maleen struck, her staff connecting with the shin of a would-be assailant. She jumped up, releasing her hold on both fear and anger, hoping Oblam and Tara would sense her even if they weren't looking.

Javon sprang to his feet, his staff colliding with an assailant about to come crashing into Maleen.

"You dare to attack a chieftess in her sleep?" Javon's booming voice accused as he stepped in front of Maleen.

"Yes, I dare," a familiar voice snarled. "She is not worthy of your loyalty, the chief seat, or any other honor greater than a harlot's bed." Lenet's insult was full of animosity, revulsion, and hatred as he stepped into the dim moonlight shining in from the small windows.

"Javon!" Maleen yelled. Another figure emerged from the shadows. Javon had been too focused on Lenet to sense him. The attacker's staff shattered as it struck Javon's shin. The massive warrior crumpled to the floor.

Maleen stood her ground as Jewel and three more of Lenet's followers surrounded her, Lenet, and Javon.

"I would offer you a fair fight," Lenet said, still sneering. "But you know as well as I do the boy has informed the others of your predicament. Not to mention Tara." He spat out the Grand Voyant's name. "That daughter of shame was arrogant enough to think she could shield you from Kayla."

As Lenet spoke, Maleen could feel the presence of those behind her nearing. One lunged forward. Maleen slammed the end of her staff into his chest before twirling around to strike her heel into the face of another. Jewel and the last man standing took a hesitant step back out of Maleen's reach. Lenet strode forward without raising his staff.

"I told you she was fast," he seethed. Even as he spoke, his closed fist struck her with enough force to send her reeling. "Almost as fast as me."

Maleen recovered and twisted her grip on her staff. She was ready when Lenet stepped back and the other two came at her. Jewel held a staff, the other a knife. Several feet away Javon groaned as he tried again to get up to help her. Knocking the knife wielder unconscious, the weapon clattered to the floor, and she kicked it in Javon's direction. Facing Jewel, Maleen made a move that surprised even her. With every ounce of strength she had, she swung her staff at the other woman's head. Jewel's head snapped back, and she fell to the floor. Dead or unconscious, Maleen didn't know as she turned to Lenet, who raised his staff.

One of Lenet's subordinates dragged himself up from the floor.

"Find Kayla," Lenet hissed at him. He was angry but showed no concern for his wife lying on the floor. "Send men to intercept the Acorans before they get here!" The man ran up the stairs, and out the door at the top.

Lenet charged Maleen. He was, by far, the best opponent here. Possibly the best she'd *ever* had to face in real combat. Maleen blocked, dodged, struck, and blocked again. She could keep up with his speed, but not his strength. She had to resort to outmaneuvering him. She backed up, sidestepped, jumped on low crates, and knocked items from the shelves. Still, he came. At last, she found herself against the wall, with nowhere to go.

Lenet continued to swing relentlessly, though he was slowing down. If he was tired, then he would be desperate. A blow hit Maleen's fatigued hands, causing her to drop her staff. It clattered to the floor near where Javon lay.

Maleen ducked Lenet's next blow but had nowhere to go as he dropped his staff and wrapped his calloused fingers around her throat. He slammed the back of her head into the brick wall behind her and lifted her feet a few inches off the floor, cutting off her airway.

Javon gave one final surge in their direction, a knife in his hand. Another of Lenet's men regained his senses and kicked the knife Javon held and kicked him in the face, sending him back to the floor.

Maleen clawed at Lenet's arms. Her nails could reach nothing but the thick leather of his bracers. Lenet's reach was longer, and he held her at arm's length, so she couldn't strike effectively. Her feet sought footing where none was to be found. Desperately, she tried to free herself, feeling her strength and consciousness waning.

Above them, footsteps and scuffling could be heard on the ground floor. Shouting came from Kelvians and Acorans.

"Sounds like your reinforcements have met mine," Lenet growled, tightening his grip. The pain of his grip on her throat was almost as bad as the pain in her head from not being able to breathe. Lenet stepped close enough to feel his breath on her cheek as he hissed in her ear, "Too late for you, of course."

That was the opportunity Maleen needed. As he leaned closer to gloat, she brought her knee up to his groin with every ounce of strength she had left. Lenet yelled incoherently as he threw her to the stone floor. As he stooped down to grab his staff, she struck out with her foot, kicking him in the face.

At the same time, the storage room door came crashing in. Recovering quickly, Lenet had his staff in hand, poised to strike. Noture rushed down the stairs and, using his staff to vault into the enemy, smashed both feet into Lenet.

Maleen crawled away from the combatants, wheezing and coughing, trying to get enough air into her lungs. An instant later, Phillip was by her side.

"Help Javon," she ordered hoarsely.

"You first." He tried to help her up.

"I can stand. He can't. Help him!" She shoved Phillip in Javon's direction and stood on her own to prove her point.

"No," Javon said weakly, his face pale and sweaty.

"No time to waste with an argument we won't win." Phillip pulled Javon up, throwing his arm over his shoulder. "You better be right behind me, Chieftess. More of Lenet's men are upstairs." He kicked a staff in her direction.

Maleen bent to pick it up. Some of Lenet's men were also here in this room, though she had to be careful. Lenet's and Tyndall's men both wore Kelvian colors, and both groups had immediately followed Noture into the room, Tara and Tyree among them.

"If you recognize them from the Western Garrison, assume they're Lenet's," Tara called, as she ducked a staff. "Except Tyree."

At the top of the stairs, Tyndall entered the room, pursued or joined by more Kelvians. Seeing men she'd encountered in her year at the Kelvian garrison, Maleen swung hard. She and Tara fought side by side once again. When next Maleen saw Lenet, he was facing off with Tyndall.

What's Tyndall doing? He's not fast enough! Noture was at Tyndall's back, keeping him from being hit from behind as he settled his personal affairs with his nephew.

Noture caught Maleen's eye through the crowd of warriors, from both sides. "What are you doing?" he yelled, getting winded. "Get out of here! I can't protect you and Tyndall!"

Ignoring him, Maleen dodged one warrior and pummeled another.

"Tara! Get her out of here!" Noture yelled to the other woman when Maleen refused to listen to him.

To Tara's credit, she ignored him as well. "Someone needs to remind him *you're* the chief," she said to Maleen, with labored breath.

The number of aggressors thinned, but so did the number of allies. Kelvian warriors lay everywhere broken and bleeding. Separated from Tara, Maleen saw Tyndall with Noture still at his back, though with more distance between them. She tried to push through to get to them when a knife flashed in Lenet's hand. He sunk it into Tyndall's side. As Tyndall crumbled to the floor, Lenet pulled the knife out and kicked him in the face. There was nothing Maleen could do.

Tyndall's breathing was shallow, but he was still conscious. Three of his men stood between him and anyone who would seek to finish what Lenet had started. Another stooped by him to stem the blood flow.

Lenet looked around him. Dread filled Maleen as Lenet's eyes met hers. She would be next. She knew it. She couldn't beat him. If she didn't get help, she'd be lying next to Tyndall. She stood ready for him, but Noture did not allow Lenet another chance at her. As Lenet strode near Maleen's position, knife ready, Noture struck.

Maleen felt relief that was mirrored in Noture's face. Lenet's eyes went wide as Noture's staff landed forcefully in the middle of his spine. He tumbled to the floor, dropping the knife. Seeing their leader down, two of Lenet's men turned on Noture, while two others lifted Lenet to his feet and ran up the stairs, with him between them.

Maleen couldn't let them go, but she could not go after them alone. Two Kelvians engaged Noture. Tara was holding her own against a man twice her size. Tian and Asher didn't seem to be in the room. They were, most likely, among the combatants upstairs.

Seeing Tyree put down an opponent, she called to him, as she ran after Lenet. "Is your first duty still to your chief?"

Tyree followed on her heels.

They reached the top of the stairs, entering a dining hall as the offenders ran out the next door, into the early morning light. Two more of Lenet's men intercepted the pursuers. Tyree dispatched one while Maleen disabled the other.

Moments later, they caught up to their quarry, hobbling in the shadows. Tyree connected his staff with the leg of one of the men who'd aided Lenet. As he collapsed, likely with a shattered knee, Lenet went down, too. Maleen swung her staff hard and fast at the third man, quickly laying him out.

His companions being no use to him, Lenet struggled to his feet. His face gave no indication of the pain he felt as he faced the Acoran Chieftess, but Maleen had seen the tremendous force Noture hit him with and had little doubt he had at least one cracked vertebra.

Before either Maleen or Lenet could take any action, Tyree spoke up. "You are under arrest for the attempted murders of Lady Maleen of Acora, and Tyndall, Chief of Kelvia."

"You spent your first three years of service to your tribe under my father." Lenet turned to face him. Pain broke through his façade of strength. "Now you aid his murderer?"

"My duty is to my chief," Tyree said. "That's the only statement my father ever made that was worth listening to."

"Your father was loyal to mine," Lenet spat out. "And now to me."

"And look where it got him." Tyree shook his head, clearly ashamed. Again, he repeated, "My duty is to my chief who now lies with a knife wound in his side, just as your father did three months ago."

"And when he died, Western Kelvia followed me. Who do you think all Kelvia will follow when Tyndall dies?" Lenet asked.

"Not his murderer, if I have anything to say about it." Tyree had acted boldly. Even his stutter had disappeared at his forceful words, but he didn't seem to know what to do next.

Maleen held back. She had to let Tyree handle the arrest. She couldn't allow Lenet to escape, but she had no real authority in Kelvia. If Tyndall died, whoever followed him as Chief could easily charge her with interfering in a Kelvian matter. If the Council agreed, then the arrest would be meaningless and Lenet would be free again. Tyree's Kelvian vestments gave him the authority for a legitimate arrest, especially for a crime he'd witnessed.

Behind them, voices called to one another. In the dark, Maleen couldn't tell who they were, but there were several of them, and they were heading in their direction. If it was more of Lenet's men, she and Tyree were soon to be in serious trouble.

As Tyree turned to look in the direction of the yelling voices, Lenet seized the opportunity. Despite the pain it cost him, he reached down and grabbed the knife one of his companions carried. His pain made him slow and Maleen easily dodged his thrust, but the man on the ground with the shattered knee grabbed Maleen's foot and twisted. The bones in her ankle shifted and she toppled to the ground. As Lenet raised the knife again, he flipped it around for a downward strike, but Tyree was faster. With his left hand, he stopped the downward motion of Lenet's knife, and with his right, he drove his own blade into Lenet's rib cage.

Lenet's eyes went wide, and his mouth fell open as he slumped to the ground. Maleen kicked the other man in the face, forcing him to let go of her foot. As she stood, her ankle wouldn't hold her. Tyree reached out to hold her steady, never taking his eyes off Lenet as he took a last rasping breath. Looking as though he was going to be ill, Tyree had a mix of sorrow, horror, and shock on his face.

"The first time you've ever killed?" Maleen asked quietly. She'd had a similar reaction and so could completely understand.

Tyree nodded.

She laid a hand on his shoulder. She wasn't the best person to share this terrible moment with him, but there was no one else.

"I only passed my com-com-combat test because Commander Rundel is my f-f-f-f-father," Tyree said flatly, as if it were the most natural thing in the world that two months ago he'd helped Tara save Maleen from being killed by the man who sat in prison. "He p-p-p-passed me when he shouldn't have to save himself the embarrassment of a son who froze in battle."

"Rundel?" Maleen didn't know what to say to that confession. "I'd never have guessed."

"No one does. My m-m-m-mother was dark. Darker than me. Part of the p-p-p-problem was I looked more like her than him. Reminded him too m-m-much of his failed marriage."

This wasn't the place to reminisce. The voices of the pursuers in the dark came closer, a female voice with them.

"That's Kayla." Tyree looked away, allowing Maleen to lean heavily on him. "W-w-w-we have to go, Chieftess." It was the first time Tyree used her title. "We need to get back to the d-d-dining hall and let them know Lenet is dead...and find out if Tyndall is still alive."

As the voices came closer, Maleen indicated a place in the shadows.

"Can't stop to hide. Kayla will sense us. Or at least me." Tyree continued on.

"No!" Kayla's voice rang out as those coming through the night found Lenet.

"It was Tyree, and that Acoran female," a nasally voice said, sounding as though it was speaking through a broken nose. "I dislocated her ankle. They couldn't have gone far."

They could hear Kayla screaming vulgarities at the others, but not one of them came in the direction of their quarry.

"You said Lenet's father died from a knife wound?" Maleen asked as they made their way.

"You kn-n-n-now very well how F-f-f-Fanton died," Tyree said bitterly. "When they arrived back at the garrison, after l-l-l-losing your trail, he had an arrow in his leg, and a knife wound in his side."

"They didn't lose our trail. We had already crossed the creek at the border. None of us were close enough to stab him. Jewel and Sampton were the only ones even carrying knives."

"I saw him carried through the gate," Tyree argued. "The next morning, I-I helped bury him."

"I know my uncle shot an arrow, but it was dark. When we found out Fanton was killed in the pursuit, we assumed that was what killed him. But if he had a knife wound, it was from a Kelvian."

Tyree said nothing for a moment.

"When Rundel accused me, Tara knew he was hiding something," Maleen said. "But she couldn't figure out what. I'm sorry to make the accusation against your father, but... If you have any doubt, have Tara question us specifically about a knife. My uncle is usually an unreadable, but you've seen Tara read him before."

Tyree sighed deeply, slowing his speech down, making it clearer. "That's not necessary. Lenet killed his own f-father...and my...and Rundel had a hand in it. Even with no loyalties to them, it still comes as a sh-shock." He ran a hand through his hair. "Every-every-everyone who pursued your escape remained loyal to Lenet," Tyree said thoughtfully. "T-t-that night I'd thought it odd that Lenet didn't take as many v-volunteers as he could to find you. If he and Rundel were planning to... It would explain why a few of us who volunteered were ordered to stay in the garrison. They knew we wouldn't have followed Lenet into Acora if we'd known. He-he played a smart game, using his father's murder to rally us to him. I'm certainly not the only western warrior who questioned his t-t-tactics."

Tyree stopped to listen to noises in the dark. Convinced no one was following, he continued. "Something else suddenly makes sense now. We were the s-s-same few who were ordered to follow a caravan that left your garrison before the slaughter. Lenet hates me. I couldn't figure out why I was t-t-trusted with that... I was not a part of the massacre in your garrison. Nor was I with Lenet in your home v-village."

Maleen looked him in the eye. "I believe you, Tyree." Though she still wished Oblam was there to confirm her trust.

Clearly annoyed at the slow progress, Tyree handed his staff to her. "Hold this." As she took it, he swept her up and hastened his pace.

As they came to the place where light flooded from the well-lit building, they could see Tian, Noture, and a few Kelvians standing outside, looking into the dark. "They're not fighting," Maleen noted. "I guess that means those Kelvians are on our side?"

Without answering, Tyree walked up to Tian.

"What happened?" Tian demanded as he helped his sister inside to a chair.

"I'm fine. Nothing Phillip can't fix." Maleen tried to clear the raspy sound from her voice. Tyndall sat, holding blood-soaked cloths on the wound in his side, leaning over a warrior. Phillip was kneeling beside the same person, hard at work. Seeing who lay there, Maleen rushed to them, all but falling in her effort. Tara lay still, a cut across her face from her ear to her mouth. Her chest heaved with effort.

"The cut is deep, but not dangerously so," Phillip said as he stitched it closed. "She got the wind knocked out of her, but she doesn't have any broken ribs. She should be all right." He looked up at Tyndall. "Thank you for trusting me, Uncle."

Tyndall clenched his jaw shut. Trusting him with the life of someone so close to him was a far cry from forgiving him. It simply meant Tyndall found Phillip more trustworthy than his garrison physician, who had already proved his loyalties did *not* lie with Tyndall.

As Tyree knelt by his chief, Maleen hoped he wouldn't feel guilty. He hadn't shirked his responsibilities to Tara. He'd made a choice to pursue a greater responsibility. Tara wouldn't blame him for going after Lenet, and Maleen hoped Tyndall wouldn't either.

Tian helped Maleen back to a chair where she sat for a moment, exhausted from the ordeal, emotionally and physically. But it was over. Looking around, she saw injured warriors held up by comrades. Others were sprawled around the floor, waiting for attention from the physician.

"If Tyndall loses Tara, he'll never know who to trust in this mess," Tian observed.

"If Tyndall loses Tara, he loses a great warrior," Maleen said. "And a loyal friend."

"We need to spread out and find Lenet," Asher reported, coming to her side as she removed her boot. "Tyndall ordered extra guards at the gates, but Oblam can't sense him. Kayla may be hiding him."

"No, she's not. Somewhere out there in the dark, you'll find an unconscious Kelvian and another with a shattered knee and broken nose. You'll find Lenet's body with them."

"You went after him?" Noture looked at her in disbelief. "Without any of us?"

"I couldn't wait for you. He would have escaped. Your last swing slowed him down, but it didn't take away any of the hate." She nodded to Tyree. "I didn't go alone. This loyal Kelvian warrior did his duty to his chief and his tribe. And for the second time, he saved my life." She wouldn't share the information about Tyree's parentage with anyone. It was his secret to share or bear alone. As for Rundel's part in Fanton's death, that was a Kelvian issue to be dealt with later, by Kelvians.

Maleen noticed the satisfied look on Noture's face. She couldn't share his satisfaction. Lenet had been a cruel enemy, but while she could be satisfied that justice had been done, she couldn't celebrate the death of a human being, no matter who he was.

As Lenet's men were separated from the crowd and moved to the prison, Maleen wondered who among the guards belonged to another faction who would see Tyndall's house brought down now that there was no blood relative to be named Heir. Kelvia wasn't likely to follow a woman, and most certainly would not consent to a chief heir who'd not been a warrior. Regardless of any claim Kayla might have to lead because of blood, she would *not* be named Chief.

Maleen was somewhat relieved when Jewel was led away. The woman was unsteady on her feet, but she was alive. It hadn't been anger, hate, or even vengeance that had driven Maleen to strike out at her. It had been an act of desperation. If she'd faced a full fight with Jewel, she would have had nothing left to face Lenet. She hadn't been trying to kill the woman and was grateful she hadn't. Knowing Jewel would be sitting in a prison cell was enough. For now.

Maleen sat, her head down, relief and sorrow overcoming her, simultaneously. Having taken care of the worst of the injuries, Phillip came to her side. "I'm fine," she assured him, "Nothing a week of rest won't cure."

Unconvinced, Phillip examined the bruises on her neck. "Considering the bruising, I'm worried about a cracked windpipe," Phillip said. "You're breathing okay?"

"I'm fine now," she insisted, knowing he could hear how raspy her voice still sounded. "How's Tara?"

"She'll be all right in a while," he said. "She's awake now."

"Lenet wasn't as fortunate," Maleen said without emotion. She held her foot so he could see her ankle, gritting her teeth as he set the bones into place and wrapped it carefully.

Moments after Phillip finished, and helped her put her boot back on, Maleen heard a woman scream at someone to let her pass. Kayla came running into the room.

"You!" She pointed indignantly at Maleen and stomped across the room. Standing over her, Kayla screamed nasty names, blaming Maleen not just for the death of her brother but for every struggle her family suffered within their own tribe. Slowly Maleen stood up, calmer than she'd felt in several days, and giving no indication of the pain in her foot. Her increased height did nothing to temper the smaller woman's rage. Maleen had enough. She would not tolerate the disrespect this woman showed, chief's family or not. Maleen raised her hand and, with an open palm, slapped the woman.

Two Kelvian warriors, still on their feet, took a step toward Maleen.

"Leave her alone," Tyndall ordered. "Kayla had that coming for a long time."

The two men relaxed.

"Feel better?" Noture asked.

"Much." Maleen rubbed her fingers together, savoring the stinging in her palm from Kayla's cheek. Seeing the proud woman sit on the floor and sob *did* give Maleen satisfaction.

EPILOGUE

6ᵗʰ Lunar, 522 AC
Acora, Northern Garrison

Maleen folded the letter from Tara. She shared Tara's concern for Tyndall and his young wife. Vastele was young enough to give Tyndall an heir, but at Tyndall's age, it was questionable as to whether he could produce one. Hope wasn't completely lost, though. Maleen's father had been older than Tyndall when he'd fathered Nolel and Jillian. She also knew her grandparents had been middle-aged when they were surprised with Noture. She could only hope, for Kelvia's sake, it wasn't too late for Tyndall.

It was easy to wish for the best for another couple, because in the weeks following Cutter's death, the signs—real ones—had appeared that Rabe's line was not gone. In fact, if Tyana and Javon were correct, Maleen would be tasked one day with choosing which of Cutter's twin children would succeed her. Javon had taken Oblam to Oak village and returned with both his mother and Maleen's, along with the children. The day they got back, Javon had found amusement in Oblam's confusion when he tried to discern the gender of Maleen's baby, not understanding at first why he sensed both.

Cutter would have enjoyed poking fun at Oblam. She could easily imagine Cutter and Javon laughing together as the boy worked logically through his confusion.

Cutter. She missed him terribly. The fact that he was murdered only made the ache worse. A warrior was supposed to have the honor of dying in battle or of pressing on until he was an old man, dying in his bed, surrounded by those who loved and honored him. Not knowing who had killed him was the worst of all.

Maleen dabbed a handkerchief to her eyes. She understood she had to take the time to mourn. She had done plenty of it already, but at the moment, there were more immediate concerns needing to be addressed, which was why she sat, waiting for her elect to assemble.

One by one, they trickled in and took a seat. Javon, wearing a purple scarf, was the last one to enter. Maleen picked up Tara's folded letter and waved it. The men could clearly see Tyndall's crest on the outside. "Kayla has disappeared, and several of Lenet's men have escaped from the Kelvian prison."

"Not a coincidence, I'm sure," Noture lamented.

"Who?" Asher asked, grave concern in his voice.

"Among others, Rundel, the day before his execution." Maleen paused. "And Jewel."

"We should've had the woman extradited," Phillip said quietly. "She should have been in an Acoran prison, not Kelvian."

"In her condition? With the animosity felt toward her from every Acoran in the territory who knows what she did? I wasn't willing to take the responsibility." Maleen shook her head. They'd had this same discussion nearly six months ago, the day of Tara's last message. The message told them Lenet's bloodline was not gone, and Jewel couldn't currently be executed for her crimes.

"Will Kayla try to use Jewel and her child for claiming the chief's seat if Tyndall dies? Maybe as Chief Guardian?" Tian asked.

Maleen shook her head. "She may try, but Tyndall hasn't given up hope of producing an heir. They'll have no ground to stand on." Maleen still wondered how Kayla had managed to convince a judge that she hadn't known Lenet and Rundel had killed Fanton. The judge obviously didn't understand how strong of a voyant the woman was. Lenet would never have been able to hide that from her. Yet, she'd feigned shock and hurt that her brother would have any part of it, and the judge had bought into her act. As for her part in the plot against Tyndall and Maleen, the judge had claimed not to have enough evidence to convict her. Other than the unusable testimony of voyants, all they had was hearsay.

"Before he died, Lenet fathered a child, and Tyndall's still hoping to father a child?" Asher raised an eyebrow. "I'm not sure if that will prevent a civil war or cause one."

"If they are successful, Tyndall's wife will hopefully help him avoid it, providing Tyndall can avoid assassination for another twenty years after the child is born." Maleen didn't raise the concern that Tyndall would be over seventy years old by the time his child came of age, and his young wife was Simoten. Even with Tara's help, she was not strong enough to hold the seat as Guardian until the child was old enough, even if Kelvia would consent to a female guardian.

"Unless one of the children doesn't live long enough for a war." Kelvian tactics once again weighed heavily on the Acorans.

"Tyndall would be better off adopting Lenet's child. If Jewel hadn't disappeared," Tian said.

Asher perked up. "Tyndall could always name his adopted nephew as his heir."

Phillip punched him in the arm then flinched when Asher drew back as if to return it. "You couldn't get me in the chief's seat for all the volcanic glass in Kelvia." He sighed. "Not that it would ever be an issue. Tyndall would let Kelvia be plunged into a civil war before he'd take that step. I do want to go home, but I'll have to wait until Tyndall's gone. Even then, it'll depend on who follows him as Chief."

"Why does Tara tell us about the prison escape? She should know we won't get involved in an internal Kelvian issue," Tian said.

"I think she wanted to warn us—to warn me—that Jewel is no longer in prison, and she may be with Kayla and Rundel."

Jewel wouldn't come to Acora yet. It would be another few months before her child was born, but then she would come. And she would bring her hatred with her.

Glossary of Terms

Age of maturity: Twenty years old, the age at which a person is an adult.

Chalent: A planet with no technology and very little metal ore. It has a tribal form of government.

Chief Heir: The person chosen to succeed the current chief. By naming an heir, a chief ensures that if he dies unexpectedly his choice of successor will be honored. The person chosen must have reached the age of maturity before he can be named.

Chief Ward: The underaged child of a deceased chief, under the care of the chief guardian who administers the tribe until the ward is of age.

Chiefs' Council: The annual Council formed by all the tribal chiefs coming together to discuss and debate issues which affect the peace and wellbeing of the entire continent.

Equin: The first three days of the new year. It is marked by the spring equinox. The term is also used to refer to the festivals which take place over the three-day holiday.

fentel: A drink made from the leaves of a *fent* tree. It is energizing and is often used as a morning drink to start the day.

first mother/father: a term used to refer to a deceased birth parent after the surviving parent has remarried.

garrison: The fort-type installations that house the majority of a tribe's warriors and their families. The size of a garrison varies depending on the size and strength of the tribe, as does the number of garrisons within a tribe.

Guardian: Also called Chief Guardian. The person who administrates over a tribe upon the death of the chief who has not named an heir until his underaged child is of age.

graebig beast: Long gray-haired mammals that stand six feet tall at the shoulder. They are used as mounts and beasts of burden. *Graebig dung* is used as a swear word.

Grand Voyant: A voyant who works for the tribal leadership.

Tamal: A fight between two chiefs to solve an issue that could escalate to war. The winner is considered to be "right" in the conflict. Only chiefs may use the Tamal, and only in extreme circumstances.

thessel: A plant with slightly toxic leaves. An extract from those leaves can make a strong, fast acting sedative. The seeds to thessel grow in pods. If these pods freeze in the wintertime, such as at higher elevations, it creates a different, less useful variation of the plant.

unreadable: a person who can hide emotions from voyants. It is sometimes a practiced skill, usually done by walking around the truth and telling partial truths.

voyant: a person who has an insight into the emotions of others.

Writing stories has always been a pastime. Writing novels has always been a dream. My favorite place to write is near the ocean in Northern California or in the middle of the woods. Nature calls to me and I love combining my love for it and my love for writing into the same pastime.

Currently, I live in Northern California where I am the Circulation and Technical Services Manager for the library of a small college. I'm not fond of the city, but if you must live in one, this is perfectly situated halfway between the mountains and the ocean

Three boys keep me busy, so finding time to write can be a challenge, but it's all worth it.

Books by Judy Lynn

Fantasy

Tribes of Chalent Series:

Book 1
Chieftess of Acora

Book 2
Guardian of Kelvia

Book 3
Physician of Simot

**Science Fiction
Coming 2023**

Commonwealth Series:

Veil of Deceit (rerelease)

Discovering Secrets

Calamity on Pala